Equal and Opposite Reactions

Patti Liszkay

To Toy,
may your life be filled

BLACK ROSE
writing™

with love luck, laughter, and
beautiful images !
Patti Liszkay :)

The final approval for this literary material is granted by the author.

First printing

This is a work of fiction. Names, characters, businesses, places, events and incidents are either the products of the author's imagination or used in a fictitious manner. Any resemblance to actual persons, living or dead, or actual events is purely coincidental.

ISBN: 978-1-61296-886-5
PUBLISHED BY BLACK ROSE WRITING
www.blackrosewriting.com

Printed in the United States of America
Suggested retail price $21.95

Equal and Opposite Reactions is printed in Book Antiqua

Equal and Opposite Reactions

Chapter One

"Sally. Hey, Sally."

Darren's voice seemed to be coming from a speaker somewhere inside her head. His image conjured itself up from a haze in the back of her mind like a genie rising from a bottle and then there he was behind her eyes, handsome, bare-chested, wearing only his pajama bottoms and swaying his hips to the sexy salsa beat of some far-off music.

"Darren?" she mumbled groggily.

"How are ya, Babe?"

He floated on the rhythm of the music to a spot next to her in bed. His hand caressed the side of her face. Her hand was wrapped around his hand, which felt small and hard and smooth as molded plastic.

Darren laughed in her ear. "Sally, what's going on? Are you awake yet?"

"Huh?" Sally's eyes creaked open. She was lying on her side, her cell phone pressed against her head. She rose on one elbow and squinted at the phone in her hand. How did that get there? She struggled to break through the soft layer of gauze that was pulling her brain back to the comforting oblivion of sleep.

But where was she? What was this dump, this strange bed, where was that Spanish music coming from? And where was Darren?

"Sally?"

Then the world came into focus and she came to the painfully surprising realization, as she had on at least half a dozen other semi-focused mornings over the past two months, that this place was her home, the music was wafting up from her neighbors below, and

Darren was…

"Sally? You fall back asleep again or what?"

"Darren? Is that you?"

"Wake up, little Sally," his voice sang to her, "it's six-fifteen Monday morning. Time for worky-work!"

Sally bolted up to a sitting position, fumbling for the clock on her night stand until she caught sight of its glowing digital numbers.

"Oh geez!"

Darren laughed again. "There now, aren't you glad I called?"

"Oh geez, I gotta get up! Stupid alarm clock, oh geez!"

"That's right, kiddo, blame the alarm clock."

Sally giggled, probably because her brain was still slightly foggy with sleep and at six-seventeen a.m. her defenses weren't yet up for the day and, like the song said, she hadn't the time for the pain, not at this moment at least, and because bits of mental debris whizzing through the cerebral fog were firing off message bites like *might as well start being mature and realistic about the whole kettle of fish (as her mother would say), she was twenty-seven years old and things could actually be worse, she and Joshua could still be living with her mother or, God forbid, her father, or, God doubly forbid, with the both of them, Misery and Company, under the same roof, and being all the time angry wasn't healthy, and why was it still so pleasant having her cold brain warmed up by the sound of Darren's voice?* The Mexicans or whatever they were below were up for the day and she damn well better be, too. She pushed back the covers and swung her feet to the floor, feeling around for her slippers. She'd read somewhere that making the effort to *sound* cheerful actually made you *feel* cheerful, so she'd make the effort. "So, Darren?" she yawned, "It's you?"

"Yeah, Babe. It's me. "

Yeah, Babe. Just like he'd have said it in the old days, the old years, when it *was* him, and only him, ever, lying beside her in the morning in the bedroom of the small red brick Hawthorne Street row house that she'd loved, lying there and talking about this and that, he maybe stroking her hair, she maybe rubbing his shoulders, talking to each other over the sound of the morning birds across the street in Wissenoming Park.

"So Darren…Did you want to, you know, talk, or something?" A

8

free-floating pang of yearning snuck up on her, an uninvited half-wish, maybe things weren't going so great with him and Trysta after all, well, that wouldn't come as any surprise would it? A tiny unwanted ember of hope sparked inside her as involuntarily as a beat of her heart.

"Well, yeah, I wanted to catch you before you left for work." A momentary pause on his end. "I need to talk to you."

"You do?" Now the ember was fanning itself into a warm glow in the middle of her chest. *Cut it out,* she told herself, *he only wants to talk.*

"Yeah. Just for a minute, okay? I got a long day, a big property to sell out in Manayunk."

"Manayunk?" Sally glanced again at the clock. Six-nineteen. She ought to tell him *okay, talk, but do make it short and sweet* and she ought not to try to draw him into any kind of unnecessary conversation because she really couldn't afford to risk ticking off Joanne, who was top of the line as bosses went but whose patience might not cover yet another morning of Sally traipsing in (another of her mother's expressions) ten, fifteen minutes late from still trying to get used to the god-awful traffic in this neck of Northeast Philadelphia, and, of course, Josh's day-care-slash-kindergarten was no longer a straight shot between home and work, and, in any case, even Sally had to admit that in general she'd been running behind the curve personally and professionally (if you could call her bottom-of the-rung admin job a profession), not to mention all the extra attention Joshua seemed to need, especially in the morning for some reason, since the divorce...But if Darren wanted to talk to her, if he'd finally come to realize that his relationship with Trysta was about as meaningful as with what he could have gotten from a cheap trinket fished out of a Cracker Jack box (if they made Cracker Jack prizes with functioning ovaries and super-sized breasts) then maybe it was important for Sally to let him know that, well, in spite of all that had gone down (and it had gone down pretty low as far as Sally was concerned), she wasn't angry and could still be there to listen. After all, she had been his wife for almost seven years; they'd married when Darren was barely out of college, Sally not even, so maybe this whole Trysta thing had been just been a wild oats-type impulse, a seven-year itch, like they say, which he now regretted scratching. "Manayunk, huh? You found something looks good out there?"

"Oh yeah, a real cream puff. That is, it could be. I mean, it's got value-add potential, you know what I mean?"

"Sure." It occurred to Sally that if Darren had picked up nothing else from his half-dozen years of grinding away for a high-end downtown commercial firm, he'd definitely mastered the real-estate lingo.

"All right," he admitted, "it's kind of a monster, actually, but I've got investors ready to shell out big-time. I'm thinking I could slice the place into twelve units, at least. It's one of those old classic city buildings that you always thought were so cute, halfway between Fairmount Park and the river. And you know these old Philly neighborhoods, today city working-class, tomorrow wealthy urban professional, that's where it's going, believe me. Say, I wish I could take you out to see it."

I'll go, she nearly said and then substituted with something almost as foolish. "Wouldn't you like to take Trysta out to see it?"

Darren laughed. Sure sounded like an unhappy laugh to Sally. She could be wrong, of course, but then he added, "Trysta's not much interested in old buildings."

"I'll bet."

"Not like you used to be."

"Still am." That was a daring remark, she knew, but wasn't he leading her, trying to communicate something to her in a call that had to be made in the early hours, before there was the risk of Trysta being awake and possibly listening in? And wasn't some hidden secret pocket of her heart still open to what that something could be?

"Yeah, you're still great Sally, you know that. And like I said, I did want to talk to you. Okay?"

"Okay." She drew a deep breath. Her heart was palpitating ever so slightly.

"Great. Listen, Sal, there's a fantastic property down in Puerto Vallarta, dirt cheap, right on the"

"What? Puerto...? What? What are you talking...?"

"*Hello,* Sally," Darren laughed, "where have I been the past week? Are you awake or not?"

The feeling was like the sudden sharp pop of a balloon in her chest followed by a harsh cold gust that took her breath away, blew out the ember and killed the glow.

"What's wrong, Sally, you got a cough?"

"No. I'm fine. Just great. Puerto Vallarta, that's where you've been. On your honeymoon. I'm awake now." Sally lowered the phone slowly from her ear until it rested in her lap. His voice travelled up from the speaker.

"Okay, good. Anyway, like I was saying, this place, it's a real peach, gorgeous, right on the beach. Great place to take Josh on vacations. Sally? You still there?"

Sally stared at a small crack in an empty spot on the gray-green wall across from her bed. She wished there were a nice picture there, or something. She'd go out and buy something. Maybe after her next pay check. But what the hell difference would a damn dollar-store picture make? The muffled *cha*-chaka, *cha*-chaka beat of the music still pulsed below her. Outside her window Roosevelt Boulevard, the great artery that pumped twelve lanes of traffic through the heart of Northeast Philadelphia, was already in full-tilt rush-hour boogie.

"Listen, Sal, it would be the best thing for Josh. He'd have a ball down there. In Puerto Vallarta, I mean." Darren paused again for Sally's reply and then cheerfully continued over her silence. "Not to mention what a great investment property a place like that would be, and then with the year-round rental income, I mean, we're talking money for Josh's future."

"So buy it."

"What? You gotta speak up, I can't hear you."

Sally returned the phone to her ear. "Buy it! Buy the frickin' thing!"

Darren chuckled uncomfortably. "Yeah, heh, heh, well…here's the deal. I'm just a little strapped for cash at the moment."

Sally laughed sourly. "Aw, no kidding." Her desire to act cheerful, to *be* cheerful, had curdled and the bad mood that she probably should have been in from the moment she woke up was settling in and in fact quickly sliding down the scale from bad to rotten.

"You know," he continued, "with me quitting Highland and Erskerberg and striking out on my own like I'm doing, start up's been a little slow, just a little, but things should be picking up, I mean, especially with this place in Manayunk and all, and there's even a second apartment building I'm about to pounce on out in West Philly, and it's gonna turn into a real cash cow really soon."

"Yeah, well that's great, but speaking of cash I've got to get to work, so"

"No, wait, just one more sec. See, I was thinking that if we could cut back a few bucks on the child support payment, just for a while, I'm pretty sure I could swing it."

"Swing what?"

"Buying the property. In Puerto Vallarta."

"*What?* Darren, what are you say...you wanna cut back on your...?" Sally sprang out of bed, a mother cobra riled from the nest.

"Let me explain what I"

"Well, screw *me*, I should have seen this one coming!"

"Sally, let me expl—"

"Boy, am I a slow learner!"

"Sally..."

"Hey, don't bother giving me a hint, I'll never get it! Hit me between the eyes with a two-by-four, why don't you, maybe then I'll get the drift!"

"Sally, I"

"I mean, why the hell did I *think* you were calling me at six-fifteen in the morning? To ask me how I'm doing? To ask how your son, who thinks you've forgotten him, is doing?" A voice behind her voice was warning her to calm down, back off, resist pulling him into yet another battle, but she was already flaming ahead. "Or how about to tell me you want to cut off your child's financial support so you can go and buy a beach house for that juicy little *squeeze* your left us for? Hmmm, I wonder which it could be?"

"Now, wait a minute, wait, that's not what I...I cannot believe you, Sally, you are not hearing what I said, you are jumping to conclusions here!"

"I'm not jumping to anything these days, thank you! I'm crawling, slow in the head as a goddamn one-eyed snail!"

"Slow? Slow? Jesus, Sally, you're spinning your wheels at a hundred miles an hour! All that negative energy, grinding away!" Then his voice softened, turned gentle, concerned. "You gotta calm yourself, Babe, you're gonna wear yourself down."

Sally wasn't sure at what point she'd started crying, but she could feel the tears rolling down her cheeks. He was right, the jerk. She took a deep breath, tried to slow down the angry wheel whirring away inside her. "Yeah, well, it's hard, you know? You try being at this end at goddamn six..." She glanced at the clock. "...goddamn six-twenty-four in the morning, see if you don't get worn down!"

"Aw, Sally, I'm sorry, I really am. Hey, don't get all upset, Babe, please, I didn't call to wear you down."

But, she thought, *you also didn't call because the sound of my voice could still turn you so inside out, make you so stupid that a few soft words could haze over all the hurt and bitterness and make you feel that if we were in the same room you'd want to throw yourself into my arms and forget everything except restarting our life together from where we left off.*

"Sal? You okay?" He sounded truly concerned for her, probably was, in his own dumb shit clueless way.

"Yeah. I'm okay."

"Good, good, I want you to be okay. I really do. Anyway, it's like I was telling you, I just want to get something good going for Josh. See, I'm thinking"

"Darren."

"Yeah?"

"Bullshit. You're thinking bullshit."

"Aw, now here we go again! I'm trying to put us on a positive beat, but you won't even listen 'cause you're still stuck in all that damn self-negativity that was the root our troubles in the first place!"

Her inner wheel revved up again.

"*I'm* negative? It's all *my* fault? Everything's *my fault?* And never mind that *you* were humping your brains out on *my* time and on Josh's time, and"

"Aw, Sally, could we please not get into that? I mean, what is the point?"

"I don't know, Darren, what *is* the point? What's going on here? Are you trying to use me again? Because if you're trying to use me, I swear"

"*Use* you? Sally, I never tried to use you, I swear to God. What happened...with us, I mean...Look, can we talk about us for a minute?"

"*Us?* How can we talk about *us* when there *is* no *us* anymore?"

"Sure there is. I mean, as long as we have Josh between us. And I swear, Sally, it's for Josh that I want to buy this place."

"Oh, right, you haven't seen the kid in what, three weeks?"

"Yeah, and I'm sorry about that, but how could I? I mean, with the new house and then the wedding and then the honeymoon, and…"

Sally felt the blood pounding in her head.

"…so it's been hectic around here, you know?"

"Oh, sure, sure, sure! Sounds real tough!"

"Aw come on, Sally, you're being totally"

"Life is just *sooooo* hard and you want to make up for it by buying Josh a beach house in Mexico!"

"Hey, I'm trying to tell you! Josh would have a ball down there!"

"Yeah. Josh and who else?"

"Well…Josh and me, of course."

"Josh and you and Trysta."

"Well…yes."

"And Trysta's three kids."

She heard a long-suffering sigh from Darren's end. "Sally, please, *please* try to hear me out, can't you at least *try?* Do you think I don't know this isn't easy for you? Do you think I don't understand what you've been dealing with?"

"No, Darren. Tell me. What have I been dealing with?"

"Well, you know… emotional issues. Changes."

"Emotional issues. Changes."

"Yeah, and anger, and all. But, Babe, it's time to put the past behind us, move on, like they say. I mean, just 'cause we split you wouldn't want to deprive Josh of the chance to have some good times, happy childhood memories, and"

"*Damn it, Darren, would you cut it out?* I'm not some, some…*schmuck* you're trying to unload one of your ratty-assed apartment buildings on!" As soon as she'd spit out the words Sally knew she'd crossed the line, pressed the big red button that launched the full-scale attack.

"Wha...? What did you…? Now, look, Sally, that was out of line, '*way* out of line! I'm in a clean business, you know that, and I've never, *ever* done anything below the belt, you know that, too!" He sounded mad now, but if anything the anger in his voice was serving to fuel Sally's own escalating rage.

"*How about what you did with Trysta, was that below the belt?*" Oh my God, she thought, I'm shouting.

"*Aw geez, Sally,*" now he was shouting, too, "*that is so off the subject, I can't believe you!*"

"*You* can't believe *me? You're talking about cutting back on Josh's support, for God's sake!*"

"*Oh, come on, you've got a job, it's not like you couldn't get by!*"

"*What? Are you saying*"

"*I'm not saying any*"

"*I know what you're say*"

"*I'm only trying to say*"

"*Because if you're trying to say*"

"*Aw, Sally, don't start, please don't start*"

"*I'm not starting anything, I'm just trying to figure out what you*"

"*All right! All right!*"

"*Why do you accuse me of trying to start, when all I*"

"*I said all right!*"

"*When all I*"

"GODDAMMIT, SALLY, WOULD YOU CORK IT THE HELL UP?"

There was a shocked silence on both ends, as if the connection had suddenly gone dead. Sally felt as if she'd been slapped or had a glass of cold water thrown in her face. She realized she was breathing heavily, that she'd been pacing the floor at a frantic speed. She caught a glimpse of herself in the mirror of her beat-up thrift-store dresser. She looked hateful. Her dark brown eyes were swollen and streaked with red and her flushed cheeks wet with tears. She must have been running a hand through her bangs, which were spiked in every direction. God, she looked a mess. She was out of control, letting Darren make a mess of her all over again, like the mess she'd been right after the divorce. She pictured Darren, probably pacing like her, probably still in his pajamas like her, though he only ever wore the bottoms. She wondered if Trysta, that fat-uddered cow, ever wore his pajama tops like she, Sally, used to. Maybe he was in his new bedroom in the new house that he'd bought way out in the newly developed western suburb of New Conshohocken where there was probably a big beautiful master bedroom with a big beautiful bathroom and a walk-in closet and a king-sized bed where he and Trysta...God, she needed to stop now. She needed to control herself. It was six-twenty-seven in the morning and already she was feeling exhausted.

***

Darren wanted to kick himself. He couldn't believe he'd lost it like that, blew the whole deal, probably. He'd forgotten how unreasonable Sally could be with all that hostility she was hanging on to. Little Sally, five-foot-three and a hundred and ten pounds stocked with the fury of a ten-megaton firestorm. He was too damn stressed out these days – except for the week in Puerto Vallarta, that had been paradise: simple, sunny, easygoing, the way life was supposed to be. And now he had an unbelievable, dropped-from-the sky opportunity to pare off a slice of that paradise for himself...well, for Joshua, really, it was all for Joshua...Why couldn't Sally see that? Did she think he was trying to hurt her? He'd never wanted to hurt her, never then and not now. Why was she making him into some kind of villain here? Did she think he wasn't stretched in fifteen different directions himself these days just trying to make ends meet? Still, she was all upset. Crying. Little Sally. He'd been a shit to jump on her like that when she was crying.

"Oh, Jesus, Sally, I'm sorry. I'm sorry, I didn't mean"

"It's okay."

"It's okay?"

"I'm tired of fighting. Worn to the bone."

"Yeah I know." Another moment of silence and then Darren tried, carefully, again. "Look, I just meant, about your job..."

Trysta entered from the bathroom brushing her long blond hair, clean from the shower and freshly blown dry. "Honey, were you just shouting at somebody? Oh, you're on the phone."

Darren covered the receiver with his hand and nodded. He was suddenly distracted by the sight of her, the way her huge pregnant belly hiked up the silky material of her nighty so that it barely fell to her hips and made him wonder if she were wearing any panties, and just the thought of the word "panties" distracted him, too.

"Well, what *about* my job? Darren, are you still there?"

"Oh, yeah, I just meant..." What *had* he meant? What had he been about to say about Sally's job? Now Trysta was leaning slightly over her vanity table massaging some lotion into her neck and shoulders. She was almost thirty, yet her skin was still so soft and creamy. And was it just the shadow of the material or was that the lower curve of her cheeks peeking out below the hem of her nighty?

"Darren, are you still there or what, because speaking of my job, I have to get to work."

"Oh, yeah, sorry, I just meant..." Hell, he didn't know what he meant, his wife's ass was short-circuiting his thought processes. "Your job, you know..." He had to block out Trysta and the thrill that was brewing below his waist or he was going to blow this chance for sure. "I mean, it's a good job."

"It's all right."

"You love your job."

"I like it. It's all right. I don't love it. Darren, what is your point?"

"My point is..." Damn, now he'd caught Trysta's attention. She was headed for the bed, mouthing, "Who is that?"

"...about your job..." He hadn't wanted Trysta around when he made the call, which was why he'd made it while she was in the shower, but he hadn't planned on the whole thing taking more than a couple of minutes, hadn't factored in Sally being so antagonistic. He should have run downstairs and called from the kitchen phone, or from his cell, or something.

"About my job?"

Trysta crawled into the bed next to him while the strap of her nighty slipped off one shoulder causing the top to slide a little down her full round breast.

"Well, you know...it's a...it pays good." He was jabbering nonsense while Trysta ran a finger down his arm, trying to get him to communicate who he was talking to. He sidled away from her then swung his feet over the side of the bed. She ran her nails lightly down his back.

"It pays good? *My* job does?"

"Well, sure. You make a decent salary. Real decent."

"I don't make squat. You know that."

"Well... I only meant... you know, considering there's only the two of you. Look at me. I've got five mouths to feed here, and then Josh over there, and then another one on the way..." Trysta's eyes lit up with understanding and he heard her say, "*Ohhhh,*" and then he knew he'd slipped, mentioned Josh's name and given away that he was talking to Sally. Still he wasn't prepared for Trysta to swing around next to him and try to grab the phone from his hand. "Let me talk to her," Trysta whispered. Darren shook his head and grabbed the phone back from her while Sally continued, thankgodfully unaware of what was going on at his end.

"Oh, and whose fault"

"...And a four-thousand-a-month house payment that's killing me..." Now he was in a tug of war with Trysta over the phone. "Let me, let me!" she wheedled softly but insistently.

"Yeah, and whose fault"

"... And then with Trysta giving up her job to stay at home with the kids..."

Trysta finally gave a good substantial yank and Darren lost the phone to her.

"*What?* Oh, well, that's just swell! Trysta doesn't have to work anymore! Tell her congratufuckinglations!"

"Oh, my goodness, *Sally?*" Trysta's voice was sweet as corn syrup. "How *are* you?"

Sally was momentarily disoriented. She frowned at the phone for a few seconds then murmured, "Oh, *great.*"

"You okay, Sal?" Trysta cooed.

"Trysta..." Sally realized she was breathing heavily again, and she strained to control herself. "Trysta, could I please talk to my hus...to Darren?" She pulled the phone away from her ear. "*Shit! Shit!*"

Trysta giggled and her voice turned even sweeter. "You mean you want to talk to *my* husband?"

Sally closed her eyes for a moment and rubbed her forehead. She took a slow, deep breath. Even with the phone away from her ear she could hear Darren's voice in the background: "*Trysta, give me back the damn phone!"*

"Honestly, Sally," Trysta continued, "I just don't want there to be any anger."

Sally returned the phone to her ear. "There's no anger, Trysta. Everything's jello and dream whip. Put Darren on, please."

"Because, you know, we've *really* got our hands full here."

"*C'mon Trys,*" Darren pleaded in the background, "*cut it out, give it back!*"

"Yeah, you really had it rough down there in Mexico all week. Let me talk to Darren."

"Oh, no, Puerto Vallarta was *wonderful!* You really should go there sometime."

"*Dammit, Trysta, cut it out! Give me that phone!*"

Trysta turned away from the phone towards Darren: *"Wait, I'm getting through to her."* Then back to Sally: "What I mean, is, you just have no idea how it is trying to care for a husband and three children and a big, brand-new house when you're eight months pregnant."

"*Aw, geez, Trysta, what in the hell are you trying to*"

"Oh, I don't, huh? *I don't?*" It was as if Sally had burst into flames, her angry inner wheel morphed into an erupting volcano. "And how about *you?*" *Don't shout, don't say it, back off, hang up,* some voice of reason vainly begged, but she drove on. "Yeah, how about *you,* you...Ms. Hot Pants! You got any idea how it is having your husband run off with some, some," *Stop! Stop now!* "SOME DUMB, SLUTTY LITTLE GOLD-DIGGER SO HE CAN GO AND BUY HER AND HER KIDS A GORGEOUS FIVE-BEDROOM HOUSE OUT IN TOOTY MONTGOMERY COUNTY WHILE HIS OWN CHILD AND ME END UP STUCK ON THE ROOSEVELT BOULEVARD IN A CARDBOARD CONDO JUNGLE WITH FUCKIN' SALSA MUSIC BLASTING AWAY TWENTY-FOUR SEVEN, AND EVEN THIS DUMP I CAN BARELY AFFORD? YOU WANT TO TELL ME WHAT YOU KNOW ABOUT THAT, HUH? AND WHILE YOU'RE AT IT, YOU WANT TO TELL ME HOW MY SON, A SIX-YEAR-OLD BOY, IS SUPPOSED TO PLAY AND, AND, DEVELOP, FOR GOD'S SAKE, IN THE FENCED-IN CONCRETE JOKE THEY CALL A BACKYARD AROUND HERE? YOU HAVE ANY IDEAS ABOUT THAT, EINSTEIN?"

Equal and Opposite Reactions

Trysta sat wide-eyed and drop-jawed. She silently offered the phone back to Darren. He grabbed the phone and glared at her, though her face now had the look of a stricken baby doe.

"Uh, Sally?" he tried, "You still there, Babe?"

"And as for you, you...*shit*," she said between breathless sobs, "you come up one day late, you come up one penny short on your son's support, and I swear to God, I'll sock it to you so fast and so hard you'll wake up on Venus with your arse-end fluttering in the goddamn breeze! *And don't call me Babe!*"

Darren sat frozen, momentarily transfixed by the hum of the dial tone in his ear. Trysta lay on the bed crying, an arm thrown across her face, her belly heaving with each loud sob. Darren smacked the phone into its cradle.

"*Shit! Shit!*"

"Y-y-you...you called her...*Babe!*"

Darren was pacing now, waving his arms for emphasis. "Blown! Screwed! All my plans, fuckin' *skewered!*"

"*Wha...what she said to me!* Oh! You're not even listening!" Trysta gave a long wail broken by coughing sobs which caused Darren to stop pacing and turn to her.

"Huh? Aw, Trysta, what's the matter with you, I *told* you not to..."

"Those *awful, awful* things she called me! She's a horrible witch! And you don't even care!"

"What do you *mean* I don't...look, you *know* Sally goes off like a firecracker these days!"

"A horrible...*exploding* witch!"

"Yeah, so then what did you have to *antagonize* her for, huh? What were you trying to—"

"*Help!* I was only trying to *help you!*"

"Help me? *Help* me? Jesus, I was in the middle of *negotiating*, trying to get some goddamn *cooperation* on this financial thing!"

Trysta hoisted her bulk up to a sitting position, and in so doing caused her nighty to slide half-way down her breasts. She pulled her long hair around so that it cascaded over one shoulder. "I'm sorry, okay? I really thought I could reach her. Woman to woman. Mother to mother. I'm just...*so sorry.*" She heaved a great sob-broken sigh that made her top slip down another inch.

Darren took in the sight of his wife. She looked pathetic, so vulnerable, her eyes overflowing with tears that streamed past the tip of her reddened nose. And then there was her golden hair falling over one mostly-exposed breast…Darren sat down on the bed next to her. He resisted the urge to feel her hair. "Look, Babe, it's just that"

"You can't call me Babe if you're gonna call her Babe!" Another heart-wrenching wail.

"I'm *not* gonna call her Babe! I *don't* call her Babe! *Ever!*

"What about just now?"

"That was a fuckin' *accident* just now! Okay?"

"Now you're cursing at me!"

"I'm sorry. I'm sorry."

"No more cursing at me! I hate that filthy language!"

"Okay. I'm sorry. I'm sorry. Okay?"

"Okay," she sniffed.

"Look, all I meant was…about Sally… you gotta handle her real carefully. Like an egg."

"A rotten, cracked, *scrambled* egg! She's so mean! Darren, why do you have to have to handle her at all? Why do we have to have *anything* to do with her?"

"Oh, well, there's just this little thing called my son, you know? Just this little, insignificant, six-year-old detail…"

"How could you marry somebody like her in the first place? What were you *thinking?*

Well, she wasn't always on the warpath. She *could* be nice. Only she's having these…adjustment problems."

"Oh, that's nice, take her part now!"

Tears, breasts, hair or not, that was too much, Trysta was going too far now, really setting him off. *"Take her part?* Why the hell would I take her part? She's putting the screws to me, and with your *generous* help I just blew any chance of getting her to loosen up!"

He grabbed a brochure from the nightstand and waved it at Trysta. *"Now* what do you think our chances are of getting that place in Puerto Vallarta?"

"I don't care!"

Darren sprung from the bed and once more began pacing the

room. "You don't care? Oh, well, that's very good, because I'm already up to my ass in bills, and now, *now* it's all fucking shot to…" Darren stopped in mid-sentence. Trysta had grabbed her stomach and was moaning in pain.

"*Oooooooh.*" She slowly slid down against the headboard until she was lying on her back. Darren dropped the brochure and hurried over to the bed.

"What? What's wrong? Are you having a pain?" He hovered over his wife, scanning her vast belly as if it were a great crystal ball that could give him the answer to her sudden malaise.

"No," she huffed breathlessly, "I'm… fine… it's… nothing… *ooooh…*"

"You're having a pain! Oh Jesus, she's having a pain!"

Trysta put her hand on Darren's arm. "My darling…please…don't worry about me…I'll be…all right…*ooooh…hand me the phone, quickly!*"

Darren grabbed the phone from the nightstand. Trysta stopped in mid-moan, pulled the phone from his hand and began pressing buttons.

"What?" Darren cried, "What, you need the squad? Stop, here, give me the phone, let me dial!"

"I'm calling Donna," Trysta said coolly. "I need to talk to Donna."

"*What? You're calling my mother?*"

"I need to. Donna works in a hospital. She'll know what to do."

"She's a goddamned HR administrator! How the hell would she know what to do?"

"She'll know what to do about your cursing," Trysta sniffed, "and the way you're treating me, and how you were carrying on with Sally on the phone this morning." Trysta made a show of continuing to push buttons.

"*No! Don't call Donna!*" He tried to pull the phone from her hand.

"You're hurting me!" Trysta cried as she pulled back.

Darren let go of his hold on the phone and unconsciously folded his hands into the gesture of prayer. "*Please, Trysta, please, don't call Donna!*"

Trysta gave a great heaving sigh and flopped back down onto her back. She threw her arm over the side of the bed and let the phone drop to the floor.

"*Ohhhh,*" she continued from where she'd left off, "*the pain, I just can't...*"

"Oh God, I'm calling the squad!"

Trysta grabbed his arm as he tried to scramble off the bed to retrieve the phone.

"No, no, please, my darling, just stay here by me, *oh, oh...*"

"You sure, Baby? You want me to"

"Rub my back." Trysta rolled over onto her side and Darren began kneading the small of her back through the material of her nighty.

"Is that better?" he asked anxiously.

"No, no, do it right on the skin!" She lifted her top over her shoulders and wiggled out of it. She was, as he'd conjectured earlier, pantiless. She turned her bare back to him.

"Rub."

Daren rubbed her back, trying not to pay attention to his stiffening penis. It didn't help that Trysta was now arching and flexing like a pampered cat.

"Ooh, oh, that's better," she purred. "You know just how to make me feel better. *All* over."

She backed her buttocks into his waist and pulled his hands around to her breasts. He tried to pull back. "Aw, Babe, no, no, you're in pain."

"You made me all better." She began slowly grinding against him.

"I can't! I can't! I gotta get to work, I got that big property out in"

"I know." She turned to face him and yanked down his pajama bottoms. He pulled her close and kissed her lustily, her lips, her face, her neck, her breasts and then he stopped suddenly.

"The kids!" Darren cried, "what about the kids!"

"Mmmmmm, don't stop, don't stop!"

"But...how long 'til they get here?"

"Who?"

"Your kids, Trysta, your kids!"

"Oh. Silvio's bringing them back to catch the school bus. We've got *plenty* of time." She wrapped her legs around his groin.

"Oh, Baby," he moaned, "move over, here comes Daddy!"

Chapter Two

What she needed, of course, was to flop back into bed and cry. And cry. And cry. No, what she actually needed was to find herself a dark space somewhere, a cellar, or even a decent-sized closet (neither of which could be found in this place, though she'd had, but never needed for this purpose, both those things at their old home on Hawthorne Street) where she could really cut loose, let her sobs escalate to screams and then scream like a wounded she-beast, the most intense primal scream therapy, scream and scream until she'd screamed herself into …what? Oblivion? Sally grabbed the comforter that she'd earlier kicked to the floor and threw it across the bed, smacking out the wrinkles and yanking the edges even. Then she punched up and straightened her pillow. Nobody ever screamed themselves into oblivion. Nobody ever screamed themselves into anything except the looney bin or a bitching sore throat. Her bedside clock now read six-thirty-five. "Shit son of a bitch," she muttered and then headed down the hall to the bathroom.

The toilet wasn't acting right, but who had time or money to worry about that? Sally scrubbed her teeth, threw some water onto her face then ran a brush through her hair. *Get over it,* she told herself in the mirror, *get over it and get on with your life, such the fuck as it is.* God knew Darren was sure enough getting on with his life. He'd honestly sounded pretty damn happy this morning, too. Or at least until Sally slammed the kibosh on his half-baked pipe-dream of buying, what, some beach house in Mexico? Was he nuts? Or still just shooting off sparks from his Puerto Vallarta honeymoon with Trysta McSlut? Hell, what *had* Trysta's last name been, anyhow? That is, the name she'd worn before she'd thrown it away and grabbed the name that had been Sally's for the last seven years. The name of the poor schmuck who'd married her the first time around. Come to think of it, Sally couldn't remember if Darren had actually ever told her what Trysta's last name had been or anything at all about Trysta's husband. Her old husband. Her used husband for whom Darren was doubtless a trade-up. In any case, Darren had never even mentioned Trysta to Sally right up until he'd sprung the D-word on her, after which most communication between them, save the strictly essential exchanges of necessary logistical information, involved yelling and/or crying. But then, what reason would he have had to mention Trysta previously, Trysta supposedly having been just some hot-looking telephone receptionist in one of the offices of Highland and Erskerberg, where Darren had no sooner started making terrific money as a newly promoted Vice-President of Strategic Acquisitions than he quit to "strike out on his own," as he put it. But why did he give up that great job, that prestigious position? Well, sure, he had talked a couple of times over a glass of wine about maybe someday starting his own real-estate development business, but to Sally that had sounded like just another dream in passing, of no more real substance than this nonsense he was now spouting about buying a house in Mexico. Seemed like Darren was always percolating some dream or other. So why had he picked now to start running after these dreams? Or maybe it had all started with Trysta. Maybe she'd started out as some whipped cream fantasy he'd mentally salivated over every day on his way to the office and then she became real, and now he was bent on making all his other fantasies come to life. Like that huge new house he just bought out in New Conshohocken. Hadn't buying a place in the suburbs also been another some-day dream of Darren's? Of course, the house in the suburbs had been the dream that Sally had always believed she'd be part of. But then how could anybody have dreamed a year ago that today Darren and Sally would be divorced? Thinking back, it was just a little less than a year ago that their marriage started sliding downhill for some reason that Sally couldn't put her finger on at the time – well, of course it was because Darren had started screwing Trysta. And now Trysta had Darren and Darren's baby and the house in the suburbs. And Sally had squat. Their nice little brick row house by the park now belonged to someone else, a guy from Darren's work whom Darren had unloaded on over a drink that he was about to divorce his wife and who, the next day, offered to buy Darren's house from him, and for a darn decent price. Of course Darren had been more than happy to sell it fast and avoid the hassle of putting it on the market. He'd laid out the facts for Sally on the day he asked for a divorce: they were going to split, the house would have to be sold. They could sell it now at a profit or wait until the divorce played out and lose a bundle of money in the process and maybe end up not being able to unload the house at all, the local residential real estate market always being in danger of falling back into the dumper. In any case, the writing was on the wall, so why not take the sensible approach? For Josh's sake. Why not sell the house now? For Josh's sake. Be grown-up and civil? For Josh's sake. Hell, Darren had made it sound like the whole break-up was for Josh's sake! But by the end of all the talking, crying, reasoning, begging, and screaming, Darren had somehow convinced Sally that she would end up in a better financial and emotional state if they sold the house first, since the opportunity was upon them, and then got through the divorce as smoothly as possible – for Josh's sake. So Sally cooperated – for Josh's sake – and the house was sold and the divorce over with almost before Sally could catch her breath and the whole process went smooth as butter (as her satisfied attorney'd noted afterwards) and things were peachy for Darren while Sally ended up broke and a candidate for advanced anger management. In the meantime Darren bought a new house and quit his job and Sally and Josh went to live with Sally's mother until Sally found this shoebox with cardboard walls for them to live in and which she'd bought instead of renting because she'd spent all her married life hearing that buying always makes more economic sense in the long haul than renting. Only now she was wondering about that. And a lot of other things, too.

Sally shoved some styling mousse into her bangs. Maybe she should have fought Darren more, dragged out the proceedings, made him squirm and made Trysta have a kid out of wedlock. Though Sally doubted the fine point of in or out of wedlock would have mattered much to Trysta. The music from below had stopped and was replaced by the sound from across the way of a crying baby. Sally pictured the young Hispanic couple she'd passed a couple of times on the roof-covered concrete landing that passed for a hallway between her unit and that of her neighbors. The woman had carried a baby in her arms. Come to think of it, there seemed to be a lot of Hispanics in the complex. Carrying babies. And playing salsa music. Oh well, so what, Hispanics were all over Philadelphia these days, a ton of them around the Northeast. Of course, there was a ton of *everybody* around the Northeast, always had been, the Northeast being the population melting pot of the city, upper, middle, and working class, blacks, whites, Asians, Russians, Italians, Irish, Jews, Middle Easterners, and most recently, of course, the hordes of the Latino invasion. *You're crying now, kid,* Sally mentally addressed the baby while twisting her dark shoulder-length hair up in a clip, *you'd better get used to it, it only gets worse.*

And she immediately felt a pang of remorse for the thought. What if it were her child, her Joshua, crying? She pictured Joshua, small for his age but so smart, with his beautiful, serious brown eyes and love of all things dinosaur and robot. Would she want someone making that kind of prediction for her own child's life? Wasn't Joshua the one bright, happy, hopeful spot in her existence? And bad as things were at the moment, didn't she wish for him to get through this rough patch unscathed, resilient, ultimately happy? She once again pulled up the thought that had been rescuing her from her worst moments since the divorce: *I've got Josh.* Darren might be living the American Male Dream, but for it he'd traded his son. Yes, Sally had handed Darren a nice, neat, quickie divorce, over with before Trysta's due date, in return for full custody of Joshua on Sally's terms, no court battles, no wounding Joshua over and over while they waged war on each other. The baby across the hall was still crying. Sally sighed. She felt bad that she'd harbored such a mean thought for that helpless baby, who was surely some other mother's beloved child. She made a wish for a happy life for Joshua and for the wailing child, whom she hoped was legal, but even if it wasn't, what did she care? She had enough worries of her own, right?

On her way back from the bathroom Sally cracked open the door of Josh's room. He was still sleeping, – the kid could sleep through anything like thirty-five pounds of brick, thank God – still wrapped up in some happy little boy dream, she hoped. She decided to let him sleep another minute or two and headed back to her bedroom. Rooting through the stingy recessed rectangle of space that passed for a closet, Sally wondered as she did most mornings how she was supposed to find anything amidst this squashed goulash of clothes. *Aw, quit bitching,* she ordered herself, *count your goddamn blessings.* She dressed and worked on a quick make-up job, deciding that just the essentials would do for today. So what if she was living on Roosevelt Boulevard in a shoebox with cardboard walls, one of half-a-hundred cardboard-walled shoe boxes stacked in square rows? She had a sudden flashback of her mother giving her a shoebox when she was six years old and helping her cut and glue squares of cardboard to make the walls of a little shoe-box house for her tiny Strawberry Shortcake figurines. They'd even made tiny chairs, a table, couch, TV and a bed, all painted from jars of bright-colored tempera. Her eyes moistened over a wave of nostalgia for the happy child she'd been. And what the hell, for all her complaining about her mother, Sally had to admit that her mother was a good mother, the avatar of motherhood, in fact, compared to Donna, that spiteful self-important shrew who'd raised Darren. Sally vowed to quit ruminating over her mother's faults, even the most annoying (like her new-found religious fanaticism and her constant nit-picking at Sally's life), and try to keep in mind her mother's good points: her generosity, her helpfulness, her naturally cheerful disposition. After all, for all Sally knew her mother might still be coping in her way with her own divorce two years ago from Sally's father; though as far as Sally was concerned her mother was better off without the man, who had a stubborn streak the size of New Jersey and who could be hard-headed as a child. Sally swore her father had actually enjoyed instigating the escalating arguments with her mother that ultimately tore their marriage apart. Yet amazingly, her father continued to pay her mother support, so Sally at least had to give him credit for that.

She heard Josh's door creak open and the light pad of his feet across the hall to the bathroom. She smiled then sat on the bed for a moment. All right, so maybe at this moment she didn't exactly have enough blessings to count but at least she had Josh, and then hey, a day that had started out as rotten as this one had couldn't possible get any worse, right?

Patti Liszkay

A blood-curdling scream tore out from the bathroom.

"*Oh my God, Joshua!*" Sally sprinted across the hall to the bathroom to find her son wailing as if the stuff gushing over the rim of the toilet were not water but his life's blood.

"Daddy! Daddy!" he sobbed.

"Oh, geez, oh geez!" Sally grabbed for the shut-off valve at the base of the toilet and gave it a quick turn while Joshua hopped from one foot to the other, flapping his arms like a little bird in a blind panic. His crying was now a sorrowful mantra of *Daddy, get my Daddy, Daddy, get my Daddy…*

"Oh, my Baby!" Sally scooped up her child and carried him to her bed where she held him in her arms and rocked him. "Shhh," she cooed, "It's all right, my Baby, don't cry. So what if the potty decided to overflow? So what?"

"Get my Daddy!"

"Shhh, it's all right, Mommy's here."

"But you have to tell my Daddy to come *right now!*"

"Joshie, Baby, you know Daddy isn't gonna," she swallowed hard, "… isn't gonna come back just because the toilet's broken."

"But, but, what if I have to go to the bathroom?"

"Oh, Baby, don't worry! Somebody else will fix it for us!"

"Somebody besides Daddy?"

"Why sure," she sniffed, wiping her eyes with the back of her hand, I'll call the plumber and he'll come right over and fix it for us, and you'll see, when you get home from school it'll be good as new."

Sally grabbed two tissues from the small box on her bedside table and wiped Joshua's eyes and nose then her own. Then she kissed him and held him close a little while longer, wondering how in the world to console a little kid who's being offered dream trips to Mexico when all he really wants is a working toilet and an unbroken home.

Chapter Three

Darren sat on the edge of the bed still in his pajama bottoms. Post-coital depression, wasn't that what it was called? Or maybe this was post-Sally depression, temporarily mitigated by a quick but hot roll in the sack with Trysta, who was back in the shower again, singing like an off-key blue-jay. He looked at the Mexican real estate brochure in his hand. Why did Sally have to be so unreasonable? Of course, Sally had always had an edge to her, he'd even liked that about her once upon a time, it had made her seem lively, self-assured, more desirable, somehow. But these days she was sharp and bristly as a porcupine in permanent defense mode. He could hardly approach her about anything, even something as important as this beach house that would be so good for Joshua.

Darren sighed. He missed his son. He really missed not seeing him for the past few weeks, but things had been so crazy-busy. Down there in Puerto Vallarta all he could think about was how much Josh would love playing on the beach, splashing around in the surf, squealing with delight each time a wave broke over him, just like he always did when he and Sally used to take him to the Jersey shore in the summer. On the sunny Mexican beach he and Josh could have some real bonding time, some time to heal and create happy memories to replace any unhappy ones the boy might be holding on to from the divorce. But was Sally willing to see any of this? Well, maybe if he just backed off a while, gave her some time. Huh, fat chance. Sally could be tenacious as a Gila monster even in her best of moods, which she obviously wasn't in now. Yeah, well, okay, he was sorry he'd had to leave her and Josh a little strapped, and that they'd had to sell the house so fast. But he'd *had* to sell it, he'd had a buyer; Rob Rushkin from work had just dropped an offer like from heaven, and, the housing market being what it was, who knew if or when there'd be another offer? Sure, Darren wished he could have hung on to that little brick house, it was such a gem, and let Sally and Josh live there like Sally'd wanted. But the mortgage payments were too high for Sally and he'd needed cash for a down-payment on the house in New Conshohocken. He'd really wanted to wait and eventually settle down somewhere in Lower Merion, just west of the city line on the other side of the Schuylkill River; owning one of those wonderful old Philadelphia Main Line properties had been his dream. But that dream had been years away even before he left his job at Highland and Erskerberg, and the reality was that he'd needed a place to live right away, as did Trysta and her three kids – well, four pretty soon – and the other reality, this he knew, was that he couldn't very well marry Trysta then not set her up with a classier lifestyle than what she'd just come from over in working-class Cornwells Heights. If only he could have gotten Sally to agree to move to an apartment while he and Trysta kept the Wissenoming house...popsicle's chance in hell of Sally entertaining that possibility for half a nanosecond. And besides, the house by Wissenoming, nice as it was, was really too small for the six of them (seven when Josh was visiting), with its three small bedrooms and only one bath. So he'd had to settle for a new house of questionable construction in a new development set down on a recently-cleared field of scrub brush in New Conshohocken instead of his old Main Line dream house. Not to mention his Puerto Vallarta dream house. Life was full of disappointments.

But it went on anyway, and he had a 9:00 am appointment with his two potential investors, a couple of big-shot lawyers, Chase Winston and Aaron Winslow, for the Manayunk property. Where he lived now was far west of the city, and the traffic on the Schuylkill Expressway east into downtown Philly could be a real rush-hour bitch. He hauled himself up from the bed and started to dress. From the dresser drawer he pulled out briefs, undershirt, socks. He was pretty sure these guys were solid on the Manayunk deal, and they'd already agreed to pay him thirty-seven thousand five, a quarter of the ten-percent development fee, up front. Thank God. Otherwise he'd be flat-out welfare broke. His stomach lurched at the thought. He took a deep breath. But he was okay, things looked okay. Unless something catastrophic happened today, his investors should leave the inspection convinced and smiling and loosening their wallets and the sale should go through within the next couple of weeks and then he could call in the contractors. From the closet he pulled out a suit, shirt, slacks, tie. He figured he could have the building ready for some high-rent tenants in, oh, three, four months. At that point he'd collect another twenty-five percent. Then when fifty percent of the units were occupied he'd collect the balance of his fee. A hundred and fifty-thousand dollars total. Then in a year, eighteen month's tops, he'd sell the building for twice what his investors had paid and they'd all rake in a righteous profit. Simple as pie. Provided all the slices fell into place. In the meantime he had to keep on the prowl for more properties, more investors. He stood in front of the dresser mirror and fixed his tie. His forehead broke out into a light sweat. No need to stress, everything would roll into place.

Chapter Four

"Every fifteen seconds your eyes should complete a rotation that includes windshield, rear mirror, side mirror, dashboard and then back to windshield."

Silvio never forgot that nugget from his high school Driver's Ed class and had faithfully practiced it for the fourteen years since. Even moments like this, stuck in west-bound traffic on the Schuylkill Expressway on a warm October morning with unhappiness eating the very heart out of him, his eyes continued dutifully making the rounds. What was it, an accident up ahead, or something? He craned for a glimpse of a flashing light, strained for the sound of a siren above the back-seat bickering of his daughters – those two were always at it anymore – and the silence of his son. Silvio looked back to make sure Zach was all right. They'd had a pretty good week; actually, but now, heading back to his mother's, how was the boy feeling now? How would he be in the days, weeks, months ahead? Well, they were all still adjusting, still raw inside. The routine was still new for all of them, and this past week that his children had spent with him, though God knows he'd been happy to have them, was probably going to set them all back. Zach was gazing absently out the side window of the van. He looked all right. Not scowling. But not smiling, either. Aw, who could tell, really? Eleven years old and needing a psychologist already. Crying shame what the divorce did to that kid. What it did to all of them. And Silvio worried plenty about his son. Worry, loss, grief, whatever, sometimes Silvio felt a heaviness forming in a spot to the left of his chest, felt it spread across his ribs and wrap itself around his lungs and spine then pulse up his windpipe and throat and finally settle in behind his eyes, squeezing so hard that that he swore the tears were being squeezed out of him.

33

Silvio closed his eyes and breathed deeply. *I'm okay*, he told himself. *I got things to do today. I got these kids to*

"Daddy, what's that car behind us doing?" Trina was kneeling on the seat facing the back window of the van. "It's going baack and forth, baack, and forth!"

Silvio turned around. "Hey!"

By then Samantha had followed her sister's lead and she, too, was kneeling against the back of the seat chanting, "baack and forth, baack and forth!"

"Stop copying me! Daddy, Sam's copying me!"

"Baack and forth, baack and forth!" Sam continued, tossing her sister a sassy look.

"Daddy!" Trina squealed.

"Hey! Hey! Trina! Sam! What do you think you're…"

"But Daddy, what's that car *doing?*"

Zach turned towards his sisters. "It's being stupid, like you two. God."

Well, the boy was speaking today. That was good. That Zach had participated in a family conversation, even if his contribution was only to antagonize his sisters, was enough to pull Silvio back from the edge of his private black hole.

"Okay, Sam, Trina, you turn yourselves around and you get back into those seat belts!"

"But we're not moving."

"Yeah, we don't have to wear our seat belts when we're not moving!"

"Yeah, you do, and now we're moving. Zach, you make sure your sisters stay buckled up, you hear?"

"Fine," Zach mumbled, and that crumb of cooperation raised Silvio's hope that today would be a good day for his son. Zach did have good days, too, after all. If Silvio could just keep the boy connected.

"Yeah, well, that guy behind us?" he said, trying to draw Zach in, "See him, Zach, in the fancy Lexus? That guy, he's thinking he's gonna try and pass me up on the shoulder. Only he can't see around my van because I'm a big guy and he's a little guy, so he can't see that there's a cop car about a hundred feet ahead waiting to zap any dodo

34

bird who thinks he's gonna pass the rest of us on the shoulder. Look at him, look, see how he's trying it, Zach?"

"Is the guy being a dodo bird, Daddy?" asked Sam.

"Oh yeah. A big one. Thinks the rest of us don't have to get to work, too."

"And to school!" Trina added.

"Yeah, school, too, huh, Zach? Hey, everybody still like their new school? How about you Zach, you like school these days? Hey, you join the soccer team yet?"

But Zach had drifted back into silence. Silvio sighed. Traffic was stopped again. This time on his visual tour Silvio's eyes lingered on the rear-view mirror. Idiot in the car behind him still jockeying to pass. Probably some rich idiot lawyer in a hurry to get to the office so he could make a bundle breaking up some poor schmoe's family. *Aw, back off it,* he warned himself. His eyes shifted to his kids in the back seat, the girls quiet for a moment. Zach too quiet. Silvio caught his own image in the mirror. He noticed that his blue t-shirt almost matched the blue of his eyes. His baseball cap was blue, too, but several shades darker. And then there were his blue jeans. Blue inside and out today, he joked to himself. He studied his face. Silvio Jablonski. The big guy with the curly hair and the great smile. That's what they wrote about him in the high school yearbook. He sure had reason to smile back then. Hell, even a year ago, when he was still 29, when they were still a family and he was ignorant as a mushroom in a cave about Trysta's carrying on...

"Yay, we're moving!" cried Sam.

Silvio pulled into the exit lane marked "Route 23" and below that "Conshohocken State Road." Why those two dumbbells had to move his kids way out here to the far west end of nowhere suburbia was beyond Silvio.

"Yay, we're almost home!" cried Trina. "Aren't we almost home, Daddy?"

"Yeah. Almost."

"Daddy, when am I going to start my tap-jazz classes?"

"What?"

"I decided I don't want to do ballet anymore. I want to do tap-jazz. They had that at my old dancing school."

"I want to switch to tap-jazz, too," cried Sam.

"No, Daddy, tell her she can't do everything I do!"

"Yes I can, Daddy!"

"Okay, everybody settle down. We'll have Mommy call your new dance school and get the dancing classes all sorted out."

"But I don't *have* a new dance school! Mommy says we can't afford it yet!"

"*You can't...?*" Silvio grasped the steering wheel tightly to keep from pounding it. "Okay, well, I'll talk to Mommy about it,"

"Daddy, will you stay and live with us and call our dancing school?" asked Sam.

"*Sa-am!*" shrieked Trina, who, being nine years old, knew better than to ask such a question.

"But I miss Daddy too much! I want him to stay with Mommy and us! Please, Daddy, please stay with us?"

Silvio's chest and throat had tightened up on him again, and he needed to focus on rapidly blinking his eyes to keep the tears from welling up.

"Daddy?"

But it was Zach who burst out, "Jesus, Sam, would you stop being so damn stupid? He already told you ten times he's not gonna! Jesus God!"

The girls squealed at their brother's swearing.

"Daddy, Zach said a swear!"

"Two swears!"

"No, three! Jesus, God, and d...."

"Yeah, I heard what he said and you two don't need to go repeating it. Zach, where'd you learn that language?" But of course Silvio knew; Trina and Sam kept him abreast of everything that went on at "Mommy's house," including "Daddy Darren's" "bad words." And what could he do about it? His tone with Zach was more conciliatory than scolding: "No more swearing, and no more 'Jesus God,' okay? I mean, not like that. And especially not in front of your sisters. And no calling little Sam stupid. She's only what, seven now?"

"Yeah, I'm only seven now," Sam sniffed indignantly.

"You act like you're five," Zach grumbled.

"I do not!" Sam shot back.

"Hey, hey, hey, what's going on here? Look, you guys were as good as gold for me all week."

"And we were good as gold for Grandma while you were at work," Trina added.

"Yeah, you were," Silvio said. "And now that you're going back to your Mom's you gotta be just as good. I want no acting up for your Mother. I don't want any bad reports like before, okay?"

"Okay," agreed Trina and Sam.

"Hey, Zach, okay?"

"Yeah, okay."

"And you help your mom and cooperate. Oh, and when he comes over to visit you be nice to little…what's his name? Darren's boy?"

"Josh!" Sam answered.

"Josh*ua!*" Trina corrected her. "He always wants his Mom."

"No he doesn't," Zach huffed. "He just wants to play with my Mario and my Wii."

"Well, you let him, okay?"

Silvio turned his van into a new upscale housing development. They drove past the residences of the suburban nouveau-gentry, homes set back on bright green lawns landscaped with expensively-coordinated shrubbery and ornamentals.

Silvio wondered if his children preferred living here to the Cornwells Heights bungalow on the other side of the city that had been their home before it became an every-other-weekend pit stop. He wondered if they were happier traveling around in their mother's midnight blue SUV than crammed together in the single back seat of his banged-up red work van. In truth he hoped they liked living here. Even though he hated leaving them here. Hated it with all his guts. But he wanted them to be happy. Not full of knots inside. Not like him.

He pulled up to a colonial-style brick house with a small front porch and a yard that appeared to be a few lawn treatments behind the yards of its neighbors. The house was set on a corner with a three-car garage facing the side street. Silvio parked on the street in front of the brick path that led to the front door. He got out of the van and opened the side door then waited for his daughters to climb into his arms.

"A couple more weeks and you girls are gonna be too big for me to be lifting you like this." Sam and Trina squealed their protests as Silvio gently lowered them to the ground. Then the two girls took off down the path towards the house but stopped short when Silvio gave a shrill whistle. "Hey, you wait for your bags!"

"But I want to see Mommy!" Sam whined.

"You get back here and you pick up your bags first."

Sam and Trina scampered back to the van while Zach helped his father unload bags and backpacks. Silvio lined up his three children before him. Good-looking kids. The two girls with Trysta's blonde hair, Zach's several shades darker, the three of them with his and Trysta's blue eyes. He kissed each child then watched while the girls ran away from him with shrieks of joy as their mother opened the front door and her arms to them. Zach lingered in silence with his father for a moment then turned to go.

"Zach, wait a minute. I need to talk to you." Zach turned back to his father.

"What about soccer? Now your Mom's back you can start going to practice."

"I don't know anybody on the team."

"Hey, you get out there on the field, start running around, you'll know 'em all soon enough and they'll know you, too. Tell your mom to sign you up, get you to the practices."

"Like she really will. The season's already started, anyway."

Silvio sighed heavily. "Okay, but look, you remind your Mother about your appointment with Dr. Cavanni, okay?"

"Mom said I don't need to see her anymore."

"Your mom said that? When?"

"Before she left with Darren. On her...honeymoon thing."

Silvio felt flashes like fireworks shooting off in his head. He wanted to put his fist through something, pry up a brick from this fancy path and put it through one of these nice living room windows, or maybe just grab Trysta and shake an ounce of sense into her. But he couldn't afford to get carried off by anger, he'd already lost too much from slamming around like a wounded bull. What he needed now was to keep his head clear, be a father, take care of business, however hard it might be. He breathed deeply for a few moments and then spoke to his son.

"You like seeing Dr. Cavanni?"

Zach looked down and absently ground one foot into the pavement.

"Hey, Zach. Look at me. You like seeing Dr. Cavanni?"

The boy shrugged. Silvio studied his son for a moment then sighed again. "Okay, then. You be good. I'll see you the weekend after next." He hugged his son and Zach hugged him back hard and then trudged off towards his mother, who was waiting for him at the door. Trysta opened her arms to her son but he pushed by her. She waved to Silvio and then turned to re-enter the house.

"Wait, Trysta," Silvio called. Trysta turned back to him and waited on the porch while Silvio walked up the path. Well, she looked good anyway. All filled out and, how did they call it? Glowing. Like she always looked when she was expecting. And then that robe she had on, made of some pale green shimmery material, slipping off her shoulder to reveal a delicate lacy strap...Silvio stopped before he reached the porch, not wanting to come any closer to her. She shouldn't even be outside dressed like that. But Trysta came down the porch steps armed with that sweet promising smile that had hooked him the first time she'd flashed it at him back in high school.

"Yes, Silvio?" She asked pleasantly, seductively pulling the top of her robe back onto her shoulder.

Silvio lowered his eyes. "What about the girls' dancing classes? And Zach's soccer?"

Trysta sighed. "Silvio. I *just* got *back*."

"Yeah, well, what are you telling Trina you can't afford it for? I give you support, right? You gave me a bill for those activities and I've been paying you for them."

"Don't *worry*, Silvio, I'll *get* them to their activities, of *course* I will!"

"Don't forget Zach's appointment."

"Appointment?"

"With Dr. Cavanni."

"That *psychologist*?" Trysta laughed. "Oh, for goodness sake, Zach doesn't need a *psychologist*!" Through the front door screen came the sound of the children arguing. "Why, he's just a normal, active,"

Trysta turned towards the sound of the bickering then back to Silvio, "...*noisy* boy!"

Silvio glanced towards the front door then met her gaze. "His teacher says he needs to see the psychologist."

"Teachers!" Trysta huffed. "I've about had it with those teachers! What do they know about children? *I'm* his mother, *I* should know what he"

"Look, do I have to make an issue out of this?"

Trysta looked slightly wounded at having been cut off by Silvio. "No...no, of course not. You know I always put my children first."

Trina and Samantha flung open the front door.

"Mommy, is Daddy allowed to come in and see our new house?" asked Sam.

"Well...I don't know..." Trysta took a step closer to Silvio. She was only flirting, he knew it, that was her way, but he felt that old stirring in spite of himself. "Want to just step inside and see my new house, Silvio?"

"Cut it out, Trysta."

Trina and Sam began hopping with overlapping squeals of delight.

"Daddy! Mommy says you can come in!"

"Daddy! Come in and see my new room! Please, Daddy, Please!"

"Daddy, Please, please!"

Silvio shook his head helplessly and turned away from them, walking down the brick path in silence.

The girls ducked back into the house and within seconds the fighting resumed.

"Aw, Silvio," Trysta called after him, "now you've got them all riled up!" She hurried up the steps and into the house. Silvio could hear her shouting at the children. A moment later she was calling to him from the front porch.

"Silvio! Silvio, couldn't you come here a minute?"

But Silvio kept walking towards his van.

Trysta shouted back into the house, "I *said* stop!" Then she jogged down the steps and along the path towards Silvio, quickly as her bulging body would allow. "Silvio! Stop!" He was turning the key in the ignition when she reached his van. She hooked her hands over the window sill and leaned inside.

"Silvio," she said breathlessly. Her face was flushed and beads of perspiration lined her upper lip and hairline. Silvio felt a pang of concern for her. He suddenly wanted to cradle her in his arms, wipe her face with his handkerchief, get her a drink of cool water.

"Silvio, couldn't you just come to the door a minute, say something to them, get them settled down for me?"

"Trysta, I, don't think I…"

"Well, it's just that…well, I mean, the kids've been gone for a week, and they're all unsettled, and we've got to get them to school, and, oh, no, there's the school bus! Darren!" she yelled back towards the house. "Ohhh," she moaned.

Silvio considered offering to drive the kids to school. He sighed. Oh, why not. Here she was, all sweaty and flustered and pregnant…

"Silvio, can you drive them for me, please? Darren's probably in there having a fit, he can't stand it when they carry on like that, and I"

"*Darren can't stand it?*"

"Well, you know what I mean…"

Silvio suddenly leaned so close to Trysta's face that she instinctively stepped back. "Trysta, my visitation time with my kids is over. The lousy visitation that you and Darren stuck me with, it's over! So I'm gonna go to work and you're gonna go back inside your house" – he didn't know how it happened, but he was shouting now – "*and figure out how to be a decent mother even if you don't have a clue how to be a decent wife! And you get those kids to school, you hear me?*"

Silvio yanked the transmission into gear and took off down the street leaving Trysta staring, drop-jawed, after him.

***

Trysta's kids were back. Damn. Darren could hear the racket from his office where he was gathering his paperwork. God, living with this tribe was going to take some getting used to, two little screaming banshees and a pre-adolescent zombie whose eyes shot hate-rays. And then there was Sally over there complaining because she got to live in a quiet, trouble-free condo with sweet little Josh, whom he only got to see every Wednesday and one Saturday a month. Like that was fair. Well, whatever Sally's feelings about the divorce, Joshua was *his* son, too, and Darren had the right to spend time with his own son. Why hadn't he called Sally's bluff during the divorce proceedings, insisted on more custody of his son? Something crashed to the floor in the living room and Samantha (or was it Trina?) screeched a high note fit to break a window. Darren sighed. All right, the truth was, he couldn't take another kid full-time, not even his own. Where the hell was Trysta? He'd better go out there and see what was going on in the living room...Aw, Jesus look at the time, why weren't those kids on the school bus? And what kind of game was that damn Silvio playing, bringing them back so late? *Where the hell was Trysta?*

***

Darren met her as she trudged back into the house. "Christ, Trysta, those kids walk in the front door and they're at it! Look, I loaded them into the SUV for you, okay? They already missed the damn bus, thanks to that idiot Silvio!" But Trysta appeared to be in no big heat over the situation. "Okay," he offered, "I could take the SUV myself today and drop them on my way to Manayunk..." He waited for her to object, to insist that she'd take them to school since he had an important investor meeting to get to... "I mean," he continued, "it's out of my way and I got that big meeting..." Still no objection on her part. "... but what the hell, I'll take them, only I gotta get out to the car before they get into my briefcase, okay?"

Trysta fell against his chest, breathing hard.

"Whoa, what's wrong?"

She burst into tears. "What he said to me! How could he call me those awful things?"

"What? Who? Silvio? Aw, don't tell me he was being an asshole again!"

Trysta nodded, still sobbing. "He purposely got the children all riled up so I wouldn't be able to control them and then he called me an awful mother!"

"Where is he?" Darren pulled away from Trysta and ran out the front door and down the path but, to his secret relief, Silvio had already driven off.

42

Darren returned to the living room to find Trysta sprawled across the sofa, one arm across her face, the other thrown behind her head.

"It's okay Baby he's gone. Only now I'm running 'way behind, and I still gotta get those kids to school." He bent down and kissed her on the forehead. "'Bye, Baby."

"But I'm still so upset!"

"Baby, I gotta go..."

"I'm upset!" She threw her arms around Darren's waist and buried her head in his stomach.

Darren glanced at his watch and rolled his eyes in dismay. He put an arm around her shoulder and stroked her hair impatiently. "Aw, Baby, it's all right, look, you gotta ignore Silvio, he's just a dumb slob."

"He'll do *anything* to upset me!"

Darren sighed heavily. "Hell, maybe we should introduce him to Sally."

Chapter Five

"So that's my sad story, Joanne. Don't fire me, okay?"

"What, just because you're dealing with the Johnstown Flood of toilets? You sure you're not making all this up? Lying in bed with a cup of coffee and a couple of hot buttered buns?"

Sally laughed. Joanne Ponticello was being kind. That was the way of this loud, over-the top, middle-aged Italian lady who'd been office manager at the accounting firm of Zarnecki and Young since before Sally'd started working there in high school. In fact it was Joanne who'd gotten Sally the little under-the-table, licking-envelopes-and-pulling-out-staples job at the office in the first place, Joanne having been on a couple of Sally's mother's church committees back at Our Lady of Peace before her mother went religion-crazy and had to go seek out a crazier church. After high school when Sally started at Philadelphia Community College she moved up a rung to legitimate part-time administrative assistant. Then she married Darren, got pregnant, dropped out of college and stayed on full-time at Zarnecki and Young at that same low rung. Of course at the time the plan was that Sally was only going to work there until Darren's boat came in and then she'd go back to school, have a few more kids and they'd all move to some sweet little property, as Darren used to refer to their future home, out on the Main Line where she'd settle in as a retro full-time stay-at-home mom, at least until the kids were all in school.

But it had seemed that Darren was on a pretty slow boat until last year when he turned thirty and his slow boat turned into a speed boat: he was promoted and got Trysta pregnant.

"Well, at least *you* waited until you were married to get pregnant," Joanne had huffed when Sally tearfully broke the news that Darren was leaving her for a pregnant telephone receptionist. And Sally'd had to laugh through her tears at Joanne's heavy-handed sympathy. Because Sally *had* in fact been married to Darren when she'd gotten pregnant. But just barely. She and Darren figured it happened on their wedding night, geez, how had they managed that? Of course, it was her first time using the pill, so maybe she did screw it up, as Darren had accused her. But she'd been twenty years old and the wedding night of their off-season weekend-special honeymoon at a cabin in the Pocono Mountains had been her first time ever, and was that such a crime, waiting 'til your wedding night? After all, she was a Catholic girl from Little Flower High school. Well, Catholic on her mother's side, Jewish on her father's. But mostly Catholic. Not that her Jewish side had injected any more sexual liberation into her psyche than had her Catholic side. And once, in one of those dark moments when she was turning over and over in her mind the endless possibilities of *why, how, why, how, why, how* could Darren have left her, she scraped up the possibility that he left her because of some long-held resentment over her having been too stingy with the put-out years ago at the front end of the relationship.

"Oh, sure," Joanne observed one day after joining Sally in the vending area where Sally was taking a crying break, "he'd of been a whole lot happier if you'd have slept with him and gotten knocked up *before* he married you, while he was still in college." She took a sip of her Styrofoam-cup coffee. "Deep-six that one, Hon."

"Well, then why *did* Darren leave me?" Sally sobbed.

"Um…how about because he's a regular size-11 shit-heel?"

Joanne's advice was somehow always a lot better than her mother's.

Still, Joanne was Sally's boss and doubtless not thrilled that Sally was calling in late for work this morning, rogue toilet or not.

"So what time do you think you'll make it in?" Joanne asked.

"Well, I just finished mopping pee-water off the damn bathroom floor."

"Good times."

"Yeah. Anyway, I'll be in as soon as the plumber shows. They said a couple of hours."

"How does that work now, does the condo send you the

plumber?"

"Nah, the condo doesn't pay for anything that fritzes inside the house, which stinks. I called some outfit I found online: 'Quick and Reliable Plumbers. Dependable Service to the Great Northeast for Forty Years.' Supposedly. You ever heard of them?"

"Well, no. Ponti takes care of the household breakdowns."

"Oh. Yeah. Well," Sally forced a weak laugh, "that's what husbands are for, right?"

"Let's don't talk about husbands."

"Not even good ones like your Ponti?"

"How old are you, Sally, twenty-six, twenty-seven?"

"Twenty-seven."

"You started young."

"That's what my mom said. It's what Darren's mom said. What everybody said. Now it's *'See? See? This is how you end up when you get married and you're both too young!'*"

"I didn't say you got married too young. I said you started young. Plunged right into life in the grown-up world instead of spending a couple of years goofing off like kids your age generally do. That's not necessarily a bad thing. Plunging right into life, I mean. And believe it or not, you got lots of years ahead of you yet and I promise you, a good man is gonna come your way, trust me. Though the most important man in your life today is gonna be that plumber, and believe me, a good plumber is better than a bad husband."

"I believe you," Sally laughed. "Only I hope Mr. Goodplumber doesn't charge me a fortune. My checkbook's about to crack."

"Hang in there, Hon. Just stay calm and you'll make it."

"If you say so then I know it's true. Thanks Joanne. And thanks so much for"

"Just get your hiney back here as soon as you can."

"Keep my desk warm for me, okay?"

"I'll lay an egg on it. And you stay calm."

"Okay. 'Bye." Sally hung up the phone and closed her eyes. *I'll stay calm.*

Chapter Six

"Silvio? I just now got another toilet. What do you say, Hon, you think you can do another toilet? "

Silvio reached for the clipboard on the passenger seat and flipped through the pile of work orders he'd just picked up from the office. Toilet, toilet, sink, tub, sink, toilet, toilet. Standard Monday morning junk jobs for this time of year. You get a bunch of guys together over Sunday afternoon football and too much beer, who knew what would end up flushed or shoved down the sink or toilet?

"Yeah, okay, Ida, but they better not be in a hurry 'cause I'm already up to my neck. Isn't there somebody else who can take that one?"

The dispatcher sighed. "Well, see, John's off today, he did the weekend, and your Uncle Bud and Kevin are gonna be half the day on that subcontracting job with Kensington Sewer and Gas, you know, routing out that backed-up sewer line 'way out on Byberry Road in Somerton, which I know you'd rather be doing, and believe me, Hon, I'd of saved that job for you if I could of, but you know Bud's rule on jobs, first come, first serve, and Kevin was here at, like, six-forty-five, so, I mean, you know…"

"Okay, Ida, okay, but they're gonna have to wait." Ever since his divorce Ida had been treating Silvio like he was made of egg shells, or something. He wished she would stop being so careful around him, it only put him in a bad mood, or on a day like today, a worse mood, only the worse his mood the more careful she got, so it was all a big vicious circle, or cycle, or whatever, but he didn't know how to tell her so.

"Oh, sure, sure," Ida cooed, "if they gotta wait then they gotta wait. Don't you worry about it, Hon, you're doing the best you can.

47

Your uncle knows it. We all know it."

Silvio made an effort not to clench his teeth. "All right, Ida, what's the address?" He put his cell phone on speaker while he flipped to a blank work order at the back of the clip board and grabbed the pen chained to the clipboard.

"Ahh, let's see…The Villas at Roosevelt. Two-oh-seven Roman Fountain Way."

"The Villas?" Silvio thought for a moment. "Oh, wait a minute…that's that condo complex? Out at Roosevelt and Rhawn?'

"Uh…yeah, I think so. Yeah, Roosevelt and Rhawn. A condo-apartment mix."

Silvio sighed. "Yeah, I know that place, that's one of Mo Ealy's. Look, I thought we weren't gonna mess with that guy any more, he's stiffed us before."

"I don't know, Hon, Bud didn't say anything about it to me, so, you know…"

"Right. Who called you? Ealy?"

"Well, no, it was a woman. Must be a condo owner."

"She speak English?"

"Yeah, she spoke perfect English."

"'Cause Ealy, his buildings are crawling with immigrants, I can tell you that for a fact."

"Oh."

"Look, the guy is not legit and I don't like dealing with him."

"Oh. Well, it wasn't Ealy who called in the work order, it was a woman, so it must be for a condo owner, not a renter."

"Holy crow, who'd be stupid enough to *buy* one of those units?"

"I don't know, but she spoke perfect English, no accent or anything. So what I'm saying, is, you shouldn't have to deal with Ealy himself, or anything. Look, Silvio, like I said, I hate laying another dip-squat toilet job on you, but, I mean, you know…"

Silvio blew out a deep breath. "Yeah, well, she's gonna have to wait."

***

All right. The plumber was called, the office was called, the bathroom floor was scrubbed along with the cheap hall carpeting into which the toilet water had seeped. What next? Take Josh to daycare or leave him home? He'd be happy to spend a day at home...but then...what if he had to go to the bathroom again before the plumber got here? Come to think of it, Sally kind of had to go the bathroom...she could drop Josh off at Happy Tots and make a bathroom stop herself on the way home...but what if the plumber showed while she was out?...nah, the woman she'd talked to on the phone said it would be an hour or two...she could get Josh to Happy Tots and be back inside half an hour...yeah, better to get him to school, not upset his routine, such as it was.

After she dropped Josh off Sally stopped at a fast-food place near her condo to use the bathroom. The warm aroma from the griddle reminded her that she hadn't eaten any breakfast. The dining area was bright, the walls hung with homey country-suburban restaurant art, the overhead muzak cheery. Suddenly a cup of fresh coffee sipped at one of those vinyl and Formica booths seemed like Nirvana. And heck, what was a small cup of coffee? A dollar? A coffee and one of those warm cinnamon rolls with the melting butter cream frosting...what, two-fifty-nine, total? She could sit by herself in that booth by the window and relax for ten minutes. What the hell, she deserved it.

By the time Sally returned home the fast-food caffeine and sugar had elevated her mood considerably, but an hour later the two coffees she'd drank came home to roost, and by eleven-thirty her urge to pee was a raging tide. The plumber was already two hours later than promised, but by then Sally didn't dare leave to seek out another public restroom. She paced the floor: what should she do? Leave and risk missing the plumber? Call another plumber? Pee in the tub? She was about to go for the last option when the sensation knock-knocking at her gut warned her that she needed to do worse than pee...*Oh, shit!* She needed a fully functioning bathroom! Fast! She heard the baby across the hallway crying again. So at least one of her Hispanic baby-carrying neighbors was home...but did the people who lived across the hall from her even know who she was? She was pretty sure they'd exchanged a "Hi" a time or two in passing...geez, why hadn't she gotten to know her neighbors? Now she was going to have to knock on these people's door, practically a stranger, and ask to use their bathroom, how embarrassing! Well, hell, she had no fucking choice. She grabbed a post-it note from the kitchen drawer and wrote a quick message for that asshole plumber: *I'm across the hall.* She considered adding *using the bathroom*, but she figured the dope wouldn't take it as the reproach intended.

Sally rang the bell of the apartment across the hallway and a moment later the door was opened by a young woman holding a chubby baby.

"Hi, I'm Sally Miller. From across the way?"

The woman nodded and smiled pleasantly.

"My bathroom is, uh, out of order. Do you think I could borrow yours?"

The woman blinked and continued smiling. Blankly. It was clear she didn't understand a word of what Sally'd said.

"Lo siento," the woman finally answered, "No hablo mucho ingles. No English."

Sally moaned, and the woman, understanding that Sally was in some kind of distress, stepped back and beckoned her inside. Sally desperately flipped back through her mind, scrounging for a few dregs of high-school Spanish. Damn, four years vegetating in Senora O'Sullivan's Spanish class at Little Flower, why couldn't she remember a word? Or a word of anything useful? Like, "Can I use your bathroom? My toilet is broken." Wait, didn't she learn how to say "Where's the restroom?" Wasn't that one of their cultural phrases to learn? To learn just in case one's toilet broke and one happened to be living across the hall from a person who only spoke Spanish? *If I pee all over her floor then she'll understand, all right! God, in another second I'm going to start dancing! Oh, please, God, make her understand!* The woman obviously understood something was wrong. She balanced the baby on her hip and gently took Sally's arm. She tried to lead Sally to a chair.

"Aqui sientate, esta bien."

"No, no, I need to go..." Wait...she had it! *"Donde esta el baño!"*

The woman looked at Sally quizzically. "El baño? Mi baño?"

"Si, si," Sally pointed at the woman, "Your...tu baño. Mi baño is... no worky..." She made several gestures for "dead".

"Oh…tu baño no functiona?"

"Si, si… mi baño no functiona!" It was coming back to her, thank God!

"Tu quieres usar mi baño?"

"Si, si, yo quieres…quiero…" Sally almost shouted it, "*Yo quiero usar tu baño! Please!*" *Thank you God! Thank you Senora O'Sullivan!*

"Oh…si," the woman nodded, "I you comprendo. Por supuesto, puedes usar mi baño. Come." The woman led Sally to the bathroom while Sally showered her with "gracias's" and decided she was going to kill that goddamn plumber.

It was actually a good thing there was no window in the bathroom. Otherwise Sally might have considered climbing out rather than facing her neighbor again, who by now probably had Sally pegged as a mental case, a weirdo, or maybe just your garden-variety walking embarrassment. God knows, if someone showed up at Sally's door babbling and desperate to take a pee and a dump in her pot Sally certainly would have thought as much.

But when Sally exited the bathroom the woman smiled and gave no hint of thinking any the worse of her toilet-deprived neighbor. In fact she was serenely rocking her now sleeping infant, who resembled a little brown rosy-cheeked cherub.

"Mi baby boy," she said and gently kissed the child's curly black hair.

"Beautiful baby boy," Sally said, smiling back, grateful that the focus had shifted from her own awkward situation.

"Baby name Dayveed."

"Dayveed?" Sally thought a moment. "David?"

"Si, yes, Dayvid. Mi baby es americano,"

Her baby is American? Which is supposed to imply that she's…?

"I," she pointed to herself, "name Lupe. Soy de Nicaragua."

"Nicaragua, huh?" Sally pointed to herself. "Sally. From Northeast Philadelphia."

"Mucho gusto, Sally"

"Mucho gusto, Lupe."

Lupe stood up, carefully cradling the baby's head. "Dayvid esta durmiendo." She closed her eyes and mimed snoring.

"Oh yeah," Sally chuckled, "He's sleeping. *Sleeping.*" She closed her eyes and pressed her palms together, tilting her head against her hands.

"Sleeping," Lupe repeated.

"Right. Just like babies are supposed to do."

"Sally, esperate aqui, no te vayas." Lupe gestured for Sally to wait there while she carried the baby to the bedroom to lay him in his crib. When she came out she gestured towards the kitchen. Sally noticed a Spanish-English dictionary on the kitchen table.

"Quieres tomar un café conmigo?" She pointed to herself then to Sally and mimed tilting a cup to her lips. "You me? Un café?"

"Oh, no...gracias...I mean, I would like to...quiero...but, no, uh, I can't." Sally shook head and shrugged apologetically.

"Oh, no puedes."

"Si, no puedes."

"No *puedo*," Lupe corrected her, "you say no pued*o*."

"Right. No pued*o*. I'm waiting for the plumber...*plumber...*" Sally tried to mime a plunging motion. "To fix my... baño."

Lupe's face lit up. "The plumber! Feex...you baño!" She imitated Sally's mime-plunging.

"Si. To fix my baño!" Now both women were mime-plunging.

"I comprendo, Sally! Mi esposo es the plumber! He feex the baño!"

"Your husband is a plumber?"

"Si!" She repeated slowly, "My husband es plumber. Feex the baño!"

"Fix the baño," Sally sighed. "Wow. Some girls get all the luck. Anyway, Lupe, I have to leave..." Sally walked towards the door. "No puedo..." She did the cup-tilting mime, "café. I'm sorry. Uh...Lo siento?"

Lupe clapped her hands. "Si, Lo siento! You good Spanish!"

"Me sucky Spanish," Sally replied and then immediately regretted it.

"Sucky?" Lupe repeated.

"No, no, don't say that word, say...oh, what the heck, you'll learn the word soon enough, the way you're living. Sucky is ...bad...malo."

"Sucky es malo?"

"Yeah...muy malo."

"Sucky," Lupe repeated thoughtfully. "Sucky."

Way to go, Sally thought, *You've just taught a Nicaraguan immigrant her first bad word.* "Anyway, thanks again," Sally said as she stood at the door to leave. "I owe you."

"I owe you?"

"No, I" Sally pointed to herself, "Owe *you.*" She pointed to Lupe. "You say, '*You* owe *me.*'"

"Oh. She pointed to Sally then herself. "*You* owe *me.*"

"That's right. Sally owes Lupe. If you can ever figure that out. Well, don't worry, I won't forget."

As she walked across the hallway Sally stopped to look back into the still-open door of Lupe's apartment. She saw Lupe in her kitchen reaching for the Spanish-English dictionary. "*You* owe *me,*" she repeated. "*You* owe *me.*"

Chapter Seven

"Hello, Joanne?"

"Sally? Where are you, Lady? It's almost, what, three-fifteen?"

"Huh, three guesses where I am. Quick and Reliable Plumbers ain't."

"Aw, gee," Joanne sighed. "Well, the day's about shot. You got any personal days left?"

"Yeah, right. The divorce proceedings on top of Josh's fifteen ear infections ate up every minute and then some."

"Oh boy. So the best I can do for you is give you a day of unpaid leave. I'm sorry Sally."

"I know, it's okay. Just don't fire me, okay?"

"Fire you? Sally, you know I'll go to bat for you as much as I can. But look, Hon – and I know you're gonna feel like this is about the worst time to bring this up, but I think this is the very time to bring it up – you really need to start thinking about finishing up that college degree. Get yourself a business degree, accounting, pre-law, even, something that will let us up-grade what you're getting here in pay and benefits."

"Me? Go back to school? Now? Aw, Joanne, you gotta be"

"Just listen to me Sally. I could promote you, I *would* promote you in a minute if you only you had a degree. I know, I know, you've been working here for years, you're smart and savvy and could probably even run the place, but that's the way it is. If you had that degree you'd be in a position to receive better pay, better benefits, and, most importantly at the moment, more personal leave. So you gotta start thinking about going back to school, start looking into how you could possibly make it happen. Okay?"

Sally sucked in a deep breath. "Okay. Sure. I will. Thanks."

As soon as Joanne hung up Sally looked at her phone and snapped, "God, Joanne, what the hell do you think is going on in my life at the moment? *College?* Are you totally out of your..."

The doorbell! Someone was outside the door and here she was shouting at the phone like some kind of nut case!

Sally took a few deep breaths then opened the door to a big muscular man carrying a large tool-box, clipboard, and a coiled plumber's snake. He looked surly and cheerless as a stiff. "Quick and Reliable Plumbers," he muttered.

"Yeah, right," Sally muttered back.

"Excuse me, Ma'am?"

"Forget it."

"You got a problem here?"

"Yeah, I got a problem. Here."

Sally and Silvio stared at each other for a moment in a silent exchange of hostility. Then Sally turned and walked to the bathroom while Silvio followed behind. She opened the bathroom door and pointed to the toilet.

"There, okay? There's my problem!"

Silvio stepped past Sally into the bathroom and studied the toilet for a moment. "Yeah, okay." He knelt and opened his tool box while Sally stationed herself over him. He looked up at her.

"Uh, Ma'am, do ya mind?"

"I just want to see what you're gonna"

"I *said* do ya *mind?*"

Sally stomped back out into the hall and stood outside the bathroom with her arms crossed. She watched while Silvio worked in silence, removing the toilet's lid and fiddling inside the tank, pulling something out, sticking something back in and then poking the interior of the bowl with his snake. He opened the valve then flushed the toilet. "Okay, it works."

Sally entered the bathroom and looked over the toilet while Silvio filled in a form attached to his clipboard.

"What about those black scratch marks you left all inside the bowl?"

He answered without looking up from his writing. "You got cleanser?"

"Yeah, I got cleanser!"

"Good." Silvio ripped off a sheet from his clipboard and Sally snatched it from his hand. She looked at the bill. "What? What's this? Ninety-two dollars?"

"You wanna pay cash, credit or debit?"

"But...*ninety-two dollars?* I mean, you're here, what, ten minutes, you scratch the heck out of my toilet, and you charge me"

"Look, Ma'am, we charge by the hour. They told you that on the phone, right?"

"Yeah, but you"

"That's how we charge. By the hour."

"For ten lousy min"

"By the hour. Cash, credit or debit?"

"What? Wait a minute, you can't charge somebody for an hour when you"

"Lady, you wanna pay me cash, credit or debit?"

Calm down, she thought, *cool it,* but it was too late. She could feel the heat of her inner Vesuvius rising, rising. "You want me to pay you? You want me to *pay you?*" She was sputtering with rage. "What the...you think you can knock around here for, for ten lousy minutes and charge me for...? I mean...I, I, I MISS A WHOLE DAY OF WORK AND YOU, YOU...WHERE THE HELL DO YOU GET OFF?" She was flailing her arms at Silvio, who looked suddenly drop-jawed and flabbergasted. "WHAT KIND OF A GODDAMN SNAKESHIT CLIP-JOB ARE YOU TRYING TO PULL HERE, CHARGING PEOPLE FOR, FOR, YOU WANNA GET PAID FOR AN HOUR? YOU CAN PARK YOUR ASS HERE AND *WORK* FOR AN HOUR, DAMMIT, AND YOU CAN START BY SCRUBBING THOSE LOUSY FUCKING MARKS YOU LEFT ON MY LOUSY FUCKING TOILET!"

She let out a wail that could have come from a wild jungle animal, or from the wildness of her own interior jungle, overgrown and out of control with frustration and sorrow. She smacked her face into her hands and crumpled down to a sitting position on the floor. Her crying sounded loud and ugly in her ears and she struggled to catch her breath against her sobbing. This time she'd let herself go. Just let herself go and cry herself to death and get it over with. Except that within two minutes she was done. Cried out. Her monsoon of tears had been merely a flash flood. She rubbed her hand across her eyes and under her nose and looked around her. The plumber was gone though his tools were still here. Sally slowly stood up, ran a hand through her hair, straightened her clothes. Now what? She looked at herself in the bathroom mirror. She looked a mess, so what else was new? And where was the plumber? Poor schlemiel had probably run for his life. Then Sally saw his reflection in the mirror and jumped. She quickly turned around and there he was, standing at the bathroom door looking pale, one had rubbing against his jeans, the other holding a bucket that held a can of cleanser and a scrub brush. Up behind him came Lupe holding her baby. And behind her stood another man whom Sally recognized as the man she'd seen before around the apartment complex with Lupe. Just the audience for her one-woman freak show.

"Uh, these people, your neighbors, I guess…see, I went out to my truck for, uh," he held up the bucket, "and when I came back they were standing outside your door."

Lupe and the man maneuvered around Silvio into the bathroom. The man was just a little taller than Lupe, presumably Nicaraguan as well, and he had nice eyes, a nice smile. A short, handsome Nicaraguan guy.

"Estas bien, Sally?" Lupe touched the man's arm. "Este es mi esposo."

"*My husband,*" the man whispered to Lupe.

"Es *my husband*. Ascensiòn."

"We heard a lotta noise," said Ascensiòn. "You okay?"

"Yeah. I am." She felt like an ass. An ass in a circus act.

"Ascensiòn es plumber," said Lupe.

"Lupe says you having a problem with your toilet," said Ascensiòn. "Is okay now?"

"Yeah," Silvio replied. "It was just her inner valve was corroded."

"Inner valve? Is pretty easy to fix. You need one? I got one in my box."

Easy to fix. Figures, thought Sally. She dredged up a smile and walked Lupe, Ascensiòn and their baby to the front door. Lupe paused at the door. "Sally, porque lloras?"

"She wants to know why are you crying." Ascensiòn turned his wife. "Lupe, dile, '*Why are you crying?*'"

"Why are you crying?" Lupe slowly repeated after her husband.

"Oh, ha, ha, I'm not really…" Sally let her smile drop. "I'm having a bad day."

"Oh, un dia malo, I comprendo," Lupe cooed. Her wide brown eyes were full of sympathy.

Ascensiòn offered Sally his beautiful smile. "You gonna see. Now your day's gonna get better. I promise."

"*If it does,*" thought Sally, "*then I really owe you.*"

***

Lupe and Ascensiòn were gone, but Silvio was still standing outside her bathroom, still holding onto his bucket. Sally ignored him while she wrote out a check for ninety-two dollars. He approached her and cleared his throat.

"Look, Ma'am, I don't want any trouble, okay?"

Sally didn't answer him, but finished writing the check then ripped it out of her checkbook with a flourish and held it at arm's length and then turned her back to him. He stuffed the check into his pocket without looking at it.

"Ma'am…Like I said, I don't want any trouble." His voice was quivering. "I'm gonna give you your hour's worth. I got cleanser from my truck."

Sally turned back to face him. "Huh?"

"I'll start with those marks on your commode.

"What?"

"Those black marks. On your john."

"You're gonna…what, scrub my john?"

"Yeah. You got anything else around here needs fixing? I wanna give you your hour's worth."

"Uh, well…" Sally was flabbergasted. "My furnace has been acting a little tricky lately…"

Sally sat on the edge of her sofa picking at her nail polish, occasionally gnawing a raggity cuticle. It had been forever since she'd had a manicure, but why the heck was she even thinking about manicures right now? The plumber had cleaned her pot and was now in the alcove off the kitchen working on her furnace. She stood up and paced the living room for a moment then sat back down. Then she wandered through the kitchen to the alcove. The plumber was on his knees hunched into the interior of her furnace. She talked to his back.

"Ahem. Look, I...I'm really sorry. It's just...I've been having a bad divorce, er, *day*, I mean."

Silvio turned to look at her. "A bad divorce day? Okay. I've had a few of those myself." He turned back to the furnace.

"You're divorced?"

"Yeah." He yanked a wrench from the guts of her furnace and stood up. "Your switch is about to go. A new one'll run you about a hundred and ten bucks with labor. I could fix it myself if I had the part."

"No kidding? You fix plumbing and heating, too?"

Silvio gave a short, unhappy laugh. "Oh sure, I can fix almost anything. Except my marriage. That I couldn't fix."

"Well, I'd of sure thought twice about leaving a guy who can fix anything," Sally joked. And immediately wished she hadn't. The plumber wasn't seeing the humor.

"My wife, she didn't want a plumber," he said sourly. "She wanted college educated. Upper class. Some rich guy to buy her a damn palace out in the suburbs!"

Silvio threw the wrench into his tool box where it landed with a loud metallic smack that made Sally jump. She suddenly wanted to lighten the situation.

"Oh yeah? Well, heh, heh, she can have my ex. For a nickel."

"Don't worry. She got what she wanted!" He swiped a rag he'd left lying on the counter, wiped his hands and then threw the rag into his bucket.

"Aw, c'mon," said Sally, feeling truly sympathetic, "college isn't for everybody. Me, I dropped out of Philadelphia Community."

"Yeah? What do you do now?"

"Admin. Over at Zarnecki and Young. An accounting firm, a big place. Out by Castor Avenue and Cottman? It's a pretty nice job. I mean, it's okay. The truth is, I really gotta find something that pays better. Now that I'm a – like they say – single mother."

"Your ex pay you child support?"

"Yeah. But he's threatening to go dead beat." She gave a short, false laugh. "If he does I'll kill him."

"Well, even if you end up broke, at least you got your kids." Silvio slammed the metal cover back over the furnace. "You know how often I see my kids, my own kids? Every other damn weekend! You wanna tell me how I'm supposed to be a father to those kids?" He bent over and picked up several tools from the floor, sniffling and pausing to run the back of his hand across his eyes.

Sally sighed. "It's gotta be tough," was all she could dredge up to say.

Silvio began throwing the tools into his box one by one, each hitting with an unnerving clang.

"You wanna hear something makes a whole lot of sense? This guy's got a wife and kid of his own, he leaves them to go play house with *my* wife and *my* kids!" He slammed shut the lid of his tool box then gave the box such a hard, mean kick that the red fanned out across his cheeks and forehead. "You wanna hear something makes even more sense?" His voice was cracking. "My wife, she takes my kids away from me to go live under some other man's roof, but *I* still have to pay for their support, because *he's* supporting his *own* kid, who lives somewhere else! Now doesn't that make a whole damn terrific load of...of..."

Silvio slammed his forearm against Sally's furnace and buried his head in his arm to stifle the loud heavy sobs that were heaving up from his chest. Sally watched him for a moment, her fingertips covering her mouth.

"Uh, I'm gonna make some coffee," she said softly. "You want some coffee?"

***

They sat at Sally's dinette table sipping coffee and nibbling at sugar doughnuts in uncomfortable silence.

"Coffee all right?" Sally finally tried.

"Coffee's good," Silvio replied.

"I like to get these doughnuts..."

"They're good doughnuts."

"I get them off the day-old rack, but they're still all right."

"Sure, just as good. I don't know why I gotta let loose like that. Like I just did."

"Ha, tell me about it. Me, the lady volcano."

Silvio tilted his head thoughtfully. "You know, that's just what it's like. A volcano. It's like this hot...flash... and then..." He shook his head.

Sally chuckled. "Hot flashes, that's a good one! On account of the *change* we're going through! Wait, did I just say that? I can't believe I just said that! God, what a dumb thing to say!"

Silvio smiled. "Don't worry about it." He stood up. "Well, let me get my tools. Thanks for the coffee." He sounded sincere. He seemed like a sincere kind of guy. And sensitive. Big and strong on the outside but sensitive at heart. And suffering. Just like herself.

"Sure." Sally followed him into the bathroom.

"You have any more trouble with this commode, you call me back. I stand by my work."

"Okay, thanks."

"And you ought to have that furnace fixed real soon. It could go any time on you."

"Well, it's always one thing or another, huh?"

"Yep. Well..."

The plumber looked as though he wanted to say something more, but he picked up his work tools then nodded and smiled at her and headed for the front door. He stopped at the door, put down his tools and turned back to Sally.

"Hey, I'm sorry about taking so long to get here. By seven a.m. this morning I had a list of jobs like you wouldn't believe. You just sorta got tagged on at the end."

"It's okay. I understand."

"Yeah, well we really need another plumber on board, you know?"

"Oh yeah? Hey how about...?" She cocked her head and hitched her thumb over her shoulder, "my neighbor. He's a plumber."

"Your neighbor? Huh, guy's about as legal as a three-dollar bill."

"You think?" Sally sighed. "Too bad. Seems like a nice guy."

"Nice is nice and legal is legal."

"I guess. Too bad I don't know how to…plumb."

Silvio chuckled. "Anyway, it's been, you know, nice talking to you."

"Same here. Kind of like a, you know, support group, or something."

"You got a support group?" he asked.

"Nah. Do you?"

"Oh, yeah, sure. I go to that "Single With Children" one. Meets not too far from here. Over at The Harmony Church off Harbison and Frankford Avenue. You know where that is?"

"Yep. I used to live right off Harbison on Hawthorne Street across from Wissenoming Park."

"Oh yeah? We've done a lot of work out there. People are fixing up those old row houses all over the Northeast, and I'll tell you, those are some houses that were built to last. It's a nice neighborhood, out by Wissenoming."

"Yeah. A really nice neighborhood. But divorces happen, right?"

Silvio looked stricken. "Oh, gee, I'm sorry, I should've figured…look, you really ought to check out my support group. It's a good group."

Sally sighed. "Yeah, I should. Only I hate to leave Joshua."

"Joshua?"

"My son."

"You got a son named Joshua?"

"Yeah. I don't like to leave him alone any more than I have to. The divorce has been rough going for him, too."

"No kidding. My son, he's eleven years old and he's seeing a psychologist. Eleven years old. Damn shame!"

"Poor little guy."

"You see how it is? The parents rip up the marriage license then you gotta scotch-tape the kids back together."

"Meanwhile you yourself are feeling like a piece of paper that's been written on, wadded up, and tossed in the trash can."

"Yeah."

"Look, I hope your little boy gets better."

"Thanks. And you go ahead and stay home with your Joshua. Kids need their parents. It's the best thing for them." Silvio picked up his tools again and put his hand on the doorknob. Sally laughed weakly and shook her head.

"What's funny?"

"Oh, don't mind me. You just reminded me of something my ex said when he called this morning."

"Oh yeah?" Silvio put down his tools again.

"Yeah. Get this. My ex, he calls first thing this morning to tell me he wants to cut back his child support."

"Nice kinda guy."

"*Oh* yeah. Now, the guy has just bought a five-bedroom house out in New Conshohocken, he just got back yesterday from his honeymoon in Puerto Vallarta, that's in Mexico, see, and"

Silvio cut her off. "Hold it! Did you say Puerto Vallarta? In *Mexico?*"

"Yeah. Why?"

"Oh geeze! You got a son named Joshua?"

"Yeah...?"

"Oh geeze. Oh, geeze!" Silvio began scavenging through his pants pockets until he came up with Sally's check. He stared at the check then looked up at Sally, his eyes wide with astonishment. 'Elizabeth S. Miller?'"

"What? Oh, yeah, that's me. Only my middle name is Sarah, after my grandmother, so I go by Sally, but...what?"

"*Sally Miller!* That's *you!* You...you were married to...*Darren Miller!*"

"What? Wait, how did you know about"

"The guy who took off with my Trysta!"

"What?" Sally began feeling a sickish, sleazyish sensation in her stomach. "Oh, my God," she muttered. "You're?"

"Yeah."

Sally and Silvio instinctively turned away from each other. They stood for a few moments in silent disbelief and mutual humiliation. Sally finally laughed bitterly.

"Shit. I never knew...I mean, they never told me...I mean...hell, I guess I never asked..."

"About me? Huh, why should you?"

"Yeah, why should I?"

They stood in silence for a bit longer then Sally said, "Jesus, what were you and me in all this, anyway? A couple of, of...mile markers left behind on Darren and Trysta's road to Shangri-fuckin'-La!"

Silvio turned back to Sally, talking to her back. He laughed weakly. "Hey, isn't there a name for people like us? I mean, like step-spouses, or exes-in-law, or something?"

How about losers, Sally thought.

"Aw the hell with it!" she heard him say. Then she heard the sound of paper ripping. Sally turned back to Silvio. He was ripping up her check.

She gasped and then laughed. "My God, what are you, crazy?"

"No, I'm Silvio Jablonski the plumber. And I don't have to charge family."

"We're family?"

"Who knows? I mean, we must fit together somehow in this mess."

"We, gee...I mean...thanks...Silvio."

"Aw, it's all right. Look, I'm gonna come by after work sometime to fix your furnace. Darn thing is about to blow."

"When you do I'll fix you dinner!"

"How about tonight?"

"Uh, would tomorrow be okay?"

"Let me see...No, tomorrow I got my support group. Wednesday okay?"

Sally ran through her mental calendar. "Wednesday, you say?" Okay, what was happening on Wednesday? Something...something... then it hit her. "Wednesday Darren is coming by...that is to say, he's *supposed* to come by and pick up Josh."

"Oh yeah? What time?"

Suddenly Silvio and Sally were grinning at each other

conspiratorially.

"Around six-thirty." Sally giggled. "I'll call and remind him."

"I'll be there." Silvio was laughing. "It'll be, huh, huh, great, huh, huh!"

Now Sally was laughing, too. "Well, huh, huh, it may not be, huh, huh, great, huh, huh, but…"

Sally couldn't finish, she was laughing too hard and so was Silvio. They laughed and laughed, the tears streaming down their faces.

Chapter Eight

There was no need to sweat bullets. Of this Darren had been reminding himself since Monday. No need to stress. None at all. The Manayunk deal was still going to come off as planned. Pretty much as planned. He hoped. He prayed. Shit, those goddamn investors, Chase Winston and Aaron Winslow, Attorneys At Law, what a couple of rich, spineless pussies!

When he'd touched base with them Friday – God, Friday, he'd still been in Puerto Vallarta and riding high – the deal had been all sewn up, they just wanted one more look-over at the property Monday morning. But thanks to the six-ring circus his home life had morphed into Darren had shown up forty minutes late and their feet had gotten cold waiting for him. Now Winston and Winslow – had they made up those stuck-up-sounding names, or what? – wanted to wait until the end of the week to, in their words, finalize the decision in their minds. *Finalize the decision in their minds?* What kind of wimpy-assed psychobabble was that? You don't finalize the decision in your mind, you finalize it on paper, signing on the damn line, dotting the i's and crossing the t's then sliding a big fat check in Darren's direction.

All right, it wasn't like the deal wasn't going to happen. Of course, it *could* not happen, Winston and Winslow theoretically could still pull out and then he'd be up shit creek...but no, they liked the Manayunk property, had still liked it on Monday morning, Darren was sure of that. Himself they were a little annoyed with, maybe enough to make him sweat it out a few days, maybe that's what the delay was really about – he'd made them wait, they'd make him wait, people were people, after all, always nursing their personal feelings first and foremost. But today was Wednesday and they would come through by the end of the week, so two more days of sweating at most. And in the meantime he had other fish to fry. Or fish to catch was more like it. He wished he had a partner or two to help him round up more investors and take on some of the work load, but then partners meant splitting the profits and he couldn't quite afford that right now. Hell, truth be told, he couldn't realistically afford anything right now, not even his Puerto Vallarta dream, not even if Sally would agree to give him a break on the child support. Truth be told, he needed her to give him a temporary break anyway, just until he had all the incoming funds from the Manayunk deal in his pocket. Maybe if he tried again with Sally, played his cards right, really smoothly – without Trysta stirring up the pot – he might be able to pull it off, milk out a little financial co-operation on Sally's end. He'd have to approach Sally in the right way, get on her good side, talk a strong case. After all, if he went broke what good would it do Sally and Josh in the long run? If presented with the big picture Sally could be reasonable. Maybe. Meanwhile he had to keep his nose to the real estate grindstone. There was that multi-unit out in West Philly, a big, beautiful empty building going for a song and with a re-development potential that made Darren's mouth water, he just needed to do a last bit of on-line research, and why did his laptop keys feel sticky? Anyway, he should first call Dustin Sunfield, owner of the local Sun Hardware stores, make sure the guy was still showing an interest in getting on board. Now was the critical time to snag that interest, feed it, water it and coax it along until it bloomed into the beautiful cash commitment that would open the door to the West property. It was almost four pm...business day winding down, should be a good time to call. Darren reached for the West Philadelphia Property file sitting on his desk. Damn, the file was sticky as well, spotted with small brownish finger prints, as were the papers inside the folder which were in disorder and where was Dustin Sunfield's card? The one with all his contact information on it? That card had been paper-clipped to a status report that was now crinkled along one side! He looked over his desk for the Sunfield card. What the hell, his desk had been ransacked!

Darren stormed out of his office into the family room where he found Trina and Sam in a screaming tug of war over a pink Barbie sports car.

"Okay, which one of you kids was in my, hey, listen to me, who got into my, hey, hey, you two stop that fighting and tell me, DAMMIT, TRYSTA, WOULD YOU DO SOMETHING ABOUT THESE KIDS!"

Trysta waddled into the family room, yawning and rubbing her back.

"Darren, what in the world are you yelling at the children for?"

"A dozen goddamn rooms in this house for them to tear apart and these kids can't keep out of *my office!*"

"What are you talking about? The girls aren't in your office. They're right here playing. Or trying to. Stop yelling at them."

Trina, who had ceased fighting with her sister in order to participate in the more interesting drama now being played out between her mother and step-father, took on the role of indignity personified. "Yeah, Darren, stop *yelling* at us. We're *trying* to play with our *Barbies.*"

"Yeah, *Darren,*" added Sam, and following her sister's cue, rolled her eyes and shot him a look of slack-jawed pre-adolescent scorn.

It was too much! *Yeah, Darren?* From an out-of-control seven-year-old he had to put up with *Yeah, Darren?*

"Is that how you talk to me?" he shouted, "To *me,* when I'm busting my elbows trying to work to get some money to keep this family afloat? How the hell am I supposed run a business with people tearing around my *office,* gumming up my *papers, losing* my important"

"Here, Darren." It was Trina, tugging at his elbow. She handed him the remains of Dustin Sunfield's torn and rumpled business card. "Little Sam wanted it," she cooed in her sweetest good-little-girl voice. "She just wanted to have the flower picture for her Barbie."

Darren looked at the tiny field-of-sunflowers logo engraved in the corner of Sunfield's card. He looked at Trina, who was now hugging her wide-eyed and clueless little sister, squashing Sam's cheek with kisses, and why did the two of them have to be so goddamn disarmingly funny and cute?

"Awww, Darren, Sam wanted the little sunflower picture for her Barbie! Isn't that sweet?" Trysta sounded as if she were about to melt into a puddle of maternal delight. "Look at them," she sighed, "aren't they cute?" Darren wanted to pull out his hair. Trina continued hugging and kissing her sister, pausing to catch Darren's eye and gaze up at him with a miniature version of her mother's smile. The doe-eyed smile of a seductress-in-training.

"Okay, well, no more rooting around in my office or there'll be trouble. Big trouble." His words now came off with the ferocity of a tiger who'd been shot with a pink Barbie tranquilizer dart. Darren tried to sharpen his tone. "Everybody understand? Girls, you understand?"

"Of course they don't understand. They're retarded, okay?"

Zach stood in the doorway of the family room with war in his eyes, a rebel who'd just found a cause.

Trina and Sam responded with their signature high-pitched battle cry and Zach stepped-up his brotherly goading while Trysta tried to shout them all down. Darren retreated in defeat to his office then slammed the door with a bang that startled Trysta and the children into sudden silence. Then from the other side of the door Darren heard, "Ooooh, Daddy Darren's in a *really* bad mood!"

Chapter Nine

"First thing upon waking up in the morning, have a tall glass of water and spend a moment visualizing one thing you're looking forward to in the upcoming day." This, according to an inspirational booklet entitled *The Heart And Soul Connection* that Sally's mother had given her, was the key to a healthy and happy start to every day. All right, so maybe Sally'd even tried it a couple of times, but the water from her tap had not proven to be any kind of elixir of happiness, and, scrounge her mind as she would, more often than not the only thing she could come up with to look forward to was the doughnut box in the break room, and anymore even the thought of a cream-filled long john wasn't enough to make her feel happy. Or healthy. But oh what the heck, she'd tried the method again this morning and for some reason today the Delaware River hadn't tasted half bad.

And as for something to look forward to, she found her mind meandering throughout the day towards this evening when Silvio Jablonski the plumber was supposed to come over to fix her furnace. Well, why shouldn't she feel just a little excited in the middle of October at the prospect of having a furnace that worked?

"Hey, what's that on your face?"

"Huh?" Sally snapped back to the here and now as Joanne smacked a pile of invoices on her desk.

"That curvy thing on your mouth." She pointed to the invoices. "These are bad boys. Could you copy and collate them by date for me?"

"What?" Sally reached for the papers with one hand and ran the other hand across her mouth.

"Oh, wait, was it a smile? Nah, couldn't have been a smile on Sally Miller's face. Sally Miller doesn't go around smiling these days."

"Aw, gimme a break, Joanne," Sally laughed.

"Only if you tell me what you're looking so not miserable about."

"Don't worry, I'm *not* not miserable. Not yet."

"But you *were* smiling just now. And it was over something real nasty, I can tell."

Sally laughed again. "Right. Look, I was just thinking about how I need to remember that a guy is coming over to work on my furnace tonight."

"*Oooooh*, getting your furnace worked on, huh? No wonder you were smiling. Tell the guy you want it real hot."

"Right."

"Say, could you tote those invoices directly over to Mr. Rynkowski's office when you're done with them? Oh, and he's still waiting for that fax from North Broad Actuary, so keep your eyes peeled."

"I'm on top of everything."

"Watch you don't end upon top of the furnace man."

"Fat chance."

"You know, I need to call your mom. What's she up to these days?"

"Oh, praying, I expect. And working for the beatific Father Tim."

"She still running the office at St. Sixtus?"

"Yeah, that crazy retro parish. All the way down in West Kensington."

"Well, we miss her back at Our Lady of Peace. And we miss you, but you I'm not even going to start on."

"Thanks, because I don't need another mother nagging me about my lost soul. *And* everything else."

"Well, your mom, she just worries about you."

"I know. She wishes I would move back in with her so she could control my every move.

"And spoil you rotten."

"Nah. She thinks I'm already rotten enough."

"Wait 'til she hears about you and the furnace man."

"Look, my mother doesn't need to know about..." Sally felt the blood rushing to her cheeks. "What I mean is, there's not going to be anything between me and...I mean, He's just a guy, who, uh, you know, he's gonna come over and, uh…"

"Come over and what? Hon, I was just joking about the furnace man. But you're not joking back, are you?"

Sally faked a cough and began riffling through the invoices on her desk. "I'll get to these right away, then."

Joanne sat herself on the corner of Sally's desk. "Since when does a repair man come at night, anyway?" A wide grin spread across Joanne's face. "Isn't Josh gonna be out visiting with his dad tonight?"

Sally sighed. "Yes, tonight is Darren's visitation night. Look, Joanne, this guy, he's just some guy…the plumber who came over the other day."

"Late? The plumber who came over late? And made you miss a whole day of work?'

"Well, yeah, but he ended up not charging me, or anything, because, well…"

"Because he made you miss work, the dumb *buttagots.*"

"Well, yeah." It occurred to Sally that this story was too long and maybe too complicated to spill to Joanne at this moment. And besides, she didn't really know what the outcome of Silvio's visit would be. Or what she wanted it to be. Maybe he *was* coming over just to fix her furnace and have some dinner and mess with Darren's mind a little (if Darren ended up even caring), and maybe that's all she really wanted the evening to be.

"Yeah, he made me miss work, and all," Sally continued, "but like I said, he didn't charge me, and then we talked some. He really seems like a nice guy, and it turns out he fixes furnaces, too, so…"

"Gotcha," Joanne said with a wink. "Anyway, a guy who fixes plumbing *and* heating, I'd be all over him myself. Is he cute?"

"I'm *not* all over him. And yeah, he is pretty cute. A big guy."

"Big paunchy or big buff?"

"Uh, buff, I think…oh, come on Joanne, I don't know, I mean, I wasn't checking the guy out!"

"Right, you'll do that tonight. He's not married, I hope?"

"No, he's not married."

"Good." Joanne hoisted herself up from Sally's desk. "I think I'll get Ponti to work on *my* furnace tonight."

Sally shook her head as Joanne walked off. How in the world, she wondered, could Joanne and her mother possibly be friends?

As if her thoughts were traveling the cross-town psychic hotline, her mother's number popped up on her tootling cell phone. Sally remembered that she'd neglected to call her mother to cancel tonight, Wednesday being her standing night to go to her mom's for dinner after Josh left with Darren. In fact they'd nicknamed Wednesday night "girls' night," since it was easier to say they were just having a girls' night than to delve into the painful truth of why both women spent nights alone. Besides, Sally's mother's preferred method of dealing with her pain was to bake it into a nice little cake smothered in a corn-syrupy icing of religious platitudes, while Sally's modus operandi in her mother's presence was to just shut up about it all. Still, it was easier to spend an evening having dinner with her mother than to sit alone in her condo ruminating over the fact that her husband was gone and even her son was in reality only half hers anymore. Of course lately Darren had become sketchy about picking up Josh for his visitation, and on those Wednesday nights when Darren cancelled or stood them up then Sally took Josh along to her mother's, thus being at least able to offer her son the consolation prize of an evening of basking in his grandmother's love and home cooking.

"Hi Mom, I was just thinking about you."

"Well, dear, you know I'm *always* thinking about you. You and your brothers. And your children. Thinking about you and praying for you."

"Thanks, Mom." Sally knew there was no one-upping this woman in the realm of sainted motherhood.

"I meant to tell you, your brother Jay has been bringing Jennifer and the children to St. Sixtus Martyr for the High Mass of the Sanctified Chrism on Sunday. St. Sixtus is the only church that offers the High Mass of the Sanctified Chrism, you know."

"That's great, Mom."

"They think it's wonderful, and the Latin? Well, the children just love it, and"

"I'll bet the children do just love that Latin."

"...and we were talking about how much Josh would enjoy"

"Right, right. Oh, say, Mom, I almost forgot. About tonight..."

"Oh, I've got the most wonderful roast beef stew, it's simmering in the crock-pot right now, with carrots and potatoes and onions, and I'm making a pan of cherry crisp for us. I've got this new recipe that uses a cake mix and a can of pie filling and a stick of butter. Somebody brought one to our last Blessed Charismatics meeting, and was it ever good! And hot from the oven with a scoop of vanilla ice cream?

"Sounds like heaven, Mom."

"Well, of course it's not *heaven*! How about my little sweet heart? Can Josh come tonight?"

"Aw, gee, no, Mom, and I can't come, either. My furnace is on the blink, I have a repair man coming."

"At night?"

"Oh, sure. They have these twenty-four-hour service places..." Okay, so she was starting to spin a lie.

"Those twenty-four-hour places will charge you a fortune."

"But I can't afford to miss work during the day." That at least was true.

"Look, Honey, let me call Joanne for you, I'll just tell her you need a day off for"

"*No! No!* Look, I can't have my mother calling my boss for me. Even if you are friends."

"Oh, all right, dear, now don't get yourself upset, I'll let you handle it. I'll just mention it to Joanne. In passing. Since I need to call her anyway."

"I already have the guy coming. Just let it go, Mom, all right?"

"How about if I bring dinner over to your house tonight?"

"Uh, no, no, Mom, I mean, that's too much trouble for you, hauling all that food over."

"Well, yes, but that's what mothers do. We go to trouble for our children."

"I know, Mom, but..." What lie could she cook up to keep her mother home? "I just think, you know, with the furnace man coming, and then Darren will be here to pick up Josh, and all...It could turn into a three-ring circus." And that wasn't *even* a lie, especially if her plot (the wisdom of which she was now having second thoughts about) to spring Silvio on Darren should take an unexpectedly nasty turn.

Her mother sighed loudly. "All right. But why don't you stop by here on your way home from work and take the dinner with you? I'll ask Father Tim to let me off work a little early so I can get home and get everything wrapped up for you. Father is so good about letting me close the church office a little early on Wednesdays. And nobody ever comes by after four o'clock anyway, and if the office phone should ring, well, Father will just answer the line in the rectory, he is so good about that. He's a saint, really. He's the one who says the High Mass of the Sanctified Chrism, and if you come this Sunday I could introduce"

"Mom, I'm not going to take your dinner!"

"But I *want* you to!"

"No, Mom. I can't do that." *Of course if you did,* suggested a selfish little voice in her head, *then you wouldn't need to stop at the store and pick up a box of spaghetti and a jar of Ragu for dinner with the plumber.*

"But then you wouldn't need to stop at the store and pick up something for your own dinner," said her mother. "Besides, I have a little something for you to give to Josh. Nothing big, just a little book I saw at the store."

"Okay, I'll pop by, but Mom, I'm *not* taking your dinner." *Though I really feel like it and wish you'd talk me into it.*

"Please, dear. I haven't fasted yet this week, and you know I like to fast once a week. So I'll do it tonight and get it over with. Please."

"No, Mom." *Next time you ask I'll give in.*

"*Please, Sally!*"

"All right, Mom. I'll take the dinner. But I'm going to feel guilty about it."

"A little guilt now and then is good for us all, dear."

Chapter Ten

Darren ceased pacing the floor for a moment to take in the sight of his wife sitting on the bed brushing her thick luxurious hair. It occurred to him that the robe she was wearing, this one a Chinesey-looking thing of red poppies on a creamy white background, brought out the rosiness of her cheeks against her fair skin. On the bedside table sat her make-up bag and mirror and a few pieces of jewelry, but what did someone with Trysta's looks need make-up and jewelry for?

"Whatcha looking at?" she asked in a coquettish voice.

"Huh? Oh…You."

"You're looking at my fat stomach, right?" She rubbed a hand over her middle.

"No, no, your stomach looks great. All of you looks great."

Trysta smiled. She put down her brush and picked up a pair of earrings from the bed-side table and began putting them on.

"It's just that…Trysta, I don't know about this."

"I'm almost ready. We've got a little time, don't we?"

"Yeah. No. Five minutes, tops."

"Then why are you pacing? Come sit by me." She patted a spot on the bed and Darren sat down next to her.

"That's better." She kissed his cheek then picked up the mirror and studied her face. "Do you like these earrings on me?"

"Look, I just don't want to aggravate her again."

"Huh!" Trysta tossed the mirror onto the bed then grabbed her brush and began pulling it through her hair with short, angry strokes.

"It's just that I'm just trying to get on her *good* side, get a little financial co-op-"

Trysta slammed down her brush. "That woman does not *have* a good side! Nobody has tried harder than *me* to be nice to her! But all she ever does is …is…say *horrible* things to me!"

"Aw, Honey, that's my point, don't you see? If you show up with me to pick up Joshua Sally is gonna get *seriously* aggravated."

"So I can't even go out with my husband, can't be seen in public with my *own* husband because *she* might get aggravated?"

"Honey, that's not what I"

"Well, what, then? Are her feelings more important than mine?"

"No, Baby, not at"

"Or are you just so *ashamed* to be seen with me now that I'm all…fat…puffy…"

"No, no, no…"

"That's it, isn't it? You're ashamed of me now!" Trysta grabbed her mirror. "Oh these earrings *do* make my face look fat!" She put down the mirror and burst into loud sobs. Darren put his arms around her and held her close while she fumbled with an earring, trying to pull it off her ear.

"Shh," he cooed, "don't cry now." He gently pulled her hand away from her ear and held her hand close to his chest. "You look great, really. Beautiful. I can't even look at you without thinking how beautiful you are."

"Really? M-M-My face?"

"Your face, your hair, your body…"

"Y-You're not ashamed to be seen with me?"

"Ashamed? No, no."

Trysta pulled herself away from Darren. "Because if you are I won't come. I'll just stay right here, cooped up like I am all day long in this house so that you and the children can have a nice home, nice meals, nice, nice…everything!"

"Baby, I never meant that you had to stay cooped up…"

"…Cleaning, doing laundry, washing dish-"

"Actually, Honey, I meant to tell you, I'm out of clean shirts, and the kitchen floor is getting a little, you know, sticky…"

"I've *told* you I need some household help! How am I supposed to manage these active children, this huge house, and, and *you*, and I'm *eight months pregnant!*"

"Baby, look, don't I help you around the house? I wash the dishes, and, okay, don't worry about the floor, I'll mop it, it'll be fine, and I can throw in some laundry, but that's not what I"

"Well, what then? What?"

Darren sighed. He spent a moment weighing the right words in his mind and then he tried again. "I just meant, was just *suggesting,* that maybe it would be better if you stayed here while I picked up Josh, not because you don't look great, because you do, but for Josh's sake. That's all."

"Oh, Sweetie, it's for Josh's sake that I want to come! I want to be there for him, be a *mother* to him from the moment he leaves behind that, that...*psycho* you were married to!"

"Aw, that's nice of you, Honey, to think of Josh and all, but"

"Well that's just the kind of person I am. I'm a mother at heart. I adore children. They're my life."

At that moment Trina and Sam came tearing into the bedroom, Zach close behind, all of them shouting and screaming at once.

"Mommy, Mommy, Trina and Zach won't let me play, they're being..."

"Mommy, Sam's a cheat, she won't play right..."

"... being mean, they're hitting me.."

"...says I hit her, but she hit me, and Zach..."

"...stupid little tattle-tales and running to mom every minute, *Mommy, Mommy, I'm just a little baby, wah, wah...*"

Trina turned to Zach and pushed him. "Quit calling me names!"

Zach pushed her back. "Baby! Baby!" Then to Sam, who was now pushing him in her sister's defense, "Stupid little Baby!"

"*Mommeee!*"

Trysta covered her ears. "Ooooh, not again, I can't stand it! Darren, *do* something!"

Darren squeezed his way into the middle of the three children, who were now engaged in a full-scale pushing war. "KNOCK IT OFF, YOU GUYS!"

The children went suddenly quiet. Darren turned back to Trysta, who was lying across the bed, her hands still over her ears.

"Trysta, uncover you ears. TRYSTA!"

Trysta uncovered her ears and sat up. "Whew, that's much better."

"*Jesus,* Trysta! Okay, what are you planning on doing with the kids while you're out with me picking up Josh? You got a sitter coming or what?"

"No. Of course not. The children will come with us."

The children immediately revved back up in protest, merely switching gears when Trysta announced that they'd be going out for ice cream afterwards.

"I want chocolate and Oreos, no, no, I want peanut butter and"

"No, Sam! You can't have peanut butter, *I'm* getting peanut butter!"

"Yes I can, Mommy, tell Trina I can have whatever kind I"

"Sam copies everything I do, Mommy, tell her she has to"

"Would you two babies quit freaking out over stupid ice-cream? God, you're giving me a headache." Zach punctuated this with a push to each of his sisters, which re-escalated the pushing fight among the three of them. Trysta tried sweetly but ineffectively to persuade her children to stop fighting, to go downstairs and put on their jackets, but they were locked in loud battle. Darren pulled in a deep breath.

"SHUT UP AND GO GET YOUR JACKETS! AND WAIT DOWNSTAIRS!"

Once again the children responded like little Pavlovian pups who were becoming conditioned to snap into silence at Darren's shouting. Except that Pavlov's dogs never gave their owner the raw throat and stress headache that Darren was developing from Trysta's kids' behavior.

Trysta, however, who always seemed to land on the other side of her children's behavioral tornadoes without a hair out of place, was suddenly sunny and animated as a blond, busty, vastly pregnant Mary Poppins. "Children," she chirped, "run downstairs now and put on your jackets and wait nicely downstairs like Daddy Darren asked you to." Trina and Sam ran from the bedroom while Zach slunk out behind them. Trysta turned to Darren, who was sitting on the bed massaging his temples. "See? They're good children, you just have to know how to handle them."

"Trysta. *Why* would we take them out for ice cream right before dinner?"

"Well, do you have a better idea?"

In fact, Darren didn't. At the moment he was drained of all ideas, good, bad, or indifferent. He stood and walked to the bedroom door. "Come on," he snapped, "we gotta go."

Trysta scooted from the middle to the edge of the bed.

"Darren? Honey? You're all tense now." She patted the bed. "Come here."

"There's no time. It's gonna take forever to get those kids into the car."

"No it won't. I promise." She patted the bed again. "Darren? Sweetheart? Please? Just sit with me for one minute before we leave? Just one little minute to get calmed down? Please?"

Darren had no desire to sit back down next to his wife on their bed. He was tense and irritable. But he was out of fight. He sat down next to Trysta. "We're gonna be late, you know."

"Shhh, my Baby." She began rubbing his back. "There now, doesn't that feel better?"

It did actually. As her hands worked their way from his trapezius to his deltoids he felt the tension loosening. "My poor baby," she cooed, "he works so hard, takes care of us all, treats us so good...somebody needs to take care of him once in a while." She ran her fingers down his spine, slipping them beneath his belt and pressing into the small of his back.

"Oh, wow," he sighed, "that feels good."

"I know." She leaned in close to him. "*Soooo* good." She breathed into his ear and moved her hands around to his thighs and began running her thumbs along the V where thigh meets crotch.

"Aw, no, Honey, we gotta go." He put his hands over hers with the intention of pulling her away from him, but he felt suddenly overcome by sensation: the feel of her hands on his body, the clean, sweet smell of her hair, her cologne, the warm tickle of her breath in his ear, the press of her breasts on his back, until he was wrapped in a state of arousal that was taking him down like sex-scented nerve gas. She undid his belt and zipper and now her fingers were playing lightly below his navel while she daubed the back of his neck with the tip of her tongue.

"Oh Baby, no, no" he pleaded weakly, "We gotta..."

"I'll go lock the door," she whispered.

Chapter Eleven

Sally sat on the couch reading to Josh, who was curled up next to her, a blanket wrapping them close together. Overnight the weather, which had been in a state of October indecision over the past few weeks, had once more turned from summer-warm to fall-chilly and Silvio's forecast for Sally's ailing furnace had come true this evening when she got home from work and tried unsuccessfully to turn on some heat.

"'And that's how Big Billy Bilabong hit the famous home run that won the game and saved the town.'" Sally snapped the book shut. "Wow. Great book Grammy got for you, huh?"

"Will you read it again, Mom?"

"Aw, Baby, I don't think we have time. Your Daddy will be here any minute now."

"Is Daddy really coming?"

"Sure. I mean, he said he's coming. He's just a little late, is all."

"But what if he forgets to get me again?"

"Aw, Joshie, Daddy never forgot you. He just…well, he got a little busy, with his honeymoon and things."

"But what if he doesn't come?"

Sally sighed. "Well…then I'll be able to read your book to you again."

"Will you read it twenty-nine times?"

'Twenty-nine? Whoa! Hey, why don't you bring the book with you to Daddy's and maybe he'll read it?"

"Okay. Mommy, what will you do while I'm gone?"

"Oh, now, I already told you. My new friend Silvio is coming for dinner. He's Zach, Trina and Sam's daddy, remember?"

"Is he coming so you won't be lonely without me?"

"Well...yeah, sure. And Silvio's gonna fix our furnace, too, won't that be great?"

Josh mulled silently over the situation, trying to make some sense in his mind of his daddy being with Zach, Trina and Sam's mom while their daddy was with his mom.

"When is their daddy coming here?" he finally asked.

Sally eyed the clock on her living room wall. "I guess he's a little late, too."

The door bell sounded and Joshua pushed back the blanket and hopped off the couch, sprinting towards the door.

"Now who do you think that is?" Sally asked him brightly.

"Daddy!" Josh pulled open the door. His initial impression was of a big blue-eyed bear standing in their doorway. Only bears didn't wear tan pants or a blue buttoned-down shirt or carry a tool box.

"Oh, hey, Silvio," Sally called. "Josh, this is Silvio. Remember? Silvio? Who I told you about?"

Silvio stepped inside the door and smiled at Josh, who continued to stare up at him, wide-eyed.

"You the lady with the volcano needs fixing? I'm late, right? Look, I thought about it, I didn't want to be here when, you know, Darren...I mean him seeing me here, there could have been a scene, and you know, I mean, that kind of thing wouldn't be good for..." he cocked he head towards Josh. "Anyway," he glanced at Josh again "I see somebody's still here." He checked his watch. "It's five after seven. I thought you said six thir"

Sally cut him off. "Hey Josh, you wanna say hi to Trina, Zach and Sam's daddy?"

Josh didn't answer, but looked down shyly.

Sally walked towards the kitchen and motioned to Silvio, who set down his tool box and followed her. When they were out of earshot she said softly, "You've gotta excuse Josh. He's real shy."

"Shy is okay," Silvio replied. "Maybe some of that shy will rub off on my kids. They're a bunch little bulls in a china shop." Silvio glanced back into the living room at Josh, who was studying Silvio's tool box. "Speaking of which, isn't Josh supposed to be over there by now?"

"Yep. Only somebody's being a bastard, as usual."

"Aw, geez. Well..." Silvio rubbed his hands up and down his arms. "Man, this place is cold."

"Yeah, well, I guess the furnace decided to blow today, just like you said it would."

"So I'm just in time, huh?"

"You sure are."

Silvio called into the living room, "So where's that broken volcano you got?" Joshua perked up and looked at Silvio, who was now following Sally back into the living room. Silvio stopped in front of Josh and squatted down to his level.

"You wanna show me where your volcano is?"

Josh giggled. *"Volcano?"*

"That's what we call the furnace in my business. Your mom says yours is on the fritz. I brought my volcano-fixing tools. You wanna see?" Silvio opened his tool box just a crack, causing Josh to cock his head to try and see what was inside.

Sally stood over the two of them. "So like I said, Josh, this is Silvio. Silvio, this is Josh."

"Oh sure," said Silvio, "I know all about Josh. My Zach says Josh is a good Mario player. Is that right? You good at Mario?"

Josh nodded shyly.

"How about fixing volcanoes? You like to do that?"

Josh thought for a moment and then nodded. Then he ran to the furnace alcove and opened the door. Sally laughed and Silvio smiled and picked up his tool box then walked over to the furnace. He opened his tool box, which Josh immediately started investigating. Silvio turned to Sally.

"Have your volcano fixed in no time, lady." He pulled open the furnace panel then knelt. He turned back to Josh while rolling up his shirt sleeves. "You wanna hand me that pliers? Yeah, that thing with the two red handles, that's right. You and me are gonna get this volcano huffing and puffing like nobody's business."

Though the chill in the house was making her shiver, Sally felt the beginning of a warm, melting sensation inside. She stood over Silvio. "Looks like you're fixing more than the furnace."

Silvio turned and looked up at her. "It's like I told you. I can fix a lot of things. Except that one thing."

"What one thing?" Josh piped up.

Silvio reached into the furnace. "Cuckoo birds. I can't fix cuckoo birds."

This made Josh giggle again. "You need another tool, Silvio?" he asked.

"Uh, yeah. How about that little wrench."

"Which one is a wrench?"

Silvio guided Josh's hand to a small wrench. "That one there's the one I need, can you grab it for me?"

"Well," Sally said, "if you guys got the situation here under control I'll go get dinner ready."

"Go get dinner ready, Mom," Josh said brightly, "Me and Silvio can fix this volcano."

Sally headed for the kitchen, her inner warm melt spreading. *Cut it out,* she warned herself, *he's only fixing your furnace and making your kid happy, which at this moment are only your two greatest desires in the world.* She moved her mother's pot of sacrificial beef stew from the stove to the table along with the loaf of crusty Italian bread her mother had insisted she take as well. The cherry cobbler was staying warm in the oven so as to be in top form for linking up with the half-gallon of vanilla ice cream in her freezer, also pilfered from her mother. *Okay, so I'm feeling guilty about taking the food off my mother's table, but of course she wanted me to, I did her a favor by taking it, or at least she said I did, but who knows what the connect is between what my mother says and what she really thinks, but, hey, wouldn't I take the food off my table to give it to my child? Only I'm not a child anymore* (She reached for two beers from the refrigerator and grinned) *Thank goodness!* She heard the *whosh* of her furnace kicking on and called towards the alcove, "Hey, is that heat I feel?"

Josh came running into the kitchen followed by Silvio, who was wiping his hands on a rag. "Mommy! Me and Silvio fixed the volcano!"

"You did? Whoa, that calls for some beef stew."

Silvio sniffed appreciatively. "Is that what's been making my mouth water the whole time?" He winked at Josh, who tried to wink back at him.

Sally began dishing the stew into three bowls. "Well, come on, you heroes, sit down and eat. *After* you wash your hands, that is."

"Silvio says I can use his special plumber's soap!"

"You got a great little volcano-fixer here," said Silvio.

"Wow." Sally glanced at Silvio. How nice-looking he was when he smiled. As soon as they were seated at the table Silvio dug into his stew and tore off a mouthful of bread. Sally could see that he was hungry, probably a big eater. Probably a bigger eater than Darren, who was shorter and slimmer than Silvio. Then Sally found herself wondering about Silvio's appetite for Trysta compared to Darren's. Well, what man wouldn't have an appetite for a dish like Trysta? She let out a long sigh. Then she noticed that Silvio was looking at her in dismay, his fork poised in mid-air.

"Is something…?" he asked.

"Oh, no, don't mind me. I was just, I don't know, thinking."

"Thinking, huh? You sure don't want to be doing that." Silvio took a long pull on his beer. "You just want to enjoy this great food. He turned again to Josh, who had moved his chair closer to Silvio's. "Aren't we enjoying this great food your mom fixed for us?"

Josh giggled. *"Mommy* didn't fix it! *Grammy* did!"

"Ohhhh, *Grammy* did, huh?" He raised an eyebrow at Sally in playful mock reproach.

Sally sighed. "Okay, cat's out. Yes, my mother made the stew. Heck, she made the whole dinner. It's a long story, see, I was"

"Nah," Silvio cut her off, "I understand. My mamma, she sends over dinner for me all the time since my div…" He glanced again at Josh, who seemed to be hanging on Silvio's every word. "Well, all the time these days. That's what mothers do. Josh, once you're all grown up, I bet your mom'll be bringing dinner over to your house, too."

"Mommy, will you bring dinner to my house when I'm all grown up?"

"You betcha."

"You're a lucky guy, Josh." Silvio's eyes locked with Sally's for a moment then they both quickly looked away.

"Anyway, this is one heck of a great stew."

"Yep, Grammy can sure cook." Sally dished another scoop of stew onto Silvio's almost clean plate. "Here, you need some more bread with that, too."

"Thanks, Sally." Silvio lost no time digging into his second helping. "Yeah, my mom, she's a super cook, too. Best Italian cook in Cornwells Heights."

"Cornwells Heights, huh? You know, I've never been. Out in Bucks County, right?

"Not too far out. Just east over the city line. But it's not bad, location-wise. From where I live you can hop on 95 and it's a straight shot over the Delaware Expressway to Frankford Avenue, the Roosevelt Boulevard, anywhere you want to get to in the city. Without actually living in the city."

"Sounds like a nice place."

Silvio shrugged. "Eh, it is what it is, but I've lived there all my life. Most of my family still lives in South Philly, though."

"Your family Italian?"

"Oh, yeah, on my mom's side. That's where the Silvio came from. My dad's Polish."

"And that's where the *Jablonski* came from," Sally added. "Silvio Jablonski. Italian and Polish. I get it."

"Sort of like that fusion thing," he said with a self-depreciating grin.

"Has a nice ring to it. I like it."

"And I like you, Sally," he blurted and then, hit by the surprised look on Sally's face, he quickly added, "Oh, hey, uh…look, I didn't mean"

"It's okay."

"No, I…forget I said it, I don't know why I"

"No, really, it's okay. I'm glad you like me, Silvio."

"You are?"

"Sure, But, I mean, you really do like me? With the way I pop off sometimes, and all?"

Silvio shrugged. "Yeah."

Sally suddenly felt shy as a schoolgirl. "I like you, too, Sil…"

It hit her that Joshua was still sitting there, elbows propped on the table, his chin propped against his fists, hanging onto every word of the adults' exchange.

"You guys *like* each other?" he asked, wrinkling his nose and squinting his eyes in childish disbelief.

Sally blushed and noticed that Silvio was reddening likewise. She cleared her throat. "Well, Josh, we"

"Can I show Silvio my dinosaurs?"

"Yeah, sure," his mother replied, thankful for the shortness of the six-year-old attention span, "soon as we eat our cherry cobbler."

"Mommy, I don't want any cherry cobbler."

"A kid that doesn't want dessert?" Silvio asked with exaggerated amazement. "That's a new one."

"I don't like the cherries."

"He doesn't like the cherries," Sally said with a shrug. "Go figure." Then to Josh she said, "Okay, you may be excused from the table, then go ahead to your room and set all your dinosaurs up real nice while Silvio and I have some coffee...you want coffee, Silvio?"

"Oh yeah, I like coffee. *And* cherries." He winked again at Josh, who again tried to wink back. Josh carried his plate and cup to the sink then ran off towards his room but then stopped and turned back. "You need me to help you fix anything else, Silvio?"

"I'll call you if I do."

Sally cut squares of cobbler for herself and Silvio and topped each with a scoop of ice cream. As she poured the coffee she asked him, "You know the way to a woman's heart?"

"You kidding?" Silvio dug into his cobbler.

"It's through her children."

"Oh." Silvio blushed again, but he smiled then gave a dismissive wave of his hand. "Well, I mean, Josh, he's a good kid."

"He is," Sally took a sip of coffee. "Funny, our kids are sort of related now."

"Yeah," said Silvio reflectively. Then he added, "I guess they'll be getting to know each other pretty well."

"Huh, provided Darren doesn't continue to screw up on his fatherly duties. Oh, man, if he doesn't show up tonight I don't know what I'll do with Josh."

"Eh, don't worry. If he doesn't show up me and Josh'll fix that broken pipe."

"What broken pipe?"

Silvio chuckled. "Believe me, if Darren doesn't show up I'll find us a broken pipe."

87

How could any woman, she asked herself, *even a woman as stupid as Trysta, be stupid enough to leave this man?*

A few minutes later Josh called down the hall from his room. "Silvio! My room is all ready!"

Silvio stood up. "I guess I better go see the little guy's room."

"I hope you like dinosaurs," Sally said.

"Oh yeah. Love 'em."

***

Darren stopped at the bottom of the exterior stairway that led to Sally's condo. He checked his watch. "Jesus, seven forty-five! How the hell did we get so late? Sally's gonna be spitting fire!"

"Oh, she'll be fine," Trysta huffed. She looked around her at the apartment/condo complex and frowned. "Goodness, how could Sally let her child *live* in such a place. Doesn't that old beat-up van over there look just like Silvio's?"

"I don't know." Darren scanned the buildings. "This place is not bad, except for being right on the Boulevard. But you gotta understand, finding an affordable condo in the Northeast is not so easy these days."

"And *Sally* has got to understand that when you have three children to look after it's not so easy as when you only have *one.* She has got to grow up and understand that."

Shit, Darren thought to himself. To Trysta he said, "Look, Hon, I don't think we should go to the door. We'll go back to the car, I'll call from my cell, Sally can send Josh out."

"No, I think we should go to the door." Trysta started climbing the stairs. "Sally needs to see us together."

"Trysta..." Darren started up the stairs behind her. "Sally *knows* we're together! I mean, it's pretty damn *obvious* we're together and have *been* together for...geez, how many months pregnant are you?"

Trysta stopped at the second floor landing outside Sally's door. "I *mean,*" she said breathlessly, "she needs to see us *together. Married.*"

Yeah, she really needs to see that, Darren thought. He joined Trysta on the landing then looked back towards the parking lot. "Hey, you really think we ought to leave those kids in the car by themselves?

They're liable to knock each other's heads off."

Trysta laughed. "Don't be silly! The children are fine. Everything will be just fine." She wrapped her arm around his and kissed his cheek. "Come on now, ring the doorbell. Ring it."

Sally had just started clearing the table when the doorbell rang. "Finally decided to get here," she muttered to herself, but as she opened the door she was taken aback at the sight of Trysta clinging closely to Darren.

"Look, I'm late," Darren began apologetically, "but"

"Oh," Sally cut him off, "so why don't you tell me something else I don't already know? And you just had to bring…" She looked Trysta up and down and shook her head. "Boy, Darren, you really know how to put the cherry on the cake."

Trysta's voice dripped Honey. "Oh, now, Sally, be nice."

Sally fixed her eyes on Trysta's bulging middle. "Or should I say, the cake in the oven."

"*Uh!*" Trysta huffed indignantly.

"Sally," Darren said softly in a tone that was more pleading than assertive, "*Please* don't start…"

"You know, Darren," Sally shot back, "this shit you're pulling, I don't have to give you Josh."

"Uh! Such filthy language!" cried Trysta.

Darren rubbed his temples. "Please, Sally, I've had a long, hard day." He sounded exasperated.

"I'll bet," said Sally.

"Well, he *has* had a hard day!" Trysta cut in defensively. "And you have no idea how hard it is caring for three chil-"

Darren cut her off and spoke to Sally. "Where's Josh?"

Sally let the question hang in the air a moment then said. "I'll get him. The poor little guy's been waiting in his room. Playing with his dinosaurs. You wait here." Then she shut the door.

Darren felt a pang in his heart for his son. While he contemplated the image of little Josh waiting alone in his room with his dinosaurs Trysta carefully tried Sally's door knob. It was unlocked. She opened the door and stepped inside to Sally's living room. She grabbed onto Darren's arm. "Come on!" She whispered.

"*No!*" Darren whispered back, quickly shaken from his

melancholy little reverie. "We're not supposed to."

"Please, Darren, I'm getting a chill!"

Darren allowed himself to be dragged into Sally's living room. "I don't feel comfortable," he whispered.

"I know what you mean," Trysta whispered back, "this place really is *awful*."

She walked back to the dining room end of the living room. She pointed to the beer bottles still on the table. "Tsk, look at this," Trysta said softly, "she's been drinking. A child to take care of and she sits here....*uhhh*," she gasped.

"What?" Darren, who had been waiting close to the front door hurried over to his wife. "What is it?"

"There!" she shrieked, "in the kitchen, look! *That's Silvio's toolbox!*"

Hearing Trysta's cry Silvio stormed out of Josh's bedroom followed by Sally. Josh poked his head out from the doorway of his room.

"*Silvio?*" cried Trysta and Darren.

"*Trysta?*" cried Silvio.

"Daddy!" cried Josh, and he ran down the hall to Darren, who, though still trying to mentally process the idea of his wife's ex having just popped out of a bedroom with his ex-wife, managed to open his arms and catch his son in a hug.

"Sorry, Silvio," said Sally. "I wasn't gonna spring it on you. I thought they were waiting outside."

"Well, you know," said Trysta, "you left the door unlocked, which I would *never* do if I lived here. And what in the *world* is Silvio doing here?"

"Come on, Josh" Sally said, ignoring Trysta's comment and question but taking the boy's hand and leading him away from Darren, "We'll go to your room and get your stuff so you can go with your daddy." Before turning to go she caught Darren's eye and shook her head while her eyes asked *how could you do this?*

Trysta meanwhile studied Silvio in bug-eyed amazement. "What in the world *are* you doing here?" she snapped.

"Yeah, what *are* you doing here?" Darren echoed.

"What am *I* doing here?" he answered Trysta, ignoring Darren, "What are *you* doing here? Who's with the kids?"

"They're out in the car," Trysta said sheepishly.

Darren, feeling that he should show a little muscle and status in front of his wife, added, "Don't worry, Silvio, the kids are fine, they're just right outside in our SU"

"Are they *your* kids?" Silvio cut him off.

"Oh, *please*," Trysta said breathlessly, "let's not fight. *Ohhhh.*" She held her stomach and doubled over its bulk as much she was able.

Darren put his arm around his wife's shoulder. "What, Baby, you having a pain?" He scowled at Silvio. "Look what you did! She's having a pain!"

But Silvio seemed unmoved. "Yeah, I know all about her pains. Only they're not my problem anymore." Silvio ignored Trysta's groans and walked towards the front door, but as he reached for the doorknob her groaning ceased suddenly.

"Silvio?" She called to him. "Where are you going?"

"I'm not leaving those kids alone in the car. They're liable to knock each other's heads off."

"No, wait!" Trysta hurried over to Silvio. "The children aren't supposed to see you now! You're not allowed to see them now!" She put her hand on his arm. "I'm not letting you! It's not your turn!"

Silvio gently moved her hand away. "I'm not leaving them alone in that parking lot in that car."

"Oh, now, look," Darren stepped in again, "those kids are old enough"

"ARE THEY YOUR KIDS?" Silvio barked, so that Darren and Trysta quickly backed a step away from him as from a riled dog that might be about to slip its chain.

"Fine!" Trysta huffed. "Darren, go out and wait with the children."

"Me?" Darren asked incredulously. "You want *me* to"

"Oh," Trysta cut him off, "I need to sit!"

"No, they're my kids," said Silvio. "I'll go stay with them."

As Silvio opened the door Trysta jumped up from the couch and followed after him. "I *said* no!" She squeezed herself in front of Silvio, trying to block his way out the door, but as he eased around her she said, "Oh, fine! *I'll* go!" Then she added, with much indignation, "Silvio, please wait in here until we leave. I don't need you stirring

the children up the way you always do. Besides, it's not your turn."
At that moment Sally entered the living room with Josh, who was
back-packed and carrying a stuffed dinosaur. From the doorway
Trysta called to Sally, "*You* just have no idea how it is trying to care
for three children when you're"

"Eight months pregnant," Sally called back. "Gotcha!"

"Oh!" Trysta huffed.

"What is it, Trysta?" asked Sally, "Hormones? Pre-partum
conniptions? What?"

"*Oh!*" Trysta called to Darren, "Are you going to let her insult me
that way?"

But Darren was focused on Sally. "What," he pointed to Silvio, "is
he doing here?"

"*Oh!*" Trysta shrieked.

"Okay, Trysta," Silvio said calmly, "are you gonna go to the kids
or am I?"

Trysta burst out with one final "*Oh!*" before storming out the door
and down the stairs to the parking lot where, rather than venturing
into the SUV, inside of which the children were, indeed, engaged in
close combat, she simply leaned against the door, arms crossed above
her belly.

Darren meanwhile felt a strange brewing inside him, like wisps of
internal storm clouds. Silvio began clearing the dinner dishes from the
table to the kitchen. "Look, Sally," Darren said calmly, "please tell me
what *he* is doing here."

"Excuse me," Sally answered him, "didn't you come to see
somebody?" She cocked her head towards Joshua, who stood looking
up expectantly at his father.

"Oh, hey Josh," Darren said, putting his arm around the boy,
"How you doing? You ready to spend some time with Daddy? Sally,
what *is* that guy doing here?"

Josh piped up, "Daddy, that's Silvio! He's Zach's dad. He knows
how to fix volcanoes, that's what we call the furnace. And he likes to
drink your flavor of beer."

Darren fixed his eyes on Sally. "Oh he does, does he?"

"Yeah," Josh continued excitedly, "And guess what, now Mommy
won't have to be lonely while I'm gone."

"*Mommy won't have to be...?* Oh great, that's just...I don't believe this, Sally!"

Silvio rinsed the dishes in silence and stacked them in the dishwasher,

Josh pulled at this father's arm. "Want me to stay home with Mommy instead?"

"Yeah," said Sally, "you want him to?"

Darren took Josh's hand. "No, I don't!" To Josh he said affectionately, "Hey, we're gonna have a good time, go out for ice cream and all." Then to Sally he said, "Geez, why do you have to put a blight on everything I try to do?"

The words poured out of her with the sudden surprising rush of a gallon of milk gushing to the floor from a carelessly knocked over bottle. "*Everything you try to do?* What, like knocking up your girlfriend while you're still married to me? Or trying to go deadbeat on your child support? Or maybe you're talking about showing up an hour and a half late to pick up your son with that over-sexed zeppelin stuck to your hip?" *Oh my God,* she begged herself, *stop it!*

"Oh, now, wait a *minute,* Sally," Darren jumped in, "you *wait just a minute!* You are going *too far!*"

Shut up now! Sally ordered herself, but she couldn't. "*I'm* going too far?" she shot back, "*I* am?"

"Yes, *you* are!"

Sally and Darren began speaking at the same time, shouting at and over each other:

"...I mean, I come here to pick up my son..."

"...Oh, right, it's my fault again, always..."

"...I find you here with *this* guy..."

"...always me, no matter that *you're* late..."

"...then you have to start..."

"...and you bring *her*..."

Silvio threw down the dish towel he'd been using to wipe his hands and came rushing in from the kitchen. He stepped between them. "*Stop it!*" he said, "*Now!*"

Darren and Sally stopped in mid-word.

"Look," Silvio said. He pointed to the sofa where Joshua lay face-down, his hands over his ears. Silvio walked over to the sofa and sat on the edge. He put his hand on the child's shoulder then gently lifted one of Josh's hands from his ear. "Hey guy," He said softly, "whatcha doing?"

Joshua turned over and looked up at Silvio. "This is what I do when Mommy and Daddy fight so I won't get upset."

Darren and Sally looked shame-stricken. Darren walked over to Josh and took his hand.

"Come on, Champ," he said, "time to go. Say good-bye to Mommy."

Josh ran to his mother and hugged her. Sally kissed his cheek. "'Bye, Baby, you have a great time, okay?"

"Okay."

Darren headed for the door with Josh then turned back. Josh quickly slipped his hand from Darren's and once more covered his ears.

"And you," Darren said, pointing a finger at Silvio, "You've got no business coming around here stirring things up with my wi...with Sally."

"*Your wife?*" echoed Sally and Silvio.

Darren grabbed Josh's hand and hurried out, slamming the door behind him.

Sally walked absently across the room then stopped by the dinette table, her back to Silvio. She leaned her hands on the back of a chair as if for support.

After a moment Silvio said, "Well, I guess I better get going." Receiving no reply from Sally, he picked up his tool box and said, "Thanks for dinner. It was real good." Silvio headed for the door then turned back. "Guess I'll see you around."

"I need a beer," Sally said. She turned to face Silvio. "You want a beer?"

Silvio set down his tool box. "Yeah."

Chapter Twelve

They sat at Sally's dinette table and sipped their beers in silence for a few moments.

"Go ahead," Sally finally said, "Say it."

"Aw, come on."

"No, no," Sally insisted, "Say it. Just lay it on without Vaseline. Hell, never mind, I'll say it myself. I'm an ass, okay? God, why do I have to do it? Make a big hairy scene every damn time? Why can't I just keep my big mouth…" She made a zipping motion across her lips.

"You ever take physics?" Silvio asked.

"Uh-uh."

Silvio studied his beer bottle a moment, rolling it in his hands. "I did. In high school."

"No kidding, you were good in physics?"

"Nah. But I liked it. I think I could have been good at it, only I didn't put any time into it. I was too busy playing football. And chasing Trysta."

Sally chuckled. "So you were chasing old Trysta back in high school."

"Ha, me and every other guy in Cornwells Heights."

"But you were the lucky stiff who got her."

"Well, I was the lucky stiff who got her pregnant."

"Oh, that's bad," Sally laughed, though she wasn't sure Silvio got his own joke.

"Aw, it was okay." Silvio replied. "It happened at the senior picnic…"

"Of course,"

"…so we had already graduated, and all, before she even knew."

"Oh, well that's good. I guess. Which brings us back to physics?"

"Oh, yeah. See, in physics you learn that for every action there's an equal and opposite reaction."

"For every action there's an equal and opposite reaction," Sally repeated thoughtfully. "That's good. I like it."

"It's true. Your ex sets off your fuse, you're gonna explode. You can't help it."

Sally laughed glumly. "So that's physics, huh?"

"Sure. You can keep the explosion inside you, you can even smile, but under your skin you are gonna be blown to bits."

"Yeah. More physics." Sally sighed. "You know, who'd of thought it would come to this between Darren and me? I mean, it didn't used to be this way. I wasn't always a walking physics experiment. I used to be normal. I was happy. And when we were first married? Boy, I was on top of the world! I'd have done anything for Darren, I mean *anything!*"

"Oh, hey, me, too. Trysta..." Silvio shook his head. "She had me wrapped around her little finger."

"Until she flicked you off." Sally made a flicking motion with her thumb and pinky.

"I was crazy back then. And stupid. But happy. Boy, was I happy! What was I, eighteen? Graduated from high school, set up with a good union apprenticeship in my uncle's business, money in my pocket, and getting married to the most beautiful girl in the world. God, I was so crazy about Trysta."

"Ah." There was a moment of pause between them. Each took a sip of beer. Then Sally spoke. "Uh, Silvio?"

"Yeah?"

"Did you ever wonder...I mean, with all those other guys chasing Trysta, and all...did you ever think that, uh, maybe the baby might not have...well, not quite have been, you know...yours?"

Silvio smacked his beer bottle down on the table. "No! Nobody ever said that! Not one of the guys ever said it, not once, not even joking around! It was, 'Hey, way to go, Silvio,' and, 'Have a cigar, man!' Or even 'tough break,' or whatever. But *nobody* thought it wasn't mine. So I don't think about it either, okay? You think about something like that it could make you crazy. So I didn't think then and I don't now!" Silvio took a deep breath. "Aw heck, what did I know? I was just a dumb kid."

"You were a good kid, Silvio."

"Nah, just dumb. But it doesn't matter, okay? Zach is my son. Nothing's ever gonna change that."

"I know," Sally said gently. Then she added, just as gently, "But there's something else you maybe ought to think about. Trysta's eight months pregnant. She and Darren have been married, what, a couple of weeks? Isn't there just a chance that this one…?"

"Oh, no!" Silvio sprung up from his chair and began pacing the floor. "Oh, no, not this time! This one is *not mine!* It's *his! He* got Trysta, now *he* gets the kid, *he* gets the pains, *he* gets the grief, *he* gets the bills! Not me, okay? Not this time!" Silvio was breathing hard and oh Jesus, he was crying again. Sally felt on the verge of tears herself.

"Okay," she said softly. "You want another beer?"

Silvio sniffed and wiped his eyes with his hands. "Okay."

***

Silvio took another long pull of his beer and then he raised his bottle towards Sally. "You know what we're doing with stuff this, don't you?"

"Yeah. Trying to forget our troubles. Our sorrows."

"Yeah. Seems you and me, we got a lot in common, huh?"

"Yeah." Sally raised her bottle. "Here's to troubles and," she hiccupped, "sorrows." Though she was actually feeling pretty good now. Mellowed out. She smiled at Silvio who smiled back and said, sounding kind of mellowed out himself:

"Wellll…maybe we ought to be trying some other way? To take our minds off our troubles and sorrows?"

Some other way? Geez, I wonder what he's getting at? Then she wondered how she felt about what he might be getting at, if what he might be getting at was what she thought he might be getting at. *Fuck it,* she thought, *he's cute, he's nice, I'm half drunk and still on my birth control pills and I'm not twenty years old any more.*

"Wellll," she responded, looking at her beer because she felt too shy to look him in the eye, "I mean, maybe if something …someone, whatever...*did* come along...into our lives...I mean, like, me into yours and yours into me, uh, mine, uh, no, *me* into, uh..." *and I'm sounding like an ass.* She tried again. "Okay, what I *mean* is"

"I know what you mean."

"No, what I *mean* is"

She was cut off by a sudden terrible racket outside her door. It sounded like a herd of elephants pounding up her steps, yammering in some convoluted elephant-language, ringing her bell and pounding her door simultaneously.

Sally hurried to the door with Silvio following behind her. She opened the door and recognized Mo Ealy, owner of the apartments and manager of her condo. String-skinny with close-cropped greying hair and a salt-and-pepper mustache, he stood in her doorway in front of a crowd of people – were they all Hispanic? – jammed onto the landing.

"Wha?" asked Sally.

"What's going on?" echoed Silvio.

Sally's neighbor Lupe quickly pushed in front of Mo so that she was standing inside Sally's living room.

"*Sally,*" she said breathlessly, her hands in a gesture of supplication, "*Ayudanos, por favor, ayudanos!*"

Over Lupe's shoulder Mo Ealy smiled the wide urgent smile of a hungry crocodile. "Say, Mrs. Miller, can we all just step in a minute?"

Before Sally had the chance to answer, a total of thirty-two men, women, and children were crowded into her living/dining room and her kitchen. Among the crowd Sally recognized Lupe's husband Ascensiòn, who was holding David. Mo closed the door to Sally's apartment.

"Now, wait just a minute," Silvio said.

"This is a two-bedroom, right, Mrs. Miller?" Mo asked.

"Uh, yeah, but what"

"Okay. Ascensiòn," he said, "send them into the two bedrooms, you can even stick a couple in the bathroom, fast, and tell them *be quiet! No habla,* okay?" He turned back to Sally, still smiling his urgent smile. "It's all right, isn't it? Your neighbors the Guzmans here, they said it would be okay."

"*What?*" Sally tried to shake her head clear of the two-and-a-half beers she'd just drunk, not counting the beer with dinner. But the whole scenario had a fuzzy, surreal quality to it.

Ascensiòn had handed the baby to his wife and was herding the crowd into the bedrooms and bathroom.

"You tell them not to *breathe*," Mo Ealy called to Ascensiòn.

"Wait, wait, what is going *on?*" Sally asked.

"*I* know damn well what's going on!" Silvio answered.

Ealy pointed a finger at Silvio. "Hey, don't I know you from somewhere?" You been around here before, right?"

Silvio ignored him. "Sally, are you involved in this racket?"

"What? I don't..."

"Now, now, it's nothing, nothing at all," Mo Ealy cut in. "Mrs. Miller, here, she just offered her place as a kind of a safe haven, didn't you, Mrs. Miller, a kind of Hotel Guadalajara, if you get my drift." Ealy chuckled nervously.

Clarity hit Sally like a bulls-eye to the brain. *"What?"* she cried, "What are you, *nuts?* What are you talking, I never, *never,* I, I, *no!* This is cra...*No!*"

"Calm down, Mrs. Miller..."

Sally and Silvio began shouting in unison.

"*I never said...*"

"*...some kinda jerk ...*"

"*...Out of your mind...*"

"*...totally illegal...*"

"*...can't hide here...*"

"*...get into big trouble...*"

"ALL RIGHT! ALL RIGHT!" Mo Ealy shouted over both of them. His crocodile smile was gone, replaced by a stony cold look which he aimed at Silvio. "And this gentleman," he said icily, "wouldn't happen to be Mr. Miller?"

"Oh, for God's sake, Mo, you know he's not!" Sally snapped.

"Well, Mrs. Miller," Mo sniffed, "I'll have to remind you that this is a family-friendly residential living community, and if you are using your home for the purpose of entertaining men, then as president of the condo association I'm afraid I'm going to have to"

"Aw, fuck off, Mo," Sally cut him off. "And quit 'Mrs. Miller'- ing me, you know damn well my name's Sally!" She pointed towards her bedroom. "And you get those poor people out of my"

"Oh, Jesus!" Ealy cried. He was looking over her shoulder out her living room window, eyes bulging.

Sally spun around to see a parade of official-looking cars, some of them police vans.

"Jesus, I gotta go," Ealy bolted to Sally's door, hurried out and then stuck his head back inside. "Look, I'll have to be handing out some keys so they don't break down the doors, you might be hearing a little commotion, doors opening and all, but just sit tight, nobody's gonna come to your place. But if they do don't let them in, don't answer, you don't have to, they don't have a warrant for you, you're legit. I'll be back in half-an-hour, forty-five minutes, an hour tops. Turn out the lights and lock your door, okay?" Then he took off down the stairs and from the window Sally and Silvio saw him running towards his office.

"This can't be happening!" Sally cried, "I just live here! I'm not involved in anything like this!"

"Huh, you are now," Silvio replied.

"Jesus, Silvio, this is unreal! What am I gonna do?"

"Well, I'd say you're either gonna make those illegals leave or set yourself up for criminal charges."

"You think it's actually a crime?

"I'm guessing."

"What if they won't leave?"

"The police are right outside."

Sally ran a hand through her hair. *"Jesus."* She walked to her hallway and hesitated outside her bedroom door. "I don't believe this," she muttered. She pulled open the door to the sound of a loud collective gasp and the sight of a dozen-and-a-half pairs of eyes wide with terror. At the same time she could hear a rustling from Joshua's room and a light shuffling from the bathroom. In her room the frightened-looking people were huddled close to the floor between the bed and the wall. There were men and women, a few old, most of them young, some with children. One young mother held on her lap a thin little boy with wide serious brown eyes who reminded her of her Joshua. Among the group were Lupe and Ascensiòn.

Ascensiòn stood up. "No se preocupen," he said to the others, "esta es nuestra amiga Sally."

Sally understood that he was telling them not to worry, that she was their "amiga." Everyone let out a breath of relief. Some of them smiled at her and she heard whispers of "Gracias" and "Thank-you." God, they looked so helpless. So desperate. So down-at-the-heels human. *Shit*, she thought. She took a deep breath. "Okay, look…" She hesitated for a moment and then continued. "I really hate to have to, you know, ask you to leave, but hiding you like this is, well, it's illegal and all, and, I mean, I'm not trying to be mean, or anything, but like I said, it's a crime, and I could, you know, get arrested, so…I mean, I don't want to have to, you know, go get the police, or anything, so if you all just left on your own…maybe you could all run around the back of the far buildings, behind the dumpsters, or something…?" Sally had the impression that everyone in the room had stopped breathing and that they were frozen in a collective stare directly at her. She pulled in another deep breath. "Anyway, you have to leave right now or I'm calling the police." There, she'd spit it out.

She could tell by the devastated expressions which ones understood English. "Ascensiòn," she said, hating herself, "could you, uh, translate?"

Ascensiòn opened his mouth to speak but to Sally's shock what came out was a long broken sob. He tried again, but a wave of uncontrolled sobs had taken over his voice. Then the tears were spilling out of his beautiful brown eyes and his crying was like a super-contagion of hopelessness: moments later every man, woman, and child in the room was crying. Except for Lupe. She set her baby David into the lap of the woman next to her and sprung from the floor and across the room until she was face to face with Sally. She grabbed Sally by both arms.

"*Sally, no, no, por favor, please, Sally, mi baby Dayveed, please!*" Then she said, slowly, desperately, but ever so clearly: "You…*owe*…me! You …*owe*…me!"

Sally stood momentarily drop-jawed. The immigrants' crying had crescendoed into a loud sorrowful group lamentation. Sally pressed her palms against her eyes. "*Oh, what the hell do I do?*" she moaned.

Then she felt a hand on her shoulder. She turned to see Silvio standing behind her. His eyes were red and teary.

"What you do," he said softly, "is tell them to be really quiet. And go lock your door. I'll turn out the lights."

***

Sally and Silvio sat in the dark at the dinette table. In a whispered voice shaky with nerves Sally told Silvio the story of how she'd made Lupe and Ascensiòn's acquaintance two days earlier. "So you see," she ended with a small humorless chuckle, "this is all 'cause of you."

"Geez, Sally, I'm sorry, I really am," he whispered.

"Silvio, cut it out" she whispered back, "I'm joking."

"Oh."

They sat in nervous silence for another fifteen minutes, each nursing a personal conundrum of thoughts until those thoughts were broken by the sound of several pairs of hard-soled shoes climbing the outer staircase. Sally and Silvio could hear pounding on the neighbors' door and a voice that called, "Guzman? Open the door please, Federal agents, we have a warrant." Sally felt slightly faint. She took in several deep breaths and squeezed her eyes shut. There was more noise of activity, and in her mind Sally could see the beefy, stone-faced agents pushing through the door of Lupe and Ascensiòn's apartment and laying siege to their little life. A few minutes later her doorbell rang and then there was the same pounding on her door and the same voice called, "Open the door, please, Federal agents." Sally gasped and began sucking in breaths to keep from fainting. She looked towards the door then and back to Silvio, who was shaking his head and motioning for her stay quiet. His face was broken out in a sweat and he was breathing heavily himself. Sally closed her eyes and began praying. She prayed the Catholic prayers and the Jewish prayers, though she was pretty rusty on both, and she silently vowed to take Josh to the High Holy Mass of the Sacred Whatever if only God would rescue her from this.

"Nobody home," the voice outside said. "Should we break in?"

"What for?" answered another voice. "We got no warrant on this one. The snakes have all slithered away."

"Should we break in by mistake?"

"*Oh, my God,*" Sally whispered, "*oh my God, oh my God, oh my God!*" Again Silvio motioned for her to be quiet.

Outside her door there was laughter then the sound of footsteps descending the stairs.

Within ten minutes the last official vehicle had exited The Villas at Roosevelt and after another interminable ten minutes Mo Ealy was back in Sally's living room.

"Oh my God, Sally, you did great!" he cried, wrapping Sally in a hug which she stiffened against. "And you!" He gushed at Silvio with open arms, but thought better than to put a finger on this big angry-looking man. Then Mo hurried around to the bedrooms and bathroom and flushed the bedraggled fugitives from their refuges.

As they processed through Sally's living room to her door each rescuee paused respectfully before Sally and Silvio as if they were royalty. They offered tearful and emotional thanks, some hugged Sally and one sobbing woman got down on her knees and kissed Sally's hand. Lupe and Ascensiòn were the last to leave. Lupe hugged Sally and Silvio and to Sally she said, "Eres mi amiga, my *friend,* por eternidad." Then she pointed to herself and to Sally and said, "Ahora I owe *you!*"

Ascensiòn gave Silvio a manly half-hug and said, "Thank you, my friend, thank you." Then he wrapped his hands around Sally's and said in a voice quivering with emotion, "You use our bathroom anytime."

A moment later the Guzmans were out the door with Mo Ealy following close behind them, crocodile-grinning once more. "Well, if you folks don't mind I'll be on my way now." But before Mo could get a foot out the door Silvio's big hand was gripping his shoulder.

"We do," Silvio said, "and you won't. Not yet."

***

Once again Sally and Silvio were seated at Sally's dinette table, this time with Mo Ealy wedged close between like them a prisoner squirming between his two interrogators.

Mo pulled in a deep breath. "Okay," he began, "you know the Chupaflor Market? Around the corner from here, a couple blocks down Rhawn Street?"

"Yeah, I know where the Chupaflor is," said Sally.

"Right, well that's where these Latinos all go to shop and wire money across the border. You know how they're always sending money back home. Take all the American jobs then don't even invest it back into the American economy, but what can you do, that's the way it goes." Silvio gave a small nod but said nothing. "Anyway," Mo continued, "tonight the Chupaflor got raided by ICE."

"ICE?" Sally asked, "That's Immigration?"

"Yeah. Immigration and Customs Enforcement. The same goons who just now muscled their way onto my property."

"So Immigration and Customs Enforcement raided this market for hiring illegals?" Silvio asked.

"I don't actually know, though I doubt that was the main intent. The green-card Guatemalans who own the place would have to be pretty stupid – I mean, open a Hispanic supermarket then staff it with illegals? Okay, they might use a couple in the back for stocking, I don't know. And then Ascensiòn, he works there, that I know. In fact I think he did say there were one or two other under-the-table part-timers besides himself. But Immigration isn't gonna stage an expensive raid over two or three undocumented employees."

"Wait a minute," Sally cut in, "Ascensiòn works at the Chupaflor Market?"

"He's in and out, takes care of all their maintenance. He works a couple of places. He does my maintenance, too."

"Ascensiòn does?" Silvio asked.

"Oh, yeah, and I'll tell you what, he may be illegal but he's worth the risk. The guy can fix anything, heating, central air, hot water, and he's a top-notch plumber. You know how hard it is to get a good plumber?" Sally and Silvio exchanged a look, but Mo went on. "Don't ask me how he picked up his know-how down there in Nicaragua, but it's great for me because I don't have to deal with these half-assed local outfits anymore."

"Like Quick And Reliable?" Silvio asked sardonically.

"Bunch of assholes, excuse me Sally," then back to Silvio, "you know about them, too?"

"Never mind," Sally quickly added, putting a hand on Silvio's arm. "You say Ascensiòn is pretty good, though?"

"Oh yeah."

"You pay him standard rate for his work?" Silvio asked.

"I give him free rent and utilities. He's getting a real deal."

"What's rent here?" Silvio asked, "Nine, nine-fifty a month?"

"Plus utilities, that takes it up over a thousand a month," Mo said defensively. "Like I said, he's getting a deal."

"A thousand a month," Silvio huffed. "You know what a top-notch union plumber makes in Philadelphia?"

Mo shrugged. "So let him go out and make it."

"Right," Silvio muttered.

"So," Sally leaned in a little closer to Mo, "what happened at the Chupaflor Market tonight?"

"Okay," Mo continued, "the Chupaflor got raided, maybe or maybe not for hiring illegals. But what ICE did show up with was a warrant to seize all records of all Western Union money wiring transactions over the past, well, I don't know, whatever period of time, with authorization to check the senders' identities."

"They can do that?" Sally asked. "Go into a business and pull up the names of the customers? Check on who's sending what where?"

"Oh, sure," Mo answered. "With Homeland Security, the Patriot Act and all, they can seize any kind of personal transaction records of anybody they want. You, me, anybody. Anyway, while the Feds are screwing around with the records, pulling up people's names and addresses, checking them, the manager of the Chupaflor calls Ascensiòn to warn him what's going on and that half a dozen suspicious addresses have popped up at The Villas at Roosevelt, including Ascensiòn's, and that the Feds would be on their way over. Now one thing I have to say about Ascensiòn, he's a good hearted-kid, maybe a little too good-hearted, if you know what I mean, and he's smart, too. He knows every one of the thirty-two illegals who live in this complex and their half-a dozen apartment locations and numbers."

"Wait a minute," Sally broke in, "All those people crammed into my house tonight, they all live in six apartments?"

"Well, yes. But most of the units are two-bedrooms. Nice and spacious. Like this one." Mo gestured to the room around him and Sally muttered, "Yeah, right."

"So," Silvio continued, "you're saying Ascensiòn ran around and told all the illegals that they were going to be raided?"

"Flew around like a bat out of hell is more like it. A regular Nicaraguan Paul Revere! And what do you think happened? They all followed him like he was the Pied Piper – straight to my office! They wanted me to hide the bunch of them, do you believe that? I told them to get lost but nobody knew where to lose themselves, so now it's my problem! It's not like I even have one vacant unit I could've shoved them all into. And even if I did, how do I know that ICE wouldn't want to check out the vacancies as well? And I want to tell you, after the grief I got a year and a half ago over this same kind of thing," Mo waved a hand in disgust.

"What happened a year and a half ago?" Silvio asked.

"You remember when the Luxor Paint factory got raided?"

"Oh, yeah," said Sally, "that big place out by the Northeast Airport. I remember that. Didn't Immigration find over a hundred undocumented workers there?"

"Yep. And followed them right to here where a whole lot of them lived. Look, there's no one law against me renting to whoever I want to rent to."

Silvio cocked an eyebrow. "Are you kidding me? Not one law?"

"Not one law. Fifteen laws, yes, one law, no. So this lawyer cites this law, and that lawyer cites that law, and the judge cites another law, and I so end with no kind of conviction that sticks but a bad case of heartburn and money out of my pocket all the same, not to mention being on a radar screen I don't want to be on. Which is why I stopped renting to undocumented foreigners, except this handful who I needed to fill up those six vacant units. I've got a family, kids of my own to support after all. But frankly, with the economy being what it is nowadays, everybody's looking left and right to rent or downsize to a condo, and suddenly I've got a waiting list. Good American families, like Sally's here, in need of good housing. I'm through renting to illegals, especially after tonight. They're all out the door."

"What do you mean, out the door?" Sally asked.

"Like I said, out the door. I mean I'm sorry to have to make them leave, they're mostly nice people and I feel for them, I really do. And I'll give them a week or so, I'm not heartless, or anything."

"Don't they have rental contracts?" Silvio asked.

Mo laughed. "Well, yeah, but…look, these people, they come over here, they're breaking the law, so they're taking a risk, same as anybody who breaks the law. They break into our borders like thieves and they've got no legal recourse and no right to ask for any and they know it. What, you disagree with that?"

Silvio sighed. "What's to disagree with there? But it's still not right to take advantage of people."

"What do you mean?" Mo shot back, "those people, *they* took advantage of *me!* I'm the one who took them in and got in trouble with the law for it, *twice!*"

"Oh yeah?" Silvio snapped, "Well what about how you"

Sally cut Silvio off. "Where will these people go? The ones with children and the old people? I mean, it's getting cold outside. It must be forty degrees out there right now."

Mo shrugged. "Not my problem. I'm sorry, but I'm not the one who got them into the situation they're in. I didn't drag their children and grandmas over here without a shred of security. They did. Aw, look, don't worry, they'll be all right. To tell you the truth, most of them will be out of here by morning on their own. Scattered and running scared. Immigration knows it, too. ICE won't bother to come back here any time soon. Not without another lead. Which they won't get on me, 'cause like I said, I'm handing the bunch of them their walking papers, so to speak."

"Yeah, well, you're a real nice guy, Mo," Silvio snapped.

"Oh, *I* am?" Mo answered sarcastically. "How about you? You want to deal with them? You want to risk your hide helping them, invite a few of them to go live with you, you're such a good guy?"

Silvio and Mo glared at each other, but Sally grasped Silvio's arm. "Lupe and Ascensiòn and their baby," she said, "they'll be out on the street!"

"No, the Guzmans won't have to go. They're my one and only exception. Ascensiòn works for me, he can stay here. For now. Like I said, at the moment there's no real law against renting to them."

Sally felt a rush of relief, but wondered why she suddenly felt emotionally attached to these strangers who, she had to agree with Mo, truly had no right to be here.

"Renting to them, no," Silvio said. "Employing them, yes."

"What, you want to give me a hard time about it? Do I have to remind you of how much trouble Sally's in if ICE was to get word of what she did tonight? They could find out, you know. Easily."

Sally pulled in a gulp of air and felt a sudden stab of fear in her stomach. Silvio's face reddened and his eyes narrowed angrily. But his voice was calm.

"You know Angelo Barbieri?" he asked Mo.

"Angelo Barbieri? Out of South Philly?"

"That's right. You heard of him?"

Mo swallowed. "Yeah. Yeah, I heard of him."

"Good. 'cause if my Uncle Angie heard about some double-crossing snake threatening Sally he'd have to do something about it, you know what I'm saying?"

Mo's eyes widened in fear and then his crocodile – now endangered crocodile – smile suddenly switched back on. "Oh, hey, nobody's threatening Sally, heh, heh, no, no, not at all, did we miscommunicate, or something?.

"Yeah, I think maybe we did," replied Silvio.

"Oh, well, I'm sorry. No, Sally's fine, you're fine, and Sally, you give me your next month's utility bills, I'm talking water, gas, *and* electric, I'll take care of them, because I appreciate what you did for the people."

"No thanks, Mo, I'll take care of my own utilities."

Mo shrugged, still smiling. "Okay, Sally, sure, that's fine, too, everything's fine, and don't you worry about tonight, it's zipped up and it's gonna stay zipped up, right?"

"Whatever," said Sally.

"That's great, well I have to be going." Mo walked quickly to the door then turned back to Silvio. "Pleasure to meet you Mr....Barbieri?"

Silvio made the slightest move of his head, which wasn't exactly a nod, but could have been interpreted as one. Mo hurried out the door.

Sally shut the door then turned to Silvio. "Who the hell is Angelo Barbieri?"

"Oh, he's my Uncle Bud's cousin's wife's ex-brother-in-law. He owns a big salvage operation down off Oregon Avenue on the river by the Navy Yard." Then he added with a smile, "Nobody you have to worry about."

"Oh. Well, good. Somebody not to have to worry about."

Then it was the two of them standing in Sally's living room, wordless and awkward, at a loss as to what two people who've just formed the bond of a shared intense experience are supposed to do next. Their eyes met and a moment later they fell into each other's arms, each suddenly pulled like a magnet to the closeness of another human being, the comforting warmth of another body, a shoulder to burrow into against the craziness of the world. And to feel for a moment safe, protected…and just for a moment, cared about.

Chapter Thirteen

Though it was close to eleven o'clock the lights were still on in Darren and Trysta's master bedroom. Trysta was sitting up in bed crying while Darren paced the floor.

"This time she went too far!" Darren huffed. "She just went too damn far!"

"It was awful!" Trysta sobbed, "So, so awful!"

Darren stopped pacing and faced Trysta. "Oh yeah? Well are you satisfied? Are you *one hundred and fifty percent* satisfied?"

"*I'm so upset!*" Trysta bawled.

"Oh, *now* you're upset! *Then* you wouldn't listen to me. Did I tell you not to come to Sally's? Did I tell you to stay home with the kids? Would you listen to me? No. *Now* you're ups-"

Trysta cut him off. "And you didn't stand up for me once the whole time! You just let Sally run me down! You didn't even try to stop her!"

"*Try to stop her?* The woman is fucking hot-wired! Hell, once Sally starts spouting you couldn't cork her up with the goddamn Rock of Gibraltar!"

"I just don't understand," Trysta sniffled, "What was Silvio doing there?"

"Well I think it was pretty damn *obvious* what Silvio was doing there! Yeah, pretty goddamn obvious!"

"But *Silvio!* With *Sally!* How could he stoop so low? How could he pick up that *trash?* After he's had *me?*"

"Aw, screw Silvio! Let 'em have each other. Who the hell cares, right?"

"Right," Trysta sniffed. "Who cares?" She broke into a long loud wail.

Darren sat on the bed. "Aw, Trys, come on." He rubbed his eyes. He was tired. Exhausted.

"I just don't understand why I have to put up with this treatment," Trysta sobbed, "I'm a good person."

Darren sighed. "Christ, I'm tired. Let's bag this damn night and go to sleep."

There was a knock on the bedroom door and from the other side a small voice piped up: "Daddy! Daddy!"

Darren sprung from the bed and opened the door. "Josh, what's wrong? Why aren't you sleeping?"

"Daddy, they're being too loud."

Now Darren could hear the sound of Trysta's kids screaming at each other. Darren looked back and forth helplessly from his sobbing wife to the sound of her screaming children. He stormed from the bedroom followed by Josh down the hall to Zach's room, apparently the children's battle ground of choice for this late-night skirmish.

"You two," he shouted at Trina and Sam, "back to bed! *Now!*"

The girls sulked back to their room, each turning to make a face at her brother on her way back.

"Thanks," Zach muttered before climbing back into bed.

"No problem," Darren muttered, though he wasn't really sure if Zach's "thanks" was heartfelt or a parting shot of resentment.

"Now me and Zach can sleep," Josh said and then he hugged his father and crawled into the twin bed next to Zach's.

***

The idea struck Trysta the moment Josh entered their bedroom, and as soon as Darren left the room she stopped in mid-sob and reached for the cosmetics case, hair brush and small make-up mirror on her bedside table. By the time Darren returned Trysta had finished a quick application of mascara along with a daub of blush and lipstick. She also gave her neck a spritz of cologne and ran the brush through her hair and then gave herself a once-over glance in the mirror. Then she slipped off her robe and tossed it to the floor. She had just enough time before Darren stepped into the room to flip her nightgown strap off one shoulder and arrange her flowing hair over the other.

Equal and Opposite Reactions

Darren entered the bedroom, flicked off the light, and crawled into his side of the bed. He turned on his side away from Trysta and mumbled, "I'm going to sleep."

"Darren?" Trysta clicked on her bedside lamp. "Darren, Honey?"

Darren grunted in response.

"I'll rub your back."

"'Sokay," he mumbled.

"Just a little?" Trysta bent over close to him and ran her fingernails lightly up and down his back, crooning, "That's right, just relax now. Is our little Joshie all tucked in?"

Darren grunted but made no effort to pull away from her.

"Poor baby," Trysta went on, running her fingers lower down Darren's back until they teased below the elastic of his pajama bottoms, "he's such a little sweetheart. And you're so good with him. You're just so good with children. You're good with my children. You're good with everybody and everything." She was silent a moment and then continued. "Darren, there's something on my mind."

"Yeah, I can tell." Darren rolled over and tried to pull Trysta towards him, but she resisted, laughing. "Oh, you! You're supposed to be trying to sleep!"

"Later." Darren sat up and grabbed Trysta. He held her while she spoke, kissing her neck and shoulders as if he wanted to ravish her.

"Darren, Sweetie, I'm worried about Joshie."

"Joshie is fine, *Mmmmm...*"

"I know he's fine now, but what about when he's with Sally?" Trysta squirmed as if trying to resist him, which inflamed him the more.

"I don't want to talk about Sally. Baby, you smell like heaven!"

Trysta pulled away from Darren. "But I'm *worried!*"

"Hey, you, come on back here!" He reached again for Trysta but she scooted further across the bed.

"I *said* I'm *worried about Josh!*"

Darren backed off. "*Geez,*" he muttered to himself. "Look," he sighed, running a hand through his hair, "I know Sally can be a bitch on skids, but you don't have to worry about Josh. She's crazy about Josh."

112

"She's crazy, period! What kind of mother is she, always blowing up like she does? And then the men she has over!"

"*Men?*"

"Well, Silvio. And who knows who else."

"Yeah, well, having Silvio over, that was going too far. What was she trying to pull, anyhow?"

"You *know* that's how she is. Crazy and trashy and mean. The worst *possible* mother." Trysta moved back up close to Darren and began running a finger up and down his arm. "Joshua shouldn't be living with her. He should be living with us."

"Well, sure, but she's got custody, so...let's not talk about Sally." Darren put his arms around Trysta and began kissing her again.

Trysta returned Darren's kisses passionately, moaning and caressing his hair. Then her eyes flew open as if she'd just come up with the idea. "Darren!" She cried between kisses, "We could fight her on this! We could get custody of Josh!"

"*Nnnnn...*"

"But we *could!*" Trysta insisted, ignoring his mouth on her breasts. "Just think...Josh would be in a stable, loving home...and it would serve *her* right!" She slid away from Darren then took his face in her hands. "Darren, we *have* to do this!"

Darren looked helplessly into Trysta's eyes. "You're driving me crazy," he moaned.

Trysta let go of Darren's face and pulled up the top of her nightie, which had slid down around her waist. "I'm sorry, darling, but this is important."

"So is this!" Darren slid the straps of her nightie back down her shoulders, but feeling her resistance he backed off. "Look, forget it," he said, "Forget about Sally. I mean, I couldn't even afford a custody battle right now, tight as things are."

"But think of the extra income we'd have if you didn't have to pay child support. We could start thinking about that place in Puerto Vallarta again."

Darren sighed. "Yeah."

"Of course, having Joshua would be the most important thing."

"Well, yeah, of course." Darren lay down next to Trysta and stared at the ceiling for a few moments. Then he propped himself up on one elbow. "Nah, it's too risky. I could throw thousands at this thing and still lose. And why would the court take primary custody away from Sally, anyway? I mean, she's his mother."

"Hmph, some mother. What if the court knew about the language she uses? And the drinking?"

"Drinking? What drinking?"

"Well, you saw yourself how she and Silvio were drinking. Right in front of Josh!"

"Trysta, *I've* had drinks in front of *your* kids."

"That's different. We're married. And we've got a nice home and a wonderful family life."

Darren considered. "Nah, forget it, Trys. There's not a chance of me getting custody of Josh. And I can't afford any more court fights."

"Neither can she."

"So there."

Trysta slid down and propped herself up on an elbow so that she and Darren faced each other like bookends. "What if you just *told* Sally you were suing her for sole custody."

Darren laughed sourly. "She'd go nuts. She'd probably try and kill me."

Trysta's eyes lit up. "That would be even better!"

"*What?*"

"If she got violent!" Trysta rolled over and pulled herself up to a sitting position so that she was overlooking Darren. "Say Sally got so mad that she hit you, or something, wouldn't that be great? Then you could press assault charges, and it would be all over for her! Serve her right, bad as she's made us feel. And see how much Silvio would enjoy visiting her in jail!"

Darren laughed uncomfortably. "Uh, don't you think that's going a little far? Look, why don't we just forget about"

"All right," Trysta cut him off, "We'll forget about getting her to hit you."

"Thanks."

"You're welcome," Trysta laughed. Then she pushed Darren onto his back and began kissing his face, neck, and chest.

"Hey, that's more like it!" Darren laughed.

Trysta pinned Darren's arms down to the bed and cooed to him between kisses, "Promise me you'll get Josh! I'll be a good mother to him, I'll be *wonderful!*" She ran her tongue up and down his chest and stomach.

"Oh, Baby, I know, but...*oh, Baby!*"

"We'll be a *family*. No more worrying about *money.*"

"No...money..."

"No more *support payments.*"

"No...support...payments...oooo, Baby!"

"We could afford our *dream*. In Puerto *Vallarta.*"

"Puerto... Vallarta...oooooo"

Trysta lifted her arms for a moment and shimmied out of her nightie. Then she re-pinned Darren's arms above his head and positioned herself so that her breasts hovered over his face and her belly pressed against his groin. *"Promise me we'll get Josh,"* she said breathily, *"Promise me we'll do it! Promise me!"*

"Uh, uh, uh, okay!"

Chapter Fourteen

Sally smacked the snooze alarm button for the third time – or was it the fourth time? Or the tenth? – sure of one thing only: that she was hung-over.

As she willed herself to wake up subsequent bits of thought, sharp as darts, pierced her throbbing brain one by one. She was in her bed. Alone. Silvio. *Silvio? Had she and Silvio…?* No, she didn't think…or wait…how far *had* they…? Where *was* Silvio? Her alarm clock began its final encore. Damn, it was twenty-to-seven and Sally had to get up and get ready for work while dealing with a hangover and probably a man sleeping somewhere in her house. She put on a robe and walked softly across the hall to Josh's room. She opened the door a crack and by the pale rays of morning light sifting through the blinds she made out Silvio's sleeping form under the covers on Josh's bed. She now recalled the moment late the night before – of course there'd been no question of Silvio driving home…how the hell many beers *had* they polished off between them, anyway? – which had left the question hanging in the air: The couch? Josh's bed? Her bed? In any case, here was Silvio sleeping in Josh's bed, so they hadn't done…*that.* But was *that* where the night had been heading, before they'd gotten caught in the middle of – and ultimately thwarted – a full-scale police raid? Sally rubbed her aching temples. Had what she remembered happening really happened? Were she and Silvio, technically speaking, criminals? Sally laughed. Yeah, right. Silvio slept with the covers pulled high, snuggled in like a child, but she could see the back of his curly hair and a bit of bare back, shoulder and an arm tucked outside the blanket. She suddenly felt slightly embarrassed, as if by watching him asleep and unaware she were crossing some line of personal space and intimacy. Still she studied the muscles of his upper back and arm a moment longer. She recalled the pleasant sensation of his arms wrapped around her last night. It had been just a quick friendly hug – or had it been a long, sexy hug? – that they'd ultimately shared before heading off – dragging off, actually – chaste if not sober, to their separate sleeping quarters.

Sally started to shut the door again and then, on second thought, opened it wide. She cleared her throat loudly but Silvio showed no signs of stirring. She stepped into the room and then stepped back out again and closed the door. Twenty minutes later, after she was in and out of the shower and dressed, she again opened the door to Josh's room.

"Silvio," she called softly and then repeated louder, "Silvio!" Finally she walked over to the bed. "GOOD-MORNING! RISE AND SHINE!"

Silvio woke up suddenly and sprang to a sitting position. "Huh?" he mumbled, squinting at Sally through half-focused eyes. Then he grasped for a blanket to pull up over his chest.

Sally quickly looked away and hurried towards the door. "I'll fix some breakfast," she called over her shoulder .

She headed for the kitchen where she began whipping together a breakfast of toast, coffee, and – in case Silvio felt more like eating than she did – scrambled eggs. She heard Silvio head for the bathroom.

"Okay if I take a shower?" he called.

"Sure," she called back and suddenly had a mental image of Silvio in the shower. "Cut it out," she muttered, but once again that warm, melty feeling from the night before was settling pleasantly in and she was smiling over the scrambled eggs when Silvio finally appeared, washed, combed and fully dressed, in the kitchen doorway.

"Good morning," he yawned, "what time is it now?"

Sally glanced at the stove clock. "Seven-twelve."

"Seven-twelve? Geez, I got a job at seven-thirty!"

"Oh, well, relax, then. You don't have to show up for a couple of hours yet."

"Don't make me laugh," he laughed, "My head feels like a football."

"Yeah? Mine's only a soccer ball. I made some scrambled eggs and toast. Think you can handle it?"

Silvio rubbed his head then his stomach. "Head feels like a football. Stomach's okay."

"Me, I'm sticking with the toast."

Silvio smiled at Sally and reached for the two platters that she'd filled, one with eggs, the other with toast, while Sally filled their coffee mugs.

"Wow, this looks good," Silvio said as they sat down at the table. "And smells good."

"How about juice? Can I get you some OJ?"

"Let me get it." Silvio started to stand but Sally put a hand on his arm.

"No, you sit, eat. I'll get it."

As Sally poured his orange juice Silvio said, "Look at this. You're treating me like royalty. Been a long time since I been treated like royalty."

"Well, you know...you did a great job fixing my furnace."

"That was nothing, the furnace."

"Saved me, what, a hundred bucks?"

"With labor at least that." Silvio gestured towards his plate with his fork.

"This is real good. Hits the spot."

Sally bit into her toast. "It does." They ate in silence for a few moments then Sally asked Silvio how he'd slept.

"Like a dead man." After a few more moments of silence he put down his fork and said, "About last night..."

"Oh, my God, tell me about it! Did all that really happen? Us and those illegal immigrants, and the police, and the whole, the whole...?" Sally shook her head in disbelief.

"I think I was dreaming about it all night. I woke up wondering if I just dreamed the whole thing up. "

"I don't think anyone would believe it if we told them."

"Sally...I don't think we want to tell anyone. I think we want to, to...get out of the way of what happened last night, you know what I mean? And I think you want to stay out of the way of those neighbors of yours. In case Immigration comes looking for them again."

"Yeah, you're right about that. I mean, Lupe and Ascensiòn are nice, and all...but then it's not like I don't already have enough problems of my own, right? Why would I want to associate with people who could bring me more?"

As if in response to her question the doorbell rang. Sally moaned. "I don't think I have the nerve to answer that!"

"Maybe you better. Or I could. If you really don't have the nerve."

"No, I guess I better. In case it's, you know...somebody."

"Yeah."

"Maybe they went away."

But a second ring of the doorbell suggested otherwise. Sally headed for the door and opened it to find a happy-looking Guzman family standing in her doorway, Ascensiòn and Lupe smiling, David burbling in his mother's arms.

"Oh, uh, hi," said Sally. Ascensiòn and Lupe continued smiling, as if they were too happy to speak. "Everything all right?" Sally asked, though they looked as if everything were.

"We want to thank you Sally, you save us last night," said Ascensiòn.

"Si, we thank you, Sally," said Lupe

"And your friend. The plumber." Ascensiòn stepped into Sally's apartment with Lupe following behind him.

"Oh, well, ha, ha, that's okay, we just..."

Ascensiòn caught sight of Silvio still sitting at the table. "Ah, hey, Maje, you still here," he cried, "we thank you, too, man!"

"It's okay," Silvio said with a dismissive wave of his hand. Then he stood up. "I was, uh, just leaving for work."

"Yeah, and so was I," said Sally, "So, uh..."

"You living with Sally now?" Ascensiòn asked Silvio.

"Oh, no!" Sally and Silvio answered together. Then they said at the same time:

"He just"

"I just"

Ascensiòn laughed. "No problem. You Sally's friend, you our friend. But I don't know your name yet, Maje. You know my name yet?" He held out his hand to Silvio. "I'm Ascensiòn." He gestured towards Lupe. "My wife, Lupe, My son, David."

Silvio shook Ascensiòn's hand. "I'm Silvio. Nice to know you." Silvio nodded and smiled at Lupe then he picked up his tool box and said, "Well, I guess we all gotta get to work, so..."

"Wait," Ascensiòn cut in. "Sally, you save us, now we gonna do something for you."

"Oh, that's all right," Sally chuckled nervously, "I'm good."

"Lupe, she's gonna teach you Spanish!"

"What? Spanish?"

"Sure, Lupe went to the teacher's school in Leòn. She can teach you Spanish."

The toast and coffee had settled in Sally's stomach like Play-Doh and she was in no mood for yet another act in the theater of the absurd that her life seemed to devolve into whenever she was in the presence of these two young illegal Nicaraguans.

"No," she said, "that's okay, I really don't"

"She speaks half-hour Spanish to you, you speak half-hour English to her, you learn while you teach and while you learn."

"Well, see, I really don't have a lot of time"

"It's how I learned English. This guy owned an auto repair shop, he used to live in this building. He wanted to learn Spanish to pick up business with the Hispanic community. We got together an hour every night, he learn Spanish quick, I learn English quick. We called it a conversation exchange. Is the best way to learn, and free!"

"Well, I just don't think I can"

"You want to learn Spanish, Sally, you, too, Silvio. You speak Spanish, it gives you more, uh, *valor*. At your job. Whatever you do. Maybe get you a better job."

"Look, no, I really don't..." Sally stopped in mid-sentence. The words *"Maybe get you a better job,"* repeated themselves in her mind. As in, *"Maybe learning Spanish – and for free – with a native speaker – who lives right next door – will make you a more valuable asset at your job. Maybe get you a better job."*

"What you think, Sally? You want Lupe to come tonight? We got some good books to use."

"Uh...how about tomorrow?"

As soon as the Guzmans were out the door Sally turned to Silvio. "Go ahead, say it."

"Sally?"

"Just say it."

120

Patti Liszkay

"Do you think I could join your conversation exchange?"

Chapter Fifteen

"*Spanish lessons?* You and the plumber are gonna take *Spanish lessons? Together?*" Joanne cocked an incredulous eyebrow.

Sally took a deep breath. "Well, see, the girl who lives across the hall, my neighbor, that is, she's a Spanish teacher, *was* a Spanish teacher, now she's, well, she's a stay-at-home mom and we'd been talking about her teaching me, so…"

Sally hoped the version she was constructing made some sense, aware that the true version of how she'd arrived at Spanish lessons made none. Still, she wanted to tell Joanne about studying Spanish because if she actually *told* people she was going to learn Spanish then she couldn't very well *not* do it. Also, if she was going to be an employee with the added value of being bilingual she might as well let the boss know about it. But mostly she just wanted to tell somebody *something*, she was *bursting* to tell somebody, even if all she could tell was a minor, semi-accurate detail of the whole surreal drama of the night before, even if she had to shape the experience so that it could be squeezed into the realm of the believable.

"Okay," Joanne said agreeably and set a folder of paperwork on Sally's desk. If Joanne had noticed anything off about Sally this morning she wasn't mentioning it, though by mid-morning Sally's achy head and queasy stomach had improved considerably. Sally reached for the folder and glanced at its contents. "These time-sensitive?"

"Yeah, have 'em checked, entered and off to IT by…what time is it now, nine? Have 'em on the way before noon. And tell IT we'd like the work done sometime before the next millennium. And by the way, learning Spanish is not a dumb idea, Girlfriend. Makes sense for you. But your plumber? He's what, an intellectual? Or does he just want an excuse to be with y-o-u?"

"Well, he figures learning Spanish would help him with his business dealings, you know, with his Hispanic customers." Sally paused a moment and then went on. "And I'm kind of feeling like it would be nice if he wanted to do it for the second reason, too."

"Ah-ha. So I take it the date went well."

"Pretty unbelievable, actually."

"Nothing I should tell your mama about, huh?"

"Geez, Joanne, I probably shouldn't even be telling you about it."

"What? Don't tell me you jumped into bed on the first date? Sally Miller, I don't believe it!"

"Oh, hey, we"

"You know, I thought you were looking a little green around the gills this morning. Stayed up half the night, didn't you?'

"No, no, we"

"I hope you at least used protection, young lady. Guy sounds like a fast mover on the indoor plumbing."

"We didn't sleep together!"

"Oh. Well, did he want to?"

"Well, I don't exactly *know*, Joanne, he didn't say."

"Which doesn't mean he didn't want to. You know how men's minds work. Always trying to get into your"

"*Joanne!*" Sally laughed, and to her own surprise felt herself blushing. "Come on," she added, "he's a nice guy."

"Even nice guys love to do it. *Especially* nice guys."

"Okay Joanne."

"Nice he might be, but you don't know him. And you're vulnerable right now. You jump in too fast you could get hurt."

"All right, Joanne."

"On the other hand, you're young, you need to get back into circulation again, start looking for a nice guy."

"He's a nice guy, Joanne."

"But don't open the cookie jar right off the bat, and if you do, hell, I'm only telling you what your mother should be telling you, make sure you got a hundred-and-ten-percent protection, I'm talking latex, and every time."

"Joanne, my mother would *never* talk latex."

"So you're gonna hear it from me, same as I tell my own daughters. Don't get stupid over this guy."

"Believe me, I don't intend to."

But in fact Sally was already on the road to stupid and she knew it. For the rest of the morning the movie of everything that had happened to her since last night continued playing and re-playing itself inside her head, re-winding, fast-forwarding, pausing, split-screening. But the image that kept super-imposing itself over all the others was that of Silvio. Silvio smiling. Silvio in tears. Silvio strong. Silvio vulnerable. Silvio asleep, innocently half-naked under the covers. By noon the faxes were sent, the data entered, the hangover faded, and Sally was lusting after Silvio.

***

It occurred to Silvio that he had never sent a woman flowers before. Never even thought of it, really. He was married at an age when most guys were too young and dumb to know about that sort of thing, and once he was married he was too busy trying to stretch every dollar to cover their family needs to think of sending flowers to Trysta. And yet now here he was, thinking of sending flowers to Sally. He looked around the florist's shop. Pashki's Flowers and Gifts. Cute little place, smelled so good inside. Funny, this little shop was right across the street from Quick and Reliable, had probably been there as long as his uncle's business, yet the place had never really caught his eye until this morning. He looked through the catalogue that had been handed to him by a pleasant little man who looked to be in his seventies, probably the store owner. Thirty, forty, fifty dollars to send an arrangement. Well, why not spend it? When did Silvio ever spend a penny on himself? But then on the other hand *why* spend it? On something like flowers? For a woman he in truth scarcely knew? Not like it was even a special occasion, like Valentine's Day or her birthday, or anything. The shop owner came up next to him and pointed in the catalogue to a photograph of a bright variegated bouquet in a colorful striped glass vase. "This one I got a special on. Thirty percent off." He spoke with a slight Russian accent. "You send this one, somebody's gonna have a nice day."

A nice day, Silvio repeated to himself. Then it hit him: *he* was actually having….*a nice day!* Not angry, not sad, not depressed, not lonely…but…okay, hung-over. Hung over but feeling good, remembering how he'd started the day smiling, joking even, sharing breakfast with someone and talking about things that didn't center on himself and his personal black hole. And then suddenly deciding to take a new step – learning Spanish – that felt like a step away from that black hole. And just the fact that today he felt good enough to feel like sending someone flowers, wasn't that a special enough occasion?

"Okay" he said with a deep breath to the shop owner, "I'll take the special. Can I have it delivered tonight? Say, a little after six?"

***

Sally sat at her dinette table, her chin resting on one hand, the other hand holding a small white card. She couldn't stop looking at the flowers or the card that had come with them. Once again she read: "Have a nice day. From your friend Silvio."

From your friend Silvio. Your friend. Silvio. She was still gazing at the flowers when she was aroused by the sound of Josh flinging open the door and scampering into the room "Mom!" he cried as she caught him in a hug.

"Hey, how's my best guy?" she cooed. "Oooo, I missed you so much! Did you have a good time?"

"He had a great time, didn't you, Champ?"

Sally looked up to see Darren standing in the doorway. Looking nervous.

"It's too noisy there, Mommy. Can't Daddy just come and visit me here?"

"Well, no, Honey," Sally answered, still looking at Darren, who now looked nervous on top of taken aback by Josh's remark. *Well, why wouldn't he be fifty shades of uncomfortable standing at her door? After their mutual trauma-rama last night? What was he hanging around for, anyway?* Sally slipped Silvio's card into her pocket then turned back to Josh. "I'm so glad you're back. Only…what's this?" She ran a hand down the front of the over-sized hoodie the boy was wearing.

"Zach gave it to me. He got a new one."

"He did?"

"Yeah. Now that Daddy and his mom are married he can have anything he wants."

"He can?" Sally raised her eyebrows quizzically at Darren.

"Oh, hey, now, that's not true!" Darren said, stepping into Sally's living room.

"Yes it is! Zach told me. His mom told him."

"Josh, come on, that is not"

"It's okay," Sally cut him off. "I'm not gonna...it's okay." And amazingly, it *was* okay. Sally realized she wasn't feeling the least bit of animosity. In fact she was feeling positively Zen. "So Darren," she asked pleasantly, "is there something you need to discuss with me? Or do you just need a place to be right now?"

"Mommy, are you and Daddy gonna fight?" Josh's eyes were wide with dismay.

"No," Darren and Sally answered at the same time.

"No," Sally repeated with a reassuring smile, "Mommy and Daddy are not going to fight. And I'm fixing your favorite for dinner."

"Chicken nuggets? With French fries? And ketchup?"

"Yep."

"And jello?"

"Chicken nuggets with French fries, ketchup, *and* jello."

Darren spoke up. "Trysta made you some chicken nuggets last night, didn't she, Josh?"

"But they didn't taste like Mommy's, and I wasn't hungry because I already ate, and then we stopped for ice cream on the way home to Daddy's. Mommy, guess what, Zach and Trina and Sam got to have ice cream *before* their dinner!"

"They did?"

"Yeah, and then *they* didn't eat their dinner either."

Darren chuckled uncomfortably. "Josh, I'm sure your mom doesn't want to hear about"

"*Nobody* ate their dinner," Josh reiterated for emphasis.

"Aw, look, it was just the one time, because the kids, see, we"

"Well," Sally cut Darren off but said with a wink, "that's what happens when you eat ice cream before dinner, huh? So Josh, tell me what else you did at Daddy's."

Josh reached into his backpack and pulled out a hand-held video game. "Guess what Zach let me borrow! His Mario! Look!"

"All *right*," said Darren. "You like being over there with Zach, huh?"

"Yeah. But I don't like the girls. All they do is yell and fight. Mommy, can I go play Mario?"

"Sure, Babe."

Josh ran towards his room then stopped and turned back. "Next time could Zach come and play with me over here without the girls?"

"Well...uh...we'll see," Darren replied.

Sally shrugged. "Okay by me.

"Me and Zach don't like girls." Josh disappeared into his room and shut the door.

Sally laughed. "There goes my reason for living."

"He's a great kid," Darren said with a smile.

"He's a fantastic kid."

"Yeah, he's something. I love being with him. I miss him."

"Well, much as I hate giving him up every week, he loves seeing you. He misses you."

Darren took a deep breath. "Sally I'd like to be with him a lot more."

"Let's not even get into what any of us would like at this point. What's done is done. So...is there something we need to talk about or what?"

"Look, Sally, I just want you to know that Trysta loves Josh, too. Like one of her own kids."

"Oh, great," Sally chuckled, "'cause I *really* want Josh to be like one of *her* kids!"

"Aw, now Sally, that's"

"True," Sally finished for him. She looked him in the eye, not combatively but trying to fathom what was really on his mind. "Darren, can I just ask you straight up how come you're here?"

"I just want to make sure Josh is okay, and all."

Bullshit, thought Sally. "Yeah," she said, "he's okay,"

"You're in a pretty good mood yourself."

"Any reason I shouldn't be?" *I feel like damn Sherlock Holmes digging for clues!*

"Those flowers from your boyfriend?"

Bingo! She thought. "Boyfriend? What boyfriend?"

"You know. Silvio."

Sally laughed. *"Silvio?* He was just over fixing my furnace." That much was true.

"Fixing your furnace?"

"Yeah. What else would he be here for?" That wasn't a lie, only a question.

"Oh, come on, Sally, I saw beer bottles on the table!"

"So? A guy comes over to fix my furnace on his own time I can't offer him a beer? And a bite to eat?"

"But..." Darren looked thoroughly confused. "How did you meet Silvio? I mean, *I* sure as hell didn't introduce you!"

"Funniest thing. The toilet was acting up so I called from the yellow pages for a plumber and *he* shows up. We figured out our mutual connection pretty quick. Anyway, he noticed my furnace was about to fritz, so he offered to come over and fix it. We being exes-in-law, and all."

"Exes-in-law?"

"Or something like that. I asked him to come later in the evening so your paths wouldn't cross," Okay, that was a lie, but that's the way it *should* have worked out, "but then *you* showed up late, and with Trysta to boot, so...bam. Instant fireworks."

"Oh. So that's all that went on between you and Silvio?"

Sally shrugged. "Sure." That was a lie, too, but who cared? "Anyway why would you care who I have over for what?"

"Well...I'm concerned about Josh is all."

"Darren, you *know* I love our son above everything in the world. He's all I've got *left* in the world. I'd never do anything that would hurt him. I wouldn't let anyone hurt him. Ever. I'd fight to my last drop of blood for him."

"Yeah, I know you would."

"I would."

"Yeah. Well, one thing about you, Sally, you're always sincere. I mean, you don't pull any crap. No games, or anything."

"Yep, that's me," she chuckled. "You get it fast and straight."

Darren laughed. "Without Vaseline!"

My God, thought Sally, *are Darren and I actually standing here having a conversation? Letting our guard down, joking around, even?*

"You know," Darren said, "it's been a long time since I've seen you smile."

"Aw look, I'm trying to turn over a new leaf, okay? I'm tired of being a walking physics experiment."

"A what?"

Sally laughed again. "Oh, nothing. I mean, I just want to calm down inside. Avoid controversy, you know?"

"Yeah. I could go for that myself."

"Okay, well, I'll see you…this is your weekend to have Josh, so…"

"Right. I'll be here Friday night. Six-thirty. On the dot. I promise."

"Okay, then."

"Oh, and, uh, we're taking the kids out to Bensalem to visit my folks this Saturday."

"Okay."

"I mean, my folks haven't seen Josh in a while. And you know Donna… I mean *my mom*...she really does love Josh, even if you and she never did"

"I *know.* It's okay. New leaf, right?"

"Okay. Well, then…"

"Well, then…what? Darren, if there's something on your mind you should tell me, you know."

"No. Nothing. Just…okay, well, see you Friday night. Six thirty."

"Right."

Darren smiled then let himself out the door.

Sally smiled and went back to gazing at her flowers.

Chapter Sixteen

Darren drove west on the Roosevelt Expressway where the worst of the rush-hour traffic, thank God, was eastbound. Though what was his hurry to get home? Trysta's kids would no doubt be screaming when he walked in the door – right before dinner was somehow always the worst time – and Trysta, she'd be all over him wanting to know what Sally said, what Sally did, what Sally threw when she found out that Darren was intending to sue her for custody of Josh. Which, of course he wasn't. And he'd only been kidding himself – and Trysta – that he ever was. He didn't have time for a custody battle and couldn't afford one if even he wanted one. Not that he wanted one. And Sally wasn't kidding when she said she'd fight to her last drop of blood – and Darren's, too, if need be – over Joshua.

Anyway, Josh was better off with his mother. Who had, surprisingly, seemed in a good mood tonight. A very good mood. And perfectly civil and accommodating to boot. Though she never did say where the flowers came from. Maybe from her mother, her mother was always bringing stuff over. Or – wait, was today Secretary's Day? No, that was in the spring. But there was some kind of staff appreciation in the fall, too, right? Yeah, that was probably it. They probably gave her the flowers at work, a gift certificate, too, maybe even a little bonus. Which would explain Sally's upbeat mood. Anyway, at least Sally wasn't dwelling on their little scene from the night before – a total misunderstanding that turned out to be that jerk Silvio's fault. And then she didn't blow up over Josh's comment about the second-hand coat from Zach and she didn't get snide about Trysta's kids eating ice cream before dinner. Hell, if only he'd waited until tonight to bring up the child support issue instead of springing it on her first thing in the morning like he did the other day she might have been a whole lot more reasonable. Geez, how off had his timing been on that one? But if Sally was really intending to turn over a new leaf like she said and let go of some of that anger, well, maybe he could approach her on the subject again soon. Okay, it had to be soon, he had no choice. Damn, tonight had definitely been one wasted opportunity with Sally, he really *should* have asked her again about cutting back on the support, laid out his whole financial and business situation (forget the house in Puerto Vallarta, that had been nothing more than a post-honeymoon sugar-brain high). He had to pull out all the stops now. Of course he'd have the Manayunk investors on board by tomorrow, but even so he needed to look to the next investment. And he needed to start talking to friends and family, give them the opportunity to get in on his development business on the ground floor, so to speak. Thank goodness Sally didn't make an issue over him taking Joshua to see his parents on Saturday. Because Darren really needed to talk to his father and a family visit would provide the perfect opportunity for him to casually bring up the subject that he needed to bring up. Provided he could get his father alone, away from his mother...well, Donna was actually his stepmother but Darren figured he owed it to her to at least *try* and think of her as his mother, seeing as Donna had raised him since he was ten years old. Darren braked then stopped behind a line of backed-up vehicles. He'd reached the Schuylkill Expressway and the point of daily congestion where he'd have to sit stuck in other people's traffic, the traffic of people jamming the freeway with expensive cars queuing up towards the exits for elegant little Main Line communities like Merion Station and Penn Wynne and Bala Cynwood. Exits he wouldn't be getting off at. Darren tapped his fingers against the steering wheel. His thoughts drifted back to a childhood memory he didn't particularly like to revisit of that chaotic weekend when his real mother dropped him off for an unscheduled visitation with his father then never came back. Except from time to time when she would show up in a sporty car to take Darren for a Saturday outing, usually in the shared company of her current boyfriend. Darren remembered how happy he'd been to see his mother those times, how pretty she always looked, her hair wind-blown and the high color in her cheeks, and what fun they would have, driving to the shore or the zoo or for lunch in a downtown restaurant. Then she'd bring him back home and hug him and hold his face in her hands and kiss him before driving happily off with her new love. Darren would then trudge back into the house where Donna would be waiting to grill him, what had they done, where had they gone, what was his mother up to? Then Donna would frown disapprovingly and make Darren go fold his laundry or get to his homework or go to his room to be grounded for back-talk while Geoffry, her own son and Darren's new big brother-slash-tormenter-in-chief got to play his video games or talk on the phone or drive off with his jerky friends in the car Darren's father had bought him for his sixteenth birthday. Well, so what, that was twenty years ago, Darren was no longer a ten-year-old child and if he wanted to have a private conversation with his father this weekend about business matters he didn't need to ask Donna's permission. He didn't need her approval for anything. Though he had to admit that lately she seemed to be cutting him more slack than he was used to expecting from her. In fact, she gave him very little grief over his divorce from Sally – aside from a few "I told you so's" – and then she and Trysta hit it right off, reminiscing together like two old war veterans over the struggles of teen-aged motherhood – Donna had had Geoffry when she was seventeen and had raised him alone until Darren's father married her fifteen years later – though Darren noticed that Donna and Trysta's very favorite subject of conversation seemed to be the evils of Sally. He inched ahead until he'd passed the last of the Main Line exits and the gridlock broke and he was finally able to pick up speed until the road narrowed and traffic thinned on the way to the newer housing developments among which was his. Well, Sally wasn't actually all that bad most of the time. Not that she couldn't pull off a real Wicked Witch of the West act when provoked. Hell, Darren had suffered more of that side of Sally than he would wish on anybody. But then tonight...wow, tonight for some reason Sally had seemed more like her old self. Like back in the good old days before she was at his throat every minute with her claws retracted. He recalled that night eight years ago when he first saw Sally. It had been at an off-campus house party that she'd caught his eye, a cute little firecracker of a girl with hair like midnight and deep sparkling brown eyes that he couldn't stop gazing into even though he was at the party with his girlfriend with whom he'd been sleeping for three years and, more recently, talking marriage. And yet a year later it was Sally with whom he walked down the aisle, his mouth practically watering for the wedding night, the night that would make Sally his and then subsequently whisk them both quickly and unexpectedly across the threshold to parenthood and life in the grown-up world.

Still, once he and Sally had gotten used to the idea of becoming parents it hadn't been such a bad world. At least for a while. They were happy at first, he landed a job with Highland and Erskerberg and his father helped him snag their house on Hawthorne Street. They'd go for evening walks in Wissenoming Park and after Josh came along they'd push his stroller along the tree-lined paths around the pond. Well, those were the days. It was too bad that things didn't work out. But if Sally could just learn to be reasonable and control her temper, well, there was no reason she couldn't find someone else someday. Anyone but that asshole Silvio.

Chapter Seventeen

"What? The Manayunk deal *fell through?*" Ed Miller slapped his hand on the glass-topped wicker patio table.

"Oh, don't tell me!" Donna Miller stepped into the sun room with a tray of vegetables and dip. "You lost that big deal? You *lost* it?"

"No, I didn't say"

"And that's not even the worst!" Trysta followed Donna through the door that led to the sun room from the family room.

"Trysta, what are you *talking* about?" Darren cried.

Trysta looked at him accusingly. "*You* know," she said quietly. "Donna, you need to talk to him."

Donna set the vegetable tray on the table between Ed and Darren then ran a hand through her chin-length blonde high-lighted hair. "Maybe I do." She looked good for her fifty-three years, trim and well-put-together in a stylish pastel-patterned knit top and khaki slacks. She turned to her husband. "Or maybe *you* do, Ed."

"Look," Darren snapped, "would everybody just...I didn't *say* the deal fell through!"

"Okay, dear, just calm down now." Donna put a hand on Darren's shoulder, which made him twitch unconsciously. He took a deep breath. "My investors just said they want to wait a little longer. See how the market is percolating next week."

Ed frowned. "*See how the market is percolating?* They said that?"

"That's exactly what they said, Dad."

"What kind of techno-gibberish is that?" Ed plunged a carrot stick into the bowl of dip. "Sounds like they're jerking you around."

"I'll say," Donna added.

"They're not the only ones jerking him around," Trysta added, her eyes tearing up.

"Aw, Trysta, come on, Hon." Darren reached for her from where he sat and put his arm around her wide waist. "I'm just trying to talk a little business with Dad. It's all right, Baby." His conciliatory tone and affectionate gesture were really more a show for his parents. In truth he felt at this moment like muzzling his wife.

Donna put her arm around Trysta's shoulder and led her, sniffling, back inside the house.

Ed watched the women as they exited the sun porch. Then he turned back to Darren. "Something wrong?"

"I don't know!" Darren threw up his hands. "Baby hormones."

"Oh, that," his father chuckled with a dismissive wave of his hand. "Yeah, that I know about." He cocked his head towards the door through which his wife had just exited. "And then there's menopause hormones. You just wait 'til you have to deal with that!" Ed reached for another vegetable. "Me, I prefer some chips or pretzels and a beer, but your mother," he patted his slightly paunchy stomach, "she's all about health food and wine these days. Gotta keep these women and their hormones happy, huh?"

"Tell me how, Dad. "

"Hey, if I knew I wouldn't only tell you, I'd write a book about it and make a million."

"A million is small change these days."

"Well, maybe that's true among you young billionaires 'way out there in New Conshohocken, but for the rest of us…" Darren's father crunched into a carrot. "You and Trysta have been living out there, what a month now?"'

"Well, yeah, just about."Darren chuckled dryly. "Seems like a year."

"*Oh*, boy," his father sighed.

"No, I'm just joking. It's just that ever since we got back from the honeymoon Trysta's kids have been a little…over the top. Everything else, though, I mean it's great. Honeymoon was great. It's all…you know…*great.*"

"Great," his father echoed flatly.

"Or, I mean, it *will* be, once I get the business going. Finances have been a little tight, being in the start-up stage, but after I pull off the Manayunk deal…anyway, it'll all come together, and soon, real soon,

I'm confident of that."

"Oh, sure," his father agreed. Then he added, "But in the meantime you've got a gargantuan house payment, child support, a pregnant non-working wife, no income...Darren, can I ask you? What are you and Trysta living on these days?"

Darren took a deep breath. "What's left of our divorce settlements. My separation package from Highland and Erskerberg. And Trysta's support check."

Ed sighed and shook his head. "All right, I haven't asked you this yet, but...how come you quit your job? I mean, who gets a great promotion, buys a house then quits his job days later?"

"Oh, well, see, the time was right, I mean, *right now*, right this *minute* is the time to get into rental properties, with the demand being so high, and I'd actually been planning on going out on my own anyway, been laying some ground work for a while already, and then, you know, with Trysta, I mean, a new life, fresh start, the time just seemed right."

"You got fired."

The animation drained from Darren's face and his body sagged down like a deflating balloon. "I swear to God, Dad, I can't figure out why. My boss just called me in out of the blue and said I wasn't working out in the position but he never gave any specifics and I don't have a clue. He gave me the option of resigning on the spot or being fired. So I resigned. Dad, I haven't told anyone, not Sally, not even Trysta. Huh, I even pretended to go into work for another two weeks afterwards so it would look to Trysta like *I'd* made the decision then gave notice."

"Darren..." Ed paused, choosing his words carefully, "Highland and Erskerberg, that's a pretty conservative outfit, isn't it? What I'm wondering is...and it's just a theory for lack of a better one...is there any chance that you got fired over what was going on...you know...between you and Trysta at the time?"

"No, no, of course not!" Darren's voice was edged with indignation. "Nobody – nobody from Corporate, that is – ever said a word about it. Not to me. Aw, look, Dad, Highland and Erskerberg is like any other office, people have affairs, discreet affairs, all the time."

"*All the time?*"

"You know what I mean. It happens. People have affairs. People get divorced."

"But do people at Corporate level have affairs with receptionists? Get them pregnant?"

"Dad, I *married* Trysta! She's not a receptionist anymore, she's my *wife!*"

"Okay, okay," Ed backed off. "Just trying to help you figure it all out."

"Aw, the hell with it!" Darren grabbed a celery stick and jabbed it into the dip. "I've got my own company now and we're gonna be better off in the long haul."

"Okay, sure. That's fine."

"In fact, I've got a couple other properties, great opportunities, just waiting to be scooped up. And did I tell you Dustin Sunfield, you know, the owner of Sun Hardware, is a potential investor?"

"Sun Hardware, no kidding. How many stores does that guy own?"

"Four in the metropolitan Philadelphia area, and he's branching out to New Jersey."

Ed whistled. "Pretty good."

"Yep. Guy's huge. And he's very interested in a property out in West Philly that I'm about to pounce on. Only…"

"Only?"

"Dad, I need a loan!" Oh God! He'd just blurted it out! *How stupid!*

His father fumbled his cucumber, flipping it into the dip. He quickly fished the cucumber out, glancing towards the door to make sure he hadn't been caught by his wife with his fingers in the dip. "Well," he finally replied, "I guess that doesn't come as a complete surprise, but," he licked his fingers thoughtfully, "you know, Aero-Missile is laying off, and me being a lowly, fifty-five-year-old," he patted his head, *"balding* ceramic engineer…" Ed chuckled lamely and then looked at his son with an expression of sincere sorrow. "Son, I do wish I could help you but,"

"Forget it, Dad." Geez, why had he brought it up? Or why had he at least not brought it up as he'd planned, working in the subject of a loan as a sound business proposition after carefully laying out for his father the details of a long-term real estate proforma, instead of squealing it out with the comic desperation of a kid crying to daddy to bail him out of the consequences of some stupid adolescent shenanigan!

"Okay, look, the truth is, it's your mother, I mean, I'd have to discuss it with her first"

Donna! Shit!

"...and you know how she is, how she's all about personal responsibility, and all, and when she finds out you got fired"

Donna! Shit!

"I don't know, she might not"

"Oh, Jesus, Dad," Darren cut his father off, "please don't bring this up with Donna!"

"*Donna?*" His father frowned. "You call her *Donna* now?"

"*Mom,* I meant, *Mom.*" *Double shit!*

"Yeah, well, you *do* sometimes forget that Donna *is* your mother, she raised you like her son when your own mother walked out on you. She cares about you, and if you're in some kind of trouble she'd want to know about it. She deserves to."

"No, Dad, no! I'm not in trouble, I don't actually *need* a loan, I was just thinking, you know, as a business proposition, but...look, just forget it, please, Dad, *please, don't tell Mom!*"

Ed sighed again. "Aw, you know I can't not tell her."

"Why not?"

"Because...well, you know how it is with your mother. I just can't *not* tell her!"

"Yes you can, Dad! Please, *don't tell mom!*"

"Don't tell mom what?"

There she was in the doorway again, this time carrying out a platter of raw chicken and hot dogs. "Don't tell me *what,* Darren?"

Darren and his father exchanged looks, Darren's pleading, his father's the manifestation of an internal struggle between husbandly obligation and the desire to protect his son.

"Aw, nothing, Mom, just some business talk."

"Something you don't want me to know about. Ed, what doesn't he want me to know about this time? Something about Sally? Because, Darren, I *know* what's been going on, Trysta has been filling me in, and I'm telling you, you have *got* to"

"Oh, no, no, Hon, it's nothing like that." The father's protective impulse had won out and kicked in. "Darren was just telling me about some of his investors. How he's always hunting for more. But he didn't want me to mention it to you because he was afraid you might worry and want to, you know, help him out in some way. Financially."

Donna threw back her head and laughed loudly. "Oh, ho, ho! I think Darren *knows* he doesn't have to worry about that! Of course I've always been there to help him in any way I can, but Darren's a big boy now and can certainly handle his own business, can't you? Ed, carry this out to the grill, would you?" She handed the platter to her husband. "And Darren, you go help Trysta." Trysta was negotiating herself down the step from the doorway to the sunroom carrying a tray of grilling utensils in one hand and a basket of condiments in the other.

The men took the burdens from the women then Ed motioned for the women to sit. "You girls sit here and relax for a couple minutes. Let us he-men do the cooking!"

"*Relax?*" Donna laughed. "That'll be the day! Darren, after you set those down by the grill you can come back inside and set the table."

"What, we're not eating out in the back yard?" Ed asked. "Look, the sun's out. It's warm."

"It is *not* warm enough to eat in the back yard. We'll eat in the dining room, but we can have the children eat out here in the sun room. Oh dear, Trysta, I hope they won't spill all over the carpeting."

"Aw, come on, Hon," Ed interceded, "it's indoor-outdoor. Hey, where are the kids? And how come they're being so quiet?"

"They're glued to the TV and their video games," Donna answered. "And that's another thing, Darren, I was telling Trysta, you have *got* to help her get a handle on those kids, I mean, poor Trysta is eight month pregnant, she can't be chasing around"

"Yeah, yeah," Ed cut in, "I'll tell Darren the facts of life, now you girls get back inside and get busy in the kitchen!"

"Oh, you!" Donna gave Ed a friendly spank before heading back inside.

Ed gave his son a wink. "When they're not busting your balls they're actually a lot of fun, aren't they?"

***

"Anyway, Darren," Donna said, cutting into the tiny piece of grilled chicken on her plate, "as I was telling Trysta, you have *got* to set boundaries when you're dealing with Sally. Otherwise she'll continue walking all over you just like when you were married. Please pass your father the salad."

Darren grabbed the salad bowl and moved it towards Ed. "Sally is not walking all over me. Here, Dad."

"No thanks, I already had salad." Darren returned the bowl to its spot in front of him.

"Well, that's not what *I* heard. About Sally. Ed, you eat some more salad. Otherwise you'll fill up on the baked beans and potato salad. Darren, pass your father the salad, please."

Darren re-passed the salad to father, who pushed it back. "What the hell are the baked beans and potato salad *for* if I'm not supposed to eat them?"

"*A little.* You are supposed to eat *a little.* In *moderation.* And I'll thank you not to curse at me in front of Trysta and Darren, I'm only looking out for your health."

"I wasn't cursing at you. I was cursing at the beans and potato salad, which are calling out, 'eat me, eat me,' when all I'm allowed to eat is the...Darren, pass me that damn salad!"

"Oh, Donna, I have the same problem with Darren," Trysta sighed. "He just can't control his language."

"Well, you see where he gets it from." Donna cocked her head towards her husband.

Josh came in from the sun room carrying his plate and cup. "Grandma, can I please be excused from the table?"

"Yes, certainly, Darling, just put your dishes in the sink for Grandma."

"And then can I go in the back yard and play soccer with Zach?"

"Yes you may, after you come and give Grandma a hug." Josh hugged Donna then skipped off towards the back door. "And Josh, dear," Donna called after him, "remind the others to bring their plates to the sink before they go outside."

"They already went outside, Grandma."

"Well, we'll have to teach them how we do things at Grandma's won't we?"

"Okay!"

After Josh had dashed out the back door Donna smiled and said, "He's just doing so well now, isn't he?"

"Oh, yeah," Darren replied. "He's always been a great little guy."

"Well, yes, but look how happy he is being with Trysta's children."

"They do get along so well," Trysta agreed, "and he's just *so* much happier when he's with us than when he's with, well, *her.*"

"Wait, how do you know he's happier?' Darren asked.

Donna answered. "Well, of *course* he's happier being around other children in a nice, spacious home instead of being stuck alone in that cramped little *dump* – I'm sorry, but Trysta described it to me – and I can't believe Sally can't do better for that child, with all the support you're paying her."

"Well," Trysta sighed, "that's Sally for you."

Ed spoke up. "Too bad you couldn't have worked out a deal with her so somebody could have kept that Hawthorne Street house. Too bad *you* couldn't have kept it. Been a lot cheaper than that new one out on Millionaire Row you ended up buying."

"Oh, Ed, of course they couldn't have kept that house! With all the children they have between them? You've got to be kidding, that house had three small bedrooms and one bath."

"Hey," said Ed, "I grew up in a house like that, same kind of Northeast Philly neighborhood, right off Frankfort Avenue. Back in the day there were plenty of big families raised in houses just like that one. Those big Catholic families? Five, six...I remember the Scanlons raised *nine* kids in one of those row houses."

"*Nine?*" Trysta laughed, "How in the world did they manage *nine* children in *three* bedrooms?"

"Bunk beds," Ed replied, "Lots and lots of bunk beds."

"Look," Darren jumped back into the conversation, "bunk beds or not, I had to sell that house. Even if I'd wanted it there was no way Sally would have let me have it."

Ed shrugged. "You offered her enough she'd of let you have it." Donna stood to begin clearing the table and Ed caught her around the waist and pulled her to him. "You pay a woman's price she'll give you *anything* you want."

Donna gave her husband's cheek a light squeeze. "You'd better watch yourself, Ed Miller, or *you'll* be paying the price! But while we're on the subject of Sally..."

"Aw, Mom, couldn't we get *off* the subject of Sally?"

"All right, I'm just going to say it once because it needs to be said. You really should take to heart Trysta's offer to raise Joshua as her own."

"What?"

"Get custody of Josh. Get him away from Sally and into the happy, stable family life he'd have living with you and Trysta and her children."

"But he's happy living with his mother. I know he is."

"See?" Trysta huffed. "I told you that's what he'd say!"

"All right, all right! The truth is, I can't afford a custody battle right now. No *way* I could afford one."

"Well then, that's too bad," said Donna, "You've over-extended yourself financially to the point where you can't even afford to care for your son. That's just too bad."

"*Wha?* What do you mean? I *do* care for my son!"

"All right, all right, calm down," Donna backed off, "I just meant"

"*I do care for my son!*"

Trysta put a hand on Darren's shoulder. "She knows you do, Honey, she just meant"

"I just meant"

"*I* care *for my* son!"

"Hey, would everybody get back in their corners?" Ed patted at the air like a referee. "How about we change the subject?"

"Yeah, how about we do," Darren huffed.

"Huh, see how Sally causes trouble even when she's not here?" sniffed Trysta.

"Well, then, we just won't talk about her anymore," Donna said cheerily, sitting back down at the table. "We'll change the subject. Oh, Darren, did I tell you how well Geoffry is doing at his new job?" She turned to Trysta. "Did Darren tell you about Geoffry's new job? You remember Geoffry from your wedding? Darren's brother?"

"Stepbrother," Darren interjected, trying to sound merely informative, but Donna shot him a sharp look before continuing, "Darren's *brother*, Geoffry, has a wonderful job, he's working for"

For some shady-sounding salvage-yard operator down in South Philly where he'll probably last about two more weeks, Darren answered to himself. *Basically useless at thirty-six but still the apple of his mother's eye, Mr. Can-do-no-wrong-just-had-some-bad-luck-poor-Geoffry.* Well, hell, at least he was working now, though Darren was willing to bet Geoffry'd done plenty of sponging off Darren's father along the way. And at least Darren and Geoffry now peacefully co-existed, which was about the maximum relationship Darren was interested in pursuing with his stepbrother. *Geoffry.* Pronounced *"Jeffry."* Donna had once sent Darren to his room for pronouncing Geoffry's name the way it was spelled, accusing him of taunting his brother, which, of course, Darren *had* in fact been doing, but, Jesus, Geoffry'd been seventeen years old at the time, and what the hell was a seventeen-year-old kid doing running to his mother over *anything,* least of all being teased by his eleven-year-old stepbrother?

"Well, Darren, what do you think?" Donna asked him.

"Huh?" Darren blinked back to the conversation going on around him.

"Honey, I think it sounds great," Trysta cooed, slipping a hand under the table and rubbing his thigh.

"Might not be a bad idea," his father added. "Might be just the thing for you right now. Just a temporary situation, something part-time, even. Won't hurt to ask him."

"You think I should...*ask him?*" *Ask who? What?*

Donna laughed. "That's what I just *said!* Goodness, Darren, you still don't pay attention. Does he pay attention to you, Trysta?"

"Oh, he does. When I can get him to." Trysta smiled at Darren and gave his thigh a squeeze.

Donna's face turned serious. "Really, Darren, do call Geoffry. Ask him if he'd ask Angelo – Geoffry's on a first-name basis with the boss already – if he'd ask Angelo if he could find you some work handling some of his properties."

"'*Angelo?*' That's the guy who owns the salvage lot?"

"Oh, Geoffry says it's a *huge* operation, and Angelo doesn't just run the salvage company, he's involved in lots of other interests, including lots of real estate. That's what Geoffry's doing right now, helping him with the real estate end of the business.

"But what does Geoffry know about real estate?" Darren felt his annoyance rising.

"Oh, well, you know, Geoffry's smart and a good hard worker when he's given the chance." Darren glanced at this father and rolled his eyes, but his father gave a small shake of his head. "But he said Angelo is looking for someone to help him with some, I don't know, some..."

"Properties?" Darren asked.

"Or something." Donna said.

"Wouldn't hurt to check it out, at least, with this Angelo guy." said Ed.

"Angelo *who?*"

"Angelo..." his father thought for a moment. "Donna, what's Angelo's last name, again?"

"I think he told me it was Barberini, or"

"Barbieri!" Ed cut in. "Right?"

'Oh, yes, that sounds right," Donna agreed. "Angelo Barbieri. Darren, I'll give you Geoffry's new cell number. Dad bought him a Google Pixel Phone for his birthday. It does everything."

His father bought Geoffry an eight-hundred-dollar Google Pixel Phone? Great!

Darren sighed. Okay, yes, at this point he could use some sure income. And he wasn't in any place to be disregarding any possible option that might offer some networking potential down the road. But then he'd never heard of any Angelo Barbieri, guy's name didn't ring a bell as anyone he'd come across in the commercial real estate scene when he was at Highland and Erskerberg. Which didn't mean this Barbieri wasn't legit, he might be an up-and-comer, someone who could be a potential investor, a real good connection. But shit, *Geoffry?* No, dammit, he'd be damned if he'd go groveling to that loser Geoffry for anything, Geoffry and his new birthday Google Pixel Phone, he'd rather eat dirt, which is about what asking Geoffry would amount to.

"You know, I really don't think..." Darren stopped in mid-sentence. He saw three faces leaning towards him, three pairs of eyes beaming in at him, his father's pleading, Donna's challenging, Trysta's promising the same thing as the hand that was now rubbing up and down his thigh. He was trapped, trapped by their faces and their eyes and their expectations and his own financial desperation. He pulled in a deep breath then heaved a sigh of surrender.

"Okay. Sure."

Chapter Eighteen

"Como se llama?"

"Me llamo Silvio. That one was too easy."

"Too easy?" Sally laughed, "You just started learning Spanish what, two days ago?"

"Yeah, and I've been practicing for two days, too."

"Boy, you don't mess around. All right, you ask me the next one."

"Okay." Silvio pointed his finger to a line in the *Spanish for Dummies* book that lay open on the table between Sally and himself. "Donde vives?"

"Uh, let me see…Vivo en mi casa?"

"Yeah, I think that's right. 'Where do you live? I live in my house.' Vivo, vives. Yeah, that works. Only I think what they probably want to know is, which city or town or country do you live in. Like, where your casa *is*, you know?"

"Why should they want to know where my casa *is*? Do they want to come visit me, or something?"

"Well, maybe they do."

"What for?" Sally held up the book. "They're already here."

"They're here, there, and everywhere and they're all habla-ing español. Speaking of which, how come Lupe isn't over here studying with us today?"

"I don't know. Maybe she'll be along. I told her you were coming at two o'clock. Of course, *you* didn't get here 'til three."

"Yeah, well, sorry, we're open weekends for emergencies and I was on call this morning."

"Like a doctor."

"You know a doctor who makes house calls on a Saturday morning? Anyway, you know how it goes, the jobs pile up and you get behind."

"Oh, yeah, I know how *that* goes!"

"I swear, sinks, toilets and sewers have as many problems as people."

"Well, at least they don't have the kind of problems we have. I mean, I wouldn't wish my problems on a toilet."

"What problems?" Silvio leaned closer to Sally, and she instinctively moved closer to him. There seemed to be some magnetic force pulling them towards each other until their lips almost met before the sound of the doorbell made them quickly pull back. They got up from the table and walked to the door together.

In the doorway stood Lupe holding a beautifully-iced chocolate cake.

"For you, Sally," she said, "Para ti."

"Para…mi?" Sally asked, relieving Lupe of the cake and taking it to the dinette table.

"Si, si," Lupe said, smiling broadly, "Para ti."

"Para…" Silvio pointed to Sally, "her?"

"Para *ella*," said Lupe, "esta pastel de chocolate es para *ella*"

"Esta pastel de chocolate es para ella," Silvio repeated. "I got it. This chocolate cake is for her."

"This chocolate cake is for her," Lupe slowly repeated.

"Right, very good!" Silvio said with the small hand-clap of approval that Lupe had gotten them into the custom of offering each other after the victory of a correctly stated sentence.

"Di 'very good' en español," Lupe commanded.

"Okay," Silvio tried, "Muy bien."

"Y muy simpaticos," Sally added, returning from the dinette.

"Ah, si," Lupe said, beaming and pulling Sally and Silvio into a group hug, "*We are* muy simpaticos!"

***

Sally and Silvio sat staring at the cake on the table. Lupe had left it and hurried off after explaining in half-English that she needed to *regresar* to her *casa* to *preparar comida* for Ascensiòn to eat.

"So," Silvio asked, "are you and me supposed to eat this or

what?"

"Before dinner?" Sally asked.

"I mean, if the kids were here we wouldn't let *them*."

"No, we wouldn't let the *kids* eat it before dinner." Then, impulsively, Sally ran her finger through the icing and stuck it into her mouth. "Ummm," she said, closing her eyes in relishment.

Silvio looked at Sally then at the cake. He, too, dug his finger into the icing.

Sally and Silvio began taking turns running their fingers through the icing and licking it off until at one point Sally, instead of licking the icing off her finger, rubbed it onto Silvio's cheek. Then licked it off. Silvio laughed then scooped up a fingerful of icing and after a moment of hesitation, rubbed it onto Sally's neck then likewise licked if off. Half-a-dozen licks later Sally, Silvio, and the by then half-naked chocolate cake moved quickly to Sally's bedroom where the two continued to strip the cake and each other, making the acquaintance of each other's bodies by taking turns rubbing on then licking off strokes of icing until the teasing licks became unbearable and they plunged into each other in a fever of arousal and chocolate-flavored desire.

Afterwards they lay in each other's arms, sticky all over with licked chocolate and sweat. "Are we a mess, or what?" Sally asked softly.

"Yeah, I guess. But it's okay."

"I think my cheek is stuck to your chest."

"That's okay, too."

"Well, you want to take a shower?"

Silvio considered a moment then asked, "Together?"

Twenty minutes later Silvio, freshly showered, lay comfortably stretched out on Sally's bed between clean sheets. Sally sat on the edge of the bed wrapped in her robe.

"I don't know what it is about you," she said, toweling her damp hair, "but every time I'm around you something totally...*unusual* happens.

Silvio laughed. "That's putting it mildly. I mean, I never did anything even *close* to..." Silvio gestured towards the remains of the chocolate cake sitting on Sally's dresser, "*that* before."

"No?" Sally hesitated a moment then asked, "Not even with Trysta?"

"Trysta who? C'mon over here."

Sally crawled over next to him and he put an arm around her. "You know," he said, "this whole thing today was pretty spontaneous."

"Spontaneous combustion. An equal and opposite reaction."

"Not to mention the laws of attraction. Only… maybe what we did today wasn't so smart under the circumstances."

"Which circumstances?"

"The circumstances that that kind of spontaneous combustion is where kids come from."

"It's okay. I'm on the pill."

"You are? Still?"

"Well, sure. I mean, once you're on it you might as well stay on it since it takes so long to get reacclimated if you…Silvio, don't tell me you don't understand how it works? Wasn't Trysta ever on the pill?"

"Yeah. I *thought* she was. Thought she'd been on it for a while now. Huh, she obviously wasn't on it when she should have been. Or else that pill didn't work for her and Darren."

"Well, if you don't take it right or skip a dose or something, it *could* not work."

"Yeah, well, that must be what happened with Trysta."

"Yeah." Sally paused a moment. "Um, that being said, I think we could agree that next time, I mean, just in case, we should also use a"

"Trojan," Silvio finished for her.

"Condom," she said at the same time.

"Thanks, Sally," Silvio said.

"What, for talking about condoms?"

"No, for talking about next time."

Sally gave him a friendly kiss on the cheek. "Okay, now that we've had dessert I'm starting to think about dinner."

"Let me cook for you this time," Silvio said. "I'm almost as good as my mama. You like angel hair pasta primavera?"

"I'm sure I'd love angel hair pasta primavera, whatever it is. Only I can guarantee that I don't have the ingredients on hand unless you can make it from Velveeta cheese and Wonder Bread."

Is there a supermarket, an A&P, or something, close by?"

"Oh yeah, there's one a few blocks up Rhawn Street at the Red Lion shopping center. Or there's the infamous Chupaflor Market right around the corner."

"Okay, I need pasta and fresh tomatoes, green onions, olive oil, garlic, parmesan, maybe a nice loaf of bread…does the Chupaflor carry that kind of thing?"

"Oh, sure, they'll have everything you need, they don't just sell Spanish stuff. I shop there myself sometimes. We could even walk."

"A walk would be great, it's a nice night. Warm enough." Silvio considered a moment then said, "Okay, then, let's try the Chupaflor."

"If we dare!"

"Aw, what the heck. The place has already been raided by the feds. What else could happen there?"

Chapter Nineteen

Juan Diego Andrade, night manager of the Chupaflor Market, had just finished reconciling the receipts from the previous shift. He stuffed the pile of cash, checks and credit slips into the deposit bag while his assistant stood waiting by the manager's desk.

"You hear anything, Luis?" Juan Diego asked his assistant as he handed him the locked bag.

"Heard from Zorayda last week. She says Nico got himself a job giving tours of Quetzaltenango to the gringos. Can you believe that, man?" Luis laughed, "Nico? A tour guide?"

"No, no, I mean, do you hear anything *right now. Here.* In the store." Juan Diego walked to the open door of his office while Luis followed after him. "Listen," Juan Diego said.

"Oh yeah, that kind of humming sound? Above the muzak? What do you think it is? Refrigerator system?"

"Guess I'm gonna find out."

As soon as Luis left for the bank with the night deposit Juan Diego made a round of the market, checking pipes, refrigerators and freezers, including the walk-in units in the back of the store. He finally traced the sound to the outdoor enclosure behind the building that housed the utility meters, air conditioning, and the store's massive emergency back-up generator. It took only a moment for Juan Diego to realize that the loud, unhealthy noise was coming from the generator – running at full power! His heart began pounding as he grabbed his cell phone from his pocket and speed-dialed Ascensiòn Guzman, silently praying to his patron saint Santiago del Mayor de Guatemala that his Nicaraguan maintenance wizard would arrive before the surge of the generator running in tandem with the normal electrical output caused the Chupaflor to explode into the roaring electrical fire he saw in his mind.

***

Sally and Silvio were approaching the crowd that the Chupaflor staff had flushed from the store when a panel truck pulled up to the sidewalk. Sally immediately recognized the driver. "Hey, isn't that…?"

"Ascensiòn!" Silvio called.

"Hola compadres!" Ascensiòn called back, flashing his smile even as he hurried from his truck to the store. Sally and Silvio followed after him.

"So what's going on here?" Sally asked.

"A little electrical trouble. Safer you wait out here, Sally." To Silvio he said, "You know something about generators, Maje?"

***

Silvio shined a flashlight into the body of the generator while Ascensiòn fingered a partially corroded length of wire. "You see right here, Silvio? Is a bad wire in the automatic transfer. This confused the generator, told it to turn on." Ascensiòn pointed to a roll of copper wire in his tool box. "You cut me a piece of that blue, there, we make it work, I'll show you how."

After Silvio cut the wire Ascensiòn took the flashlight and directed Silvio in the replacement of the defective wire. When the repair was finished Silvio held the generator's heavy front panel steady while Ascensiòn screwed it back into place.

"See?" said Ascensiòn, "now we got the system cooled down and reset, is fine and ready to switch on next time they need it."

"I gotta say, I never worked on a commercial gas generator before," said Silvio.

"I worked on a lot of them, only never this big. In Nicaragua the electricity is bad. Goes off for a couple hours every day. In Leòn where I come from all the stores and restaurants have generators. The generators are bad, too. They're old and they break all the time. I learned to fix them from my father who learned from his father. *Leòn Reparaciònes,* that's my family's business, we fix things that break. In Nicaragua everything is bad now, everything breaks. Electricity, plumbing, everything. A lot of work for us to do but nobody can pay anymore. So *Leòn Reparaciònes...pffft!*" Ascensiòn made a "blown away" gesture with his hands.

"And so you and Lupe came up here."

"A man gotta work. Support his family. Is the most important thing."

"Yeah," Silvio sighed. "I know." He patted the generator. "Well, you see how things sometimes go bad up here, too."

"Oh, no, here everything is good. Is beautiful here, Maje."

***

As soon as they exited the Chupaflor Ascensiòn and Silvio were surrounded by the anxious staff led by Juan Diego, who'd spent the past forty-five minutes pacing the sidewalk in front of the market. Ascensiòn proceeded to explain in Spanish the generator's problem and repair while Silvio nodded politely to the group then hurried over to Sally, who'd spent the time practicing her Spanish with some of the Chupaflor employees.

"Aw gee, Sally, you're still here," he said apologetically. "I'm sorry it took so long. You know, you could of gone home."

"Well, yeah, I could of if I'd wanted to. You should actually apologize to these people, though. I've been torturing them with my terrible Spanish."

"Your Spanish is pretty good," said one of the clerks who was standing close by.

"Thanks for letting me practice on you," Sally replied, "and for your patience."

"Okay, well, let me just say 'bye to Ascensiòn and then we can get going," said Silvio.

Silvio and Sally walked back over to Ascensiòn, who was still talking to Juan Diego.

"Hey, Silvio," said Ascensiòn, "I'm gonna pay you for helping me, Maje."

"Nah, I didn't really do anything. Besides, I learned something, it was like a free class on gas generator repair."

"Silvio, you need some groceries while you're here?" asked Juan Diego, "I got the freshest vegetables."

"Yeah, but I'll take a raincheck." He put an arm around Sally's shoulder. "It's such a beautiful night, I'm taking my girlfriend out to dinner."

***

Had Sally been sitting before an elegant place setting at Le Bec Fin dining on sautéed foie gras and stuffed breast of squab she could not have savored the experience any more than she did sitting across from Silvio at a Formica-topped table in a booth at a strip-mall pizzeria and diving into a slice of deep-dish pepperoni and mushroom pizza.

"I'm telling you," Silvio said between bites, "Ascensiòn knew what he was doing with that super-sized generator. The guy's *good* at what he does. Really good. And here he can't even make a legitimate living."

"Not to mention that he could be found out at any time and sent back to Leòn, Nicaragua."

"Yeah, well, he's walking a mighty thin rope, him and Lupe both."

"What about David? What happens to that baby if they get sent back? I mean, the kid is an American citizen."

Silvio shook his head. "I sure don't know. Wish I could do something, but..." He shrugged.

"Yeah, I know. I mean, what *can* you do?"

They continued eating their pizza in thoughtful silence for a few moments and then Sally spoke up. "Silvio, doesn't it feel good?"

"What?"

"Thinking about someone besides yourself? Worrying over someone's problems beside you own?"

Silvio considered a moment then he smiled. "Yeah. Yeah, it kind of does."

Again they ate in silence until Sally said, "Silvio, what you said to that guy, Juan Diego, tonight…about me, you know, being your girlfriend…"

Silvio blushed. "Oh, look, I'm sorry, I shouldn't have assumed…"

"No, it's okay. I mean, it's okay with me if you want to, you know, date. Be, you know, *together*."

Silvio reached across the table for Sally's hand. "I know we haven't known each other all that long, but I do feel like we're already together. I really…I mean…I like you, Sally. A lot."

"I like you a lot, too, Silvio. And believe it or not, I even like how crazy my life has been since I've known you. I mean, finding out we're exes-in-law, meeting Lupe and Ascensiòn, that insane night with Mo and the illegals and the ICE, the Spanish lessons,"

"The chocolate cake," Silvio cut in, "don't forget the chocolate cake."

"Believe me, I'll *never* forget the chocolate cake!"

He touched Sally's cheek. "You're so pretty. You have such a nice smile. I feel like I want to kiss it right here."

"Kiss what?"

"Your smile."

Sally leaned across the table. "You can."

Silvio looked around the restaurant self-consciously then leaned in towards Sally and kissed her. "Okay, that's something else I've never done before. Kissed a girl in a restaurant."

"How'd you like it?"

"I feel like I want seconds."

Sally said softly, "Well, I don't think anyone's watching. We might be able to get away with it one more time."

Silvio reached under the table and caressed Sally's knee. "I didn't mean kissing."

Chapter Twenty

"So now you're *dating* the plumber?" Joanne and Sally retrieved their vending-machine lattes and sat down at a table in the far corner of the break room. "You just met the guy, what, a week ago and now you say you're *dating*? Like, you're *together*?"

"Joanne, I *like* the guy. A lot. He's nice."

"Nice he may be. I'm just saying he sounds like a fast mover."

"Fine, so what is the correct number of times you're supposed to go out with a guy before you say you're *dating* him as opposed to just *seeing* him?"

Joanne opened her mouth then closed it again and laughed. "Aw, what the heck do I know? Relationships, it's all" Joanne made a circular motion with her fingers, "wheels within wheels. Okay, so you say he's nice?"

"Totally nice. Awesomely nice. He was so kind to Joshua. And he's a great plumber."

"Well if he's all that and a great plumber, too, then what are you gonna do? But now I'm putting on my mother hat again, okay? You just be careful with this fella. Make sure you don't get hurt."

Sally gave a short laugh. "Make sure I don't get hurt? How? I mean, you can make sure you brush your teeth and make sure you take your vitamins and make sure you buckle your seatbelt, but what do you do to make sure you won't ever get hurt?"

Joanne sighed. "Okay, I guess if anyone ever actually figures that one out they can patent the formula and make a zillion and three dollars."

Sally looked into her coffee cup and smiled. "If you take off your mother hat I'll tell you something else about Silvio."

"Oh boy."

"He's fantastic, you know, in bed."

"*Oh* boy! You're telling me you went ahead and *did it* already?"

"Yeah."

"I should have guessed. So that's how come now you're dating."

"Uh-huh."

"And you're grinning like the Cheshire cat."

"Well, he's definitely taken me down the rabbit hole. He's an adventure, Joanne."

"An adventure, huh? Okay, the mother hat's going back on. You make sure that every time he takes you down the rabbit hole he's using"

"Latex, right. Every time. We talked it over."

Joanne's eyebrows arched upward. "You talked it over? You and the guy actually discussed… protection?"

"Yep. He's the one who brought it up."

Joanne nodded appreciatively. "Huh. Okay, that's good. Really, it is. I'm actually starting to be impressed with this plumber. He sounds responsible."

"Well, yeah, I mean, he's got three kids to take care of as it is. And I've got Josh. So we both know about responsibility."

"Honey, there's plenty of guys out there, even having four kids in the equation wouldn't be enough to give them religion on the topic of responsibility."

"Yeah." Sally sighed. "Case in point Darren. I mean, knocking up Trysta the same time he's telling *me* we need to wait to have another child? Can you honestly *believe* that? God, every time I think about it I could just…"

Joanne made a "T" shape with her hands. "All right, kiddo, time out. We don't need to go to Darrenandtrystaville today, okay? Let those two stew in their own juice."

"Sure. The juice of sex and happiness that they're ecstatically stewing in all over their five-bedroom house, with their three kids and a baby on the way, but right, what do I care?"

"*Why* do you care?"

"Because…the truth is…I mean, if I lived in some alternate universe, or something…the truth is I'd love to have another baby or two myself. Not to mention a husband. And a nice home with a little back yard, thank you."

"Who says you won't have those things in *this* universe?" Joanne put an arm around Sally's shoulder. "You quit raining on your own parade now, okay? Just take the good things as they come along, one at a time, and tell me everything about Mr. Wonderful Plumber that you can squeeze into, oh, five minutes."

"Thanks Joanne." Sally hesitated a moment then continued. "Only there's actually a whole *lot* about Silvio that I haven't told you."

"Oh yeah?"

"Yeah." She took a deep breath. "I did find him through his business ad online, that much was coincidental, but Silvio Jablonski turned out not to be just some random plumber."

Joanne's eyes widened and she leaned in closer to Sally. "Oh yeah?"

***

Two coffees later Joanne sat staring at Sally in wide-eyed disbelief. "So what you're telling me, basically, is that I'm sitting here swilling latte with a, a *fugitive*, an *accessory* to a *crime?*" Joanne opened her purse and pulled out a pack of cigarettes then stopped herself and tossed the pack back into her purse. "Damn this smoke-free shit!"

"I know, it's all so crazy! I mean, I've never been in trouble in my life."

"So now you're trying to double-up to catch up, huh? You and your ex-husband's wife's ex-husband, like just that much of the story alone isn't weird enough."

"Well, we"

"*Really,* Sally?" Joanne cut her off, "I mean, Jesus, Mary and Joe the Carpenter, do you have a *clue* how serious it would have been for you if you'd been caught?"

"No," Sally answered meekly. "How serious?"

"Well...I don't know, *plenty!* Look, I'm not a bigot but those people, the illegal ones, they're parasites, they have no business being over here in the first place and *they* know it, *they* took the risk, whatever happens to them, *they* asked for it. I just cannot believe a smart, savvy cookie like yourself would put your behind on the line like that, not to mention what would have happened to your kid and your plumber's kids if you'd gotten caught!"

"I *know*, I *know*, but what were we supposed to do? If you could have seen those poor people, frightened to death, some of them crying, with their babies and children, and, and old *grandmas*, for God's sake. There was even a scared little boy who looked like Josh. I mean, how could I turn in a little boy who looked like Josh? What would have happened to him if they'd arrested his parents? I couldn't turn them in, Joanne, I just couldn't do it. And neither could Silvio."

Joanne sighed. "Okay, well I guess you and Silvio are definitely together. Aw, Hon, you know I can't fault you for being kind-hearted. But what'd you have to tell me about it for?"

"I'm sorry. I just had to tell someone."

"Okay, fine, you told me, now you don't have to tell anybody else, right?"

"Okay."

"'In fact, you didn't even tell me, okay?"

"Okay."

"And you're gonna stop hanging around with that illegal couple with the baby, right?"

"Ummmm....right."

"You're lying, aren't you?"

"Yeah. Don't tell my mom, wouldja?"

Chapter Twenty-One

"Come in, Darren, sit down, sit down."

Darren entered Angelo Barbieri's office and settled into one of the comfortable burgundy leather wing-backed chairs across from the burnished mahogany desk behind which sat a big jowly man in a pearl grey designer shirt, sleeves rolled up. The man had a ring of grey hair around a bald head, a bulbous nose and large penetrating brown eyes. Darren still wasn't altogether sure exactly what he was here for, it was Geoffry who had talked to Barbieri and set the whole thing up. Geoffry told him Angelo was definitely interested...but interested in what? Hiring Darren to manage properties? To procure properties? To unload properties? Or for something that had nothing to do with properties?

"What do ya think?" Angelo Barbieri asked. He waved his hand around the office and smiled broadly. "Pretty classy for a room on the second floor of a salvage warehouse, huh?"

"Yes. Very nice, Mr. Barbieri. Very nice." Darren looked around at the modern art work that lent vibrant splashes of color to the pale buttery off-white walls. Angelo swiveled his chair around and spread an arm towards the wall-to-wall, floor-to-ceiling window behind him that offered a panoramic view of the Philadelphia Navy Yard. "I had this window put in special. Triple-paned plate glass. Look, you can see the ships."

"Oh, yeah," Darren said appreciatively. "Very nice."

"I like the ships. You like ships?"

"Yes. I do." For no reason that Darren could have verbalized this man was making him uncomfortable. He suddenly had the urge to get up and leave. But just as suddenly that urge was subdued by the mental image of his computer screen lighting up with demands for payments due: mortgage payments, insurance payments, car payments for Trysta's new SUV, utility bills, credit card bills, and those insidiously unfairly calculated child-support payments. Week after week, month after month, year after year to come, he would never be able to open his e-mail without being electronically jumped by one bill collector or another hounding him for money, a league of money-hungry vampires sucking the dollars from his dwindling bank account, dollars of which he desperately needed to find a new source.

"Yes," Darren repeated, stretching his lips into a smile, "I do like ships."

"Yeah, well, I like 'em, too." Angelo nodded towards Darren's brown leather shoulder-style briefcase. "So you got anything in that man-purse for me to look at?"

A slight grimace crossed Darren's face as he pulled out a crisp, clean copy of his resume and handed it across the desk to Angelo. "I worked for Highland and Erskerberg for seven years, most recently as Vice-President of Strategic Acquisitions."

Angelo perused Darren's resume. "Strategic Acquisitions, huh?"

"Right," Darren continued. "I currently"

"I heard," Angelo cut him off, still eyeing the resume, "that you got canned for strategically acquisitioning your way into the cooch of a hot little secretary."

It took a moment for Darren to absorb that he'd actually heard what he thought he'd heard. *"Huh, wha, excuse me what did you...?"*

Angelo burst out laughing.

Darren sprung up from his chair, sputtering with anger, *"How dare...she is my wife!"*

"'Ey, *Paisan'*," Angelo laughed, "it's a joke, a *joke!* We like to make the *battut'* around here, we're always joking about the *moglie*, the women. Your brother, he's the worst of the bunch, a real *oobatz*. I figured you'd be the same."

The same? Darren thought, *the same as that useless idiot Geoffry? Who's got nothing better to do than sit around making crass jokes about my wife with this, this glorified South Philly goomba?* Darren wanted to rip his resume from Angelo Barbieri's hand, but instead grabbed his briefcase with a flourish, making sure to carry it by the handle, not over his shoulder.

"Hey, hey," Angelo laughed, "come on now, Darren, if you're gonna work for me you gotta be able to take a little joke now and then. Come on, sit down, tell me more about your real estate business. You do fix and flips or what?"

"I don't believe this is going to work out," Darren replied coldly and then he turned and walked towards the door.

"No? Oh, well, that's too bad, because I got about three-quarters of a million dollars burning a hole in my pocket. I'm looking to invest it, your brother tells me you got some projects. I want to invest it before the end of the year. Tax purposes, you know?"

Darren stopped with his hand on the door knob while Angelo continued talking.

"I meet a young guy like you, just starting out, looks like he's got some talent, some fire – I can spot these things right off, I'm a good judge of character that way. I might be willing to look into the portfolio of such a person. I'm happy with the initial results, then I got some business associates also looking to invest right now, oh, I'm thinking two to three and a half million. For starters."

Darren's hand was still on the door knob. *Almost four million.* More than enough to snag the Manayunk property and, added to Dustin Sunfield's investment, the West property. For starters.

"I got a lotta connections all over Philadelphia and South Jersey. I do business with somebody makes me happy, I make sure the word gets around. Of course I won't work with somebody's got no sense of humor, gets his *budell'* all in an uproar, can't take a deep breath and roll with the punches.

Darren closed his eyes and took a deep breath. Then he turned back to Angelo Barbieri and once again willed his cheek muscles to pull his mouth up into a weak smile.

"Right, yes, ahem, sorry about the misunderstanding," Darren mumbled. He returned to the desk, sat down, and reopened his briefcase. "As I was saying, Mr. Barbieri,"

"Call me Angelo."

"…Angelo, Miller Realty Corporation is in fact a commercial redevelopment entity involved in the strateg…uh, the attainment of properties for development or redevelopment, that is, identifying and analyzing value-add opportunities"

"Fix and flips," Angelo cut in.

"Yes, that's right, in other words, procuring an existing structure, changing it, and"

"Unloading it for a profit," Angelo finished for him.

"Correct," Darren said, struggling to stretch his smile wider. He then went on to describe his current projects, the Manayunk and West properties, swallowing his annoyance at Angelo's constant interruptions and questions, most of which were in fact perfectly legitimate ones for a prospective investor. When Darren finished his presentation Angelo sat in thoughtful silence for a moment and then he said, "So what I'm hearing is that Miller Realty Corporation doesn't actually have any investors at the moment?"

"I'm expecting to finalize the Manayunk deal within the next few days and my West property investor should be on board shortly thereafter."

"Who are they, these investors?"

"Well, Mr. Barbier...Angelo...the privacy of my clients regarding"

Angelo stood up and smacked the top of his desk. "Did I ask about the privacy of your clients? Listen, kid, don't try to bullshit me about these bullshit "clients" of yours! I'm not stupid and I don't fuck around! I do business with somebody, I gotta know who he does business with, you understand me?"

If Angelo had reached across the table and slapped Darren's face he couldn't have been more stunned. He stared in amazement tinged with fear at Angelo Barbieri, who retreated as quickly as a cobra after a strike. Angelo sat back down at his desk and leaned comfortably against the back of his chair, his hands behind his head. He smiled and said in the friendliest of tones, "You know what I'm saying, Darren?"

Darren swallowed hard and nodded. He realized that he was now in a moment of decision. He realized that in that brief show of temper this man had actually opened the door and given Darren a view of what he'd be in for working for Angelo Barbieri. This was the moment Darren could step through that door or he could walk away. If he walked away then he walked back into the grip of the money trap that his life had become with no guarantee that his elusive investors wouldn't continue to stall him until they finally drifted away and disappeared, life boats once within reach now gone, leaving him to drown in a sea of debt. But he also understood that if he walked through that door into Angelo Barbieri's world then he'd be in the grip of that big fist that might one day come down on him with the same speed and force with which it struck the table just now. Yet if he walked through the door he could walk out again at any time, couldn't he? He'd be free to do that, wouldn't he?

Darren cleared his throat, reached into his briefcase and riffled around for the Manayunk papers. Not that he needed the papers, he knew every fact and figure by heart. What he needed was a little more time, just a few more seconds before leaping into the inevitable. Finally he pulled out some papers, perused them for as long as he felt he could and then cleared his throat again and looked up at Angelo Barbieri.

"Well, my principal investors for the Manayunk building are Chase Winston and Aaron"

"Winslow," Angelo finished for him.

"*What?* You *know* Winston and Winslow?"

"Winston and Winslow, Attorneys at Law. Yeah, I know 'em. Couple of *finoinks.*"

"Excuse me?"

"Couple of faggots."

"Winston and Winslow? You're saying they're, what...*gay?*"

Angelo laughed. "Gay as pink ink, kid. Winston's the bull, Winslow's the bitch. Aw, come on, don't tell me you didn't know that about your own investors?"

Darren shook his head.

"Oh yeah, old Winston and Winslow, they cater to the legal needs of the cock jockey community. The rich cock jockey community." Angelo rubbed his chin thoughtfully. "Yeah," he continued, "I could see those two going in for a property in Manayunk. A nice little up-and-coming spot like Manayunk, okay it's a wopbox now, but it'll be the next gay mecca, you wait and see. Hey, you got some numbers you can show me?"

"Yes, I do, in fact," Darren reached into this briefcase then handed a folder to Angelo, "here's the proforma that shows the expected returns on the Manayunk property."

Angelo studied the proforma then he set it on his desk. "Who else is playing real-estate footsie with you besides those two *ferracadoozas?*"

"Dustin Sunfield. He's interested in the West property."

"Yeah, I've heard of Sunfield. Sun Hardware, right?"

"Right."

"I've heard of the guy but never done business with him. You're on your own with Sunfield."

Darren nodded, though he wasn't sure exactly what that statement implied, or how who Angelo did or didn't do business with was any of Darren's business.

"But you get Sunfield on board for that West property, you let me know, okay? Maybe I'll be interested, too."

This time Darren hesitated, but only for a moment, before nodding.

"Okay, so now I know a little bit about your company, we can get to the business at hand. Can you handle some residential work or you only do commercial?"

"No, I'm licensed to broker for both commercial and residential real estate."

"Good. Because I have a row house out by Moyamensing Avenue. I bought it for my daughter to live in, she wanted to be in the city, running around like those little *fighett's* on those TV shows, but what are you gonna do? Now she's getting married, so she wants the house in the suburbs, something to put some nice furniture in, some dishes, some kids. I want to get her a little place for a wedding gift, something nice but not too expensive, three, three-fifty tops. Go ahead and find something for her out by Audubon, maybe Perkiomen, King of Prussia, that's where she likes."

"Three to Three-fifty? In those communities? Are we talking a condo?"

"No, she wants a house."

Darren blew out a long breath. "A single family at that price out in those places won't be an easy find, but…"

"But you'll look around, you'll find something. I'm paying you a commission now, you understand?"

"Of course," Darren said, feeling somewhat giddy at the prospect of a paying client. Or was Angelo Barbieri his employer now? Either way, Darren felt the debt noose loosening from around his neck."

"And I'll need a renter for the house on Moyamensing. I don't want to sell it just yet. Can you find me a renter?"

"Yes, I believe I'll be able to. Renting is a very popular option these days, very recession-proof."

"Yeah, well, we won't talk about recession." Angelo made the two-fingered sign to counteract the *maloik,* the evil eye. "What kind of rental income are we talking about?"

"A single family on Moyamensing Avenue? I'd have to see the place, and it depends on the address, the neighborhood, whether we're talking East or West, but"

Once again Angelo stood up and banged his hand on the desk. "*East or West?* What, you think I'd set my daughter up in a neighborhood full of greaseballs and street trash?"

"Oh, no, of course not, I only meant…"

Angelo sat down again and said calmly, "She lives in a good neighborhood, East, over by Queen Village Pennsport. I bought the house six years ago for one ninety-nine-nine when the bottom was out of the market and then I put another five thousand into it to make it nice for her."

"Sure, sure of course," Darren quickly conceded, "you wanted it nice for her."

"It's a nice place."

"Sure, of course, a nice place."

"So continue."

Darren cleared his throat again and then continued. "Well, so let's say the house, your daughter's house, is currently appraised at around two, two-fifty, then we're talking, let me see…" Darren did a mental calculation, "probably anywhere between eighteen and twenty-two hundred a month rent. I'd have to pull comps." Angelo gave him a blank stare and he explained, "compare the rental prices of comparable properties in the area."

Angelo nodded. "Okay, well, you go ahead and pull your comps, only don't sit around pulling it all day. You get the place rented, I'll pay you half a month's rent commission, no make that a full month, and a hundred fifty a month to manage it."

It hit Darren that he, not Angelo Barbieri, should be setting his service fees, yet he nodded acceptingly at Angelo's proposition.

"And then I got a couple other units that need a new manager, you interested?"

Darren continued nodding as if his head were on a spring.

"Good. I'll need you to go collect rents for me up in North Philly. They're some rough neighborhoods, you understand? Allegheny Avenue, Lehigh, around there. The guy I have now is afraid of the Blacks and Mexicans after he got roughed up a little. Can you handle, say, about thirty-two units, fifty bucks a unit?"

Darren's head froze in mid-nod and his jaw fell open. *Thirty-two units? In the most treacherous, crime-ridden no-man's land in the city? For what, sixteen hundred dollars a month?*

"Well, what do ya say, Darren? You wanna go collect rents from the spics and spooks for me? Don't worry, I'll give you a baseball bat to use."

Darren's stomach lurched. "Uh, well, Angelo..."

Angelo burst out laughing. "Holy shit, if you could see your *face!* You thought I was *serious!* You thought I was *really* gonna send you out to North Jababaland to collect rents!" Angelo slapped his knee in glee and laughed so hard the tears ran down his face. "Your *face,* kid, you had to see your *face!*" Then he wiped his eyes and sputtered out the last few chuckles. "Aw, it's like I told you, kid, we love to joke around here. You stick around you'll end up a crazy guy, too, just like your brother, you'll see!"

Darren willed himself to get up and leave. Now. He stood up.

"Hey," Angelo continued with the most good-natured of smiles, "you know I'm just dicking your balls a little, right? What, you need to use the john, or something? Otherwise sit down, we gotta talk about how I should invest the rest of that seven hundred and fifty thousand."

Darren slowly sat back down. He opened his mouth to speak just as a red light on Angelo's desk phone lit up and through the speaker came a female voice: "Mr. Barbieri, your wife and daughter are here to see you."

"Aw, Dina, tell them stop by later, I'm in a business meeting."

"*Angelo,*" a different female voice whined through the speaker,

"You said come by at eleven, it's eleven... *Angelo*, I'm *here*, come *on!*"

"Fine, come up!" Angelo barked into the phone. *"Bah-fungool,"* he muttered.

"Uh, maybe I can talk to your daughter about the house while she's here?" Darren suggested deferentially.

"Nah, that's my other daughter."

A moment later Angelo's office door flew open and in bounced a little girl in a pink fur-trimmed coat, her long brown hair curled and pulled back in a big pink and white bow. Behind her followed a model-thin woman who appeared to be in her early thirties. The woman's long blonde hair was cut in stylish layers and her face was half hidden behind a pair of large round-framed sunglasses. She wore a fashionably over-sized black leather jacket and a black mini-skirt over black patterned tights and black suede boots.

The little girl hopped onto Angelo's lap and threw her arms around his neck. "Daddy!" she cried.

"Whoa, Abington," he laughed, "how's my little princess?" He kissed her loudly on the cheek.

"Mommy and I are going shopping! We need some money!"

Angelo laughed again. "What do you think Daddy is, the bank?" To the woman he said, "Hey, Nicole, how come this one's not in kindergarten?"

His wife rolled her eyes and the little girl cried, "Oh, *Daddy*, don't you *remember?* There's no kindergarten today!"

"Teacher's meeting," Nicole said, "remember?" She'd pulled a nail file from her purse and was filing the edge of a perfectly manicured nail.

"Teacher's meeting?" Angelo cried, "I'm paying $18,000 a year so the teachers can take a day off to shoot the bull?"

*"An-*gelo," sighed his wife.

*"Dad-*dy!," sighed his daughter.

"All right, all right, go shopping, put Daddy in the poorhouse!"

The little girl giggled and Angelo pulled out his wallet. He counted out a sheaf of bills and handed them to his daughter. "Tell mommy not to spend this all in one spot."

Abington Barbieri jumped off her father's lap and handed the money to her mother, who thumbed through the bills as adeptly as a bank clerk. She looked up at her husband.

"Three hundred and fifty dollars? God, Angelo, you are such a *Jew!*"

Angelo laughed and pulled several more bills from his wallet and handed them across the desk to his wife. "You bring me back some change, okay? And listen, you watch what you buy for the *bambine'* here, I don't want to see her dressed like a little hoochie mama."

Nicole grinned and stuck out her tongue at her husband and then walked around desk to give him a quick kiss on the forehead. "C'mere, Abbi," she called to her daughter, "give Daddy a kiss."

After he'd waved them out the door Angelo turned back to Darren and chuckled. "You play you pay, huh?"

Darren chuckled lamely.

"So," Angelo continued, "what were we talking about here, Bobby Darren?"

"Bobby Darren?"

"Yeah, you know... 'Bobby Darren?'...'Mac the Knife?'"

"Mac the Knife?" Darren smiled blankly.

"Yeah, you know." Miming a microphone in one hand and swaying his shoulders, Angelo began singing, "*Oh, the shark has...real sharp teeth, Babe...and he keeps them...pearly white...*" Angelo raised his eyebrows. "No?" Then he laughed and waved his hand dismissively. "Okay, so where we?"

"You were, uh, interested in investment possibilities?"

"Oh yeah." Angelo picked up the Manayunk prospectus and looked it over again. "Okay, here's what I'm thinking, and this is just an idea. Supposing I get in on this Manayunk deal. And the West deal, if you can get that Jew Sunfield to spring."

"Uh, Mr. Sunfield seems very interested. Definitely interested."

"So are those two backdoor men Winston and Winslow."

"You think so?" As soon as he'd said the words Darren could have kicked himself for accidentally letting his insecurity slip out.

"You'll see. When you hear from them you'll let me know. And if you snag Sunfield you'll let me know." Angelo swiveled his chair around then sat back and gazed out his window. He appeared to be deep in thought, his hands behind his head. Darren sat in silence until Angelo turned back to him. Then Angelo put an elbow on his desk and propped his head in his hand. He blew out a long breath. "Okay," he said, "I'll tell you what. How much more you need for the West Property after you get Sunfield's share?"

"Well, Mr. Sunfield hasn't actually said how much he's willing to put up...." Darren sensed this was the moment to grab. "But if I had another investor on board he would maybe"

"Yeah, I get your drift," Angelo cut him off. "Tell me about the West Property again. Run the whole deal by me."

"Okay, the property is a rehabbed apartment building from the 1930's, beautiful, art deco-style, a gem. It's in foreclosure now, unbelievably irresponsible financial management on the part of the previous owners and it's sitting empty, ten units, *empty!* Anyway, the bank is willing to practically *give* the building away at seven-hundred-nineteen-eight, a steal, for *ten units*, and we're talking spacious, well-built apartments that could be resold as condos once the neighborhood has turned and reached its full development potential, which will be very soon, which is happening even as we speak. In fact next year Anderson Consulting is relocating its corporate headquarters to Drexel Hill, just about a mile from the property. They'll bring dozens of young white collar professionals looking for high-end urban housing. Look, for under a million dollar investment I'll be able to re-sell those ten units, I mean they'll be *walking away from me* for three-fifty, three seventy-five a pop! The time to grab this space is *now!*" Darren was suddenly excited, on edge, tingling with nervous anticipation.

"You're making it sound good. I'll tell you what. You call Sunfield and you tell him you got another investor putting up half on the West property. That's how much on my end now, about three-fifty?"

Darren pulled a calculator from his briefcase and did a quick calculation. "Three fifty-nine nine, plus half of another two hundred thousand, more or less, for the contractors, the renovations, and then half of the ten-percent developer's fee." Darren had to stifle his elation. A partner to share the initial investment was likely to provide the spark needed to light a fire under Sunfield.

"Right," Angelo said thoughtfully. "I'll tell you what. For your ten percent developer's fee you have Sunfield pay seven percent, I'll pay three."

"What? Mr. Barbieri, I can't do that! Sunfield would never stand for that, nobody would!"

"Okay, okay." Angelo held his palms up in a gesture of backing off. "Sunfield pays five percent."

"Yes, that is standard. Sunfield pays five percent and you pay"

"Three percent. And you settle for an eight percent fee."

Darren stared at Angelo for a moment in disbelief. *Eight percent? The balls on this guy!* "No," he finally said, "I'm afraid that won't, for a developer's fee, that *definitely* won't..."

"Sunfield pays you the five that he's expecting to pay in increments as the deal moves along. And I pay you three. And in return for this discount you collect the first twenty-five percent...no, *fifty* percent of my share of your fee up front. Today."

Darren was even more stunned by this proposition of Angelo's than the last. "You're saying...you're saying you're willing pay me *today? In advance? Fifty percent?* Before Sunfield has even signed on?"

"You object? It's illegal, or something?"

"Well, no, it's not illegal, but..." *But I can't believe I could have that money in my hand today!*

"Look, I believe in you. You'll snag Sunfield or you'll snag somebody else, right? So I risk paying you something today, and for my trust in you you're gonna give me a two percent discount. That work for you?"

"Well..."

"Go figure out on your little machine how much I'm paying you today."

Darren tapped in the figures on his calculator then said, "Fifty percent of three percent comes to ten thousand seven hundred and ninety-seven dollars."

"That work for you?"

Darren had to stifle the grin that threatened to take over his face before it morphed into a whoop of joy. "Well, yes, yes, I believe it would work, Angelo. I'll just have to draw up the papers."

"You do that. And while you're at it go draw up another deal with the queers. Factor in a third partner for – okay, I'm gonna run a little over budget here – but factor me in for half a million on the Manayunk property."

"All right. Very good," Darren chuckled and then his elation deflated slightly. "Um, about Winston and Winslow..." Darren hesitated, not sure how forthcoming he should risk being concerning their recent skittishness.

"Hey, don't worry," Angelo said as if reading Darren's mind, "like I said, they'll get on board. Very soon. You'll see. You be ready with that new contract, which they will be creaming themselves with joy over, believe me. And one more thing. When you talk to Sunfield, tell him your new investor in the West Property wishes to remain a silent partner. Don't give him my name, you get it? Give him my attorney's name. My attorney will represent my interests, you understand?"

"Well, uh, actually it would be a little unusual to invest through an attorney on such a relatively small transaction..."

Angelo tapped his fingers on his desk. "*Small* transaction?"

"But of course we can work it that way if you want," Darren quickly added with a nervous chuckle. "Perfectly legal."

"Good, good." Angelo leaned forward, his elbows on the desk. "I like doing business with you."

"Real estate *is* my business, Angelo. And I'm good at what I do."

"Yes, Bobby Darren, you are." Across Angelo's face spread a grin as wide and friendly as a shark's and behind narrowed eyes ran the thought, *but mostly you're easy. And cheap. And oh, so clean.*

***

Chase Winston and Aaron Winslow sat down across from each other in a booth at their favorite Society Hill coffee shop. Aaron stirred a packet of artificial sweetener into his black coffee and eyed his partner's tall whip-cream-topped vanilla caramel macchiato.

"Good lord, Chase, I know you're as aggravated by this whole Manayunk situation as I am, but attempting to self-induce diabetes is not the answer."

Chase ignored the comment. "I *told* you we should have closed the deal weeks ago with that *pisher* real estate agent."

"Who wasn't such a *pisher* that he hesitated to court the likes of Angelo Barbieri."

Chase Winston shook his head and blew out a sigh of frustration. "We should have moved sooner. Had it signed, sealed, and moving along before Miller found any more investors to climb on board."

"Look, Chase," Aaron said defensively, "you had the same misgivings as I did about this Miller. That day he showed up at the building forty minutes late and looking frazzled as a fart in a blender? Remember? Your enthusiasm for the guy was as cooled as my own. At the time."

"At the time," Chase echoed sardonically.

"Not to mention that he was in no way established in the field. Didn't have one other investor in his repertory at the time."

"At the time."

"At the time."

"Well," Chase continued, making no effort to hide his annoyance, "now he *does* have another investor on the Manayunk property with whom we will have to share what promises to be a sizable profit if this Darren Miller is as market savvy as he *now* appears to be."

"Look," Aaron offered, "another investor is not necessarily a bad thing for us. It's less of an upfront cash commitment and shores up confidence in the project as a whole. And Barbieri, whatever our personal feelings about the man, *is* a secure investor with a ton of financial clout."

"Who is latching onto us like a parasite, mixing his dirty money with ours so that it will come out clean at the other end."

"Chase, we don't *know* that Angelo Barbieri is using this investment to launder dirty money."

"Oh, *no*, we don't *know*, we haven't a *clue*," Chase said sarcastically. "In any case I don't like the idea of associating with the man."

"On the record, as far as we know Angelo Barbieri is just another member of the business community. He's had dealings with many legitimate businesses, including our own at one time."

"And many legitimate businesses *won't* deal with him. *I* don't want to deal with him. Not anymore."

"Fine. Shall we pull out of the Manayunk deal, then? Let Miller go find someone else who has no qualms about investing in a sure profit-reaper because one minor partner has...run a few stop signs, so to speak?"

"For God's sake, Aaron, you know as well as I do the situation we're in now! It's not that fucking simple! This conniving little prick Darren Miller has locked us into a situation that we either have to go along with or back out of, thus saying "fuck you" to Angelo Barbieri. Is that what we want to do? Flip the bird to a short-fused three-quarters Mafioso?"

"No," Aaron replied, "as a matter of fact I don't particularly want to do that."

The two sat for a moment sipping their coffees in irritable silence and then Aaron spoke up. "All right. Let's figure this out."

"Yes, Aaron, let's."

Aaron moved his coffee aside and with his finger drew two invisible intersecting lines on the table to form four imaginary quadrants. "Supposing we set up the situational possibilities on a sort of Cartesian coordinate plane, as it were, utilizing a variation of Pascal's wager."

"Fuck you."

"Come on, Chase, look at the possible outcomes." Aaron placed his hand on one of the quadrants. "Possibility number one: we abandon the whole thing altogether, with no reverberations from Angelo Barbieri, assuming Barbieri has bigger fish to fry than to waste time – not mention the risk – on revenge over a *potential* deal that was really nothing more than an unformed plan anyway."

"Good outcome for us."

"*Not* good for us if with Barbieri's solid financial backing Miller finds other investors and the plan *does* take form and money is made and we lose out."

Chase reached across the table and put his hand in the second quadrant. "Possibility number two: we pull out of the deal and Angelo Barbieri breaks our legs."

"He breaks out legs *and* we lose out on the deal. Also not good for us. Now let's look at the next potentiality." Aaron pointed a finger in the third quadrant. "Here we stay in the deal and, because of our having signed on the dotted line of a perfectly legal transaction – which happens to also have Angelo Barbieri's name on it – and that's all we're doing, signing the dotted line then handing over some money to a developer – we're not getting into bed with Barbieri per se..."

"Per se."

"But, all right, supposing that our indirect, once removed business association somehow causes our *'pristine reputation,'*" Aaron made dramatic air quotes around the words, "to be sullied. That's possibility number three. And finally," Aaron drummed his fingers several times in the fourth quadrant, "we invest alongside Angelo Barbieri, we all make a healthy profit, we go our ways, Barbieri goes his, and no one's the worse for wear."

"So those are our possibilities, huh?"

"Most likely. Which one do we bet on?"

Chapter Twenty-Two

Silvio and Sally lay comfortably in each other's arms just this side of drifting off to sleep.

"*Me encantan los miercoles por la noche,*" Sally said softly.

"Yeah, I like Wednesday nights myself," Silvio yawned and then he added, "I mean, '*yo tambien.*' Me too."

"We're getting pretty good, aren't we?"

"Oh, yeah. But I think we need more practice." Silvio began kissing Sally's face and neck.

"I meant our *Spanish,*" Sally laughed, and Silvio laughed with her. They wrestled playfully for a moment then settled back into each other's arms.

"What about your Mom?" Silvio asked. "Does she mind that you're spending your Wednesday nights with me instead of with her?"

"Nah, she doesn't mind at all."

"Sally? Have you even told your mom about me?"

"Of course not. She thinks I'm taking a Spanish class that meets on Wednesdays, which is pretty much true. Oh, I mean I'm sure she suspects something, since Joshua has been telling her about my "friend" Silvio who comes over to study Spanish with me. But sometimes my mom is smart enough not to ask too many questions about issues she doesn't particularly want to have to deal with. Like the possibility that I could be sleeping with someone."

"'Don't ask, don't tell.'"

"Bingo. So what about your mom? Have you told her about me?"

"Not yet. She's still hasn't recovered from Trysta."

"Right, right." Sally kept inside herself the question she really wanted to ask Silvio: *What about you? Have you recovered from Trysta yet?* Which question, if Silvio even felt like tackling it, would then lead to the question about where *she* was on the road to her recovery from Darren. And that wasn't a place she needed to go right now. Not now, when she felt so good, so happy in Silvio's arms. She changed the subject. "So… do you think Lupe and Ascensiòn have figured out what we do after our Wednesday evening language lesson?"

"They probably think we do this every night after every language lesson."

"Spanish being such a turn-on."

"Well, yeah," Silvio chuckled then turned thoughtful. "All right, you want to know what really turns me on? It's seeing Lupe and Ascensiòn together. Happy. In love."

Sally sighed. "Yeah, you can sure see that they're in love. And with that chubby adorable little baby between them…recipe for one cute, cozy, happy little family."

"Guess I wish I had me some what they've got," Silvio sighed.

"Me too. Someday."

"Okay now, would you look at us? Lying here talking about two poor refugee illegals who are living by the skin of their teeth and could lose *that* any day, and that's what we're wishing we had."

"Yeah," Sally chuckled dourly. "Meanwhile they'd no doubt give anything to have what *we* take for granted. Some crazy world, huh?"

Silvio held Sally a little closer. "You and me, we don't have it so bad right now, though."

"I feel wonderful right now, Silvio. I really do."

"Me too."

"And in a crazy way, I feel like Lupe and Ascensiòn are part of what brought us together. Or brought us closer together. Gave us more to share. Experiences, I mean."

"Well, yeah, they've provided some shared experiences, all right," Silvio chuckled.

"I just wish there was some way for them to get, you know, green cards, visas, whatever."

"Visas, that's what they'd need to start off with. Only, being illegals…" Silvio shrugged. "Look, if Ascensiòn could get a work visa, I'd ask my uncle to hire him in a minute. But there's just no way."

Sally thought for a minute then she said, "Maybe there *is* a way".

177

Equal and Opposite Reactions

Silvio propped himself up on one elbow. "What, are you saying you've got an idea?"

"Well, no, but," Sally shrugged. "I'm just saying maybe there is a way. I mean, you never know, do you?"

"I think that..." Before Silvio could finish his thought he was distracted by the ring of his cell phone. He reached over to the night stand for his phone and looked at the number on the screen. "My Uncle Bud. I better get it."

Silvio turned on his side away from Sally to take the call from his uncle. By the time he was sitting up in bed Sally was drifting off to sleep. By the time he was pacing the floor Sally was deep in a dream. After he hung up he walked back to the bed looking like a man in shock. He crawled in next to Sally and gently rubbed her shoulder. "Sally?" he said softly, but she responded with an unconscious sigh. So he let her sleep and instead announced softly to the empty room, "I'm gonna be rich."

***

John and Kevin had called in the last jobs of the day and Ida had already turned on the answering machine and left for the night. The doors were locked and the lights were off at Quick and Reliable Plumbing except for inside the office of Bud Danessa where Bud and his nephew Silvio sat at a cleared-away corner of Bud's beat-up work desk digging into an order of cheese steaks from the pizzeria down the block.

"You're not gonna be rich, I can tell you that right now," Bud said to his nephew between bites. "Comfortable enough, yes, rich, no. At least not right away. So don't go building yourself any mansions in your mind out there on the Main Line. Not right away."

"Right, Uncle Bud, I'll be sure not to build any. Not right away."

The men ate in silence for a moment then Bud said, "On the other hand, Quick and Reliable Plumbing is a good business with a solid customer base. You continue to manage it decently you can expect to take home right off the bat at minimum twice what you're making now, and that's *after* you've paid the staff, suppliers and the tax man, all of whom get paid before you pay yourself, you'll remember that,

178

right?"

"Right, of course."

Bud blinked several times and rubbed his eyes with the back of his arm. Silvio put down his sandwich and wiped his hand on a napkin. Then he put a hand on his uncle's shoulder.

"Hey, Bud, you sure you're ready to do this?"

Bud sniffed. "Aw, don't mind me. Yeah, I've been thinking about doing this for a while now. I was gonna bring it up to you back at the beginning of the year, but then you were having your, you know, domestic problems. I figured it'd be best to wait until things settled a little."

"Right. Probably was a good call."

"So you tell me, Silvio. Are *you* ready to do this? Being a business owner, it's no small job."

Silvio pulled in a deep breath. "Uncle, Bud, you gotta know, owning Quick and Reliable, it's a dream, it's, it's…I mean, yeah, I'm ready. I'm ready right now."

Bud smiled. "Yeah, I can see you are ready. And I wouldn't be selling you my life's work for a dollar if I didn't think you were."

"I am. But it's gotta be what you want, or I"

Bud cut him off with a wave of his hand. "The business needs to expand. We both know this."

Silvio nodded.

"And the fact is that I'm going on seventy years old and my heart's not into expanding. My heart's into leaving the hard work and long hours to somebody else and spending some time with my grandkids before they get too big for me to spoil 'em rotten. And I figure it's time to start making that bucket list. I mean, how many good years do I got left?"

"Hey, you don't need to be thinking that way, you got a lot of good years left, a whole lot. Come on."

"You're young yet, Silvio, but guys my age are dying. Cancer, heart attacks, they're dropping like flies every day. I can't ignore this."

"Well, you should, Uncle Bud."

"All right, I will, but I still want to get my affairs in order, is that okay with you, kid?"

"Aw, sure, Bud, I didn't mean to say…"

"It's okay, I know what you meant. Anyway, look, even though this outfit will be yours to run however you want, you're gonna need some guidance. On the business and accounting end if nothing else."

"I'm gonna need guidance on a lot of things and I hope you're gonna be the one to give it to me."

"Yeah, well I figure I'll hang around, do some work when I feel like it, take some jobs, show you any ropes you need to be shown."

"Good. I'll need you here."

"Who you really need is Ida. She knows the books inside and out and could run this place-single handed. You lose her you'll have to hire two people to replace her."

"Don't worry, Bud, I'll sure hold on to Ida. And you, too, as long as I can."

"Well, it's like I told you on the phone the other night, I'll need a little something to pad my savings and my 401K and then some to put away for Celeste, should I go first, with a little left-over gravy to leave my kids."

"Sure."

"So in return for the good price I'm giving you for the business, and not only the business, you understand, but the building, furniture, all the inventory and customer base, you'll get it all…"

"Whatever kind of deal you want is good by me."

"Okay, so here's the deal I'm thinking. You'll pay me a part-time salary – I don't need benefits, I got my Medicare and Social Security – you'll pay me until I die, don't wince, I'm not planning on going today and then when I'm gone, I'm gone, you're free okay? And in the meantime, any value you add to the business, that will be all yours. Don't you start crying now. Here, let me tell you about the big vacation I'm planning." Bud pulled open a desk drawer and took out a colorful brochure depicting a palatial cruise ship sailing on a sparkling sea set against a sun-lit blue sky. He handed the brochure to Silvio. "Look at this. What I want to do, not right away, a year or so down the road, I'm thinking, is take the whole family, kids, spouses, grandkids, on a cruise, one of these Carnival lines, see? Down to the Caribbean."

Silvio looked at the brochure photos. "Sounds great. Looks great."

"Yeah. And we'll go first class all the way. One of those ships that has everything on board, the Vegas shows, the casino, the swimming pools, a beauty spa for the ladies. And the food…they say the food on those cruises is out of this world, you'd go just for the food."

"Hey, *I'd* go just for the food! I think it's a terrific idea, Uncle Bud. You should go for it, the family'll have a great time."

"I hope so," Bud sighed. "And I hope it will bring us all together and heal the bad blood."

"Bad blood? What bad blood?"

"The bad blood there's gonna be when my kids find out I'm selling you the business for a dollar.

"*What?* You haven't told Rick and Jeannine about selling to me?"

"No, they don't know this yet."

Silvio was dumbstruck. "Does Aunt Celeste know?"

"If I tell your Aunt Celeste today it'll be on the 6:00 news by tonight. I'm gonna have to break it carefully to the family. Use the right words. Time it just right. Even then…" Bud shrugged. "We'll see."

"Aw, geez," Silvio sighed.

"Aw, come on, don't let this crap rain down on your parade. I had to tell you because you need to know what's going on but you shouldn't feel bad. I mean, look at my kids. Rick's a lawyer married to a doctor and Jeannine's a doctor married to a lawyer. What would any of them want with a plumbing business?" Bud shook his head. "See, the problem is not that I'm selling the business. There's already been some talk about that. 'Sell the business, Dad,' they say, 'sell it now, the time is right.'"

"Only they weren't talking about selling it for a dollar."

"No. Not for a dollar and not to you. You know how Rick takes care of the legal end of things for me?"

"Yeah?"

"I told him I was thinking, just *thinking* of leaving Quick and Reliable to you, and…" Bud blew out a long sigh.

"He didn't like the idea."

"Acted like I was planning on giving away his first-born to the gypsies."

"Great. You know, I thought him and Jeannine were acting funny to me at Grandma's birthday this past summer. I figured it was over, you know, my divorce." Silvio contemplated for a moment. "Come to think of it, everybody was acting funny to me then. Some of 'em are still acting funny to me."

"Yeah, you're right, they *were* treating you funny. But *then* it actually *was* over your divorce. I didn't mention this idea to Rick until *after* Grandma's birthday. At which time he immediately told Jeannine, who right away called their mother, who also didn't like the idea on top of having a fit because I told our son something before I told her…our son, who is *supposed* to be my attorney and give me client confidentiality…" Bud gave a disgusted wave of his hand. "I ended up in the dog house good with everybody for even *entertaining* such an idea. So I backed off, dropped the subject altogether and haven't brought it up since. Consequently they think I've come to my senses and forgotten all about it."

"This is not making me feel good."

"So let me finish. You know how we've done some give and take on jobs with that big outfit, Kensington Gas and Sewer?"

"Yeah?"

"Well, last week Kensington offered to buy me out."

"*What?*"

"Four hundred forty thousand dollars. Furniture and inventory included."

Silvio gave a long whistle. "Four hundred forty thousand. That's way out of *my* league."

"Anyway, *this* time I made sure to tell Celeste the news first, only like I said, anything I tell Celeste…" Bud put both hands put to his mouth and mimed birds flying away. "So of course the kids now know about the Kensington offer and they assume I'm selling to them even though I never actually said I would. I did think about it, tossed it around a little, but…" Bud sighed. "It's not an easy decision, turning over my business to someone else. Even to you. But selling it? To strangers? Cutting myself off completely from my life's work?" Bud shook his head. "You know, I started Quick and Reliable almost forty-four years ago. I was younger than you, even." He looked around his office. "I love this place."

"I know you do, Bud. I love it, too."

"Yeah, you always did, Silvio. From the time you were a little kid, you loved hanging around here. You mother would bring you over, you'd be poking around, digging into my tool box. My own kids? Never had any interest, what can I say?"

"You can say one's a doctor married to a lawyer, the other's a lawyer married to a doctor."

"How'd that happen?" Bud chuckled. "Anyway, like I said, neither of them is interested in my plumbing business. But money? Huh, that's something everybody's interested in, right? Hell, I'm sure Rick's having some assistant to an assistant to an assistant draw up a sales contract for me right now with Kensington."

"So what are you gonna tell Rick?"

"Well, I'm gonna tell him to put your name on the contract and write in the sale price as one dollar. And I'm gonna tell him I want the sale to happen as soon as possible. Right away. You okay with it happening right away?"

"I'm okay with it happening yesterday, but if your family's not gonna go along with it…"

"Hey, I can *guarantee* the family's not gonna go along with it. Not right away. But they will eventually. They'll come 'round sooner or later. I'm hoping it'll be sooner. But if it turns out to be later…" Bud massaged his temples for a moment with one hand. "See, that's why I want it done right away. Do it and let people be angry if they're gonna be angry, and then get over it. And the sooner they get angry, the sooner they can *start* getting over it, you see what I'm saying?"

Silvio nodded.

"And something else," Bud continued, "I don't want to go to my grave with this thing unsettled. I want Quick and Reliable to pass from me to you now, so that I can live out my life knowing my life's work is in good hands. That it will go on. Be…" Bud's voice began to crack again.

"It's okay, Uncle Bud…"

"…be taken care of."

"It will be."

"I don't want there to be any possibility of a legal fight over the disposition of Quick and Reliable after I'm gone. By that time I want any conflict to be history. So I'm taking care of it now. So I can live out the rest of my life and not have to worry about it."

"Sure, Bud, I get what you're saying."

"I know you do, Silvio. So," Bud pulled in a deep breath, "so I'll break it to the family, get Rick to draw up the papers, or if he won't then I'll have to get somebody else, and hopefully in a week or two, or however long it takes, you'll be running this place."

"Wow. Great."

"Though like I said, I'll still be coming in, working, doling out the advice if you need it."

"I'll need it."

"Hopefully you'll have some ideas of your own. You know, for expanding the place."

Silvio hesitated for a moment and then he said, "Well, Bud, I kind of do have something I was thinking about."

"Oh yeah? Well, shoot."

"Well, you know how we've been having more Hispanic customers lately? Mexicans, Nicaraguans, and all?"

"*Nicaraguans?*"

"Well, you know, Spanish speakers, wherever they're from. Seems like they're everywhere these days, right?"

Bud rolled his eyes. "Tell me about it."

"I haven't told you this but I've been taking Spanish lessons."

"You?" Bud chuckled, "*Spanish lessons?*"

"Yeah. To use on the job. "

"Hmm." Bud nodded appreciatively. "Okay."

Silvio continued. "And then I was thinking, since we need to hire another guy or two anyway it would be smart to look for someone who speaks Spanish."

"You want to hire a Spanish plumber?"

"Then we can advertise 'se habla español' like they do and cater to the Spanish community."

Bud rubbed his chin. "I mean, I guess it's not a bad idea, in theory, but…"

"What?"

"Well, you'd have to find a guy, first of all."

"I figure I could start looking around."

"You know he'd have to be legal."

"Well, yeah. Of course."

"I don't think I'd write that 'se habla español' in the ad. Might put some people off, you know what I mean?"

"It was just a thought."

"You could just put "Spanish spoken."

"Yeah, that would definitely be better."

"Yeah." Bud contemplated for another moment. "Boy, if we got a healthy slice of the Spanish customer base we could be avalanched."

"That's what I was thinking. I mean, it's the wave of the future, right?"

Bud lifted his plastic cup. "To the future."

Silvio tapped his uncle's cup with his own. "To the future."

Chapter Twenty-Three

Lupe carried in a plate of sugar doughnuts from Sally's kitchen and set them on the dinette table. "Donde esta Silvio?" she asked, glancing out the dining room window for a sign of Silvio's red van.

Ascensiòn reached from where he sat at the table and patted Lupe's hand. "Say it in English, Mi Amor."

"Okay." She turned towards Sally, who followed her from the kitchen with a pot of coffee, "Where is Silvio? He work late?"

"Yeah," Sally replied. Then she added, speaking slowly, "Silvio tiene que trabajar tarde. He has to work late. Pronto va a ser... a ser.." She set down the coffee pot then reached for the Spanish-English dictionary sitting in the middle of the table among the other language books. She flipped open the dictionary and after a moment said, "...el...*jefe*." Then she repeated, "Silvio va a ser el jefe de..." Again she flipped through the dictionary then said, "...de la empresa."

Lupe and Ascensiòn's faces lit up and Ascensiòn cried, "Silvio is going to be the *boss*? Of the whole *company*?"

"Que bueno!" Lupe cried, "Is *fantastico*!"

Joshua looked up from where he sat on the floor playing with David. "Mommy, is Silvio going to be the boss of the all the plumbers?"

"Yep, he sure is," Sally replied happily.

"Which word means boss?"

"*El jefe,*" Sally carefully enunciated.

"Yay for Silvio!" Joshua cried and then he got up from the floor and skipped to the table. He reached for a doughnut and said, "Puedo tener, uh...how do you say doughnut in Spanish?"

"We don't have these in Nicaragua," Ascensiòn explained. "You have to just say 'Puedo tener un doughnut?'"

186

"You don't have *doughnuts* in Nicaragua?"

"Is okay," Ascensiòn chuckled as he held out the plate of doughnuts to Joshua, "we have lots of beans and rice."

"Puedo dar un doughnut a David?' Joshua asked.

"No, you no to give doughnut David," Lupe answered with a smile. "I give him." Lupe picked the baby up from the floor and set him on her lap then offered him a few crumbs of her doughnut to eat off the end of her finger.

To his mother Joshua said, "Puedo tener, um, milk?"

"Di 'leche,' Maje," Ascensiòn said. "Milk is 'leche.' You say, 'Puedo tener un vaso de leche?' 'Can I have a glass of milk?'"

"Puedo tener un vaso de leche?" Joshua repeated.

"Kiddo, you are incredible," Sally said as she poured Joshua his milk. "You're learning so fast, you're leaving me in the dust."

Lupe looked confused. "He leaving you in…the dust? *El polvo?*"

"It's slang, like we talked about. *El argot*, remember? It means he learns faster than me." Sally explained.

Lupe nodded. "Ah, si. The children, they learn fast. They are like, like…las esponjas." She drew her hands in towards her mouth and made a sucking sound.

"Oh yeah, like *sponges*," Sally translated, imitating Lupe's depiction of sucking in.

"Sponges," Lupe repeated and then gave one more long imitation sponge slurp, which made Josh and baby David laugh.

There was a jiggling of the front door knob and a moment later Silvio walked in. "Hey, guys," he said as he set his tool box down in the living room. "Sally, you know the front door was left unlocked again?"

"Hola, jefe!" Ascensiòn cried, springing from his chair to give Silvio a handshake and pat on the back while Lupe applauded, followed by Josh and Sally and even baby David on his mother's lap, who made everyone laugh when he burst into a big smile and clapped his hands along with others.

"Whoa, what's going on here?" Silvio chuckled. "What'd I do?"

Joshua ran to Silvio and gave him a hug. "Eres el jefe!" he cried.

"I'm el *what*?"

"El *jefe*," said Ascensiòn. "The *boss*. Sally tells us you're the big boss pretty soon."

"The boss of *all* the plumbers!" Josh added.

Silvio blushed. "Oh yeah. Well, I'm taking over my uncle's business."

"Felicidades," said Lupe.

"Dile '*Congratulations,'*" Ascensiòn corrected his wife.

"*Congratulations,* Silvio," Lupe dutifully repeated.

"Thanks, thanks, guys."

Josh ran back to the table and grabbed a doughnut from the plate and offered it to Silvio. "Aqui tienes, Silvio, quieres un doughnut?"

"Hey," said Sally, "you don't want to pick up the food in your hand, you pick up the plate and then let the person pick out their own."

"Lo siento," Josh apologized.

"Don't worry about it," Silvio chuckled, biting into his doughnut while settling himself into a chair at the dinette table, "it's *nada.*" Silvio patted his knee and Josh climbed onto his lap. "Boy, this guy's Spanish is getting pretty high-tech," Silvio said, patting Josh's head.

"Oh, yes," said Lupe, "he talk like a *Nicaraguensito!*"

"He sure does," Sally agreed.

"And listen to you," Silvio said to Lupe, "Your English is getting so good, you're starting to sound like a real Americ..."

Silvio stopped short and cleared his throat while his face reddened with embarrassment.

"Silvio, they don't have any doughnuts in Nicaragua," Joshua cried, breaking the awkwardness of the moment. "Only beans and rice!"

"And platanos fritos," Ascensiòn quickly added, "that's fried bananas, Maje."

"You eat *fried bananas?*" Josh asked incredulously.

"Son deliciosos!" said Lupe. "I make you some."

"And we used to eat chicken sometimes," said Ascensiòn. "But not too much. Only when we have the money."

"Not too much chicken in Nicaragua," Lupe repeated solemnly. Then she added brightly, "In America we can to eat chicken all the days! And we no have to, to..." she mimed decapitating and plucking a chicken.

"She means in America you don't have to run around and catch the chicken first, like we do in Nicaragua."

"You have to run around and *catch the chicken?*" Josh cried.

"Sure we do," said Ascensiòn.

"We just have to buy ours from the A&P," said Josh and then he added, "I wish we had to run around and catch *our* chicken!" He hopped off Silvio's lap and chased an imaginary chicken around the room for a few moments and then he stopped suddenly. "Wait a minute," he cried, "do you have to *kill* the chicken?"

"Well, yeah, Honey," his mother answered. "Somebody has to kill the chickens we eat, too, you know."

"Oh." Josh silently considered this newly revealed fact of life. Lupe looked up from the Spanish-English dictionary, which she'd been studying during the conversation.

"We also to pull the, the…" She glanced back down at the dictionary, "…*feathers!*"

"*What?*" Josh cried.

"Oh sure, Maje," said Ascensiòn, pulling Josh, onto his lap. "Is okay, that's how we eat. When I was like you my grandpa teach me to chop off the head of the chicken and then I pull out the feathers. Was my job."

"Oh." Josh frowned, deep in thought, and then he turned to Silvio. "Silvio, do you think it could be my job to catch the chicken if I lived in Nicaragua?"

"Oh, yeah," Silvio replied. "You'd be great at it."

"I guess I could chop off the head, too, so mom and me could eat it." Josh made a chopping motion with his hand.

"Yeah, you could," said Ascensiòn. "You always take good care of your mama. She's a lucky mom."

"Yeah, I am," said Sally, feeling her eyes tear up.

"We all so lucky here," said Lupe. "So happy with good friends."

Then around that little dinette table passed a moment that, had it been captured on canvas, could have passed for a twenty-first century slice of Norman Rockwell Americana. But the moment quickly evaporated when Ascensiòn stood up and said, "Now I have to work." To Lupe he said, "Lista, Querida? You ready?" Lupe nodded and stood as well. "Good-bye, good friends," she said, "I sad to go now."

"Wait, you have to go to work *now?*" Silvio asked. "Weren't you working all day?"

"Yes, but I got another job. Got to buy lots of chicken for this little majeito." He cocked his head proudly towards his son. "There's so much good work in America, everywhere you look day and night, the jobs, they fall from the sky. Why do people say there's no jobs in America?"

Because not everyone wants to work sixteen hours a day doing menial labor for a wage you can't live on, Sally answered to herself. To Ascensiòn she said, "Where are you working?"

"Hallmark Janitorial Services. Night crew."

Sally stood and walked the Guzmans to the door. "So you'll be, what, cleaning?" she asked. "All night long?"

"Is just until three am."

"Then he can to go home sleep," Lupe added.

Ascensiòn put an arm around his wife's shoulder. "And to work on your *infinitivos*, Mi Amor."

***

After Sally finished kissing and tucking in Josh for the night she returned to the kitchen where Silvio was washing the dishes. She grabbed a towel from a rack next to the sink and began drying. "You know," she said, "it kills me that Ascensiòn has to make ends meet by scrubbing floors and toilets all night."

"Yeah," said Silvio, "Especially since he could be making good money as a top-scale plumber. It's like I said, I'd hire him in a minute if he had the papers."

They continued cleaning the kitchen in silence for a moment then Sally said, "So do we know for an indisputable fact that there's no way he *can* get papers?"

"Huh, if there was any way, believe me, there'd be a whole slew of illegals out there getting papers."

After another moment Sally said, "And do we know for a fact that there *aren't* a whole slew of illegals out there getting papers?"

Silvio laughed. "And if a tree falls in the forest and nobody hears it, does it really fall?"

"You know, I don't know if the damn tree falls or not, but I'm about to enter that forest and find out if there's any way in hell an illegal can snag a green card."

"How you gonna do that?'

"Oh, well, I don't know, I guess I'll go on line, find out what I can. And I can run the situation by Joanne. She knows a lot about a lot of things. She might know some direction to point me in. And she's, you know, trustworthy."

"Okay, if you say so. Maybe I could even run the situation – hypothetically, of course – by my cousin Rick."

"Is that the lawyer married to the doctor or the doctor married to the lawyer?"

"The lawyer."

"Who's not talking to you because your Uncle is selling you his business for a dollar?"

Silvio sighed. "All right, well, maybe I shouldn't ask *him* right away. But look, maybe between the two of us we'll open a door."

"Or at least find a key that opens a door."

Silvio paused a moment then said, "Speaking of doors, you gotta stop leaving your front door open like you sometimes do, I mean, around here that could be dangerous."

"Well, I only leave it unlocked when I know you're coming. To make it easier for you."

"I can ring the bell. I can wait 'til you get to the door. It's not that hard."

"You having a bad day, or something?"

"No, I'm having a good day, only you keep leaving the door unlocked for *me*, one of these days *you* could end up being surprised, and not in a good"

"*Okay*," she cut him off. They continued doing the dishes in silence for a moment and then Sally said, "All right, so sometimes I forget to lock the door. I'm not perfect, okay?"

Silvio put down his dish rag and took Sally in his arms. "Yeah, you are," he said, kissing her forehead. "You just gotta remember to keep your door locked."

Chapter Twenty-Four

"Okay, Girlfriend, first of all, I thought we weren't going to talk about your two little amigos anymore. In fact I thought you were going to nip that association in the bud. Isn't that what you promised me?"

"Um, I don't exactly think I ever did promise that."

"Yeah, I don't think you did either. I think it was just wishful thinking on my part." Joanne sighed and took a sip of her vending machine latte. When she'd accepted Sally's break room lunch date she'd had a premonition that she might be in for a revelation of something sticky wrapped around something not altogether legitimate, which pretty well described the subject under discussion. "But all right," she continued, "I'll be honest, what I know about Immigration law is the same as what everybody else knows about it. There's no way a person here illegally can suddenly, or even not suddenly, become legal. Having an American-born baby makes not a drop of difference. Makes it worse if you ask me. Your friends made a sketchy choice and now they're going to have to lead a sketchy existence."

"Well, yeah, that's what you always hear, but…." Sally shrugged, and looked so downhearted that Joanne added, "of course, I'm not an Immigration lawyer."

Sally suddenly perked up. "That's what I need! An Immigration lawyer!" Then she deflated just as quickly. "Like I could even think about calling a lawyer."

"Yeah, well, lawyers, they do charge by the minute, a lot of them."

"Huh, my divorce lawyer charged by the nanosecond. No wonder I caved so fast."

"Aw, Hon, why don't you not go there. In fact, I'm just gonna say this for your own good…"

"Yeah, I think I know what you're gonna say."

"Right, what I'm gonna say is that these people may be perfectly nice human beings, but the fact is that they created their own situation, and if you're smart you'll realize that it's not gonna do you or them any good for you to go getting all tangled up in their ball of yarn. I mean, you really think it's gonna do anybody any good?"

Sally's optimism went flat while her annoyance expanded, both with Joanne and with her own dumb, naïve self, and worse, she was now climbing on board the defensive. "Well, I don't know," she quipped sarcastically, "it did *them* some good the night I hid them from the feds."

"Aw, would you *please* let me forget you told me about that?" Joanne shook her head. "All right, look, I don't know these people from Adam and Eve, but I can tell you they seriously took advantage of you that night. And you ask me, they're still taking advantage of you, period."

Joanne's words might as well have been darts hitting a raw nerve,

"Lupe and Ascensiòn are *not* taking advantage of me!" *Don't yell at your boss,* her inner voice of reason tried to warn her, *no matter what, do not lose it with your boss!*

"Emotionally and possibly legally," Joanne continued. "God, Sally, you're a smart girl, how can you be so totally *clueless?*"

That did it, the word *clueless!* "That's right, Joanne," Sally snapped, mentally smacking aside her inner voice, "you *don't* know them! And fine, maybe they *are* taking advantage of me, but you know what? If I was in their shoes I'd do the same damn thing! I'd do whatever the hell I had to do in order to protect Joshua!"

"What," Joanne shot back, "like breaking the law and pulling other people down with you? People like Silvio with children of their own? And by the way, remind me again how what you're doing is in Joshua's best interest?"

Sally stood and whisked up the napkin and plastic wrap left from lunch and stuffed them into her empty paper cup. "I better get back to work," she huffed.

Joanne watched Sally's back as she sprinted from the break room. "Huh, you're welcome," she muttered.

***

"*What?*" Silvio looked up from the pot of spaghetti sauced he'd been stirring and stopped in mid-stir. "You went off on your *boss?*"

"Totally lost it," Sally poured a pot of spaghetti into a colander over the sink. "Dumb move, huh?"

Silvio stared at her, drop-jawed speechless for a moment. "You mean...*totally* lost it?"

"Well maybe not *totally* totally, but..." Sally sighed. "Aw, shit."

"Geez." Silvio shook his head and returned to his sauce.

"Look, I don't think she'll fire me, or anything. That is to say, she didn't fire me today."

"Yeah, well, let's hope she doesn't fire you tomorrow. Because with the job market the way it is...Sally, you could be in big trouble."

"Yeah, I know, I know. I feel really awful about it. And not just because Joanne's my boss and could fire me. I mean, she's more than a boss. She's always been more like a friend. Like a second mother to me. And I go and yell at her when she was only trying to give me some sensible advice."

"You *yelled* at her?"

"Well, not exactly...sort of."

"Aw, Sally..."

"I know, I know, I'm an idiot. Go ahead, say it."

"The volcano."

"Yeah. The damn volcano." Sally finished setting the table and called down the hall to Joshua that dinner would be in five minutes.

Silvio set the sauce on the table. "You got the parmesan?" he asked.

"Right here." Sally reached into the refrigerator for the cheese. "It's just that I felt so frustrated. And kind of stupid, even. Joanne said Lupe and Ascensiòn are using me. Do you think they are?"

"Aw, I don't know. Maybe they are. On the other hand, they're teaching us Spanish."

"And I'm teaching Lupe English."

"You hid them from the law."

"Lupe let me into her house that time to use her bathroom. And she didn't even know me."

"I helped Ascensiòn fix that generator and he taught me how to fix one for myself. So I guess that's the way it goes. The human condition. Give and take."

"User, usee. Bad luck leading to good."

"Good luck leading to bad."

"Equal and opposite reactions. Oh, my God! What if Joanne fires me? What'll I do?"

Silvio considered in silence for a moment then he said, "You better show up at her office first thing tomorrow and apologize."

"Believe me, I'm gonna show up begging forgiveness on all fours like the dumb ass that I am."

***

The email arrived at Sally's desk shortly after Sally did, just as she was mentally putting the finishing touches on her apology before heading down to Joanne's office. *Please see me*, Joanne's email said. That was all. Just three little words that jumped off the computer screen and hit her in the stomach with a thrill of dread. She read the words and re-read them, telling herself that it was surely no big deal, that Joanne called people down all the time. *Of course she's not going to fire me*, Sally thought as she walked to Joanne's office, fighting the jitters that seemed to radiate from her chest out to her finger tips. *"Why am I even thinking about that? She'll probably just chew me out, or something. Maybe even give me a written reprimand. Screw up my personnel file, but I deserve it. She won't fire me, though. Not Joanne.* She hesitated a moment at Joanne's doorway before entering her office.

"Come in," Joanne called to her. Joanne smiled coolly and she sounded cordial enough, nor did her face reveal any left-over rancor from the previous day. Still Sally felt a twinge of fear on top of her jitters as she stepped into her boss's office. She cleared her throat, but before she could speak Joanne said, "Sit down first."

Sally settled into one of the chairs on the other side of Joanne's desk. She noticed a slip of yellow paper on the desk but couldn't make out what, if anything, was written on the paper because Joanne was covering it with the palm of her hand. *Dear God*, she thought, *Please don't let pink slips be any color other than pink.*

Joanne's finger played along the edge of the paper for a moment then she cleared her throat. "About yesterday, Sally, I've thought it over, and I think that"

"Oh, geez Joanne," Sally blurted, "I'm sorry, I'm so sorry, I behaved like a real ass, just totally out of line." In her head she added, *And please don't fire me!*

"Apology accepted. However"

"Oh, no, I mean, I shouldn't have waited until this morning to apologize, I should have done it yesterday, it's like I said, I was wrong, totally wrong, I'm sorry, I'm so, so"

"Sally," Joanne cut her off, "enough. I accept your apology. Okay?"

"Okay," Sally replied in a small voice. *Just please don't fire me!*

Joanne pulled in a deep breath. "However, that being said, I can see that I could advise you until I'm purple in the face, you're not going to drop your two... *friends,* or whatever they are. Are you?"

"Joanne, I swear to God, I'll never, *ever* bring up the subject of Lupe and Ascensiòn again, *ever.* Consider me advised, *totally* advised, it'll be like you never heard of them, I promise."

"Too late, kiddo, I already *have* heard of them. A whole lot more than I wish I did, believe me. And that's one cat you're not going to be able to stuff back into the bag. Anyway, no matter what you're telling me and what you're telling yourself it's pretty clear they've got their hooks into you and you're going to end up associating with them, looking for some harebrained rip-off scheme to get them legal, jeopardizing yourself and possibly those around you, whether I hear about it or not. Right?"

Sally, open mouthed, hesitated for a moment and then she cried out, "No, no, I don't ever have to see them again! I *won't* ever see them again if you don't want me to, I promise!"

"Right," Joanne sighed. "And I'll believe you for about five minutes. Look, you need to calm down." She picked up the yellow paper from her desk and handed it to Sally. "Here. This isn't something I ever thought I'd be doing, but since you wouldn't listen to reason, I can't have you"

"Oh, no, Joanne *please!*" Sally burst into tears. "*Please* don't fire me! What will I do? How will I support Joshua? I'm barely making it as it is, *please*, Joanne, *please*, just give me one more chance, I promise, I"

"Wait, stop!" Joanne stared at Sally in wide-eyed disbelief. *"Fire you?* Hon, you think I'm *firing* you?""

"Please, please, don't..." Sally stopped in mid-sob. "You... you're *not* firing me?"

"Firing you? Well....no! Of course I'm not firing you!" Joanne stood up from her desk and hurried around to Sally. She hugged Sally's still trembling shoulders. "Girl, what the hell made you think I was gonna *fire* you?"

"Well, you called me in, and then that piece of paper, I, I thought it was a p-pink slip."

"Pink slip?" Joanne held up the paper. "Uh, what color is this?"

"I didn't know if pink slips were actually pink, or if that was just an expression."

"No, they're actually pink."

"Oh, thank God, thank God!"

Joanne reached for the box of Kleenex on her desk and offered it to Sally. Sally grabbed a Kleenex, blew her nose and then said, "See, I thought you were going to fire me for being such a certifiable bitch to you yesterday."

"Oh, my God, if I fired every employee who was occasionally bitchy to me I'd be running this goddamn outfit by myself! No, of course, I'm not gonna fire you. Aw, come on, dry up those waterworks. *Fire you?"* Joanne shook her head.

"Oh, *thank you*, Joanne, thank you for not firing me!" Sally blew her nose again. "But then...what's the yellow slip?"

"Oh." Joanne picked up the paper from her desk and sheepishly handed it to Sally. "It's a...God, I can't believe I'm doing this!"

"Doing what?" Sally looked at paper and blinked in confusion.

"Giving you the number of an Immigration lawyer."

"An Immigra...*what?"*

"Like I said, you're hell-bent on being Mother Teresa of Roosevelt Boulevard. But you go pursuing this 'save the immigrants' crusade on your own I can guaranflippintee you'll do them more harm than good and maybe end up in a kettle of hot water yourself." Joanne sighed. *"Sooo...* I called a good friend of Ponti's and mine."

Sally read the name printed on the paper. "'Charleston Tilley? Family and Immigration Law?' He's your friend?"

"One of Ponti's best friends, to be exact. They go back, oh, heck, close to forty years."

"Wow. Where'd they meet? School?"

"High school. Ponti played basketball for Bishop Neumann, Charleston played for South Philadelphia. They were both chosen from their schools to play for the class of 1971 city-wide all-stars team. Somehow they struck up a quick friendship and one day after practice Ponti invited Charleston back to his neighborhood. Not the smartest move."

"Why?"

"Charleston is black. Ponti is Italian."

"So?"

Joanne chuckled. "Thank God things have changed enough that you don't get it. But back then, even as late as the late sixties, early seventies, you bring a black kid into an Italian Philadelphia neighborhood…"

"Yeah, I guess I get it."

"Anyway, Charleston and Ponti practically got stoned – and I don't mean the kind of stoned you kids like to get nowadays – I mean they had stones, rocks, and other stuff thrown at them for going together to grab a couple of slices at the local pizzeria. Long story short, things got nastier and the police were called. Oh, the whole messy episode eventually got sorted out and some lame apologies were made, but not before Charleston and Ponti were arrested and taken away in a police cruiser…in handcuffs. And not before Charleston was kicked off the all-stars team."

"What about Ponti?"

"Ponti was not kicked off the team. He *was* taken aside by the coach – the *white* coach – and given a stern warning about hanging out with the wrong people. Ponti immediately quit the team."

"Oh my God, what a shitty experience!"

"Shitty experience it was for sure, but you ask either one of them they'll tell you it was the experience they bonded over."

"But what an awful ordeal for a couple of kids to have to bond over."

Joanne shrugged. "Eh, don't feel too bad. Today Charleston's a successful attorney living out in Huntington Valley and Ponti's an accountant, while most of those dumb stone-throwing yahoos ended up steam-cleaning carpets or clerking at a Qwiki-Mart. Oh, and the racist all-stars coach got canned the following year and last anyone heard he was humping the night shift at a Shop-Rite. So it's all good."

"Well, it's like the song says, 'What goes around comes back around'. Or it should, anyway. Sometimes."

"Yeah, well sometimes it does and sometimes it doesn't, but in the meantime you should call Charleston."

Sally looked over the slip of paper again. "So I should, what, call him at this number?"

"Call the number during business hours, you'll get Maria, his assistant. Tell her you're a friend of Joanne and Ponti's and that Charleston said to call for an appointment. And then she'll give you one. *Capish?*"

Sally sighed. "Aw, gee, Joanne, I really appreciate this, and all, but..."

"You know what *pro bono* means?"

"Pro bono? You mean...he's willing to help Ascensiòn and Lupe without charge?"

"Hey, he didn't indicate whether there was anything he *could* do to help them or whether, if he could, he'd do it without charge. But he's willing to talk to *you* pro bono about their situation. Of course I wouldn't get your hopes up at this point."

"Oh. Okay. And it's really okay to call him?"

"Call him."

"Okay. Joanne, you know, I'm really grateful to you. For your help." Sally felt her eyes filling up again. "And especially for not firing me over my tantrum in the break room."

"Aw, you're welcome," Joanne chuckled. "But while we're on the subject, how about going a little easier on me in the future when I'm trying to give you some decent advice?"

The tears rolled down Sally's face. "I promise, Joanne, I'll never be mean to you again."

"Okay, well, that makes my day." Joanne grabbed a Kleenex and daubed it on Sally's cheeks. "There. You okay now?"

Sally nodded. "Uh-huh."

"Geez, you really thought I called you in to *fire* you?"

"Honestly, Joanne, I couldn't have blamed you if you did."

"Hon, you are too hard on yourself." She patted Sally's hand. "So go ahead and smack yourself in the head a couple more times then let it go. And call Charleston Tilley."

"You really think he'll talk to me?"

"Call him."

Chapter Twenty-Five

At seven-twenty the following Wednesday evening Sally and Silvio sat in the waiting room of the downtown law office of Charleston Tilley. His assistant, a young Hispanic woman dressed in a smart cream-colored jacket and slacks, sat silently at her desk typing at her computer keyboard.

After several minutes the office door opened and two trim middle-aged black men stood in the doorway, one dressed in a well-cut charcoal grey suit, the other wearing a tweed sports coat, sage green polo shirt and khaki pants. The man in the sports coat dabbed his reddened eyes with a handkerchief. The other man rested a hand on his shoulder and said, "Remember, what I told you, Robert. Worrying is paying a dividend to disaster before it's due."

"Well, I'm gonna try to remember that," Robert replied. "Thanks, Charleston."

The two men shook hands and with his hand still wrapped around Robert's Charleston said, "We still on for Saturday?"

Robert shook his head. "I don't know, Baby, I"

"Oh, come on, man," Charleston cut him off, "I already got the racquet ball court for eight am." Charleston mimed swinging a racquet, "stroke's gonna get rusty. Look, you gotta push on through this one, trust me."

"Yeah, okay," Robert sighed. "I'll see you Saturday."

"I better be seeing you Saturday."

"You will. Thanks, Charleston, thanks. Give my best to Ruth."

"I surely will, Robert."

After Robert exited the office Charleston called after him, "Eight am!" Charleston then looked around the waiting room and caught sight of Silvio and Sally. He wrinkled his brow and pointed a finger at them as if trying to remember their names. After a moment he said, "Joanne Ponticello's friends."

"Sally Miller and Silvio Jablonski," his assistant added, looking up from her keyboard and smiling at Sally and Silvio.

"Right, right. Regarding the Nicaraguan plumber." Charleston spread an open arm towards his office. "Please come in."

Charleston Tilley's office was small but had a warm, pleasant feel to it. The walls were painted a deep soothing café-au-lait and the wall behind his desk was lined floor to ceiling with handsomely bound books and periodicals. There was a window that overlooked the fountain at Logan Circle across from City Hall and on the wall opposite the window hung a print by Philadelphia artist Edwin Lester of a beautiful little black girl toting a bible in one hand with a butterfly poised on her other hand. Sally and Silvio took in all these details while sitting across from Charleston, who sat at his desk reading silently from a small wire-bound note pad.

"So," he finally said, still looking down at the pad, "We've got an illegal alien plumber."

"Ascensiòn Guzman," Silvio said.

"And his wife, Lupe," Sally added. "From Leòn. Nicaragua."

"Right." Charleston jotted down a few more notes then he looked up. "It is your interest, then, Mr. Jablonski, to seek a work visa for Mr. Guzman? And," he glanced at Sally, "a spousal visa for his wife as well?" Silvio and Sally nodded and Charleston considered a moment then he said, "Just one question. Why? Why are you going to all this effort for the sake of an illegal? Mr. Jablonski, could you really not find a suitable American employee?"

Sally and Silvio glanced at each other and then Silvio replied, "Well, the guy's a good plumber. Best I've seen. He can also do electrical, generators, anything. And then with the Spanish speaking, he could expand my base. And you know, it's not easy to find an experienced top-notch plumber these days. "

"I see," Charleston replied. "Anything else you can tell me?"

Sally and Silvio glanced at each other again.

Charleston gave each of them a direct look. "Mr. Jablonski, Ms. Miller, you are both obviously dedicated to going to bat for these people and you're asking me to do the same. If there's anything else going on, any personal motives or agenda you might have, you need to tell me. If I'm going to take this case, and I'm not yet sure if I can or will, I need to know the situation from all sides and angles, inside out and upside down, all pertinent information included.

Again Sally and Silvio exchanged a glance then Silvio spoke up. "Anything we tell you, is it gonna stay right here behind these walls?"

"Anything short of a felony."

"Well..." Silvio hesitated a moment then continued, "How bad would it have to be to be a felony?"

"Assault, robbery, rape, mur"

"What about hiding an illegal from the law?" Sally piped up.

Charleston chuckled. "Technically we're all three of us guilty of that right now, aren't we?"

"Oh. Okay, well..." Sally gave Silvio an inquiring look and after he nodded back at her she began, "See, it all started one day when my toilet broke and I needed a plumber..."

"So she called my company, Quick and Reliable..."

"He was supposed to show up at, like, nine o'clock but he didn't come until after three, so"

"Wait." Charleston stopped her and from a desk drawer he pulled out a Dictaphone transcriber. After he'd positioned the microphone in front of Sally and Silvio he said, "Could you please start over again?"

***

After Charleston pressed the "off" button of the Dictaphone he sat back in his chair with his elbows resting on the arms, his fingertips touching. He appeared lost in thought for a few moments then he said, "When you said you hid the Guzmans from the law you were speaking quite literally."

"Yeah," Silvio mumbled.

Charleston was silent for a few more moments then he said, "I've been in this business for quite some years, I've handled quite a few cases, but I must admit, yours is the first of its kind." He paused a moment. "*Thirty-two* people? In two bedrooms?"

"And a bathroom," Sally said sheepishly.

"But it's a pretty small bathroom," Silvio added.

Charleston stared incredulously at Sally and Silvio for a moment then his professional formality fell away and his face broke into a wide grin. *"Good Lord,"* he laughed, "this is surely one for the books, it most surely is! *Thirty-two people!"*

Sally felt herself blush with embarrassment and she noticed that Silvio's face had also reddened. She wanted to get up and leave and imagined that Silvio did, too, but Silvio spoke up.

"So I guess we're a couple of idiots, huh?"

"Yeah, we're sorry we took up"

Charleston wiped at the tears of laughter that filled his eyes. "If you two are idiots then, believe me, the world ought to be full of such idiots. Let's just be thankful you weren't caught, in which case there would have been precious little I could have done for you. And don't worry, I'll be erasing the recording and I'll transcribe only the pertinent information myself."

"Does this mean you can help us?" Sally asked. "Lupe and Ascensiòn, I mean?"

Charleston immediately recovered his professional demeanor. "I truly don't know yet. I'd have to find out a few things from the Guzmans. First and foremost, is legal status something they want to pursue?"

"Well, of *course* they do," Sally replied. Then she added, "I mean, isn't that what all illegals want? Papers, documents, whatever?"

"I guess we never actually asked them," Silvio added.

"Might be an important question to ask," said Charleston.

"Yeah, okay," Sally mumbled and then she continued, "All right, so let's say we ask them if they want to be legal and they say yes."

"Then I would be willing to talk to them. Although…" Charleston paused, then continued, "Mr. Jablonski, you say there is a general shortage of qualified plumbers in the Philadelphia area?"

"Well, yeah, good plumbers, yeah. You can ask my Uncle Bud, he's been complaining about it for years. And I want to start expanding the business as soon as I take it over from my uncle. But it won't be easy finding enough good plumbers, especially before I'm established on my own reputation."

Charleston thought for a moment then he said, "Mr. Jablonski, would you say that once you've established your company, say, in a year or two, as a reputable business, that you'll have an easier time finding employees as needed?"

Silvio shrugged. "Yeah, it may be a little easier then, provided I can find some good help in the meantime, you know, to get things off the ground, expand like I want to. But I gotta have good workers, you know? And, I'm telling you, Ascensiòn is the best plumber I've ever met. Besides my Uncle Bud, that is. And he speaks Spanish. Ascensiòn does."

Charleston nodded. "Supposing we could arrange for you to acquire a temporary work visa for Mr. Guzman to work for you for a year or two, help you out while you establish your new business. Would that be satisfactory to you?"

"Well, I mean…are you saying he could only stay for a year or two?"

Charleston pulled in a deep breath. "All right, I'm going to lay out for you a couple of possible scenarios I can envision under the circumstances. And by possible I mean, just that, an eventuality within the realm of possibility, not necessarily the realm of certainty. First, there is a category of visa known as the H-2B. It is a temporary work visa that you, the employer, must apply for in the name of the individual you wish to hire, in this case Mr. Guzman. To qualify for an H-2B visa an individual must have a valid job offer from a U.S. employer who is in acute need of someone to perform a temporary specific job for which the individual has the specific skill. The H-2B visa is generally issued for a year, though an extension of another year, possibly two, can be granted. Mr. Guzman will have to show proof of an intent to return to Nicaragua upon the expiration of the visa."

"So this H-2B visa will buy him three years, tops."

"Him and Lupe," Sally added.

"Lupe will be eligible for an H-4 spousal visa for the same period of time, that's right."

"No way they can get a green card?"

"The only way an individual with an H-2B can attain permanent status is if he or she has a close family member who is a citizen or permanent resident who could petition on their behalf. Does Mr. Guzman or his wife have someone? A parent or sibling?"

Silvio scratched his head. "Well, I don't know." He turned to Sally. "They ever say anything to you?"

Sally shook her head.

"How did they arrive here? What brought them to Philadelphia?"

Sally shrugged and Silvio shook his head.

"It's something you might look into. In any case, it won't affect your ability to procure an H-2B for Mr. Guzman. I frankly think the H-2B might turn out to be the most beneficial option for you personally, Mr. Jablonski. See, Mr. Guzman could theoretically stay here for three years, assuming you wished to keep him for the full three years. If, on the other hand, things were to, say, not work out, you as his employer would be perfectly justified not to take steps to extend his visa past the one year period. Or, if after a year or two or three the Guzmans were to decide that they wished to return home permanently, say the economic situation in Nicaragua were to improve within that time period, or they missed their home, or for whatever reason..."

"Well, sure, that could happen, too," said Silvio.

Sally spoke up. "But assuming the plumbing job works out and they love it here and end up wanting to stay permanently and become citizens?"

"Well, there are two possible routes to that end. The first is that they initially come over on a H-2B visa and then"

"Excuse, Mr. Tilley," Sally cut in. "Did you say 'come over?' I mean, there're already here, right?"

"Oh, they'll have to return to Nicaragua before we can start any visa process."

"*What?*" Sally and Silvio cried, both bolting upright in their seats.

Charleston raised his eyebrows in surprise at their reaction. "Of course they'll have to return. They're both over here illegally. No kind of visa can currently be offered to an illegal."

"*Shit,*" Sally muttered and then immediately apologized.

"No offense taken," Charleston said, suppressing a smile.

"All right," Silvio sighed, "If that's the way it is then that's the way it is. So they'd have to go back to Nicaragua. For how long?"

"That all depends," Charleston replied. "For the H-2B, not long. These temporary visas are generally plentiful at the beginning of the year. It usually takes about forty-five days from the time the petition is filed until the individual can enter the country to begin his or her employment. So if they were to return to Nicaragua fairly quickly and you put in the paperwork right away they could theoretically be back here by the first of the year."

Silvio shrugged. "Well, that much sounds pretty good."

"Then, as I was saying, if, after the expiration of his H-2B, you wished to bring Mr. Guzman and his wife back again – after they'd again returned to Nicaragua as required – you could always file to obtain permanent labor certification for him, which is the first step to attaining an employee-based green card. That process generally takes two to three years."

"Two to three *years?*" Sally exclaimed.

"Well, theoretically six months to three years, but from my experience I'd lay out two or three years as more realistic. Of course if the Guzmans wish and you are not opposed you could go for the option of skipping the H-2B period and jump right into the permanent labor certification process. Cut out several years from achieving the final prize of a green card."

Sally looked dismayed. "But two or three years back in Nicaragua where there's no work and not enough to eat? After having lived here? That's awful! Isn't there any way to speed up the process?"

"Mrs. Miller," Charleston said, speaking slowly and patiently as one would to a child, "Getting a permanent employment-based green card is a fairly involved multi-step process and, as I said earlier, the first step just takes that much time. Now I know that having to wait so long can be a frustrating experience, but that is the reality that the Guzmans will have to understand and accept if they and you, Mr. Jablonski, wish to pursue this option. You know, there's something we as Americans tend to forget, and that's that America, even in these hard economic times, is still the land of opportunity. Even a life of poverty here is a great improvement over the life of those in the poorest countries, among which Nicaragua surely is. Which is why there are so many human beings clamoring to get across our borders and take up life here. But the life your friends the Guzmans are living is a life on the edge of well-being. It's a game of chance that they could lose any day and that ultimately will not serve them well, I assure you. Do your friends want to take the risk?" Charleston let the question hang in the air for a moment, then he continued. "Sadly, there is simply no getting around the fact that if the Guzmans want to reach the Promised Land they're going to have to spend their years in the wilderness."

Sally opened her mouth to reply but Silvio took her hand in his and cut her off before she could speak. "Yeah, okay," he said, "we'll tell them all that."

"All right, we will," Sally agreed. "But how do you recommend they get back to Nicaragua? I mean, they're illegals, it's not like they can buy a plane ticket, or anything."

"No, they cannot buy a plane ticket." Charleston hesitated a moment and then he said, "They could, however, exit this country in the same manner by which they arrived."

"You mean...what, sneak back across the border?"

Charleston shrugged. "It would be the quickest, least complicated way.

"But what if they get caught?"

"Do you mean what if they get caught while they're crossing back over the Mexican border? Or what if they get caught right now?"

There was as moment of silence as Silvio and Sally absorbed his meaning.

"Right," Silvio sighed, "so it all boils down to the same thing."

"That it does. It all boils down to the ever-present possibility of them being caught, arrested and deported, and formal deportation for 'unauthorized presence' in the U.S. carries serious consequences, as you must know, these days more than ever. They'd be blocked from pursuing legal immigration for ten years, at the very least. At worst they could be apprehended and charged with a criminal offense."

"Oh, geeze," Sally muttered.

"And the longer they stay here the greater become the odds of them getting caught. But assuming they could make it to the border before that happens, crossing the U.S. border into Mexico should pose no problem. They could just walk or drive or take a bus across – provided they chose a traditionally tourist-friendly border crossing station...Brownsville, Texas, for example, or San Ysidro California, or any number of other places. They should avoid setting foot in

Arizona, of course. But look, they figured out how to get over here, figuring out how to get back is the easy part. It's not as if they'd have to deal with the dangerous thugs they most likely dealt with getting into the country. This isn't to say they won't face dangers getting back to Nicaragua once they've reached Mexico. And needless to say, the sooner they were able to make it back home the sooner you could apply for a visa for Mr. Guzman, who would then be starting off with a pristine record, no complications. Assuming this scenario all works out. Which it could very well not. Say, if they were caught tomorrow."

"So any way you cut it, if they want to be legal they've got to go back first."

Charleston nodded. "Anyway you cut it. There is one more option for the Guzmans, considerably more complicated, less risky and more risky at the same time."

Sally raised her eyebrows. "Uh, how can something be less risky and more risky at the same time?"

"Different categories of risk. I'd rather not go into that option today." Charleston glanced at this watch. "If I do I'll end up late for dinner with my wife. However I could explain it to you and the Guzmans when you bring them in to see me. If, that is, they're interested in pursuing legal status and enduring the possible hardships involved. Because if, in fact, they're not interested in going this route, then…" Charleston shrugged.

"Then they're not interested," Silvio finished for him.

"So then, if you have no more questions for now I think we can wrap up this meeting and plan to schedule another for you and the Guzmans, if you and they wish."

Charleston stood and Sally and Silvio followed suit. They thanked him and he shook both their hands then walked them to the door of his office. Sally stopped short at the door. She turned back to Charleston and said, "I guess I actually do have one more question. I believe you are a top-notch attorney. Not only because Joanne told me so, though that would be enough in my book, but because, well, I believe you really are.

"Thank you, Mrs. Miller."

"Hey, I second that, every word," Silvio added.

"And I believe," Sally continued, "that you must have more clients, paying clients, than you can handle. So my question is, why are you helping us for, you know, pro bono?"

Charleston smiled, and once again they saw his professional demeanor relax. "Well, I expect it's because I have more *paying* clients than I can handle." Still smiling, he looked down and rubbed his chin as if enjoying a private joke. "I'll tell you, though," he said, walking over to his window and pausing there to look out over the city scene beyond, "it's like this. I have two fine children who've never wanted for anything and who I was able to send to private colleges. One is an architect, the other is finishing her PhD in biomedical engineering. I've got a nice manse out in Beth Ayres and another nice one out on the beach at Cape May. I just renewed my membership at the Huntington Valley Country Club, where my wife Ruth and I play with our mixed doubles team on the tennis court. In other words," he glanced back at them, a playful grin again lighting up his face, "I've got money falling out my backside." He turned back to the window. "But I don't forget where all that money came from and to whom it really belongs in the end." He raised his eyes heavenward. "Or, as my kids used to say back when they were young and too cool to walk like normal homo sapiens, 'keeping it real.' Besides, I'll recoup my loss on Lupe and Ascensiòn on some Main Line fat cat willing to pay me handsomely to get his daddy's inheritance tipped in his favor. See, I've stood on the other side, my face pressed against the glass, watching how the other America lives, longing for my chance to pursue my true destiny...when I was young that's how I used to think of my future in my mind...*my true destiny...*" Charleston chuckled. "And by good fortune and the willingness of some good people I was given my chance. So once in a while I repay it when I can. And I was given an opportunity today, when two good people walked into my office wanting to give a young man and his wife the chance to find their true destiny."

Sally felt moved, teary, and Silvio sniffled slightly. Charleston stared out the window a moment longer then turned back to Sally and Silvio, his professional formality recovered. "So, Mrs. Miller, Mr. Jablonski, you'll talk to your friends, find out if they're interested in the possibilities we discussed. If they would like to come in and see me then have them call Maria and make an appointment. Does that sound like a plan?"

"Sure does," Silvio replied.

"I suggest you come along with them – at least you, Mr. Jablonski."

"Maybe I should stay home and watch Baby David," Sally said.

Charleston frowned. "Baby David?"

"Lupe and Ascensiòn's baby. David."

"You're telling me the Guzmans have...a *child?*"

"Well, yeah," Sally said, "we mentioned it, didn't we?"

"I'm pretty sure we did," Silvio added, "didn't we?"

Sally and Silvio both wore sheepish expressions. Charleston rubbed his forehead wearily. "Tell me," he said, "how old is this baby...David?"

"Oh, around six months," Sally answered.

"And where," Charleston's voice had an edge of fated resignation to it, "was Baby David born?"

"Here," Sally answered. "In Philadelphia."

"So," Charleston sighed, "the Guzmans have a child who is an American citizen."

Sally and Silvio nodded, each of them beginning to turn over vague uneasy notions of the implications of this new information.

Charleston opened the door of his office and said to Maria, "Could you please call my wife and tell her I'll be late – very late – for dinner?"

Chapter Twenty-Six

The beer was draft, ice cold, just the way Ed Miller liked a good glass of beer. He raised his mug and took a long pull, savoring that first taste then sighing with contentment. How long had it been since he'd had good glass of beer? Donna didn't care to keep beer in the house, except sometimes for company, and then it had to be some high-end bullshit brand, Stella Artois, Schofferhofer, names he couldn't even pronounce that came in arty bottles and tasted funny. Otherwise it was either one drink before dinner, or wine with dinner, or he could sometimes get away with both if they had company or were eating out, and that was fine, he certainly enjoyed a Glenlivet over ice and a glass of wine or two with dinner, but dammit, sometimes a man wanted a good cold glass of draft. Especially while watching the game with his son and chowing down on piles of spicy wings and ribs, which Donna also would not approve of, but a man also couldn't live on grilled chicken and citron-seared ahi-ahi tuna.

Still, Donna hadn't objected when Ed had mentioned that he'd made a date with Darren for the following Saturday to watch the Eagles-Steelers game at Phil's Tavern, a sports bar out in Blue Bell famous for its great food and colossal portions. "As long as I don't have to come along to make sure you don't go overboard," she'd said, patting his stomach, unaware of the double entendre of her statement, as if on some level she clairvoyantly knew that he was in fact intending to do something besides eating that she would surely interpret as going overboard.

Ed glanced at this watch. He was early. Darren should be here any minute. After a few more sips of his illicit beer he was feeling mellow, relaxed, and less troubled about the next liberty he was about to take behind his wife's back.

Though the bar was filling up with Eagles fans jockeying for a spot around one of the multiple flat-screen TV's, Ed had taken a table away from the crowd in the dining room where they'd be able to talk when they needed to but still have access to the TV screen, thus lending truth to the excuse of going to the bar to watch the game.

Catching sight of Darren looking over the bar crowd Ed stood and waved him to his table. Darren hurried over to his father and greeted him with a handshake that expanded into the kind of hearty back-pat that passed in public for a male hug. Right away it occurred to Ed that his son seemed better than the last time he'd seen him, not all stressed and nerved-wracked as when he'd been over to the house for lunch with Trysta and the kids...though Lord knows, taking those three little screamers of Trysta's out of the equation would be enough to exponentially lower the general stress level of any situation. Anyway, Darren looked happy, and Ed was considering whether he should get right down to business or let Darren chill a little with a drink when Darren burst out with news of his own.

"Dad," he said, a wide grin lighting up his face, "I got the Manayunk Property!"

Ed smacked the edge of the table. "The Manayunk property? You did? That's great!"

"And I closed another one, a building out in West Philly over by Drexel Hill. My major investor is Dustin Sunfield. You know, the owner of the Sun Hardware stores?"

"Sun Hardware, no kidding! Well hey, it looks like your ship's finally coming in."

"We're talking a whole fleet, Dad. I also picked up a client who wants me to rent out his house on east Moyamensing by Queen Village Pennsport. "

"Queen Village Pennsport? Pricey real estate out there, huh?"

"Yeah, yeah, it'll bring in a good rent which will mean a higher commission for me. The same customer also wants me to find him a house in King of Prussia, Perkiomen, you know, that area."

"Which should also bring you a hefty commission."

"*Oh* yeah. And then, wait'll you hear this, I got a call last week from Highland and Erskerberg. They're hiring me back as a contractor."

"*What?* They're hiring you *back?*"

"Yep. I was in the HR office yesterday signing on the dotted line."

"Wow. That's..." Ed's eyes widened and he shook his head in amazement. "Okay, so tell me this, what the hell did they fire you for in the first place?"

Darren shrugged. "Today I asked the guy in HR the same thing. You know what I was told? Two words: 'Probably streamlining.'"

"*Streamlining? Probably?*"

"That's what the man said."

"So why didn't they tell you that when they let you go? Why'd they make you think it was your fault? Is that any way to treat a valuable employee? I mean, you were a major asset."

"So I was led to believe."

"Seriously, what kind of bullshit game do they have going on over there at Highland and Erskerberg? They hire you, they fire you, they hire you..."

Darren shrugged. "I don't know, but at this point I'm a player and I'm not asking any questions."

"Maybe you *should* be asking ask a couple of questions."

"Dad, they're reinstating my health insurance!"

"No kidding? Okay, *that's* good."

"Yeah." Darren blew out a long sigh of relief. "Jesus, two weeks ago I didn't know how I was gonna pay for the baby. Not to mention Trysta's doctor's bills, I mean, they were starting to pile up."

"Well, they will do that. But hey, good for you. See, a good man will always come out on top. Eventually." Ed wasn't at all sure if this was true, not even eventually, but what the hell, he wanted to say something nice to his son.

"Thanks, Dad," Darren replied.

This conversation over Darren's good news was giving Ed pause in his purpose. He'd come here intending to offer Darren a $35,000 loan. But given the turn in Darren's prospects, did he really need the loan? Would he even appreciate his father offering at this point, or would the offer be taken as a double blow to his pride, aggravating the blow he'd taken by having to ask his father for money in the first place? Had Donna actually been right in stating that Darren should be left alone to handle his business himself? Well, Darren did, in fact end up pulling himself out of a ditch on his own ability and now appeared to be cruising along just fine. But on the other hand, Ed's parental conscience had been bothering him ever since he'd turned his son down on the loan. After all, hadn't he done plenty for Geoffry? Hell, Donna'd never complained when it had been *her* son who'd needed some propping up. And let's face it: Darren, for all the pussy-based problems he seemed to bring on himself, was basically a good kid. Ed cleared his throat.

"Darren, I've been thinking over that little matter you asked me about last time, you know, the loan you were needing? Well, I have these old bonds stashed away, worth thirty-five thousand now, and"

"Oh that," Darren quickly responded, "No, ha, ha, that was just, you know, just a little jumping the gun on my part, no, I'm fine, all squared away."

"Good, good. Well, just thought I'd offer. In case you still needed it."

"Nope. I'm good."

Ed felt relief mixed with a twinge of remorse for not having offered his son the loan when the boy had needed it. But at least now he wouldn't have to have a go-round with Donna.

They ordered plates of wings and ribs, most of which would be polished off by Ed (his son being what Donna called a mousey eater for a man, unlike her Geoffry who had a good manly appetite, though that kind of appetite and the developing paunch that went with it she roundly discouraged in her husband) and they ordered two more beers. They watched the game for a while and talked some sports and then Darren filled in a lull in the conversation by suggesting in a carefully worded proposition that his father utilize the thirty-five thousand dollars of intended loan money to come on board as a Miller Realty investor.

"I could turn a sure, solid profit on an investment of that size in just a couple of years, the rental property market being inversely robust to the weakened condition of the mid-range residential market."

Ed chuckled uncomfortably. His son looked so eager, he sounded so confident, like a young, competent professional...well, Darren *was* a young professional and competent, if not particularly in his personal life, certainly in his profession, right? He'd been promoted to a vice-president in his company before he was let go over some corporate bottom-line bullshit. For a moment Ed considered his son's proposition. But only for a moment.

"You know," he chuckled, "I think I'll just put that money back under my mattress."

"Oh." Darren looked slightly let down. "You sure you want to take that route, Dad? I mean, we could get that money working for you. In a real profitable way."

"Oh, I guess we could," Ed sighed, "but you know, I'm just not sure how your mother, at this point, would feel about"

"Right, say no more," Darren cut in with a knowing look that made Ed want to defend his wife, but he opted to let it pass.

"Anyway," Darren continued, "if you change your mind..."

"Sure, sure, I'll let you know."

Sure, sure, Darren thought. *And Donna will amputate your balls for you in case you do.* The men turned their attention back to the game. Well, Darren thought with satisfaction, at least his father would go home and tell Donna how well his son was doing. Really, things were starting to look up for him. Of course he hadn't shared with his father the fact that most of his present business originated more or less from Angelo Barbieri. That the first day Darren met Barbieri the guy signed on as an investor in the West property and later that very afternoon paid Darren his fee of $10,797. And not by check or bank draft as Darren would have been expecting, but with an envelope containing an assortment of legal tenders, among which were a cashier's check for $2500, A personal check from Barbieri for $1500, $5,000 cash...unusual, of course, but nothing illegal about being paid that way, nor were any of the amounts of cash or check great enough that he'd be required to notify the IRS...but unusual. Most puzzling of all the contents of that envelope was a check for $1,797 from an outfit called SP Wrecking. Well, all right, Barbieri ran a salvage operation; wouldn't a wrecking business on the side sort of go hand in hand? No, what knocked Darren off guard was that the check was signed Geoffry Steubing. Geoffry. His stepbrother. *His idiot stepbrother!* Sure, Darren had known that Geoffry was working for Angelo Barbieri – after all, it was Geoffry who'd set up his initial meeting with the guy –

but what was he doing signing checks? Barbieri would never hire a shit-for-brains like Geoffry to do his accounting and write his checks...would he? Worse, it would now be only a matter of time before Geoffry was bragging to his mother and Darren's father that he'd drummed up some business for Darren with his boss...except that Geoffry obviously hadn't done that kind of bragging yet, since Ed Miller appeared to have no idea who Darren was actually doing business with...Well, hell, who cared? Darren's business was Darren's business, and right now that business was going damn well, as was his life in general now that he was raking in a little cash. And the fact that Highland and Erskerberg had hired him back...well, that was about as sweet as it came, and Angelo Barbieri had *nothing* to do with that. No, the fact that they'd no sooner fired him than they wanted him back as a contractor meant only that he'd been let go as a salaried company employee strictly for the sake of budget-tightening. The company had surely taken a hit from the recession, everybody had, for God's sake, and the least those bastards could have done when they sacked him was let him know that he was a victim of downsizing instead of making him feel like he was at fault, a worthless loser. And now they'd come crawling back to him – man, how he would love to be able to tell them to take their job, sit on it and spin! On the other hand, there was no denying that he was glad to be back with Highland and Erskerberg; he felt vindicated, his pride salvaged.

"How's Trysta?" His father's voice called him back from his thoughts.

"Huh? Trysta? Oh, yeah, she's great. Trysta's great."

"She feeling all right?"

"Oh, well, you know, the little aches and pains, the moods they get, you know. But she's good, over all. Her kids even seem to have calmed down a little."

"Well, you know how it goes, you're stressed, you pass it on to your family. Believe me, I'm speaking from experience. But now your business is doing better, you're doing better, your family life is doing better."

Darren nodded. Yes, things were okay at home, and the sex was definitely better than okay; even with Trysta the size that she was he couldn't complain about the sex. *The sex.* The sounds and images on the television screen faded out as other images from the past faded in: Trysta, back when she was a receptionist for Highland and Erskerberg, sitting at her desk, smiling at him as he passed by, looking luscious as a lemon cream pie; his male co-workers joking about the smoking blonde hottie at the reception desk, and Darren secretly glad for the joking, since he had his own Trysta Jablonsky fantasy going on, and any guy who was joking about her wouldn't be someone who was seriously interested in pursuing her...his own fantasy interest swelling into serious interest as she began flirting with him at a moment when he was feeling on top of the world after his promotion to vice-president, a moment when he was feeling that he deserved a little celebratory fling...funny, at first he had no intention of their little hook-up moving beyond the realm of a brief, ultimately forgettable time or two, but then the sex was amazing and time stretched on until they were undeniably involved and the next thing he knew she was carrying his child and they were both in the midst of terrible divorces. Of course once the divorces and their relationship were out in the open his co-workers no longer made bawdy jokes about Trysta, at least not in his presence; still he found himself feeling resentful about the jokes from the past and jokes he imagined still being cracked behind his back. Then he was fired and now here he was slowly cobbling his way back to financial solvency, and was the sex really worth it? Worth all the stress, the money problems, the screaming kids, the child support and visitations, the fights with Sally...truth be told, if he could turn back time and do it all over again might he not just run in the opposite direction of Trysta's beckoning smile and body back to his happy home with Sally with whom the sex, truth be told, was far from bad? Sally was, of course, a considerably smaller package than Trysta...he recalled her small round breasts, her slender waist, her cute little backside...

Goddamn, what the hell am I thinking?

"*Holy smoke,*" his father shouted, joining in the collective whoop of joy that arose from the bar and jabbing his hands towards the TV image of the running back racing towards the goal line, "there he goes, there he goes...*Yes! Yes!*"

Darren joined in the jubilant roar, shouting until his voice was loud enough to banish the rogue thought that had crept into his brain.

Chapter Twenty-Eight

The following Monday morning Jeremy Andrews, Highland and Erskerberg's CEO of Global Acquisitions, appeared to be following with rapt attention a laser-point presentation on the fluctuating status of current industry regulations. But in truth his mind was wandering, drifting round and round a huddle of vaguely bothersome thoughts. He owed nothing to Angelo Barbieri. Not a thing. Not one dime. Of this he was sure. Unquestionably sure. Jeremy fingered the edge of the laminate-covered prospectus sitting on the table before him. So how did Barbieri have the unmitigated gall to come to him asking, no, *demanding* that he re-hire someone he'd just had fired? Jeremy's glance made the round of the corporate underlings sitting around him at the long oak table in the frosted-glass paneled office in which executive meetings were held. It had been a complicated enough process getting rid of that Darren Miller character even though he was no essential player, thank God, just some young up-and-coming cog in the organizational wheel. Still, Jeremy'd had to work his way downward through Corporate to get to Miller's immediate supervisor, who was not happy to hear not only that it was required of him to fire one of his rising stars for no discernable reason, but that he was forbidden to offer Miller any reason for his dismissal other than that the position "wasn't working out." *Well, too bad*, thought Jeremy. *That's show business.* And every other type of business. The subject of the presentation turned to available funds for maintenance of foreclosed commercial entities; Jeremy made a quick note in the margin of a prospectus page, he'd have to get someone to look into that...of course if Miller had known the real reason for his firing he might well have gone tearing down to HR to file a grievance followed by a lawsuit that would have blown both Highland and Erskerberg *and* Jeremy Andrews off the map. Fortunately Miller had slithered away from Highland and Erskerberg soundlessly as the stingless moral jellyfish that he was, after which he should have and *would* have subsequently disappeared from the corporate memory of Highland and Erskerberg had he not slithered off instead to plead his grievance to Angelo Barbieri, whose tentacles were substantially longer and, Jeremy surmised, considerably sharper. (Seriously, who would have guessed in a million years that a young middle-class marshmallow like Darren Miller would be in any way connected with the likes of Barbieri? *Unbelievable!*) Now Barbieri was back on the scene to haunt Jeremy Andrews like an imprudent business deal – though his one and only venture with Barbieri had been anything but, yielding a financially satisfactory, if legally squishy, outcome for both parties. But that was in the past. Jeremy presently felt no compunction to accommodate the whim of some mafiaesque nematode. In fact the fact that this Darren Miller was somehow associated with Barbieri gave Jeremy an inner surge of moral justification for having disposed of him in the first place; no one connected to the likes of Angelo Barbieri had any business working for a prestigious and reputable firm like Highland and Erskerberg. And yet it was Miller's mysterious connection to Barbieri that was the thorn of the problem (what exactly *was* the connection? Were they, God forbid, somehow related?) and the obvious reason that Jeremy was compelled to once again jump through hoops over Darren Miller, this time to get him *back on* the Highland and Erskerberg payroll...because, in truth, *who honestly knew what retribution a thug like Angelo Barbieri was capable of inflicting of if his demands weren't met?* Thank God Barbieri seemed to neither know nor care about the provenance of Miller's firing, and had been satisfied with a contractor's position for Miller – the process of pushing through a contract position had been enough of an embarrassment for Jeremy Andrews, but a requirement of re-securing Miller's former vice-president's position could have pushed Jeremy himself into a perilous place; all it would have taken was some snooping corporate crusader to come along and stir up a hornet's nest of questions, the answers to which could have been professionally and personally disastrous for Jeremy...but fine, the deed was now done, Angelo Barbieri was off his back and Darren Miller was more or less back on the payroll, and what difference did it really make? Not a bit, Jeremy concluded. He glanced at his watch and decided that it was about time to adjourn this meeting and herd everyone back to work. No, not bit of difference did this whole passel of nonsense make as long as he'd never again have to hear another word about Darren Miller...or Miller's wet-nightmare of a pregnant wife.

Chapter Twenty-Eight

"Do you all understand what I've told you?" Charleston Tilley made sure he'd met eyes with each member of the small group sitting around his desk. Lupe and Ascensiòn nodded, this time without either of them glancing for help at Maria, Charleston's assistant and Spanish translator, who sat beside them. Sally and Silvio, sitting on the other side of the Guzmans, nodded as well.

"In short, Mr. and Mrs. Guzman," Charleston summarized, "by turning yourself in to Immigration and submitting to voluntary deportation you may be able to avoid the ten-year re-entry ban that will be imposed upon you should you be arrested and subsequently deported for being in this country illegally."

The Guzmans nodded again. "And for David," Lupe said, stroking the head of the baby sleeping in her lap, "tell me again please?"

Charleston nodded at Maria, who resumed translating as he spoke. "As I explained, you can get an American passport and a visa for your son so that he can legally enter Nicaragua and return to this country with you in the event of your husband obtaining permanent labor certification." Charleston addressed Ascensiòn. "You understand, Mr. Guzman, that the temporary H-2B visa will be out of the question now, as your intent to return to Nicaragua with your American child would be highly suspect, assuming you are granted voluntary deportation. The best plan of action, I believe, will be to pursue permanent labor certification for you, Mr. Guzman, along with the spousal visa for your wife." Charleston turned to Silvio. "And you are still intending to go through with the process of hiring Mr. Guzman, even though the wait is now likely to be much longer?"

"Yes, Sir," Silvio replied. "I am."

222

"As I explained, it's altogether possible that the process could take two or three years, though I will work to get it expedited as quickly as possible.

The Guzmans looked somber while Maria translated. Ascensiòn took his wife's hand and played with her fingers. Then to Charleston he said, "And you helping us with this..." he whirled his hand to indicate that he couldn't find the word.

"This process," Charleston replied, "yes, and as I've explained, I will be handling your case *pro bono,*"

"*Gratis,*" Maria translated.

"...as I am expected to do on occasion in my profession. It will ultimately be up to the Immigration judge to decide whether you may be granted voluntary departure, but I believe you have a strong case, seeing as Mr. Jablonski has taken your part and is arranging employment for you that would diminish the danger that you might again attempt to re-enter this country illegally. It may well work to your benefit that you have a close relative, your son, who is an American citizen and who can file, through me, an immigration petition on your behalf, which, if granted, will entitle you to apply for a green card. Does this make sense to everyone?" Maria finished translating the last phrase and the others in the room nodded. "So Mr. and Mrs. Guzman, you'll need to decide whether you want to take this route, and decide fairly quickly, I'd advise, as every moment you spend here without documentation is a moment you are in danger of being caught and deported."

Lupe looked at her husband with a look that pleaded for an answer to their dilemma, while Ascensiòn shook his head as though the answer were beyond his power. Baby David's eyes fluttered open and he whimpered and grabbed for his mother's breast. Lupe instinctively began to lift the hem of her blouse to nurse her baby and then stopped. "Uno momento, Caro," she cooed, rocking him while she spoke to Charleston. "We can to have a moment, Ascensiòn and me?"

"Certainly," Charleston replied, gesturing towards the door to his waiting room.

The little family stood and left Charleston Tilley's office, the young parents down-cast and frightened-looking, the baby patiently sucking his fist. The air in the office was now as heavy and solemn as in the stained-glass sanctuary of a church. Charleston sat at his desk with his head bowed as if in deep contemplation or prayer. Silvio and Sally felt that they were expected to follow Charleston's lead and so sat in silence as well, exchanging glances every few minutes. The only sound in the office was the whisper-light tapping of Maria's fingers on the keyboard of the notebook computer balanced on her knees. From the other side of the door could be heard a muffled patter of Spanish punctuated at one point by sobbing, first Lupe and then Ascensiòn and then both together. Then the door opened and the family re-entered, Ascensiòn and Lupe sad and red-eyed, baby David rosy-cheeked with contentment. The couple remained standing. Ascensiòn took a deep breath.

"We will do the voluntary departure," he said.

Charleston nodded while Sally and Silvio let out sighs of relief.

"We will go back to Leòn," Ascensiòn continued, "to wait for our visas to come back to America. Then I will work for Silvio and we raise David to be American."

"Okay," Silvio said with a smile, "so that's the plan."

"Yes, that's the plan," Ascensiòn agreed. "But is only the plan. Maybe the plan don't work. Maybe we have some trouble back in Leòn. Things aren't so good there now. Sometimes you have to pay them just to get your mail. Sometimes you pay them and you don't get your mail anyway."

"Do you have access to internet in Leòn?" Charleston asked.

"Oh, yes, lot of internet cafes."

"Then we'll make sure all communications come via email."

"Okay. But things happen anyway. Maybe Silvio can't get visas for Lupe and me. Maybe he change his mind."

"Hey, I'm not gonna change my mind," said Silvio.

"He's really not," Sally added, taking Silvio's hand, "He's a good man."

"Yes, yes," Lupe and Ascensiòn agreed together. "And Mr. Tilley, too," Lupe added.

"And I agree with you on all points," Charleston said with a smile. Maria began translating again as Charleston continued. "But Ascensiòn is perfectly right. Something *could* happen that would

224

prevent the Guzmans from returning to the United States once they left. And though, as I said, I wouldn't be taking your case if I didn't believe it was a strong one, the possibility always exists that your petition for visas could be denied for some reason or other. On the other hand, if you continue to reside here illegally it's only a matter of time until you'll be caught and deported. In which case your option of returning legally will be virtually non-existent. So any choice you make today will involve a risk. It's up to you which risk you're willing to take."

Lupe stepped forward. "We regressamos to Nicaragua. We wait for visa. We confiamos en"

"*Trust,*" Ascensiòn corrected her.

"We trust," she continued, "we trust en you, Silvio, and you, Mr. Tilley, our good friends." Then she turned to Sally. "Sally, our good, good friend. You will to, to…?"

"*Keep,* Mi Amor," Ascensiòn said, and then he turned to Sally and continued for his wife. "Sally, will you keep our son until we return to America?"

Maria gasped and Silvio's jaw dropped. Charleston appeared to have momentarily lost his composure.

"*Huh?*" asked Sally.

"Will you to keep our baby David until we return to America?" Lupe repeated.

All heads instinctively turned towards Sally, who hesitated, shrugged, and then said, "Um…okay."

The room broke into the chaos of five people speaking and gesturing at once and hovering over Sally who sat in in silence, shocked at what she'd just agreed to.

Finally Charleston raised his hands and voice. "Everyone, please, settle down, could we please…?

The talking ceased and everyone turned to Charleston. "Mrs. Miller, did we understand you to say that you"

"Yes," she cut him off, "I'll take him. "

"You'll take"

"Baby David. Until Lupe and Ascensiòn return from Nicaragua. I'll take care of him."

Charleston blinked several times, cleared his throat and then glanced at his watch. He sighed and turned to his assistant. "I'm sorry, Maria," he said wearily, "would you mind calling my wife again?"

***

Forty-five minutes later Ascensiòn and Lupe lingered at Charleston Tilley's office door with Maria, who cooed in Spanish over David. Sally and Silvio, meanwhile, walked down the hallway towards the elevator. Sally stared straight ahead while Silvio looked as if he wanted to say something. They waited by the elevator for the Guzmans in silence until Sally blurted out, "Okay, say it, just say it. I know what you're thinking, so just go ahead and"

"I'm taking back my kids."

"Right, just go and...what?"

"I'm going to sue Trysta for custody of my kids."

Sally stared at him. "Silvio...are you *serious*?"

"Are you?"

"Are we both crazy?"

Silvio chuckled weakly. "I guess so."

"Yeah," Sally sighed.

They stood in silence for a moment then Silvio said, "But I don't care, you know? Because now that I've taken over my Uncle Bud's business I'm gonna have the income to re-open the custody settlement. I've been thinking and thinking about doing it, but I wasn't ready to take the step until now. I mean until *right now*, like when I heard you say you'd take David. So I'm gonna do it, too. I'm gonna take back my kids. And I'm gonna ask Charleston Tilley to represent me, not that lawyer I had last time who didn't give rat's behind."

"Wow." Sally shook her head and then smiled and took Silvio's hands. "Go for it. Get your kids back. I'll be right beside you, cheering you on."

"I'll be counting on you to." He took her into his arms and kissed her until she eased away from him.

"What about Trysta?"

Silvio shrugged. "What about her? She can get her own lawyer."

He began kissing her again, and again she pulled back.

"I mean, how badly do you think she's going to fight you on this?"

"I don't care what she does."

"But do you think you have a chance? Of winning custody?"

"I'm sure as heck gonna fight until I do."

"Silvio...does Trysta know that you've taken over your uncle's business?"

Silvio shrugged. "I haven't told her anything. None of her business. I mean, my child support is set. And once I have the kids back I won't have to pay her a penny, so like I said, it's none of her business. I don't care about her."

"You don't?"

"Not a bit." He kissed Sally again, and it blossomed into a kiss that they never wanted to end, a kiss that they so lost themselves in that several moments passed before they noticed Lupe and Ascensiòn standing next to them, beaming with approval.

***

"You *what?*" Joanne's eyes were wide as nickels and several diners sitting near them in the fast-food place they'd chosen for lunch instinctively turned their heads towards the source of the disturbance. Joanne lowered her voice and leaned across the table towards Sally. "You *what?*"

Sally fiddled with her straw. "My life being crazy as it is these days, what's another baby on board?"

"Honey, this is not something to joke about! Seriously, what's going on? Did you give a minute's thought to how you're going to take care of, I mean how you're gonna *support* another child? Did you think for a minute before you agreed to this insane idea?"

"*Before* I agreed? No. *Since* I agreed? Yes. I've given it many minutes of thought. Many hours, in fact."

"And? And?"

Sally shrugged. "I guess I'm doing it."

Joanne shook her head. "You're doing it. You're *doing* it. My God, Girlfriend. And Charleston did not nip this scheme in the bud

227

because?"

"Well, I guess because Ascensiòn's request about knocked the wind out of his brain, too. I mean, Silvio, me, Charleston, even the poor translator, we were all like..." Sally made a face depicting wide-eyed, drop-jawed astonishment.

"No shit," Joanne chuckled humorlessly.

"But then I impulsively said okay."

"Great. Geez!" Joanne rolled her eyes. "Okay, so you said yes, and then after Charleston regained his composure...?"

"Right, he then proceeded to lecture us all about needing to think this situation through before committing. He explained what kind of process would be involved. That's all he could do, really. Short of refusing to help us on the legal end. Which he didn't do. So it's settled. Lupe and Ascensiòn are returning to Nicaragua so they can come back legally and I'm going to be David's foster mother while they're gone."

"For how long?"

"A few months to a few years. Or...I mean...you know, anything could happen."

Joanne sighed. You really want to do this?"

"Tell you the truth, Joanne, I've kind of wanted to have another baby for a while now. I mean, I sort of forgot about it after Darren and I broke up. But now...well, maybe I was meant to be a mommy to someone else's baby, I don't know. Somehow, having Silvio...it just makes me feel like, well..."

"Yeah, I know, I've heard all the songs and seen all the movies. Geez Louise."

"What I mean is, even with everything else going on in my life I actually think I can probably handle another baby."

Joanne let out a long sigh. "You know, I actually think you probably can, too. I just...I'm a little in shock, is all."

"You and me both."

"So what does your Silvio think of all this?"

"Well, his response was to blurt out to me that he's intending to sue Trysta for custody of his kids."

"*What?*"

"Yeah. Believe it or not. But hey, we're not spreading this all around the town."

"Jesus, Mary and Joe DiMaggio!" Joanne sighed again and shook her head. "You know, you and your boyfriend are gluttons for punishment. Or else you like kids a whole lot more than me."

"What do you mean?" Sally laughed. "*You've* got four kids. And you always worked. And from what you've told me things weren't always so easy for you and Ponti when you were young."

"Yeah, well I guess I'm a glutton for punishment, too." Joanne sighed. "You crazy girl. All right, fine, go ahead and count me in on team Sally Miller."

Sally reached across the table and hugged Joanne. "How come you always say the right thing?"

"Oh, come on, Sally," she replied, awkwardly wrapping an arm around Sally's shoulder for a moment then easing her away, "look at this, we're putting on a show for the lunch crowd."

"Oh sorry," Sally said, moving back to her seat. She felt her eyes welling up. "Am I gonna get fired for hugging my boss?"

"No, but your boss will sure as hell never again go out with you for fast food. Look, if Silvio goes through with this custody thing it's altogether possible that his ex is gonna drag him through hell. Especially since he's got this big income increase in the mix. Not to mention the new love of his life, namely y-o-u."

"Trysta doesn't know about his promotion or his involvement with me."

Joanne laughed. "Oh, Baby, you think the ex-wife doesn't have ways of finding out about these things? You think Josh – he's what six now?"

"Yeah, six."

"You think little six-year-old Josh who *luuuves* Silvio and has probably figured out that you do, too, doesn't share information? Even if you told him not to?"

"Well, no, I never told him *not* to talk about Silvio and me, but"

"So he does talk, believe me. And does he know about Silvio's new business?"

"Oh sure, he talks all the time about Silvio being," Sally chuckled, "*boss of all the plumbers!*"

"Then Trysta and Darren know, too. Or they will in the near

future. Trust me."

Sally thought it over for a moment. "Yeah. Yeah, I do believe you."

"And you also better believe me that Lady Trysta's wrath is gonna burn ten times hotter when she learns that one, her ex is dating her husband's ex, two, her ex is now making a boatload of money, and three, he now wants her kids back. Sounds like a perfect hell storm a-brewin'. "

Sally sighed. "Yeah, well, I expect that is pretty probable. But what the heck, Silvio's already been through hell once and he's ready to go another round to get his kids back. Let's face it, not having his kids is hell for him anyway. I know it would be hell for me. I'm telling you, if I didn't have Josh I'd be a basket case. Sometimes I wonder how Darren can live without him."

"Well, sad to say, sometimes men – not all men, and your guy is one of the honorable exceptions – but an awful lot of guys are ruled more by their dicks than anything else. Even their children. If their dicks are happy, they're happy."

"If that's the case then Darren is definitely happy. Beyond happy. He's living in fucking Nirvana."

Chapter Twenty-Nine

"Oh, come on, Trysta, cut it out, nobody died!"

"Stop yelling at me," Trysta sobbed.

"I'm not ye-"

"Yes you are! Can't you stop pacing?"

"I'm not pacing!" Darren stopped pacing and leaned against the dresser across from their bed, his arms crossed.

"All you ever do anymore is pace the bedroom floor and yell at me!"

"Yeah, well all *you* do anymore is sit on the goddamn bed and cry!" *Oh, Jesus,* Darren thought, *did I really just say that to my wife?*

Trysta's crying exploded into a gusher of tears propelled by great sobs that took her breath away as she tried to get out the words. "You...you...*uhn, uhn,* cur-..*uhn, uhn,* -sing...*uhn, uhn,* at...m-m-m-me...*uhn, uhn...*" She fell back onto the bed and threw one hand across her face, the other across her stomach. "*Oooh...*" she moaned.

"Aw Trys..." Darren regretted snapping at his pregnant wife, but less because he felt he'd wronged her than because of the effort it would now take to get her to stop crying. He had to get Josh back to Sally and he wanted to leave soon before the rush-hour traffic turned the Expressway into a parking lot. He moved to the bed and sat down next to her. "I'm sorry...please..." Darren reached for his wife, his hand hovering above her heaving, trembling form until it landed on the most accessible spot, the vast mound of her middle, which, as if channeling her mood, gave him a good substantial kick.

"Hey," Darren chuckled in spite of himself, "did you feel that?"

Trysta smiled briefly and then frowned, brushed his hand off her stomach and turned away from him.

"Aw, come on Honey..." He continued murmuring variations on

the theme of apology while Trysta whimpered and sniffled but refused his efforts at conciliation. He sighed and looked around the room as if seeking an answer in the expensive furniture and upscale décor, which he was paying for by the month. He looked back down at his disconsolate wife. And yet he was right, dammit! All Trysta ever *did* seem to do anymore was sit on the bed and cry! Jesus, was Sally this volatile when she was pregnant with Josh? Darren couldn't remember. Hell, she probably was, considering what a shrew she'd been during the divorce process. Geez, didn't these women ever run out of tears?

Darren suddenly felt weary. It occurred to him that he'd been feeling weary for some time now. For weeks, it seemed. Since his return from the honeymoon, to be exact. Of course most of it had been the stress of starting a new business, a new marriage, a new divorce, a new home (a fucking *expensive* new home in a neighborhood that he was taking to less and less by the day), a new family situation, a fucking *chaotic* family situation between trying to keep Trysta's three little tornadoes under control and trying to fit his own son into the mix. And yet somehow Josh seemed to be the most resilient of them all these days, despite his mother's emotional inner mercury. And then there was Silvio, that fucking useless loser Silvio, who was the reason he and his wife were up here in the bedroom again snapping at each other's throats. Bad enough Silvio didn't take more responsibility for his kids instead of leaving them practically 24/7 for their seven (or eight, or however many) months pregnant mother and Darren to sort out. But now, fucking Silvio, by some stroke of cosmic irony, had been handed on a silver platter his very own business, signed, sealed, and delivered by his uncle. Shit, must be damn sweet to have somebody else do all the work for you!

As if channeling his thoughts, Trysta moaned, "It's just so unfair!"

"Aw, Baby, what do we care anyway? And, look, how do we *really* know what's going on? I mean, just because Josh talks about Silvio's new business, and, and how Silvio's gonna be rich, maybe he's just, you know, fantasizing, or something. After all he's only six years old, you know how kids are."

"Silvio will be making all that money!"

"Hey, *I'm* making good money now, I mean, with those new

contracts I've got, and"

"And who do you think he'll be spending it on?" She practically spat out the words.

Sally, he muttered to himself.

"Sally!"

"Now come on, we don't know that he's...*involved* with Sally."

"No? That's all we hear from Josh! It's 'Silvio this,' and 'Silvio that!'"

"Yeah, well, apparently they're all taking Spanish lessons, or something, from Sally's neighbors. Mexicans. Or something."

"That's what *she* tells you! And you believe her?"

"Look, *she* doesn't tell me anything, it's Josh who"

"You *really* believe Silvio goes over there for, for, *Spanish lessons?* Why would anybody be taking *Spanish lessons?*"

"I don't know, so she can get ahead at work. So he can get the customers. Hell, maybe *I* should be over there with them learning the damn language, I mean, half of Philadelphia can't even speak English anymore!"

"They're sleeping together!"

"They damn well better *not* be!" Darren sprung up from the bed while Trysta plunged into another round of wailing. Darren began pacing again. Why did he give a duck's dick who either of those two were sleeping with? And yet in truth, just the thought of Silvio sharing the same air space with Sally was enough to make him grit his teeth. He stopped and leaned his arm, bent elbow, against the wall. But *why? Why should I care?* He turned back to his wife. "Trysta," he said calmly, "stop crying. Now. Listen to me."

The calmness in his voice took her off guard. She stopped crying and gave him her attention. "What?" she sniffed.

"From now on you and I are going to forget about whatever it is Sally and Silvio are up to. We're not gonna give 'em the satisfaction. We're gonna keep it strictly business with those two, okay?"

"Okay," she replied in a small voice.

"We're not gonna notice them, we're not gonna fight about them, and we are not gonna care about them, okay?"

"Okay."

"Right. I mean, what reason could we possibly have to care about them?"

"Josh," Trysta answered.

"What?"

"Sally is exposing your son, that poor little child, to those people, those Mexicans. We don't even know who they are, they could be illegals, they could be dangerous!"

"Aw, Trysta, I'm sure they're not dangerous, Sally would never"

"There you go again, putting Sally over your son's safety!"

"I wasn't putting Sally"

"You have *got* to find out who these Mexicans are! You should call Immigration!"

"I'm *not* gonna call Immigration! Look, this is what I'm talking about, could we just stop all this"

"Well then you at least have got to get Josh out of there!"

"No! We've already been through this! I'm *not* gonna fight Sally for custody!"

"And we've got to find out how much money Silvio is making!"

"We do not *care* how much money Silvio is making! And speaking of Josh, I've got to get him back home, so if we could just agree to"

"We've *got* to get Josh living with us over here!"

"No!"

"*What?* You don't even care about your *own* son?"

"Of course I care about my son!"

"You do? You *do?*"

"Yes, I *do!*"

"Huh, then give me *one* good reason why you'd leave him with your horrible, irresponsible...*slutty* ex-wife instead of getting him here to live with us!"

"Well, for one thing, he doesn't *want* to live here with us!"

"*What are you saying?*" He *loves* being here! He loves my children, he loves our home, he loves *me!*"

"*Daddy! Daddy!*" The voice was muffled from the other side of the bedroom door.

"Josh!" Darren and Trysta both hurried over to the bedroom door. Darren opened it to his son who stood on the other side, sobbing. Joshua wrapped his arms around his father and buried his head in his father's waist.

"Hey, Champ, what's wrong?"

"Aw, what's wrong, my Sweetie?" asked Trysta, stroking the child's head.

"Stop, Daddy, *stop!*"

"Stop what?" Darren eased Josh away from him and looked into his face. "Stop what, Buddy?"

"Fighting."

Trysta giggled. "Oh, Honey, Daddy and Mommy Trysta weren't *fighting*. We were just talking about *you*, and how much you like being here with Daddy, and me, and Zach...you like it here with Zach, right?" Joshua nodded but continued to pull in sob-wracked breaths. Trysta reached for a tissue from the night stand next to her bed and wiped his nose and cheeks. "There, now. You're all better and everything's just fine, okay?" Josh nodded again. Trysta kissed his forehead then said, "Honey, how would you like to stay and live here with us?"

Josh let out a wail and pulled towards his father. "Daddy," he cried, "Take me home *now!* I want *Mommy!* There's too much fighting here!

"Okay, okay, come on, Champ," Darren said, shooting Trysta an annoyed look, "It's time to go. Say good-bye to Trys...Mommy Trysta."

"Good-bye," Josh sniffled.

Trysta took Joshua's face in her hands and kissed him on both cheeks and then ran her hands down his shoulders. "Honey, I'll sure miss you. Will you miss me?"

Josh looked up at his father then back at Trysta. He nodded uncertainly.

"And Zach. I bet you'll miss Zach, huh?"

"Trysta, please..." Darren said.

"Zach sure likes you," she continued. "Wouldn't it be just wonderful if you and Zach could play every day?"

"Yes," said Josh.

"Trysta..." Darren tried to stay calm, though his voice was tinged with impatience, "we have to go. *Now*."

"Well," Trysta drove on, ignoring Darren, "Maybe we could make that happen, okay?"

Josh's face broke into a smile. "Okay."

"Oh, come on, Trysta…"

"Daddy," Josh said happily, "Can Josh really come over and play *every day?*"

"No, Champ."

"But Mommy Trysta said so!"

Darren's annoyance had crossed over into anger and he shot Trysta a look over Josh's head. "She meant…something else."

"Oh." Josh pulled away from Trysta and took his father's hand.

"How's Silvio?" Trysta asked. "Does he still come over to your house?"

At the mention of Silvio's name Josh once again brightened, while Darren rolled his eyes and shook his head in in exasperation.

"Silvio can't come for Spanish as much because now he, um, exherited his Uncle Bud's business and he's in charge of all the plumbers, but he can come sometimes."

"Oh," Trysta replied sweetly. "Is he, um… making lots of money now?"

"Yes. He's the richest plumber in Philadelphia."

Both Darren and Trysta registered wide-eyed surprise at this revelation.

"Hey, Champ," Darren chuckled uneasily, "Did *Silvio* tell you that?"

"Well, he told me he's the richest plumber in the world, but I think he just meant he's the richest plumber in Philadelphia."

"Oh," Trysta and Darren replied together.

"Wellll," Trysta gushed, "you be sure and tell us if Silvio comes over to see your Mom, okay?"

"Daddy, can I go and say good-bye to Zach?"

"Sure, Buddy," Darren replied, "I'll be right down."

As soon as the quick patter of Josh's feet could be heard on the stairs Darren slammed the bedroom door. "What the hell!" he shouted and then, glancing at the door, immediately softened his voice, "what the hell are you thinking setting up that poor little guy like that?"

"Oh, now, Sweetheart, I was just trying to find out what's going on. I mean," she wrapped her arms around Darren's neck, "we both

236

want to know what's going on, don't we? For Josh's sake?"

"We have *got* to leave Josh out of all this, this..." he reached up and removed Trysta's arms from around his neck. "I've gotta go."

"Oh, no, *no,*" Trysta pled sweetly, wrapping her arms back around her husband and pulling his body close to hers. "Darren, darling, please, *please* don't push me away!"

"I'm not pushing you away, I just have to get Josh back to Sally!"

She ran her hands down his back until they settled over his buttocks. *"Promise* me, *promise* me, you'll try to get Josh back."

"Aw, no, no, *no!* How many times do I have to *tell* you..." She began squeezing ever so lightly and he instinctively put his arms around her waist.

"Come," she whispered into his ear, leading him to the bed.

"I *can't,*" he protested, "I've gotta get Josh...Trysta, *please...*"

But faster than he could protest, faster than seemed possible, Trysta had stripped and spread herself out on the bed in the most provocative position imaginable.

"Aw, Baby, I...I..." *I'm not aroused!*

It was true. The effect of his voluptuous wife unfurled naked before him was...*nothing!*

"Daddy!" came his son's voice from behind the door, "Daddy, hurry up, take me home, the girls are starting to fight again!"

"I gotta go, Trysta, I *can't* right now!" And it was true. He actually *couldn't* right now. Couldn't if his life depended on it. And thank God Josh was there to give him an excuse. "Cover up, I gotta open the door and Josh is right outside."

"Josh, Sweetie," Trysta called, "you wait downstairs, Daddy will be right there!" She patted the bed next to her. "Now *you,*" she said breathily to Darren, "come right *here.*"

"I can't! I *can't!*" Darren turned hurried out of the bedroom before Trysta could leap from the bed and reach for him.

"Promise me! She called after him, the words, ringing in his ears as he hurried away from her, "Promise me! *Promise me!*"

***

237

The Schuylkill Expressway was no longer a glorified traffic jam. It had morphed into a drive-in movie that played on a split screen in Darren's mind the simultaneous double feature of "Trysta: Hot, Delicious And Dying To Be Ravished" and "Why Am I Not Turned On?"

The cars idling on all four sides of him were somewhere off in the distance; even his son sitting next to him in the passenger seat, looking out the window and humming some little computer game ditty, hovered on the edge of his awareness as he flipped through scene after scene of his wife at her sexiest, as well as scenes of great sex from the past, present, and future fantasies yet to be fulfilled. He focused on arousing himself, *willed* his penis to rise, but as soon as he felt the barest tingle there was the ubiquitous sound track loop of Trysta calling out *Promise me* across every image, *Promise me, Promise me, Promise me,* moaning it, demanding it, crying it, shrieking it, destroying his desire at the root. He tried mentally blocking out the sound of Trysta's wheedling voice, putting the volume on mute, zooming in on her fabulous anatomy, but it was no use, she continued to hold for him the all the appeal of a blubbery beached whale. And this was bad. If his new wife suddenly held no sex appeal for him this was *very* bad. But even that scenario didn't terrify him as much as another, much worse possibility: that the problem wasn't Trysta; that the problem was himself. What if he could no longer, well, *function*? What if the combination of stress, financial worries, family drama and 24/7 work hours had exacted a terrible physical toll? *What if his junk had turned to junk?*

Darren's forehead broke out into a light sweat. He was being stupid, of course, totally over-reacting. What guy didn't experience the same thing once in a while? After all, he and Trysta had just had a big fight, wasn't that enough to put any guy out of the mood? And then again, what about the fact that Trysta was, what, eight months pregnant now? What guy was even *expected* to find his wife attractive at this stage? Well, no guy, of course! In fact, Darren was probably 'way ahead of the curve in that department, having continued to sleep with his wife this far along in the game. And then hadn't the baby just kicked him, wasn't she kicking him all the time these days? Hell, they probably shouldn't even be *having* sex anymore, Trysta's time being so close. And his lack of desire, well that was probably just nature's way of telling him to back the heck off! Sure, it all had to do with the baby. Soon as the baby arrived and Trysta was up to it they'd be back at it again like rabbits! But until then he was off the hook. Darren heaved a sigh of relief.

Then a moment later it hit him: *I'm relieved? I'm relieved that I don't have to have sex?* Wait, what about when Sally was pregnant? He scoured his brain to try and remember if they'd held off towards the end...and what he came up with the memory of Sally trying to scoot away from him in bed, terrified that if she went into labor afterwards then somebody, doctor, nurse, *cleaning lady*, for God's sake, *somebody* would somehow figure out that she'd just had sex! Like she could've gotten that way *without* having sex! Darren half-smiled. *Sally.* The little Jewish-Catholic Puritan back then. *But they'd had sex!*

"Daddy!"

He'd always been able to get it up, right until the end!

"Daddy!"

What had happened to him? Could it be, was it within the realm of possibility that he'd become...

"DADDY!"

"Huh?" Darren was startled back to the here and now as Josh reached across the seat and grabbed at his sleeve. "What? What is it, Champ?"

"Daddy, I told you and *told* you, they're *beeping!*"

The car in front had left them far behind and Darren was now fully aware of the angry orchestra of horns that were directing their frustration in his direction. He stepped on the gas and unconsciously sank lower into his seat.

"Daddy," Josh continued, still pulling at Darren's sleeve, "Can Zach please, please, *please* come over to my house?"

"Oh...well," Darren replied, not completely able to put aside the disturbing possibility he'd just latched onto, "I don't know...I guess you have to ask Zach first."

"I already *did* ask Zach! He said he'd bring his Wii and *all* his games that I like."

"Okay. But then we have to ask Mommy."

"I asked Mommy *such* long time ago! She said it's okay with her if it's okay with you."

"Oh, well, sure…it's okay with me…but, you know, Zach's dad has to agree, and I don't know if Silvio"

"He already said okay, too!"

"Oh yeah?" Darren couldn't resist. "So, uh, when did Silvio say it was okay, Champ?"

"When I *asked* him! Daddy, will you *please, please* bring Zach over next time so he can see my house?"

"Um, you know, maybe we should run it by Mommy Trysta first…" *Shit, she'll never agree to it…*

"No! I don't want to ask *her!*"

"Hey, hey, is that any way to talk about your Mommy Trysta?" *She'll go through the roof!*

Josh turned away and looked out the window, his arm resting against the pane. There flashed through Darren's mind a sudden vision of himself as a child, alone, looking out a window, a vague, wispy memory of longing for what he couldn't have. He reached over and patted his son's shoulder.

"Okay, well, I guess Zach can come over, then." *Trysta will never agree to it…*

"Yay!" Josh reached over and hugged his father's arm. "Thank you, Daddy!"

"You're welcome, Champ." *She'll go totally ballistic!*

Josh bounced happily in his seat for a few moments then said to his father in a more serious tone, "But, Daddy, let's not tell Mommy Trysta, okay?"

"No? Why not?" *Like I don't know damn well why not!*

"Because she'll just say, 'Oh, no, you can't do that, I'm eight months pregnant and I have three children and I'm gonna have a baby!'"

"Okay, okay." Darren chuckled in spite of himself. *Even a six-year-old has it figured out!*

"Daddy, is Mommy Trysta really gonna have another girl?"

"'Fraid so, Champ."

"But Zach and me want a boy, so we can have another brother."

"Well, it's gonna have to be a girl this time."

"What's her name gonna be?"

"Her name? Her *name*?" *Jesus. What* were *they gonna name her? Had they even talked about names? In fact, other than at the doctor's office, when had they ever talked about the baby at all? That wasn't right, they'd have to sit down and talk about the baby. At least pick out a name, for God's sake. They knew it was a girl. Geez, another girl in the house! What if this one turned out to be little screamer like Trysta's other two? Darren didn't think he could take that. But shouldn't he and Trysta at least be sitting down and talking about the baby? Didn't he and Sally talk about Josh all the time before he was born? Though he couldn't actually remember them ever setting aside a time to deliberately talk about their baby…it just sort of happened, in normal conversation. Oh sure, he and Sally were in shock at first, a little scared…no, really scared at first. But they'd just sort of pushed through their fear of parenthood and, well, it all worked out. Until it fell apart. Maybe people only talked about their first child. God knows, with Trysta's three to contend with and his own son as well, not to mention all the time and stress running his own business took…still, they should talk about the new baby sometime.* Darren expanded that thought, tried to envision himself and Trysta sitting and talking, maybe on the living room sofa, maybe at the kitchen table…and still all he could see in his mind's eye and hear in his mind's ear was Trysta on the bed, legs spread, crying, *Promise me, Promise me, Promise me!* A sickly feeling crept over him…not only did he not feel like sleeping with his wife…*he couldn't stand the thought of talking to her!*

Chapter Thirty

Sally entered her apartment, purse slung over her shoulder, keys in one hand, mail in the other. Still perusing the mail, she dropped her keys into her purse and slid open the accordion-style door to the small closet by the entrance. She hung up her purse, but as she slid off her coat her line of vision travelled to the other end of the room to her dinette table on which sat a vase holding a large, cheerful bouquet of hyacinths, carnations, and alstroemeria. She did a wide-eyed double-take then hurried over to the table, dropping her coat and mail on the couch on her way.

"Where in the heck did you come from?" she laughed, but she already knew. She replayed the moment this morning when she'd slipped Silvio her house key, a little unsure about what kind of ceremony should be involved, what words she should use, should she be matter of fact about it or treat it as a milestone in their relationship? Which, of course, it was; after all, giving a guy your key was sending a message: Key to my house? Key to my heart? Key to my bed? To my trust? To my baggage? To my expectations? To yours? What if a guy wasn't ready? Or just didn't want the key to all that stuff? Finally she'd just laid the key down next to his breakfast plate. "Here," she'd said.

"What's this?" he'd asked, a big smile lighting up his face so that she knew that he knew what it was the key to and that he was delighted to have it, whatever the implications.

"It's to the house," she'd answered, "you know, in case…"

"Sure," he'd replied then added, "Thanks."

Then they'd left it at that, he adding her key to his ring and joking, "You won't regret this."

"I already don't," she'd replied and then, even though they'd both

242

needed to get to work, the moment was just so right that a good-bye kiss led to a wrap-around hug that they could hardly break until they fell onto Sally's bed to savor each other's bodies one more time.

Sally smiled again at the memory as she read the card attached to the flowers. "Love to give these, but not as much as I love you." She read and re-read the message. *I love you… I love you…*the words that Silvio had never yet spoken, but had chosen to convey in the shy, sweet voice of a card nestled in flowers. Flowers…the language of love…or was something else the language of love? Did Silvio really mean love, like *love*-love? Or was he just tossing the words off lightly, as in "love ya, Babe." "Who loves 'ya?" "Happy birthday, Love, Whoever." Only he'd neither minced nor embellished the words. He'd chosen them straight up: *I love you.* So maybe he actually meant…*I love you.* Which then begged the question…*Did she love him back?* She hadn't yet even thought about it, but here she was, her heart pounding, her stomach doing flips, her breathing fast, a smile on her face that she couldn't undo even if she wanted to, and the desire to be with him right now and for as far down the road as she could possibly conceive… *I'm in love,* she thought and for the second time in her life all those silly songs suddenly seemed perfectly reasonable, for she did, in fact, feel like singing, like dancing, but more than anything else she felt like hearing Silvio's voice, hearing him *tell* her that he loved her and then telling him that she loved him, too.

She dialed his cell number, and though she hadn't counted on leaving it in a message, after the beep she blurted it out, "I love, you, too, Silvio! I love you! And I love the flowers! And I want to hear your voice right now, so call me, call me, *call* me!"

At that moment the door opened and Joshua came bounding in, dropping his backpack by the entrance way. "Mommy," he cried breathlessly, "Daddy says Zach can come over to *my* house next time!" He ran to his mother's arms and she lifted him up, holding him close and kissing him over and over. She noticed Darren standing in the doorway but for the moment she ignored him. "Oh, I'm so glad to see you," she said to her son, "but, *ooof,*" she set him down again, "you're getting heavy!"

"When can Zach come over?" Josh asked. "Daddy said it's okay! And *no girls!*"

"Great, no girls," Sally laughed. She nodded towards Darren, who still stood smiling in the doorway. "Let me run it by your dad again. Go ahead and hang up your stuff."

Joshua picked up his backpack then dashed off to his room.

"They ought to be able to bottle that," Darren chuckled.

"Yeah, six-year-old liquid energy."

She looks good. That was Darren's first impression as he stepped inside the house. Eyes sparkling above her smile, her black hair done up with a simple clip. She always did look pretty with her hair up. She was wearing a sea-green top that accentuated her slender frame and fitted black pants that, he noticed, nicely complimented her butt. She walked over to the couch and when she bent over to pick up her coat and her mail he was reminded of what a tight little ass she had, how he'd used to cup it in both hands while kissing her face, her neck, her breasts. And then, with no effort at all on his part, his erection returned. *He wasn't impotent after all!*

"Well, you're looking pretty happy," Sally said as dropped the mail on the table, on which sat a vase of flowers.

Weren't there flowers on that table a couple of weeks ago? "Nice flowers," he commented, fishing for a clue.

"Yep," was all she offered as she brushed by him to hang up her coat. "So it's okay with you and Trysta's not gonna throw a hissy if Zach comes over here?" She stood across from him, almost close enough for him to touch.

And in fact he felt like reaching out and touching her. "Should be fine. I'll just have to run it by Trysta."

"Maybe it would be better if Silvio dropped him over here on a weekend when it's his turn to have the kids. To avoid controversy."

"Yeah, okay, maybe that would be better." *Was Silvio in the habit of coming over here on weekends?*

"Did Josh have a good visit?"

"Oh yeah. He had a great time. He loves being over there."

Sally put a hand on her hip, rolled her eyes and laughed. "Yeah. All right."

"What I meant was"

She waved her hand. "It's all right. I know what you meant. At least he's got a friend in Zach. A big brother, I guess. I'm glad for that,

I really am."

"Yeah, that's what I meant."

"Okay, well, I guess we'll touch base, then. About Zach." Her body language was directing him towards the door but he didn't move.

"Right. About Zach."

"Right. I think the door's still unlocked, so…"

"You really ought to keep it locked."

Sally chuckled. "Yeah, that's what Si…I mean, I'm working on it." Sally walked around Darren and opened the door. "See you."

But instead of leaving Darren took a step closer to Sally. "I'm glad you're so happy these days."

"Yep. I'm glad you're so happy, too." Sally leaned against the open door. She looked so cute. So inviting. *Was she inviting him?* His penis stiffened once more. Maybe she was lonely. Maybe she'd like him to stay a while. They could close the bedroom door. Do it quietly. What difference would one friendly little poke make? After all, they were married for, what, seven years? How many hundreds of times had they already done it? What difference would one more time make?

"I'm glad you and I are, you know getting along." He moved closer.

"Okay. I guess that's good, too." *What was he up to?* Sally wondered. She stepped away from him and cocked her head towards the open door. "Well, see ya."

"Sal?" He stepped towards her. Now he was in her personal space.

"Yeah?" She took a step back.

"Sometimes I miss the old days. I mean, how it was when we got along."

"Oh, Jesus, let's not get into that."

"Into…what?"

She looked into his eyes. And he was looking into hers. That old look. The way he used to look at her. A warm feeling rose up inside her. That old feeling. The feeling that a few weeks ago would have made her fall back into his arms. But not now. *Please, not now!*

She took another step back and said, "Into, you know, how it used to be."

He stepped closer to her and said, "Used to be good sometimes, huh?" He put his hands on her shoulders. A friendly touch, really, but it made her heart flutter.

"Well, yeah..." *Stop this! Stop it right now! Pull away, push him out, slam the door shut!*

But now his arms were around her, and really, what was the harm in a friendly good-bye hug? After all, they were married for seven years, right?

But the hug advanced to a kiss, *stop it!* but it was really all right, *no it wasn't!* it was just a good-bye kiss, *no, it wasn't!* the good-bye kiss they'd never really had, and it felt so nice and so normal that the little warning voice melted away in the heat of the moment and they became so lost in each other's arms and lips that it was a long moment before they became aware that Silvio had just stepped in through Sally's open door.

Silvio's face was dark and his eyes were so narrowed that it was impossible to tell whether the emotion behind them was anger, disbelief, grief, or some shocked, confused mix. "If you're gonna leave your door wide open why do you bother to give somebody your key!" He threw her key to the floor then hurried out the door and down the stairs while Sally stood frozen, wide-eyed, her hands covering her mouth.

"*Silvio!*" She finally cried, running out of the house after him, but by the time she reached the bottom of the stairs he was in his truck, ignoring her cries, pulling away in his van as she ran and called after him until he was out of sight.

"No!" she cried breathlessly, "Oh *no!*"

"He's your lover." Darren was standing behind her.

Sally whirled around to face him. "What? What do *you* care? What the *hell* do *you* care?"

"Not just some guy who was fixing your furnace."

Sally pushed him aside and ran back to the stairway to her apartment. Darren ran after her and blocked her way at the bottom of the stairs. He put a hand on her arm. "Look, Sally, I'm..."

Sally pushed him away. "What did you come into my house for?" she sobbed, "why did you *do* that? What do you *want* from me? What in this cold, stinking world could you possibly want that you don't already have? Dream wife? Dream house? Dream vacations in Puerta...fucking...*Mexico?*"

"I really didn't mean"

"A goddamn dream life is what you have, Darren! And what have *I* got? Two dollars in the bank, two sorry bucks worth of self-respect, a plumber who, who *used* to care about me! God damn you, Darren, You want to take everything away from me! *Everything!*"

Sally pushed him hard then ran up the stairs, slamming the door behind her.

Darren stood for a moment looking up the stairs at the closed door. "You're wrong, Sally, he said, softly. "I'm not going to take everything away from you. I'm not, okay?" Then he walked to his car and unlocked the door. He opened the door but before he got inside he turned back one more time towards Sally's apartment. "I'm sorry," he said to the air. "For a lot of things."

***

Silvio's heart felt like a rock in his chest, beating so hard and heavy that it must surely break through his ribs. That same old feeling had returned and was squeezing the air out of his lungs, leaving him panting for breath. He finally pulled over for fear that he'd pass out. He closed his eyes and pulled in a few gulps of air, trying to calm himself down. *Get a grip*, he told himself, *get a grip!* After a minute his breathing slowed to normal. But was it truly possible? Had he really just seen...*that?* He tried to shake the image from his brain, replace it with one more innocent, find some room to have misinterpreted what he'd seen. But there *was* no mistaking what he'd seen. And could there be any mistaking what was going on between Sally and Darren? No, the way they were holding each other, kissing each other, they were one stop from the bedroom. It was pretty clear what was going on between Sally and Darren. But then what the *hell* had been going on between Sally and *himself?* Hadn't Sally left him a message not fifteen minutes earlier telling him that she *loved* him? But how could you love one man while you're throwing yourself into the arms of another? Silvio's eyes brimmed over and large teardrops rolled down

247

his face and plopped onto his shirt. How could Sally forget about him just like that? Had he been nothing more than a distraction for her that she could so easily toss him aside the minute Darren re-appeared on the scene? The same way Trysta had tossed him aside after three kids and almost twelve years of marriage. Must have been much easier for Sally, they'd only been together, what, a few weeks? But she said she *loved* him! He felt so confused. His cell phone was ringing. It was Sally. Huh, he had to laugh, was she *kidding?* His thumb hovered over the *answer* button, but he willed himself not to press it. The phone rang itself out then a cheery little arpeggio indicated that she'd left a message. In spite of himself he pressed *ok* and listened to "Silvio, please let me explain" then he erased the rest. *Explain?* She thought she could *explain?* What the hell did she think she was gonna *explain?* He *saw* what was going on! Did she think he was a *complete* schmuck? Huh, probably. Sure, why not? Considering how he'd been had by Trysta and now by herself. Silvio sighed in sorrow and shook his head. Were all women unfaithful by nature? No, that couldn't be…what about his mother? And his grandmother? And his aunts? No, he was sure *they* weren't like that…or were they? He sure never suspected Trysta, or Sally until he'd caught her red-handed…a new round of sobbing welled up and he sat in his truck and gave in to it until his phone went off again and he almost didn't check it but then he did and saw that it was Ida which meant that it was work and work he couldn't ignore, but he also couldn't answer with his voice all fogged up from crying, so he'd better just cut out the crying and pull himself together and get back to work. Good Lord, when had he become such a damn crybaby? Now that he thought about it, he couldn't remember crying a tear ever until the day that he learned that Trysta was leaving him and taking his kids with her, and since then crying seemed to be all he did. Well, he wasn't going to do it anymore. He was through crying over women gone bad. Through with women altogether. From now on he'd devote himself to his children. And he'd get them back, away from those two self-centered, cheating children Darren and Trysta, barely fit to be parents at all. His children would be far better off with him. But then…somewhere towards the back of his mind hadn't there lurked the idea that maybe he'd be raising his kids with Sally in the picture? And Sally raising hers with him? Hadn't the thought that they might be sharing the challenges – and joys – of a blended family, hadn't that thought strengthened and sustained his resolve to enter into another round of custody battling? And what about the Guzmans and his plan to hire Ascensiòn, to help him get his work visa? Another plan that was wrapped around his relationship with Sally, another of their shared life projects. His resolve not to cry anymore melted and there he was, tears again streaming down his face. No matter. He'd fight it. He'd be strong and fight the tears of weakness the same way he'd fight everybody and everything that he needed to. He'd do right by his kids and by his promise to the Guzmans. On his own. Still…. he didn't understand about Sally. He didn't understand at all.

Chapter Thirty-One

Joanne passed by Sally's desk, stopped and then backed up until she was facing Sally. Sally appeared to be intensely riveted to the document on her computer screen. "Hi," Sally mumbled without looking up from the screen.

"Hi," Joanne returned. She looked into Sally's face and squinted and then picked up the box of tissues sitting next to the keyboard. "Please tell me you're down with a sinus infection."

"That's it," Sally sniffled, taping away at her keyboard while trying to keep her head low.

"Sounds like a real killer."

"Uh-huh," Sally replied, her eyes brimming over. She reached for a Kleenex and wiped her eyes then blew her nose.

Joanne sighed. "*Oh,* shit, I'm afraid to ask,"

Sally continued tapping away and sniffling.

"Okay, you want to talk about your killer sinus infection?"

"No. Yeah, okay."

"What are you doing for lunch?"

"Packed."

"All right, well…" Joanne glanced at her watch. "It's 11:15. I have some unmitigated bullshit over in Receivables that I need to square away first, but how about you finish up your entries and meet me in, say, an hour?"

"Vending room?"

"Yeah. No. Whatever you've got doesn't need to be spread around here. How about we meet and eat in my office? "

"Okay, thanks."

"You can thank me by hiking next door to the Starbucks before you come and picking us up a couple of ventis, my treat. You could use the fresh air and I could use anything black. No, give it a splash of skim, okay?"

"You're an angel, Joanne."

"Yeah. Tell that to the poor *stugatz* in Receivables whose ass I'm about to ream."

***

An hour and fifteen minutes later Sally sat in Joanne's office, her heart poured out, her eyes cried out, her coffee and sandwich untouched. Joanne shook her head. "Sally, Sally, Sally."

Sally sat for a moment with her head down like a child preparing for a scolding and then she looked up at Joanne. "Aren't you going to tell me what a dumb, stupid, irresponsible...*shit* I am?"

"Doesn't sound like I need to, Girlfriend."

"What's wrong with me, Joanne? Can't I hold onto *anything* in life? Do I have to lose every good thing that comes my way?"

Joanne leaned in and put her hand on Sally's. "Listen, Honey, I'm not trying to be harsh. But you've got to back off from the self-pity. It's gonna do you no good."

"Fine," Sally snapped. "What am I *supposed* to do?"

Joanne pulled back her hand. "Not snap at me, for starters."

"Sorry," Sally muttered. "It's just I feel so bad. Like I could d"

"Don't say it, don't even *say* it!" Joanne made the sign of the cross. "Eat your lunch."

"I can't."

"*Eat.* I still expect an afternoon's work out of you. And drink that coffee, it cost me four-fifty."

Sally obediently sipped her coffee and began eating her sandwich.

"So, do you want him back?"

"Who, Silvio?"

"Silvio, Darren..."

"Darren? Oh, God, no!"

"Good. 'Cause any way you slice him, the guy's a bastard."

"I don't know, Joanne. I mean, maybe I somehow *encouraged* him, *invited* him, I don't know. And then when he kissed me I didn't exactly push him away...and screw me, I *could've.*"

"Would've, should've, sure. Only instead of pulling away from the trap you dove into it head first. But hells bells, girl, would you *please* quit giving that toadstool you were married to a pass on every piece of shitty behavior he pulls? Would you please?"

"I just thought we were getting along is all. And the worst thing is, I *have* to get along with Darren. I *have to.* For Josh's sake. But after this how can I?"

"Yes, you're right, bastard though he is you do have to get along with him. And how you're gonna do that is just something you'll have to figure out. Grit your teeth and suck in your gut. And Jesus, don't you ever, ever, *ever* again"

"Oh, believe me, "Sally cut her off, "I wouldn't touch Darren Miller again with a ten-foot pole. Unless it was to ram it up his"

"All right, that's more like it."

"I don't know, Joanne, I can't decide who I hate more, Darren or myself."

"Should definitely be Darren. Who, by the way, and I'm just asking…did you pick up the slightest vibe from him that he might be, you know, wanting *you* back?"

Sally chuckled humorlessly. "Yeah, right. I don't believe for a minute he wants me back. He was just Darren being Darren. Probably just another fleeting fantasy for him. Or maybe a quick trip down memory lane."

"Or maybe things aren't quite as peachy with Trysta as they were back when she was still a peach hanging on the vine, so to speak."

"I don't know. I don't care. I wouldn't take him back if he came crawling to me on his knees with a basket of hundred dollar bills between his teeth." Sally took a large swig of her coffee and tore off a bite of her sandwich."

"Okay, so something good has come out of this." Joanne hesitated a moment. "Silvio, on the other hand?"

"Well," Sally finished chewing, swallowed, and then wiped her sleeve across the tears that were again brimming over her eyes. "I believe it's over with Silvio, too."

"You sure? Come on, I mean, what actually *happened?* You *kissed* a guy, right? For one *moment.*"

"Darren isn't just some guy. He's the guy who wrecked Silvio's life."

"Not to mention yours. Aw, Hon," Joanne sighed. "Okay, come on." She stood up and placed her hands gently on Sally's shoulders then let go suddenly. "Aw, Jesus!" she cried, "*now* what the hell are you gonna do about those little Nicaraguans of yours? Have you thought of *that?*"

"Yeah. I don't know."

"You don't know? You don't *know?*"

"I wish I'd never gotten involved."

Joanne threw her hands up. "*Now* she comes to her senses! And hey, aren't I giving you next Monday off so you can take your little flock to see the Immigration judge and then Social Services?"

"Yeah," Sally sighed. "We have an appointment with Charleston and the Immigration judge. And then I guess Social services. If it all works out with the judge, like Charleston said it probably would. I'm driving Lupe and Ascensiòn and the baby. Silvio's meeting us. Joanne, what am I gonna to do?"

"I'll tell you what you're gonna do." Joanne counted off on two fingers. "Either one, you're gonna follow through on what you promised or two, you're not."

"I can't not. Can I?"

"Can you?"

"No," she muttered. "I can't."

"What about your ex-friend Silvio?"

"I don't think he would screw Lupe and Ascensiòn just because he hates me. Besides, he still needs a Spanish-speaking plumber, right?"

"You're asking me?"

Sally sighed. "The whole plan will fall through unless I take their baby."

"Today is Friday. Better spend the weekend doing a psychological inventory check on yourself. You've either got the equipment you need to do this on your own or you don't." At that moment Sally looked so small and young, so like a lost child, that Joanne again put a hand on her shoulder. "Aw, look, just let this whole mess go 'til tomorrow. Call up one of your friends after work, go out for a drink, or something. You still have friends, right?"

Sally shrugged. "I can't go anywhere. I'm broke. And I have to stay home with Josh anyway."

Joanne sighed. "Look, if you want, you and Josh can come along with Ponti and me tonight to the Knights of Columbus pot-luck."

Sally laughed in spite of herself. "Um, that sounds really nice, but…"

"Yeah, I didn't think you'd want to go. I'd of been worried about you if you *had* wanted to go. Hell, even *I* don't want to go!" Sally laughed again and then Joanne continued. "But seriously, you don't want to be alone. Go have dinner with your mom."

"My mom? I *really* don't want to talk about my life with my mom."

"So don't talk about your life with your mom. Just go eat dinner with her. Do you both good."

"I wish you were my mom."

"I'm not your mom. I'm your boss. And," Joanne glanced at her watch, "You need to get back to work. As do I."

"Right." Sally stuffed the remains of her lunch into her paper bag then stood up to leave. "Thanks again, Joanne."

"You're welcome." Joanne waved a hand towards her door "Leave. Call your mother. Make it short. Then get back to work."

Sally stepped through Joanne's office door then turned back. "Joanne… will I be okay?"

"You'll be more than okay. In the meantime, 'The woods are something, something, dark and deep.'"

Sally sighed, remembering the quote from ninth grade English. "'But I have promises to keep. And miles to walk before I sleep.'"

"Right. Not to mention a ton of invoices to process, which need to be finished before you leave *or* sleep."

***

"Good Afternoon, Saint Sixtus Martyr Catholic Church, please join us for the High Mass of the Sanctified Chrism, Sundays at 10:20 am, everyone is welcome, this is Mary."

"Mom, does Father Tim know you're answering his phone with an infomercial?"

"Sally? What's wrong dear?"

"Nothing's wrong."

"Are you sick? You sound like you're down with a sinus infection."

"No. Just a little sniffle. I'm fine. I just thought maybe Josh and I would come over for dinner. If it's okay."

"Oh dear," her mother sighed. "Everything's not all right, is it?"

"Mom..." Sally felt her composure melting away, her throat tightening, a throbbing behind her eyes.

"Of course it's fine for you and Josh to come over," her mother quickly intercepted, backing away from the risk of lancing a painful subject and giving Sally a moment to collect herself, "in fact Father Tim said I could leave early if I wanted to, so I'll leave right now and I can stop at the store."

"Mom, you don't have to leave right now. *I* can stop at the store and pick up something for dinner."

"No, no, I want to make a pot of chicken soup with the thin noodles you like and I'll get a nice loaf of fresh bread from Hegley's."

"I don't want you to have to do all that work," Sally said, though without much conviction, as the thought of a warm bowl of her mother's home-made chicken soup with a thick slice of buttered bread was already calming and comforting her.

"Oh, no, it's no work," her mother replied cheerily. And what about dessert? Apple cake or brownies?"

"Mom, you really don't have to...brownies."

"With ice cream."

"Okay."

"You'll feel better, you'll see."

"I already do."

But by the end of the day Sally no longer felt better; in fact by the end of the day she was so spent from grief, emotion, and the fatigue following a sleepless night that all she had left was a simmering bad mood, not improved by a call from her mother.

"You haven't left work yet, have you?"

"I'm still here Mom."

"Oh, good, because I've got the soup on but I just realized that I forgot to buy the thin noodles. Could you stop and pick up a bag on your way over? You could try Walmart. You know, the one out by the Northeast Airport?"

Jesus, how could you forget the frickin' noodles? Sally wanted to snap, but instead she closed her eyes, rubbed her temples and said, "Okay. I'll get the noodles."

"And then Hegley's was sold out of their fresh bread, do you believe that?"

"It's okay, we'll be all right without the bread."

"But Walmart's Italian loaf is good too, and they put out a hot batch at 4:45, so…"

"Okay" Sally sighed, "I'll get the Italian loaf."

"And then can you grab a bottle of Jolly Juice for Joshua? I thought I had a bottle but I'm all out."

The juice was at the other end of the store from the bread. "Mom, he'll be all right. He can drink milk. Or water. Kids don't drink enough water."

"But the only milk I have is skim. And you don't want him to have to drink skim or *water* at his grammy's."

Then why the hell didn't you pick up the juice yourself? she thought, but she said, "Okay. Noodles, Italian loaf, and Jolly Juice."

"And a pound of butter, too?"

Fuck me, she silently fumed, *the butter's at the farthest end of the store from all the rest of the shit she wants!* She pulled in a deep breath. Aw, hell, why was she being so bitch-brained? Of course she wouldn't refuse to pick up a few things for her mother, who was only trying to fix her a nice dinner. Was it her mother's fault she lost Silvio, couldn't sleep and felt as if her life were falling apart?

"Butter," Sally sighed, "got it. Shall I get you some whole milk, too?" After all, the milk was in the same aisle as the butter and she felt guilty for her previous inner nastiness.

"Okay, if you wouldn't mind."

"I wouldn't mind. Do you need anything else while I'm there?"

"Well, I used up the last of the eggs on the brownies. I don't know why I always run out of eggs. I guess it's because you can't see how many are left through the carton. Don't you think a clear plastic egg carton would be a good idea?"

"Awesome idea. And I don't mind grabbing some eggs."

"Really?"

"Really."

And she meant it. In fact, the thought of helping out her mother, of being useful, improved her mood by several degrees. She'd just swing by Walmart on her way to Josh's daycare, she'd be in and out, with few enough items that she could use the express lane. Then she'd be on her way to a nice comforting bowl of chicken noodle soup in her mom's cheery little kitchen.

But forty-five minutes later, by which time she was cruising around the Walmart lot searching for a parking spot, she was questioning why the hell her mother had been so clueless as to send her on a noodle chase a block from the Northeast Airport during rush hour and why she'd been dumb enough to go. *Probably don't even carry the goddamn noodles,* she fretted as she hurried towards the pasta aisle. But the Airport Walmart did, in fact, carry the noodles, which she tossed into her cart along with the milk, butter, eggs, Italian bread and Jolly Juice. And luck of lucks, there was an open spot on one of the self-check lanes. It was one of the new high-tech lanes, just like a regular cashier lane with a full-length belt, only without the cashier. Sally dashed towards the lane and had parked herself in front of the self-check machine before she noticed the massive pile of groceries at the end of the belt and the owner of the pile, a tall, slim, casually-but-expensively-dressed woman who appeared to be in her mid-thirties holding a cell phone in one hand while she bagged with the other. The woman was so engrossed in her phone conversation that she'd neglected to push her groceries off the end of the belt so as to consolidate them at the end of the counter and free the belt for the next customer; nor did the woman bother to put down the hinged divider attached to the side of the belt. Sally cleared her throat and shuffled for a moment to give the woman a chance to notice and rectify the situation, but the woman seemed unaware of Sally's presence. Finally Sally called down the aisle, "Say, could you flip down the divider?"

"Oh, my God," the woman laughed obliviously into the phone, "I'd of channeled my inner amazon if he tried that on *me!*" Sally sighed. By now she'd sized up the woman as the type who came to Walmart when she was in the mood to slum it, something to reverse-brag about to her suburban posse over a leisurely mom's morning out at Starbucks.

"Um, excuse me," Sally tried again, calling a little louder, "The divider?"

"No, really, I'm just as bad," the woman continued, "I definitely let people push me around too much."

Sally heaved another sigh then tramped down the aisle and planted herself in front of the woman. *Just ask nicely*, she warned herself. "Excuse me, she said with a strained faux-pleasantness, "but I'm in kind of a hurry, so"

"Wait a minute, Jen," The woman stopped, put a hand on her hip and heaved a long-suffering sigh. She turned and looked at Sally dead-on. "Excuse *me*, but do you see *this*?" The woman waved an arm across the vast domain of her groceries, which still reached so far up the belt as to be beyond the reach of the hinged divider. She shook back her bobbed hair and returned the phone to her ear. "I swear, Jen, the *caliber* here." She continued her one-handed bagging.

Sally felt little bubbles of lava heating up inside her. *Okay, cool it*, she told herself. *Just ask again, nicely*. "Like I said, I'm kind of in a hurry," *you selfish bitch*, she added silently, "so if you could just kind of scoot your groceries a little, then we could put down the divider. I'd be happy to put down the divider. If you could scoot your groceries."

The woman ignored Sally, but reduced her bagging speed to a leisurely slow passive-aggressive drag.

Selfish rich suburban bitch! Sally took a few steps forward, reached across the woman's groceries and grabbed the divider, aware that she was now deep into the woman's space, hip to hip. "*Please* move your groceries," she growled, "So that I can *put down this divider!*"

"*You* move," the woman snapped back, giving Sally a hard hip-bump to get at her groceries.

"*Uh!*" Sally gasped, dropping the divider. *Fuck it*, she thought, then she stormed back up the lane and began grabbing her noodles, milk, butter, bread and Jolly Juice, scanning them and tossing them onto the belt, down which they travelled until they ran into and settled amidst the woman's groceries.

"What? Hey, excuse *me*," the woman barked, "Would you *mind* waiting *one minute* until I've finished?"

Sally continued checking out and throwing her items onto the belt, aggressively ignoring the woman.

The woman stormed up the aisle to Sally. *"Stop it!* Can't you see your groceries are getting mixed up with mine?"

Sally got right up into the woman's face. "Well then how about *putting down* the divider like a marginally *considerate* human being would have done, and then you can just *unmix* them up!" *Oh, Jesus,* Sally thought, *am I gonna get myself arrested for disturbing the goddamn peace?*

"I *do not* have time for this nonsense! How would you like it if I just bag your groceries along with mine and take them all home?"

"Oh yeah?" Sally shot back, "Well how about I just bag *your* goddamn groceries along with mine and take them *all home!* Now *you* move so I can get to the goddamn bags!"

By now all activity in the vicinity had frozen, the eyes of the other shoppers fixed on the two quarrelling women. The only person who seemed unaware of the altercation was the skinny, pimply-faced eighteen-year-old boy who was monitoring the self-check-out lines.

"Uhhh!" the woman cried. "I'm calling someone!" Five seconds later she returned with the hapless monitor in tow. "She just *threw* all her groceries on top of mine and, and, and *threatened* me! And I *insist"*

I threatened her? Suddenly the possible repercussions of the situation were hitting home with Sally. She wished to hell she'd opted to just cool her heels and wait while Mrs. Fucking Crazy Lady loaded her fucking groceries.

"…that you make her get her groceries away from mine *right now!"*

The poor befuddled youth looked as if this was not what he'd signed on for when he dropped out of school and took this job. "Um, you want me to call the manager or something?" he asked.

"Yes!" the woman cried.

"No!" Sally cried at the same time. "Oh for God's sake!" Sally began grabbing her groceries and tossing them back into her cart. "There!" she said when she'd retrieved the last of her parcels. "Problem solved, *okay everybody?"*

The boy shrugged. "Okay." He returned to his station while the woman quickly and bitterly finished bagging her things, still not putting down the divider, alternately making "do you believe this?" gestures to her fellow customers and shooting Sally poisonous looks. Sally finally grabbed a magazine and attempted to bury her head into it to hide from the undertone of public commentary being directed her way. And she thought as she closed her eyes against the lone tear that trickled down her cheek, *Will my life ever be so bad that I won't be able to find some way to make it worse?*

Still, she managed to pull herself together and keep up a front of indifference until she finally got her groceries packed and left the store. She even managed a smile when she picked up Josh and a round of forced chirpy banter that she kept up until he leaned over and patted her knee. "Are you happy Mom?" he asked.

"Sure am," she said with a catch in her voice.

"Me too!"

Sally smiled and rubbed a sleeve across her eyes.

When they arrived at Sally's mother's house her mother was waiting at the front door. Josh dashed into his grandmother's arms but she looked past him to her daughter, her eyes brimming with concern. Then she said cheerfully to her grandson, "Now you go into Grammy's bedroom and you can sit on Grammy's bed and watch my special TV for a little bit while Mommy and I finish fixing dinner. Okay?"

"Yippee!" Josh whooped and dashed up the stairs.

"You want a little snack first?" his grandmother called up the stairs.

"No!" He called down.

Sally carried the groceries to the kitchen and put the bread and butter on the table, the milk, eggs and juice into the refrigerator. She handed the noodles to her mother then fell into her arms and sobbed, burying her head in her mother's shoulder like a child. Sally's mother held her close. "Whatever it is," her mother cooed, "it'll be all right. You'll see."

"No, Mom," she sobbed, "It's over."

"Shhh." Her mother stroked her hair. "You'll see, you'll see." Then her mother sat Sally at the table and handed her a box of tissues from the counter. She ladled some soup from the stove into a mug and set it before her. "Here, the broth is good even without the noodles. Please, dear, please sip some for me."

Sally wrapped her hands around the warm mug and sipped. Her mother's soup was delicious and calming. Her mother cut a thick slice from the loaf of bread and buttered it generously. Then she poured her daughter a glass of milk. Sally ate and drank hungrily.

"How about a brownie now? With some ice cream?" Sally's mother carried the pan of brownies over from the stove.

"I can't eat any more."

"Then why don't you go lie down and sleep? Josh and I can have a nice dinner together."

"All right." But Sally continued sitting at the table, suddenly feeling too exhausted to move. "See, Mom...there's this man."

"Silvio. I know."

"You do?"

Her mother sighed. "Josh told me."

"Oh yeah." Sally rubbed her eyes wearily. "And that makes it even worse. Josh is crazy about him."

"I know."

"And I've, we've, gotten kind of...involved. With these people. A Nicaraguan couple."

"You mean Lupe and Ascensiòn? And the Spanish lessons?"

"You know about them, too?"

"Oh, yes."

"Well, yeah, then, Lupe and Ascensiòn. And there's more."

"Oh, dear."

Sally nodded. "Long story short, they and Silvio and I have been working with an Immigration lawyer. Lupe and Ascensiòn are going back to Nicaragua to wait on a work visa for Ascensiòn so that Silvio can hire him to work in his plumbing business and they can come back legally as a family."

"That's very good of Silvio."

"But they have a baby son born over here, so carting him down to Nicaragua then back here again would be too complicated. And dangerous. They can't possibly take the baby with them. So I...offered..."

"So you...*offered?*"

Sally nodded, unable to say any more.

"To what? Take care of their baby?"

Sally nodded again, and burst into another round of sobbing.

"Oh, *Honey,*" Her mother sighed, shaking her head. "How in the world could you possibly *do* that? How could you take care of another baby?"

"But I *could,*" Sally sobbed. "I *know* I could. I figured I'd have Silvio's help, and yours..."

"Well, of *course* I'd help you." Her mother sat down next to Sally and stroked her hair. "Of course I would."

"I know, Mom. But last night Silvio and me... we... he...we're *over.* But everything else, Lupe, Ascensiòn, the baby, *isn't,* and now I don't know what I'm going to *do.*"

Sally's mother wrapped her arms around her sobbing daughter and rocked her for a while. Then she said softly, "I've had to claw my way out of many's the dark abyss and with God's help so will you. Never forget that He's given you the gift of that dear little person upstairs who needs you. Maybe there will soon be another little one in your life if it's His plan. So you'll have faith and you'll find strength and you'll do what women have been doing since the beginning of time. You'll forget about your own needs and do what needs to be done."

Sally nodded and for a few moments pondered notions of faith, God's plan, and the ache in her heart softened by gratitude at having that one dear little person, maybe two, who needed her to do what needed to be done.

Chapter Thirty-Two

The little group sat in a courtroom of the Philadelphia Immigration Court waiting their turn before the judge. Charleston Tilley glanced left then right then shook his head imperceptibly. There was something wrong with the configuration: Sally sat at one end of the row with Silvio at the other, separated by Lupe holding David, Ascensiòn, Charleston, and Maria. Definitely something wrong. In fact from the moment they'd met up outside the courtroom he'd sensed a wide wall of silence between Sally and Silvio, breached only as needed for brief, ice-tinged exchanges. But the coldness that stood out in such contrast to the warmth shared between them in previous meetings was neither Charleston's problem nor even his business in and of itself; what was troubling him was that Silvio and Sally had clearly undertaken this project as a couple...so what were they today? A quarrelling couple? An ex-couple? And if, as experience had taught him, couples who split on hateful terms were perfectly capable of abandoning the interests of their own children then what chance would these helpless immigrants have if Sally and Silvio were through with each other? He wanted to grab the two of them by the ear and drag them out into the hall to find out exactly where their heads were. But to what end? It was too late for them to change their minds, any of them; the Guzmans were in the system now, sharp and clear on Immigration's radar screen, and if Sally and Silvio suddenly cut them off then they and their child would be left in the most pitiful straits. Charleston looked around the room and caught sight of Sonia Terhorst, the tough Immigration and Naturalization attorney who'd be present at the Guzman's trial to represent the interests of the United States Government. Sonia nodded his way and he nodded back. As far as Charleston knew, Sonia seemed willing enough to play soft ball with him today, but she'd definitely needed persuading prior; he'd practically had to get down on his knees and beg her to take it easy on his clients, laying out the soundness of the scenario and talking up Sally and Silvio's promised commitment as his main point of persuasion. He suddenly regretted having taken on this weird, convoluted case. Why in the world had he ever let Joanne Ponticello persuade him to meet with her little office protégée and the plumber boyfriend? But then that's what he did, didn't he? Met with people in sore need who had little chance of finding legal representation elsewhere. Only this case was something else altogether, and he could certainly have put the brakes on the whole messy project back at that first meeting. Except that Sally and Silvio had seemed such decent youngsters, open-hearted, idealistic, responsible. And how often did one in his business see that in people, young or old? He'd found it refreshing. Uplifting. Calling to the spirit within him that yearned even at his age to do some good for this sorry old planet. And he'd wanted to be a part of it. Well, maybe they were still those same two youngsters. Charleston pulled in a deep breath. He needed to find out one way or the other. Right now.

"I'll be right back," he whispered to Maria and then he motioned to Sally and Silvio to follow him out into the hall where they found a place to stand close to the wall and out of the way of the busy hallway traffic. As he looked from one to the other Charleston felt a sinking sensation, for he recognized the stiff body language and stricken expressions of two people for whom the cord was broken, the love expired. He weighed his words carefully before speaking.

"Mrs. Miller, Mr. Jablonski...I just want to emphasize the seriousness of the commitment each of you has made to the Guzman family. They are in this courtroom today because of you both, because of your generous support. And I know you understand that this family's well-being depends upon your continued generosity and support. I know you understand this."

Sally and Silvio nodded.

"I understand what you're saying," said Silvio.

"Me, too," said Sally. "Totally."

"Good, good. And you're still on board? Both of you?"

"I am," said Sally.

"Me, too," said Silvio.

"Good, good." Charleston felt a rush of relief. They were still committed, thank God. "That being said, then, while I can't guarantee any outcome, I have a feeling that with the ground work we've laid things are likely to go favorably both with the Immigration judge and in Family Court." He turned to Sally. "I've prepared the paperwork granting you emergency custody of David Guzman. Assuming today's hearing transpires as we hope it will, I'll then have the Guzmans sign David to your custody. It will be at least another month before you can be granted official temporary custody, but at least the Guzmans will be free and clear to immediately return to Nicaragua without anxiety over the welfare of their child." Charleston had already explained this process to Sally, but he wanted her and Silvio, too, to hear the words again, as if the words could add another layer of fortification to their commitment.

Silvio spoke up. "So you figure we probably don't have anything to worry about? With the judge, I mean?"

"Hopefully not. Just remember to answer all the judge's questions in an honest and straightforward manner, as I know you will. The same with the Government attorney, should she opt to question you. And remember," Charleston added with a smile, "every answer to the judge ends with 'Your Honor'. Okay?"

"Okay, thanks," Silvio said.

"Yeah, thanks," Sally added.

Charleston felt a tug at his heart, for there was no quick shared smile, no momentary glance, no slight brush of the hand, no intimate little communication of any kind between Sally and Silvio. Sad. After all these years Charleston felt he knew every possible scenario from A to Z that could tear two people apart. Knew 'em like the back of his hand. Couldn't offer him one he hadn't already heard. Still, once in a while he came across a case the true resolution of which, he believed, lay not in divorce but in forgiveness. But try telling that to someone who'd been wounded bone-deep. So Charleston, except for one naïvely ill-conceived effort years ago when he was still a young and inexperienced attorney, never did try, it was none of his business. Nor was whatever had driven Sally and Silvio apart any of his business. Still, two such good kids, it was a shame.

***

"Mr. Tilley, would you please have your clients approach the bench?"

Charleston, Maria, Sally and Silvio filed up to the bench while the Guzmans lagged behind until Ascensiòn finished tucking David into Maria's front-pack baby carrier. They waited while the Immigration judge spent a few moments taking a final look over the brief before her. The judge raised her eyebrows and sighed. "Well," she said, addressing the group, "I must admit that this is a highly unusual case. In fact I don't think I've seen another case like yours. However, Mr. Tilley, you seem to have everything well-organized. Mr. Jablonski, you're still committed to seeking permanent labor certification for Mr. Guzman?"

"Yes, Your Honor. I am."

She addressed the Immigration and Naturalization attorney. "Ms. Terhorst, do you have any further evidence or arguments to present as to why voluntary deportation should be denied to the Guzmans?"

"No, Your Honor," the Government attorney replied.

Thank you, Jesus, Charleston thought. *You too, Sonia,* he added, casting a grateful glance her way.

"And Mrs. Miller, are you still committed to taking temporary custody of David Guzman?"

"Yes, Your Honor." Sally answered.

The judge paused a moment then she said, "Mrs. Miller, if you wouldn't mind, may I ask how old you are?"

"Twenty-seven, Your Honor."

The judge glanced down at her brief again. "And I see that you're a single mother?"

"Yes, Your Honor. I'm, you know, divorced."

The judge nodded. "And you do understand the tremendous responsibility involved in what you've volunteered for?"

"Yes, Your Honor. I do."

The judge looked at the others. "You understand, all of you, that the process involved in obtaining permanent labor certification may take some time? In fact there's no guarantee that it couldn't take years. Mrs. Miller, Mr. and Mrs. Guzman, do you understand that?"

266

As soon as Maria finished translating the Guzmans nodded.

"Yes, we understand, Your Honor," said Ascensiòn.

"Yes, we understand, Your Honor." Lupe repeated mechanically. She sniffed then kissed David's head.

"I understand too, Your Honor," Sally said.

"All right then. Just one more thing. Mrs. Miller, I am rather curious as to what motivated you to offer to care for David Guzman through all of this. It seems a mighty undertaking for such a young person who obviously has much on her plate already." The judge waited while Sally collected her thoughts.

"Well, Your Honor," Sally began, "I am a divorced mother, as you said. I have a little boy, Joshua. He's six years old. It's because of Joshua that I'm doing this." Sally paused, searching for the right words. "Joshua means more to me than anyone or anything else in the world. My divorce, it's been rough on him. But I still want him to be happy. I want him to feel loved, you know, secure. I want him to have what he needs. I want the world to be a good place for him. I want that more than I want anything else. And I know that how I feel about my Joshua, Lupe and Ascensiòn feel the same about their David. They love him just as much. They want the same things for him as I want for Josh. So that's why I have to help them. Because they're just like me. And their David is just like my Joshua. Josh and I, we don't live in a big house. But there's enough room for one more little guy. And I don't make a lot of money, but I make enough to support myself and my son, even if his father goes deadbeat, which is not totally outside the realm of possibility, the way he's been talking lately. Josh's father, that is. But as I was saying, Your Honor, whatever I have I'll make it stretch enough to cover one more, I don't care if we all have to live on peanut butter, Wonder Bread, and thrift store clothes, I'll make it work. I mean, this is America, right? And, seriously, I don't think we realize how much we all have, even if we don't have a lot. Because we really *do* have a lot compared to people like Lupe and Ascensiòn...how they lived in Nicaragua, I mean...we just have so much here."

Sally suddenly felt terribly self-conscious. *Okay, how corny was that? Are they rolling their eyes, or what?* She looked around at the others then at the judge. "I mean, we all do have a lot here, don't we?"

To Sally's surprise the judge nodded, along with Charleston, Maria, Silvio, the Guzmans, even Sonia Terhorst, the Government attorney. Aware of the how quiet the courtroom had become, Sally glanced over her shoulder to see some of the spectators watching her and nodding as well. Feeling more self-assured, she turned back to the judge and cleared her throat.

"So I figure, and I didn't always feel this way, but now I do, that there must be enough to share with people like the Guzmans, who just want to make a living, do their part, you know, provide for their child. They're even willing to do the hardest thing a mother...or a father...at least some fathers...good fathers, that is..." Sally instinctively glanced at Silvio, who met her eyes then looked away as quickly as she did, "...anyway, it would be the hardest thing in the world for me to leave my Joshua. But if for some reason I had to leave my baby boy I'd want to leave him with someone who'd care for him like their own child. The way I'm going to care for David."

As soon as Maria finished translating the only sound that could be heard was the quiet sobbing of Lupe and Ascensiòn, who kissed their child's face, hands and head over and over while the tears streamed down their faces. Sally felt a surge, the realization that her thoughts were now so clear, her resolve so crystallized, that whatever words she might still need in order to plead her case were there for her, needing only to be spoken. "So, see, Your Honor," she continued, wiping away with one hand then the other the tears that spilled over her eyes and ran down her cheeks, "I realize I'm young and maybe I've been weak..." Once again she flashed a glance towards Silvio, who didn't look away this time, "...in the past. But now I'm strong and I have two little guys who need me, and with the support of a couple of good people, my mom, my friend Joanne Ponticello, Mr. Tilley of course, and...well, I guess that's about all the support I actually have these days, but I promise you, Your Honor, Lupe, Ascensiòn..." here she turned to the Guzmans, who now wept with breathless sobs, "I'm going to do what needs to be done. No matter what." Sally again wiped at her eyes. "Well, that's all."

From around the courtroom came a smattering of applause, which the judge quickly cut short.

"All right, thank you, Mrs. Miller." The judge stared out into courtroom with a look meant to serve as a warning to anyone who might be inclined to disrupt the orderly proceedings of her court. Then she looked back at Sally. "I must say, you've pled your case quite well." She paused a moment, seeming to weigh her thoughts before speaking further. "Mr. and Mrs. Guzman, in view of the auspicious outcome towards which your case seems to point, I've come to the decision – and a rare decision it is – to grant you voluntary deportation." She turned towards Charleston, disregarding the cries of Lupe and Ascensiòn as they hugged each other then Sally and Silvio as well as they could with the baby between them. "Mr. Tilley, I suggest you and Mrs. Miller contact The Department of Human Services right away to start making the arrangements for Mrs. Miller to be appointed David Guzman's foster-care provider."

Charleston nodded soberly. "Thank you, Your Honor. In anticipation of a tentatively favorable verdict I've already contacted The Department of Human Services to send a caseworker who will be meeting with Mrs. Miller and visiting her home for the required inspection. The background check has already been done. Human Services has agreed to allow Mrs. Miller to forego the standard training sessions since this is, as you pointed out, such a specialized case."

"That it is," the judge agreed.

"We expect that Mrs. Miller should have preliminary clearance for emergency custody by next week."

"Well, then, in that case we can expedite the process somewhat." The judge addressed herself to the Guzmans, who, at Maria's whispered urgings, had calmed down and now stood attentive to the judge's words. "But of course, it all depends on how quickly you can return to Nicaragua. You'll have thirty days to return. Thirty days." The judge paused a moment to make sure that her words had sunk in. "I suggest you be prepared to leave as soon as Mrs. Miller's preliminary clearance comes through. Once you you've returned to Nicaragua we can start the process for the permanent labor certification for you, Mr. Guzman, and the H-4 visa request for you, Mrs. Guzman. The sooner you both return the sooner we can start the process." She gave Maria a moment to finish translating then looked at Lupe and Ascensiòn with raised eyebrows. "Is that clear?"

"Yes, Your Honor," Ascensiòn replied. "We will go soon."

Lupe stood silently, swaying from one foot to the other, her arms around David in his carrier.

"All right, then," the judge said, "Any questions?"

"I think we're good here, thank you, Your Honor." Charleston replied.

"In that case, your voluntary deportation is hereby granted. Mr. Tilley, if you'll take the Guzmans to the clerk they can pick up the necessary documentation. And good luck to all of you."

Each member of the group politely thanked the judge then they left the courtroom quietly. They walked down the hallway in silence, Ascensiòn with his arm around his wife's rigid shoulders, Charleston talking softly to Maria and Sonia Terhorst, while Sally and Silvio stayed far apart, having positioned themselves so that the others served as a barrier between them. Ascensiòn stopped to lift David from Lupe's carrier.

"Espera, Lupe, let me"

"No," Lupe muttered.

"Please, let me carry him for a"

"*No!*" Lupe snapped, pulling her baby close.

"Okay, okay, Mi Amor," he said, backing away.

"*No,*" she shouted at her husband, "*No! No! No!*"

"Lupe, por el amor de dios…"

Lupe began wailing hysterically, "No! No puedo! No puedo dejar a mi niño!" *I can't leave my child.*

"Calma, Lupe, calma," her husband begged, looking around anxiously, helplessly, at the people gawking as they hurried by. Ascensiòn tried to subdue her with the help of Sally, Silvio, Maria, Charleston, even Sonia Terhorst, but she wrapped her arms tightly around her baby and pushed at them with her shoulders and hips, sobbing breathlessly all the while, "*No puedo dejar a mi niño!*"

Sally was the first to notice the two security guards hurrying through the crowd. "Oh, my God, Silvio," she whispered frantically, instinctively touching his arm, her first natural gesture towards him since the unhappy scene with Darren.

"Aw geez!" Silvio dashed off towards the guards.

Ascensiòn meanwhile managed to wrestle David, now crying as

loudly as his mother, from his carrier. Without the weight of her baby Lupe slumped to the floor, limp as a rag doll, and though Charleston, Maria and Sonia tried to lift her to her feet her small frame seemed to be made of lead. *"No puedo, no puedo,"* she moaned. Sally took in the sight of Lupe's suffering and wiped fresh tears from her own eyes. She lowered herself to the floor then took Lupe's face gently into her hands and looked into the woman's tear-reddened eyes. "Si, si, puedes," she said softly. "Eres fuerte. Una mujer fuerte. Una madre fuerte. Eres muy fuerte. Puedes hacer lo necesario. Yo te lo prometo." *Yes you can. You are strong. A strong woman. A strong mother. You are very strong. You can do what you have to do. I promise.* She repeated the words over and over until Lupe finally nodded and lifted herself to a sitting position. Sally helped Lupe to her feet then Lupe fell into Sally's arms and Sally rocked her and shushed her as a mother does her trembling child. "You're all right, Hon," she cooed, "you're all right."

Meanwhile Silvio had intercepted the security guards. "See? She's all right." The ex-football player stood like a protective barrier in front of the Guzmans. "Like I was saying, she's just having a little meltdown is all, you know how that goes, but she's okay now, right?"

The guards looked at each other, exchanged a *"these people"* expression, then turned and ambled back down the hall. Silvio turned around to see Sally watching him over Lupe's shoulder. He cocked his head towards the retreating guards, she nodded and mouthed "Thanks," then each looked away and Silvio hurried off in search of an exit.

Chapter Thirty-Three

It seemed as if the halls of the Philadelphia Immigration Court had turned into a sea of people. Silvio less moved through it than was carried along as it flowed into the elevators then spilled out onto the sidewalk at the corner of 9th and Market. He turned the corner and walked quickly towards the 9th Street parking lot, his brain whirring to the beat of his own footsteps. That was that, anyway, it went good, went great, really, Ascensiòn and Lupe had their voluntary deportation, that was great, really, they'd be leaving in a couple of weeks then he'd apply for the permanent labor certification, he could look forward to eventually having a good Spanish-speaking plumber on his team, that would be good for business, great, really, that's all that mattered, Sally would be taking care of their baby but that wasn't his concern except in that it made the process flow more smoothly, otherwise nothing regarding Sally concerned him anymore, she was nothing to him and he hoped he was nothing to her, of course he was nothing to her, she'd proved it clearly enough when he'd caught her, he'd caught her, he'd caught her...Aw geez, what was he doing crossing 10th Street, had he walked right past the parking lot or what? He turned around and re-crossed 10th Street, his face red with anger, his pace as close to a run as one could get on the crowded city street. He turned into the parking lot and hurried to his truck, climbed inside and slammed the door, just making it before breaking into loud, chest-wracking sobs. He pounded the steering wheel then buried his head in his hands. When did it end? When the hell did it end? She didn't love him and that was that. That was that, that was that, that was that, he told himself over and over until his sobbing subsided and he was wept out, his anger faded into a big, dull, aching sadness. He sighed heavily. Aw, Sally. And yet today in the court room it was like she couldn't keep her eyes off him, what was that all about? And why couldn't he keep his eyes off her? He had to admit she'd been, well, awesome. Even with the tears rolling down her face she'd kept it together and convinced the judge. Convinced them all. But surely none of them had felt as if their heart were being squeezed right out of their chest, the way he'd felt at the sight of her, so small and pretty, so strong and vulnerable at the same time that all he'd wanted was to do was hold her in his arms and dry her tears and when she talked about how much she loved Joshua....no, he wasn't going to start bawling again. He wasn't a twelve-year-old girl, after all. Anyway, that's one thing you have to admit about Sally, she loves that little boy. Silvio felt his heart tighten again. He had to admit that he was pretty attached to Joshua himself. He missed the little guy. Did Joshua miss him, too? Why was he going there? What difference did it make who missed who, there was nothing to do about it. He wouldn't let Sally use him again, tell him she loved him while she waited around for her useless ex-husband to show up so she could throw herself at him again. Only...what did she mean about she was weak in the past but now she was strong? She'd looked right at him when she said it. What was that all about? Did she mean...? Silvio pounded the steering wheel in helpless frustration. *Aw, who the hell knew what she meant, he couldn't take it anymore!* All that mattered was his own children, he'd get custody of his children and then Trysta, Sally, Darren, he could be done with the whole miserable lot of them! All that mattered was his children. Now that the voluntary deportation business was out of the way he was ready to call Charleston Tilley and ask him to take his custody case. He hoped Charleston would represent him but if he wouldn't, well, he'd just find somebody else. If it took every penny he had he was determined to get his kids back. His kids were all that mattered. All that mattered in the world. *But Sally...he just didn't understand.*

***

"So you're telling me, Mr. Jablonski, that you were granted no custody at all? No partial legal or physical?"

Silvio shook his head. His hands were his lap, his fingers

interlocked but twisting and tugging against each other as if struggling to break loose. His face was a study in anguish.

"Are you all right, Mr. Jablonski?" Charleston asked.

Silvio nodded. "Yeah. She got it all. Sole legal and physical custody of our kids. All I get is two weekends a month. And whenever else she needs me."

"Whenever else she needs you?"

"To take the kids for her. Like when she went on her honeymoon with her new husband. To Mexico. She asked me to take the kids then."

"And you did?"

"Yeah, I did. They're my kids. "

"This, 'whenever else she needs you'...is that part of the custody agreement?"

"No, but like I said, they're my kids. They need me, I'm gonna be there, custody or no custody. And I pay for their support, every month on the dot, you know that, right?"

"Right, right." *Son,* Charleston thought, *you are too good for this.* "Mr. Jablonski, when you were going through your divorce did your attorney not suggest some custody options that you might have pursued?"

"Huh, what she suggested was that I was lucky to get what I got then she sent me a bill." Silvio sighed. "You have to understand, after Trysta left me I was broken in a million pieces, I mean, I was in no shape to pursue anything. It was like I was standing in front of a train." Silvio whisked his right hand over his left in a quick motion that suggested being run down and flattened. "It was all I could do to get up and go to work every day. But now..."

"Now you're better."

"I'm good enough."

"Tell me, how are you and your ex-wife getting along these days?"

Silvio shrugged. "She gets what she wants and everybody's happy."

"And when she doesn't get what she wants?"

Silvio pondered a moment. "I guess I can't think of a time when she didn't get what she wanted."

"I see. So what changes, exactly, do you want to happen within the current custody agreement?"

"I want my kids with me. I want physical custody, I want legal custody. I'm not saying they can't spend time with their mother, too, all they want, I'm willing to work that out. But I want to see them when I get home from work. I want to help them with their homework, make sure they're doing good in school. Make sure they're getting to their soccer, their dancing classes, all the things they used to do. I give her enough support to pay for those things, you know? And I want to make sure they know how to behave themselves. I want to go to teacher meetings. I guess the way it is now I'm not even allowed to go to teacher meetings."

"Is your ex-wife not getting your children to their soccer and dance classes?"

"I don't know what the heck is going on over there but as far as I know the kids aren't doing anything these days except playing video games and acting out."

"I see. I believe you told me your children currently live in New Conshohocken while you live in Cornwells Heights?"

"Yeah, that's right."

"Would you have them switch schools again to live with you?"

"Look, my kids are out of control since the divorce. My little girls do nothing but bicker and carry on, Trysta can't handle them, her Mr. Wonderful new husband can't stand them, and can I blame him, rich jerk that he is? My seven-year-old keeps asking me to come and live with her, and my son...he's in therapy."

Charleston shook his head sympathetically. "I'm sorry to hear that the situation is so difficult. I'm sorry about your son."

"Yeah. Eleven years old. And the worst is, his mother doesn't even see it. She doesn't take him to his psychologist appointments. She says our son is fine. She says his teachers don't know what they're talking about. "

Charleston turned on his Dictaphone. "Do you mind, Mr. Jablonski?"

"No, I don't mind." Silvio cleared his throat and continued. "Like I was saying, his mother doesn't want to take him to his therapy appointments." Silvio paused a moment then continued. "Okay, you

275

gotta understand, Trysta and me, we were kids when she got pregnant and we got married, right out of high school. We had no money, and with a baby on the way and me just starting my plumbing apprenticeship, Trysta had to work, she worked through all three kids. It was my mother who raised our kids for us while we worked. Maybe Trysta never got enough experience, with my parents always being there to do for us and the kids. See, my parents, they just live a couple neighborhoods over from us."

"What about Trysta's parents?"

"Trysta's parents? Well, her father, he's real strict, everybody does what he says, including Trysta's mother. I thought he was gonna kill me at first, when he first found out about Trysta being pregnant and all. He disowned Trysta for a while. But then after Zach was born he came around with Trysta, me he still has a hard time swallowing, and he sees the kids enough, but they have to toe the line with him, if you know what I mean."

"Yes, I see."

"But yeah, the kids see Trysta's parents, too, not that she takes them over anymore. But hey, I make sure when I have the kids that they visit their grandparents. Her parents, my parents, we're all there in Cornwells Heights, one big happy family. Or so I thought, dumb me. Then this Darren comes along from out of nowhere and *wham*, we're *all* hit like with a freight train. Next thing I know my wife and kids are gone, living in a big house way the heck out in New West Moneyland, and my eleven-year-old son can't take it. I want my kids back. I want to give them their life back."

Charleston turned off the Dictaphone. "In all honesty, Mr. Jablonski, it's not in my power or yours to give your children back their old life, much as I sincerely wish that it was. But I'll do my best to help you get a better custody arrangement than what you've got now."

"Thank you," Silvio said, sniffing and wiping his eyes with the back of his hand.

"The fact that your ex-wife seems to be remiss in her parental responsibilities towards her children – not getting your son to his therapist appointments, neglecting to see to your children's activities, her inability to deal with your children's behavior, not to mention the intolerance of her husband towards your children – I believe all this will inventory in your favor."

Silvio registered a look of hesitation. "Okay, in all fairness I have to admit I guess Trysta's just overwhelmed these days. I mean, all of a sudden having to deal with the three kids on her own, the big house, new part of town, and then being eight months pregnant, and all…"

"Mr. Jablonski," Charleston said bluntly, "you have to understand that a custody battle almost never involves fighting fairly. Only fighting, and using whatever weapons we can pull from our arsenal. Now, from what you've told me I can almost a hundred percent guarantee that you are in for a battle, possibly a long, hard and ugly one. And before we plunge into the war zone you need to make sure you are up to the fight. And forget all notions of 'fairness'."

"Geez."

"I've been in this business a long time. I know of what I speak."

"Yeah, okay, I know you do."

"And you're ready to go through with this?"

Silvio pulled in another deep breath. "Like I said, I'll do what I have to do to get my kids back."

"I'll do my best as well. But even so, and even though Pennsylvania law prohibits awarding custody to a particular parent based solely on gender, there exists the possibility that you will not be awarded sole physical custody. But the good news is that you most likely will be awarded at the very least partial legal and physical custody. I do believe that we can improve the situation as it exists now."

Silvio swallowed hard. "I know, Mr. Tilley. I trust you. You're a good man."

"Thank you, Mr. Jablonski." *Coming from you,* thought Charleston, *that means a lot.*

Chapter Thirty-Four

"'Eyyy, Bobby Darren, whyn't you show up five minutes earlier?"

"Uh, I believe our appointment was for three o'clock?" Darren checked his watch. "Am I late?"

Angelo Barbieri laughed. "Nah, you're ten minutes early. But you'd shown up *fifteen* minutes early you'd of caught Geoffry. He just now left. Hey, didn't you see him on your way in?"

"No," Darren replied with the plastic smile he'd become accustomed to forcing onto his face in the presence of Angelo Barbieri, "I didn't."

"Aw, well, too bad."

Yeah, Darren thought, *would've just made my fuckin' day!* "Yeah, it's too bad I missed him."

"Yeah, too bad you did. Geoffry, he's a real card. Keeps us laughing. Him and his big mouth!"

Darren suddenly had the distressing vision of Geoffry and his big mouth bragging to his mother and Darren's father about setting up Darren with Angelo Barbieri. As if reading his thoughts Angelo added, "But hey, don't worry, Geoffry knows when to keep his mouth shut. He only runs his mouth about what I let him run it about. You know what I'm saying?"

Darren nodded. Of *course* he knew what Barbieri was saying. Of *course* Geoffry was too damn stupid to think or act for himself. Of *course* he was destined to get by in life only as someone else's flunky. Or by sponging off his mother. But then...what was he doing signing checks for Angelo Barbieri? Darren screwed up his courage then felt resentful that he should have to just to ask a perfectly legitimate question of a client. It was his *right* to ask questions, his *responsibility*, this involved his *business*. Screw it.

278

"Angelo, can I ask exactly what it is that Geoffry does for you? I mean, I understand that he's involved in real-estate projects, but"

Angelo cut Darren off with a burst of laughter. "*Real estate projects? Geoffry?*"

"Oh," Darren chuckled nervously, "I guess I'm just not exactly *sure*, exactly, what he, well…*does.*"

"You don't know what your brother does? What, you don't talk to your own brother?"

"Uh, stepbrother, actually."

"Well, yeah, he can be kind of a dick, sometimes, your stepbrother."

"Oh, heh, heh, yeah."

Angelo whirled his chair around so that he was looking out his massive window at his magnificent view of the Navy Yard. "This has got to be the best view in the world." He continued gazing out the window as if Darren weren't there. It was all Darren could do to keep from drumming his fingers on Angelo's huge walnut desk. *Why the hell did Barbieri call me in today? Just to dick around with me, waste my time? Show off his goddamn view from his goddamn window?* Angelo whirled back around, a look of consummate satisfaction on his face. He gestured back towards the window. "What a ya say, Bobby D?"

"Excuse me?" *Bobby D? Now I'm Bobby D?*

"You ever seen a better view?"

"Well, heh, heh, I guess not." Darren swallowed his irritation. The subject of Geoffry seemed to be dead. But dammit, he'd asked Barbieri a question, he deserved an answer. He continued gingerly. "It's just that I noticed one of the checks you gave me, from SP Wrecking, was signed by Geoffry, so I wondered…"

"South Philadelphia Wrecking. That's mine, too. That okay with you, Bobby D?"

"Yes, of course," Darren replied, irked at the condescension in Barbieri's voice.

"Geoffry's my, uh, financial officer."

"Your *financial officer? Geoffry?*"

"Like I said, he knows how to keep his mouth shut." Barbieri leaned across the desk and lowered his voice. "So how about Geoffry's stepbrother? Does *he* know how to keep *his* mouth shut?"

279

Darren felt a chill run down his spine. Was that a threat of some kind? What was this meeting about? What did Barbieri want from him?

Angelo laughed and sat back in his seat. He waved away the subject as he would a joke. "So you know you're a genius, right? My Amy loves the house you picked out for her. Gotta keep the girls happy, that's the ticket, right? Now you just gotta unload the rental on Moyamensing. You working on that?"

Darren grabbed onto the subject with the eagerness of an insecure swimmer being offered a life preserver. "I've had five enquiries, four showings, three appear to be solid potential tenants, two with sterling credit scores. It's a nice place, we've priced it right, I'm figuring it'll be off the block by next week and bringing you some income by the first of the month."

"That's good. Money in my pocket and yours, right?"

"Right," Darren chuckled, making sure that his smile was still stuck securely on his face.

"So, I have an associate out of Cherry Hill. Howard Sill. You know him?"

"No." *Why the hell would I?*

"Well, it's just that he owns CH Concessions. In the Pensauken New Jersey Industrial Park? He's looking for another investment. Real estate. Something small for starters. I told him you'd take care of him."

I'd take care of him? Since when am I obligated to you to decide who my clients will be? Darren cleared his throat. "Well, you can have Mr. Sill call me and we can discuss the matter."

"You find him something. Just a little something. He's a Jew. You know how those guys are." Angelo held up his hand and rubbed his thumb and fingers together. "But hey, he's a good friend."

Like I care.

"So you'll go find him something."

Kiss my ass.

"Then you'll call me and you'll let me know."

Yeah, right.

"He's got about two-and-a-half million to play with."

Go fuck your...two-and-a-half million?

"Like I said, he's a good friend."

Two-and-a-half MILLION?

"So you figure you can find him something?"

Two-and-a-half million? I'll find him something faster than a speeding bullet! Darren's irritation at Angelo Barbieri melted away in the warm glow that was suddenly radiating from his cerebral cortex, a warmth which likewise melted away his plastic smile, replacing it with a smile of genuine, heartfelt, fourteen-carat joy. "Well, heh, heh," he chuckled, "of course I could find him a nice little investment property within his price range."

"Something nice."

"Absolutely, absolutely! In fact, hey, I can tell you right off the top of my head, there's a beautiful multi-family on the market right now in University City, ten units total, six three-bedroom, four one-bedroom, the area is *totally* up and coming, I can guarantee it's gonna be the *hottest*, most *sought after*"

"Yeah, yeah, sounds nice. How much?"

"Well, I believe the asking price is somewhere around two million eight, and *that's* a steal, believe me, but"

"But?" Angelo again interrupted.

"We could offer two million three then if need be settle at two million five."

"Cash on the barrel head."

"Cash? Your friend wants to pay cash?"

"An investment, you know?"

Wow, thought Darren, feeling hotter and happier by the minute. "Okay, sure, I think we should be able to snatch it off the market at two million five cash. Definitely. "

"He'll need a building manager. You can do that?"

"Yes! Absolutely! Tenants, rental collections, maintenance, everything!"

"So you'll get on it."

"I'll contact the listing broker today."

"And you'll get back to me."

"Absolutely," Darren beamed, his heart full of Christmas day. Angelo Barbieri nodded with the serene smile of a cobra contemplating a tasty bird's egg.

"You'll get a good commission on this one, eh, Bobby D?"

This time Darren felt only the tiniest twinge of pique at the "Bobby D" crap. And that Barbieri would remark on the size of Darren's commission, *that* was, well, crass, Darren's commission was his own business after all, but then that's how Barbieri was, he philosophized, rough around the edges, but fine, Darren would deal with it. "Two point five percent of the selling price, paid by the seller, is normally what the buyer's agent would expect to get on a sale of this nature."

"How much is that for you?"

Geez, over-the-top crass, Darren thought. But okay, fine, it's not like it was any big secret. "Well," he mentally calculated, "depending on what we're able to get it for, that would be somewhere between"

Barbieri raised a finger. "You'll get your get your two-and-a half percent from the seller. And Howard, he knows from me that you're reliable and you do good work. So he wants to give you an advance.

"An advance?"

"Today. For accepting his business." Angelo opened a desk drawer and pulled out a manila envelope. He slid the envelope across the desk to Darren. "Should be a hundred and eight thousand in there."

"A hundred and eight thousand?"

"Go ahead. Take a look."

Darren instinctively did as he was told and looked at the contents of the envelope. Ninety-five hundred in cash. Eighty-five hundred in a check from CH Concessions. Ten money orders from various banks in varying amounts equaling the difference. All the money orders were signed by Geoffry.

"Small amounts," said Angelo. "Under the radar. No problem."

No problem? Darren thought. "Uh, Angelo, I'm not sure"

Angelo raised a finger. "You'll put the hundred and eight thousand in the bank. An escrow fund, or whatever you want to call it. After the closing of my friend's deal, when all the paperwork is done and all the agents have gone home, you'll remember that hundred and eight thousand sitting in the bank and you'll write Howard ten checks for seven thousand each and you'll keep the change. Thirty-eight thousand. Over and above your two-and-a-half percent. That sound like enough for you?

"Wait, wait, you're telling me"

"A little extra bonus, a commission, you know? Just for doing business with my friend. No law against a commission, right?"

"Well, I...I'm not...I'd have to...look, I'm a little confused. This Howard Sill, he wants to give me a hundred and eight thousand today..."

"Put it in the bank, spend it, invest it, whatever you want."

"Then he wants seventy thousand back *after* the sale?"

"That's right, Bobby D."

"But...*why?*"

Angelo shrugged. "Eh, he's a Jew," as if that explained it all. "But still a good guy, very successful, well-respected in the business community."

"When will I meet him? I mean, he and I really need to discuss all this before any contract can be drawn up."

Angelo Barbieri sat up straight in his chair then leaned in slightly towards Darren. He folded his hands on his desk. "Mr. Sill prefers to broker this transaction through me." His tone was suddenly business-formal, one that Darren hadn't heard from him up until this moment. "I often act as Mr. Sill's agent in cases where I have more contacts or experience in a particular market, as it were."

As it were?

"Now I appreciate," Barbieri continued in his business-formal tone, "that commercial real estate is your specialty and that you are very competent. And I *assumed* that you had a bead on how business is conducted within the... *corporate community*. Do you, Darren?"

"Yes, of course," Darren replied, feeling at once sheepish, defensive, and slightly insecure, at the same time reassured that this business was probably all perfectly legal, if a little unconventional inside his own frame of experience, which was, of course, limited regarding all the possibilities within the *corporate community*, as Angelo had put it. In fact this would be a good opportunity for Darren to delve into some of the more arcane details of corporate business, good, valuable experience that would up his worth as a real-estate broker. And the envelope on the table was calling to him.

"Darren? Are you having any problem with this?" The edge in

Barbieri's wasn't *exactly* intimidating, but...

"No, no."

"Okay, then. Let us proceed."

"Yes. Of course."

Angelo Barbieri got up from his desk and walked over to the wall from which he removed a large painting. Behind the painting was a wall safe. Darren watched in puzzlement as Barbieri open the safe then pulled out a suitcase which he lugged over to his desk. He deftly rotated the digits on the suitcase's security lock then unzipped the top. Inside was an array of hundred-dollar bills, checks, cashier's checks, money orders, even rolls of quarters.

"What is...?" Darren looked down at the money then back up at Angelo.

"Mr. Sill's real estate investment. I did tell you he intends to pay in cash. Didn't I just tell you that? Didn't you just agree to... the agreement?"

"But..." Wait, what agreement *had* he just agreed to? "When you said he was going to pay in *cash...*"

"I meant that he was going to pay in *cash*. In advance."

"*In advance?*" Darren gestured towards the money. "With this?"

"What, you think it's monopoly money?"

"But why in the world would he want to pay in advance? For something that, that...really doesn't even *exist* yet."

"But you'll make it exist, right?"

"*Make it exist?* How can I...? Look, how do we know the seller will accept our offer? How do we even know this property is still on the market?"

"Didn't you just say it was?"

"Sure, last time I checked, but...I mean, I haven't even talked to the agent! This is *crazy!*"

"Crazy? What? Not two minutes ago you told me you could definitely snatch the thing off the market for two million five, that's *exactly what you said!*" Angelo smacked his palm against the desk for emphasis on the last four words.

"No, no, I said I *thought* I could. But, look, look, at this point there are any number of obstacles that could"

"Okay, calm down, quit jumping through your ass, you'll give yourself *agida*. If this property's not on the market you'll find another one just as good. You'll talk to another agent. My client Mr. Sills, he's reasonable."

"*Reasonable?*"

Angelo gestured towards the money. "Take this, count it out then take care of it. Tuck it away. Today. Then go talk to your agent. You're getting a thirty-eight thousand dollar commission to take care of this, right?" His tone was testy, but Darren was too agitated to notice.

"Angelo, I can't take this suitcase full of money! What would I do with it?"

"That's your job. How do you expect to be successful if you don't even know how to handle creative financing?"

"*Creative financing?* This isn't creative financing! It's, it's…"

Money laundering. The voice inside his head whispered the word then shouted it so loudly that the picture he had refused to get all along was suddenly, unequivocally, undeniably clear. *Money laundering!* That's what this whole crazy-quilt business was about, the baffling piles of cash and checks, the impossible-to-figure-out payments, Angelo hiding behind his attorney, Howard Sill hiding behind Angelo, all components of a financial shell game; and the advance payments, the thousands of dollars, that had been to dazzle his eyes with the look of cash, the feel of it in his hands, a taste of more to come, bait on a hook to reel him in.

"It's how the business works," Angelo finished Darren's sentence for him, his eyes narrowed, snake-like. "You understand that, Bobby D? *It's how the business works.*" He pounded his fist on his desk and made Darren jump and then his face broke into a jolly grin and he pointed a stubby finger at Darren. "Gotcha! Hey," he laughed, "we really gotta get you to loosen up! You need to take a few lessons from that stepbrother of yours, heh, heh!" Angelo sat back in his chair. His face now held the kindly look of a benevolent grandfather. "Aw, kid," he said, "something bothering you? Seriously, what's bothering you?" But he answered his question before Darren could. "Wait, wait…you don't think there's something off here, do you? Is that it? You think there's something off here?"

"Well, in fact, Angelo, I'm not sure there's *not* something a little…off."

Angelo burst into huge peals of laughter. "Holy jumpin' jack-whores, wait 'til that one gets out! Bobby D thinks *Howard Sill* is some two-bit scam artist!"

"I didn't say that," said Darren, feeling uncomfortable, off balance.

Angelo slapped his desktop again and whooped in glee. When he recovered from his laughter he said, "I'm sorry Darren, you crack me up!" He took a moment to wipe the tears from his eyes. "Howard Sills is a *millionaire*. Three times over. More than three times. The guy belongs to the fuckin' Cherry Hill Chamber of Commerce! You ought to see his office, makes this place look like skid-fuckin' row! You wanna talk to his accountant? Find out how much he paid in taxes? I'll tell you how much he paid. A fuckin' shitload!" Angelo reached for his phone. "Here, we'll call his accountant. Then we'll call my accountant. You wanna talk to my accountant? Heh, heh, heh!"

Darren sat fuming at Angelo for treating him like a fool even though he now felt like one.

"He'll get a kick out of this one, heh, heh, heh," Angelo laughed as he punched the buttons of his phone.

"No, I *don't* want to talk to Howard Sill's accountant," Darren said petulantly. "Or yours."

Angelo put down his phone and when he'd recovered from his laughter he continued. "Look, kid, Howard Sills is just a very successful guy who makes a lot of money. *I'm* a very successful guy who makes a lot of money. Now, when Howard and I were your age, did we think we knew it all? Yes we did. Did we know it all? No, we didn't. Howard and I had to learn the ropes, just like you have to. And if I'd of had someone to show me the ropes who appreciated my brains and drive the way I appreciate your brains and drive, believe me, my climb up the ladder would of been a lot easier. Now look around you," Angelo gestured around him. "Does this look like the shitty dive of a criminal?"

"No, of course not, and I didn't mean"

"You know where criminals end up? Jesus, use your common sense. I'm fifty-eight years old. All the years I've been in business? Believe me, by now I'd be looking at the view from a prison cell instead of" Angelo gestured towards his fabulous view of the Philadelphia Navy Yard. "You seriously think I'd be running an outfit like this if I were involved in some kind of fraud?"

"No, of course not." Had he really thought that very thing less than three minutes ago? How stupid could he be? Jesus, he could have totally blown the whole deal and made an ass of himself in the bargain!

"No, no, that's what you were thinking, right? You were thinking that Howard Sill and myself are involved in something shady and we're trying to drag you into it, right? Isn't that what you were thinking?" The benevolent tone was gone, and Darren felt as if he were the suspect sitting on the wrong side of the interrogation table. Tiny drops of perspiration broke out along his forehead.

"No, no, I didn't think that at all," he lied, contradicting himself, but he was desperate to explain himself, clear up the misunderstanding, get back on Angelo's good side. "It's just that…"

"Yeah, yeah, tell me what it is…"

"It's just that…this suitcase…you're telling me there's two-and-a-half million *dollars* there?"

"Eh, give or take a few. We'll count it, you and me right now. I could call old Geoffry in to help us count it. Should I call Geoffry?"

"No, no! Don't call Geoffry!"

"Okay, okay," Angelo laughed, his jolly spirits returned. "Don't worry, I'm just dicking with you, you gotta know I love to dick with you. So yeah, there's two million five there."

"But why all that cash? In a suitcase?"

"Concessions. They all deal in cash."

"They do?"

"Sure. All the time. I deal in cash myself a lot of the time. It's the nature of the business."

"But…*Two-and-a-half million dollars?*"

"Eh, like I said he's a millionaire. And a Jew. That's how they like to do it."

"They do?"

"Yeah. See, Darren, the thing you gotta understand about Jews, especially the really rich self-made ones like my friend, they like to do things different. You know a lot of Jews?"

"Well, yes. My wife…my ex-wife…is half Jewish."

"See? Your *ex*-wife. You know what I mean, then."

Darren had no idea what Angelo meant, but he said, "My wife…ex-wife…she really wasn't so bad."

"Not as good as what you got now, though, eh?" Angelo chuckled with a lascivious grin that Darren chose to ignore. "But hey," he continued, "let's be honest, these sweet little cupcakes, it takes a lot of icing to *keep* 'em sweet, eh? Keep 'em pretty?" Angelo again rubbed a thumb and middle finger together. "A lot of *icing*, you know what I mean?"

"Yeah," Darren sighed.

"And then when they start popping out the little cannoli's…" Angelo finished the sentence with a wave of his hand. But it was enough to remind Darren of Trysta's three kids, the baby on the way, the money-draining house he'd had to buy to accommodate them all, his support payments for Josh, the never-ending demand for cash that he needed to supply. Darren glanced again at the contents of the suitcase.

"Go ahead, look at it," Angelo said. "Take a good look. It's a lot of cash, huh?"

Darren looked. Yes, it was a lot of cash. It was ten times, a *hundred* times more cash than he'd ever seen in his life. And Howard Sill, whoever he was, had this kind of money on hand, had it to spare, like change in his pocket. *What must it feel like to have that kind of money?* Darren had the sudden sensation of all stress falling away, of floating on a soft cloud of plenty, no worries, life humming along like a Mercedes sports car, warm as a beach house in Puerto Vallarta. The sight of the money was mesmerizing him and he felt the whimsical desire to run his fingers through it, to lift it up in his hands and breathe in the aroma of it. This was the kind of money *he* should be making, he *deserved* to be making! And why *shouldn't* he receive a $38,000 commission from Howard Sill? Darren was a broker and he could have *required* a $38,000 fee for his work if he'd wished, what he charged a client for his services was his own prerogative. In fact, he *should* be charging top dollar for his expertise, and from now on he would, and if anything he owed Angelo Barbieri and Howard Sill a debt of gratitude for making him realize this. Nor was it illegal to transact for one client through another. Unusual, maybe, from Darren's experience, but far from illegal. No, Angelo Barbieri and Howard Sill were just two successful entrepreneurs who had the foresight to recognize Darren's real-estate expertise, *genius* was the word Angelo had used, and the wisdom to compensate him commensurately. They *appreciated* him! They *valued* him!

No they don't, interrupted the voice in his head, *they don't give a rat's ass about you! They don't give a screw about your expertise! Barbieri is lying to you, bullshitting you up one side and down the other and he and his buddy Howard Sill are using you to clean their dirty money…if this Howard Sill even exists!*

"That money giving you a nice hard-on, Mr. D?"

Darren, aghast, realized that he did have the beginnings of an erection, now fading fast.

Angelo grinned, back to his old South-Philly-salvage-yard-boss persona. He held up a fist. "That kind of money, that'll give you one. Just like back when you used to watch that *succose* little wife of yours wiggle by your office, eh?"

Darren's initial outrage at Barbieri's insult against his wife was quickly replaced by the realization that, that…*Barbieri was right!* He looked at the money again and imagined Trysta's image superimposed over the bills, naked, luscious, irresistible bait on a permanent hook. He shut the suit case lid. He pulled up his courage and looked Angelo Barbieri in the eye. "No."

"No? *No?* What the hell do you mean *no?*"

Darren swallowed hard and tried to sound grown-up. "I'm sorry, Angelo, I can't take your client at this time." He reached into the inner pocket of his suit jacket and pulled out a business card which he proffered to Barbieri. "If Mr. Sill would like"

Angelo Barbieri grabbed the card from Darren's hand and threw it. "What the fuck kind of bullshit are you trying to pull? You been handed thirty-eight thousand dollars right now, *in your hand,* for doing what? *Nothing!* You tell me, what's two-and-a-half percent of two-and-a-half million? Fifty, Sixty thousand dollars?"

"About that."

"Plus the thirty-eight thousand? What, you think you can just piss on ninety-eight thousand dollars? A dumb little *jibone* like you?

Darren made a show of glancing at his watch. "I have to go now."

"*Go now?* Where the fuck you think you're going?"

"I have to pick up my son."

"You sit your ass back down and you take care of this, you hear me, Bobby D?"

"The name's Darren," he said with as much bravado as he could muster and then he bravely turned and walked towards the door.

Angelo stood and shouted after him. "The name's shit if you walk outta here! You think you're gonna find anything out there? You think anybody but me's gonna hire a stupid fuck like you to *manage real estate*? The only thing you know how to manage is your wife's pussy!"

Darren shook with anger and fear, but he kept walking towards the door.

"Hey, hey," Angelo called after him, "You like having your old job back? At Highland and Erskerberg?"

Darren stopped short. *How did Barbieri know that he had his old job back? Did Geoffry…?*"

"It's only a contractor's job, but it's got some nice health insurance, huh? Especially with your wife about to pop. Those *bambini* cost a bundle!"

Why the hell was he going on about health insurance? Darren felt a shiver of anxiety.

"But eh," Angelo shrugged, "it was the best I could do for ya, Bobby D."

Darren felt as if he'd been punched in the chest.

"But you don't need it? That's fine. I'll call my buddy Jeremy over in, what is it, Global Acquisitions? Tell him he doesn't owe me anymore."

"*Jeremy?*" *He couldn't possibly mean Jeremy Andrews, chief of Global Acquisitions…No, that was impossible!*

"Lemme see, I've got old Jeremy's number right here in my cell phone somewhere…"

Darren turned around to see Angelo Barbieri scrolling down the screen of his phone.

"I'll have to ask him if he's still dating that big-titted hottie. Guy's not married. A lot smarter than me and you, eh, D?" He looked up from his phone. "Hey, what's the matter, you look like a ghost! Like you're gonna faint! Want me to have Dina bring you up a glass of water or something?"

Darren, his voice too dry to speak, shook his head.

Barbieri continued scrolling down his phone. "I'll tell you, though, you lose that job, I don't know how the hell you're gonna keep that *commere* of yours in toys. Not to mention kids. Ah, here it is. Jeremy. Andrews."

"No, wait," Darren cried hoarsely.

"Oh, you want me to wait? You don't want me to call my friend?"

"Just…just wait. Please. Wait."

Barbieri shrugged and put down his cell phone. "Okay. Whatever you want, Bobby D. Why don't you come back and sit down again and we'll talk it over?"

Zombie-like, Darren moved towards Angelo Barbieri's desk while the voice in his head pointed out to him that it wasn't his shit-for-brains stepbrother who was Barbieri's flunky. It was himself.

Chapter Thirty-Five

Darren stared blankly at his laptop screen and tried to drown out the noise coming from the rest of the house. More than anything he wanted to take off, go find someone to talk to. Not someone to spill his guts to or ask advice of or confide in or deconstruct his life decisions with; no, he just wanted someone to hang with, grab a beer and argue about the Eagles or the 76'er's with, feel normal with. But who would that be? One of his co-workers from Highland and Erskerberg? An old college friend? The male half of one of the couples he and Sally used to do things with? He pulled out his phone, scrolled through his contacts and sighed. He was totally out of touch. With everyone. Since he'd gotten involved with Trysta it seemed he never saw, never called, never so much as texted, well, *anyone* not related by obligations of shared DNA, marriage, or work. The ties that bind. Not that he'd sensed a warm, open-armed welcome upon his return to Highland and Erskerberg; people now seemed slightly stand-offish, not exactly unfriendly, just not as friendly as before. And definitely not reaching out to re-kindle any kind of social connection outside the office. And his old school friends had pretty much all drifted away years ago, shortly after college when they'd entered the young single life and he'd entered marriage and fatherhood. And as far as their couple friends were concerned, well, since his divorce those friendships had been replaced with a colossal silence. But then he wasn't stupid enough to think that any of the wives would allow him to insert Trysta into the slot where Sally'd been then pick up where they'd left off. But hell, why even think about trying to re-connect with anybody? When would he have time? All he could realistically think about was keeping his ass in gear, juggling his contract jobs at Highland and Erskerberg and keeping on top of his property management business. *Angelo Barbieri's contract jobs. Angelo Barbieri's property management business.* Darren shook the thought out of his head. He needed to forget about everything except the task at hand, which was to make an overture to the broker for the University City property. He needed to get on it. Right now. He stared at his laptop a while longer then closed the lid. He picked up his phone, rolled through his contacts twice more then finally stopped at his father's number.

"Hello."

"Dad?"

There was a long sigh on the other end. "Look, Darren, I'm sorry about all this. I *told* your mom to keep out of it. I *told* her to keep her mouth closed. I *told* her it's your business, not ours."

Darren felt a great flutter of panic in his stomach. *What did Donna know about his business? How did she find out? It was Geoffry, that little fuck! Who had Donna told? What had she said?* "Okay, okay," Darren massaged his temples and struggled to sound calm, "what *exactly* does she know about"

"That's just what I told her," his father cut in, "what does *she* know about it? And believe me, *I'm* not judging you."

"Yeah, okay, that's great, Dad, but what the fucking hell does Donna"

"Hey, hey, I know you're mad at her, I don't blame you, I *told* her not to make that call, but Donna is still your mother and you have no right to deny her or disrespect her, no matter what she said."

"Aw, fuck, *fuck!* Do you *know* what she said?" Beads of perspiration were breaking out on his upper lip and across his forehead.

"All right, *now* you're over-reacting," his father said sternly. "Whatever your mother said, you know she was only trying to help."

"*Help?* With *what?* Who did she call? What did she tell them? What has she been spreading around about my business?" He his heart was hammering in his chest.

There was a pause at his father's end. "Oh. You mean she didn't call *you?*"

"*Me?* No, she did not call *me!*

"So you weren't calling me about her calling you?"

293

"I wasn't calling you about *anything!* I was just...*calling!* Dad, what the *hell* is *going on?*"

"Oh, heh, heh," his father chuckled weakly, "I guess we have a little misunderstanding, then."

"*What?*"

"A little misunderstanding is all. See, your mother told me she was going to call *you* to...look it's nothing, really nothing at all, just a little misunderstanding, heh, heh, don't worry, forget it. So how's work? Any new properties?"

New properties? So his father was clueless about the Angelo Barbieri business which meant Donna was too, thank Christ! "Dad," he said, his heart beat slowing to normal, "Could you please tell me what exactly is going on? What did you tell mom not to call me about?"

Another sigh on his father's end. "Aw, it's nothing. Okay, it's just, you know how the women like to call each other all the time, yack, yack, yack, whine about this and that, cry in each other's tea and then they feel better. You know what I mean."

"I have no idea what you mean."

"All right. Trysta called Donna."

"Trysta called Donna?"

"To bitch. About you."

"So? Trysta calls Donna to bitch about me all the time!"

"Well, this time she must have super-sized it, because Donna said she was gonna call *you*. Read you the riot act, I guess. But I told her not to."

"So that's *it*? *That's* all this is about?"

"Yeah. And I told your mother what goes on between you and Trysta is not our business, it's yours. You and Trysta need to work things out on your own. That's exactly what I told her."

Darren blew out a sigh of relief that came straight from his gut. Fuck, here he was about to have a heart attack over petty female bullshit!

"But look, if your mom does call, you know, just let it ride. It's just, you know, women bitching to each other about every little thing. It doesn't mean anything."

"Right."

"I mean, you know how mom always wants try and help with

things."

"Sure. I better go."

"Wait, what were you calling about, again?"

"Oh. Nothing."

"Nothing? Is everything okay?"

"Everything's good."

"Okay. Well, if everything's"

"Great, everything's great."

"You sound like you're about to have a coronary.

"I'm fine."

"Because, what, you thought that your mother was telling people about your business?"

"No, really…"

"You meant your real-estate business?"

"Well, yeah, but I mean, I just meant…"

"Okay, now I don't get it. Wouldn't you *want* her telling people about you? Wouldn't talking about you *help* your business? Isn't that what you'd want?"

"Dad, really, it's not that. It's not mom. She's fine."

"Okay. Thank you."

"I'm sorry. It's just…I've had a stressful day is all."

"Oh. Sorry to hear that. Well, you have your hands full over there."

"Yeah. But I do have a new property."

"Oh yeah? That's great. Does it look good?"

"Yeah, pretty good. A guy's interested in an apartment building in University City. The asking price is two million eight but I need to get him down to two-and-a-half million is all.

"Well, hey, that's really great!"

"Thanks."

"You wait 'til your mother hears about *that*. She'll be real impressed, you'll see. Real proud."

"I haven't closed the deal yet."

"You will. You'll see. You're in the big leagues now eh?"

"Yeah," Darren chuckled.

"Learning the ropes."

"Yeah, only…Geez, Dad, you wouldn't believe the kind of bullshit goes on in this business."

"Hey, bullshit goes on in every business. Even mine. Bullshit like *you* wouldn't believe. But if you're smart you're always figuring how to hold your nose and navigate your way through it."

"Huh, that's exactly what I seem to be doing these days."

"That's all you *can* do. Believe me. You get down and dirty and then you get back up again. That's life in the big leagues. You can't sweat it."

"Yeah?"

"Trust me. But hey, you worked it and snagged yourself a potentially huge deal. You should be feeling pretty good about yourself."

"Thanks Dad."

"One more thing. You *really* need to relax."

As soon as he hung up Darren flipped open his laptop and pulled up the University City property. His dad was right. He *had* gotten down and dirty, held his nose and navigated his way through Angelo Barbieri's bullshit to land a potentially huge deal. That's all that really mattered, right? And he'd land a whole lot more deals, with or without Barbieri's help. So fuck it, he was just going to have to get used to life in the big leagues and quit sweating it... *And you can go fuck yourself, Geoffry!* Damn, he *was* feeling good about himself, re-energized, ready to push this deal on through! He pulled up the University City property on his computer and found the number of the broker. He picked up his phone and as his thumb hit the first digit his brain was jolted to Timbuktu and back by the most ungodly scream. Like someone was being skinned alive. Then there were two screams, then three, then the screams morphed into an angry, plaintive, argument, one, two, three, four voices, an aria of arguing, the noise moving close, closer, closer, until it was right outside his office door and then the door flew open and the whole conflagration of shouting, screaming and tears spilled into his office.

"You have *got* to do something!" Trysta cried breathlessly.

"*Do* something? What the hell am supposed to?...*Everybody shut up!*"

The uproar immediately ceased. "Look, you guys have got to take this somewhere else. I'm trying to *work,* this is *important,* for God's sake."

"That's all you ever *do*, anymore," Trysta sniveled.

"Yeah, that's all you do," whined Trina.

"Yeah, you don't even take care of us anymore," snipped little Samantha.

"Aw, come on!" These kids were seriously irritating the crap out of him!

"Bunch of assholes," Zach muttered angrily.

The two girls' hands flew to their mouths while they bounced and squealed with shocked laughter.

"Mommy, Zach just said"

"Mommy, Zach said a…s…s…"

"*Zachary Jablonski!*" His mother cried then she turned to Darren. "See? You see what I'm going through?"

"Assholes," Zach repeated and stormed from the room.

"Now you wait just a minute!" Darren flew after Zach and grasped him by the arm before it occurred to him that he had absolutely no idea what to do next. He let go of Zach's arm and wondered what kind of hell this kid must be going through, trying to grow up in this female-flavored insane asylum.

Then it hit him. "Wait," he said, "don't you have a, you know, a psychologist's appointment today? Aren't you supposed to be there right now?"

"He does *not* need a *psychologist!*" Trysta and the girls had filed out closely behind Zach and Darren. "What he needs is a *father*, but Silvio is useless and *you're* too *busy* to"

"What time is the appointment? Five o'clock, right?"

"Forget it," Zach mumbled.

"Yes, forget it," Trysta huffed, "he is *not* going to see that, that *quack.*"

"Quack, quack," giggled the girls as their brother stomped off.

"You two stop that!" Darren cried. "Trysta, you've got to take him! I can't do it, I've got to work." *And I need you all out of the house,* he thought. Again he hurried after Zach. "You're going to your psy…doctor's appointment."

"No I'm not.'

"Yes you are!"

"No he's"

"*Yes he is,*" Darren cut Trysta off. "Come on, you've *got* to take him."

"Oh, really?" Trysta stood with her arms crossed above her belly. "And what am I supposed to do with the girls?"

"Well, you'll take them with you. Let them color in the waiting room, or something."

"Huh!" Trina cried, "I am *not* coloring in the waiting room!"

"Yeah, coloring is for *babies*" added Sam. "We're *not* going!"

"Trysta, please, I've *got* to get some work done!"

"*Huh!* I am *not* dragging my poor children out of their home just so *you* can bury your nose in your laptop."

"Aw Trys, come *on!*"

"I'm not taking him. Period." Trysta turned her back and stomped over to the sofa where she plopped herself down with a loud grunt.

Shit, Darren mumbled under his breath, *shit, shit, shit!* "All right, Zach, let's go. Where's your doctor? Right across from the mall, right?" *I can't believe I'm doing this!*

Trysta popped up to a sitting position. "What, *you're* taking him?"

"*I'm* taking him." *I'm crazy! I've got to get on that University property!*

"Oh, no you are not! You are *not* taking my son to see that *quack!*"

"I *said* stop it!" *Aw, what the hell, I can't get anything done in this mad house, anyway!*

"Mommy," said Samantha, "Daddy Darren doesn't want you to say quack anymore."

"*Nobody* says that word anymore, you got it?"

Trysta grabbed her stomach. "Oh, no" she moaned breathlessly, "I...I think I'm"

"Then lay back down. Zach, you go put on your..." To his surprise he saw that Zach was already waiting by the door with his coat on.

"Daddy Darren will you take us to the mall?" Trina chirped sweetly.

"What?"

"While Zach is at his doctor's?"

"I need a present for Zoey's birthday party," cried Samantha.

"Can we buy her a Barbie outfit at the mall?"

"Aw, no, I'm sorry, no."

"Why not?" Trina and Sam cried together.

"Because," Darren, said as he hurried back to his office while the girls trotted after him, "I'm going to grab my phone, see? And my laptop, see? And I'm going to put them into my briefcase and take them with me and get some work done while Zach is at his appointment. And you two are going to stay here. With your Mom."

The two girls let loose a chorus of protest as they formed a hopping, shrieking moving wall around him, pulling at his arms, his elbows, his briefcase as he tried to make his way back to the front door.

"We want to go!"

"I *need* to buy a"

"I don't *want* to stay here!"

"Why does Zach always get to"

"It's not *fair*! We *never* get to"

Darren stopped when he got to the living room. He held his briefcase up protectively close to his chest and looked over the two bouncing, squealing heads.

"Trysta!" he shouted, "Hey, you've *got* to *do* something about these two!"

Trysta closed her eyes and threw her arm across her head. "*Ohhhh*," she moaned.

"*Aw, Jesus*," he muttered in defeat. "Okay, okay," he barked, "you two grab your coats then everybody hurry up and jump into the van! *Now!*"

"Can we eat supper at the mall?" asked Trina as she hurried into her coat.

"Fine! Come on, Zach, help your little sister with her coat."

"Fine," Zach muttered. "But they better hurry the hell up."

"Zachary," Trysta whimpered weakly, "if you do *not* stop that awful language..."

"Forget it," snapped Darren, "Let the doctor fix it."

"Huh, like that *quack* could fix"

"I *said* stop it," Darren cut her off.

"Mommy," said Samantha, "Daddy Darren doesn't want you to

say quack anymore."

"Fine," Trysta sniffed. "Ohhh," she moaned.

"Just forget it," Zach spat, walking away from the door. "I'm not going!"

Again Darren grabbed Zach's arm and stopped him from removing his coat. "Yeah, you are." He slid Zach's coat back over his shoulders.

"No I'm not," Zach repeated then allowed Darren to steer him quickly to the door. "What about her?" Zach cocked his head towards his mother.

"*Ohhh,*" Trysta moaned.

"She's okay, that's how they are when they're pregnant, she just needs some rest." Darren hurried over to the couch and patted Trysta's shoulder. "You're fine, right?"

Trysta moaned more piteously.

"See? She's fine!" He gave her a quick kiss on the forehead.

"Hurry *up,* Darren," squealed Trina, "you're making Zach *late!*"

"Yes, hurry *up,*" echoed Samantha, "you're making Zach *late* for his *doctor!*"

"I don't need to go to any damn doctor, anyway" Zach huffed.

"Yes you do," Darren snapped as he herded Zach and his sisters out the door. "You need to go to your doctor." *And I need to get the hell out of here!*

Chapter Thirty-Six

The caseworker looked fresh out of school despite her up-swept hairdo, black-framed DKNY glasses and leather briefcase which she'd snapped open on Sally's dinette table and from which she'd withdrawn a form-laden clipboard and a silver Cross pen. She wore a fitted navy suit with a pin-stripe cream-colored shirt and pencil skirt that would have looked killer-stylish had she weighed about thirty-five pounds less. Still it did make her look official, especially with the Philadelphia Department of Human Services ID she wore around her neck which displayed her photo, chubby-faced and drop-dead serious, above the name "Jordan Edelsmith." The expression on her ID photo was the same one she now wore as she tramped through Sally's apartment on five-inch power heels like a general inspecting a thoroughly substandard field division.

"So you've got two bedrooms? And only one bathroom? That's all?"

"Well, see," Sally replied, talking a little too fast, "there's only Joshua and me, so one bathroom is plenty, and we really only need two bedrooms, see, David, he can sleep in a crib in my room, there's plenty of room for a crib, see? Crib, changing table, whatever a baby needs, heh, heh."

"Hmmm," Jordan Edelsmith replied. "So where is he?"

"Oh, well I don't know, I mean, I expect he's with his parents, his mother, whatever. Across the hall. That's where they live, right across the hall. Do you want me to go see if"

"I'm *talking* about *your* son," the caseworker cut her off. "Joshua?" She glanced at her clipboard to verify, as if Sally had not introduced her son less than five minutes earlier and repeated his name within the past twenty seconds.

"Joshua? Oh, well, he was standing right here, he's probably"

"I'm in the living room, Mom," Josh called. "I'm reading my book."

The case worker gave Sally a raised-eyebrow look of disproval. "Do you often lose track of the whereabouts of your child?"

"What? No, no, I *never* do, *never*. Look, it's a small condo."

"Yes, I can see that."

"So he's never out of earshot."

"I just hope," Jordan glanced at her clip board again, "*Sally*, that you understand the responsibility that you're taking on."

"Of *course* I do, and I"

"Do you have a kitchen?

"A kitchen? Yes! Of course! We just passed it!" *Are you stupid?* Sally thought, *Or just being a bitch?*

"Really? I must have missed it."

A bitch, Sally decided, *a snarky little bitch.*

Jordan Edelsmith walked back down the hall to Sally's kitchen. "Kitchenette," she mumbled as she checked off something on her clip board.

"Look, Jordan,"

"Ms. Edelsmith," the caseworker corrected her.

"*Ms. Edelsmith,*" Sally continued, struggling hard to keep her annoyance at bay, "I *assure* you that I have everything here I need to take care of a baby."

"I'm sure you believe you do. But you have to realize that for an unwed mother like yourself"

"Divorced." *You over-privileged little twit!*

"...taking care of two young children is much more difficult than taking care of one."

"I *know* that!"

"Now, calm down, Sally," Ms. Edelsmith said firmly, putting a hand on Sally's arm, "you just have to understand"

If she tells me I have to underfuckingrstand one more thing I'm gonna lose it!

"...that I'm just warning you that you cannot let a baby out of your sight. Not for one moment. I've seen far too many cases of parental neglect, and believe me,"

"Parental neglect, are you *kidding me? I have NEVER"*

"I *asked* you to calm down." She squeezed Sally's arm ever so slightly, which had the effect of making Sally want to smack Ms. Edelsmith's designer glasses off her condescending young snout. Sally took a deep calming breath instead. *This is a test,* she told herself, *to see if I'm easily rattled.* She took one more deep breath.

"I just meant," Sally tried again, gently easing herself from the girl's grip, "that of course I would never let a *baby* out of my sight. But Josh is six years old."

"I'm six years old," Josh echoed, sidling up to his mother.

Sally wrapped her arms around his shoulders. "And he's a very good boy and a big help to me."

"I see," sniffed Ms. Edelsmith. She knelt, as gracelessly as her narrow skirt and heels necessitated, so that she was eye-level with Joshua. She looked sublimely uncomfortable, even with a wide smile pasted on her face. "Hello, Joshua," she crooned.

"Hello," he replied uncertainly.

"My name is Jordan. Would you like to have a little baby in your house?"

"Yes."

"Really?" Her smile widened while her eyes narrowed in disbelief.

"Yes."

"Do you like babies?"

"Yes."

"Do you know lots of babies?"

Josh looked at her in confusion then turned to his mother for clarity.

"Well, yes," Sally answered for him, "he knows Baby David, and his little cousin, and"

"Excuse me, Sally, I'm *talking* to *Joshua.* Now, Joshua, do you know a lot of babies?"

"Yes," he replied.

"Does Mommy make you help a lot around the house?"

Josh's eyes darted up to his mother's and then back to Jordan's. "Yes," he answered unsurely.

"What does she make you do?"

"Now, wait a minute, Jordan," Sally cut in.

Jordan stood up. "It's *Ms. Edelsmith*," she looked Sally squarely in the eye, "and I am required by law to check for all possible signs of child abuse."

"*Child abuse?* Are you *crazy?*"

"I *strongly* suggest you calm down, Sally. Now, if there's no abuse or neglect you have nothing to worry about. But I'm warning you, I know the signs."

"The signs? *What* signs?"

Jordan bent down again and put her hands on Josh's shoulders, forcing aside his mother's hands. "You don't have to be afraid, Joshua. You're safe now. Does mommy bring men into the house?"

Josh, still perplexed, looked again from Jordan to his mother.

"Oh my God," Sally cried, "this is retarded!"

"Sally, we do *not* use that word!"

"Oh no? Well, how about *stupid?* How about *idiotic?* Because that's what this whole crock of sh...nonsense is!"

"Okay, Sally, that does it, you are out of control!"

"*I'm* out of control? *I'm* out of control?"

"M-Mommy?"

Sally looked down to see tears rolling down Josh's cheeks, his chest heaving with silent sobs.

"Oh, my Baby!" Sally swooped her son into her arms and held him close. "Don't cry, don't cry, we're just talking, that's all, everything's all right."

"You *think* so?" Jordan asked archly.

"Shhh, don't cry, my darling," Sally cooed, "it's all right, it's all right." Sally carried Joshua to the couch and rocked him, cradling his head against her shoulder, still crooning softly, "It's all right, my baby, it's all right."

"I wouldn't be so sure about that!" Jordan Edelsmith marched over to Sally's table, flung open her briefcase and tossed her clipboard inside. She crossed her arms and faced Sally, whose attention was still centered on her son.

"Shhh," Sally whispered.

"Sally," said Jordan Edelsmith in a tone of high authority, "you need to understand that, from what I can surmise, I now have serious questions about whether you are a competent parent."

The words burst from her, uncontrollable as a swarm of angry hornets. "Oh yeah, *Jordan*? Well *you* need to understand that from what *I* can *surmise, I* now have serious questions about whether you graduated from college ten minutes ago or fifteen, and whether you're a competent *anything!*" And no sooner had the words left her mouth than she desperately wanted to suck them back in. *Shit,* she thought, *shit, shit, SHIT!* "Joshie," she whispered in her son's ear, "you take your book and finish reading it in your room, okay?" Joshua, at six years old already too adept at reading the signs, hopped from his mother's lap, sprinted to his room and shut the door. Sally, meanwhile, hurried from the couch back to the table where the caseworker stood, seething.

"Ms. Edelsmith, I'm so, so sorry!"

"I'm sure you are!" Jordan Edelsmith slammed shut her briefcase and smacked down the clasps. "But it's a little too late for that, isn't it?"

"It's just that I've been under a lot of stress lately."

"I can see *that,*" Jordan snapped. "I can also see that not only should you *not* be cleared for foster parenting, you are not fit to be raising your own child!"

"What?"

"I'm sorry, Sally, but I am going to recommend that you be declared an unfit parent."

"*What?*" Sally laughed in disbelief. "You're kidding me right? *Right?*"

"I am not." Ms. Edelsmith flipped open her briefcase again and riffled through some papers. "You're out of control and I'm filing a child endangerment report. I'm required to under the law." She pulled out her cell phone. "In fact under the circumstances I'll have to call my supervisor to arrange for an emergency removal of your child. Today."

"What? Wait! No! No!" Sally instinctively grabbed the caseworker's arm. "Don't! *Please!*"

"Let go of me. Now. Or I'm calling the police."

"Oh, God, oh, God, *please don't!*" Sally quickly let go of Jordan's arm.

Jordan stood with her thumb poised over her phone. "As soon as I call you can expect an officer to come and take your son into the custody of Human Services."

"No, no, oh *no!*" The tears were rolling down Sally's cheeks, her hands folded in supplication, "Please, *please,* I'm, sorry, I'm sorry, I'll do anything, please, *please, don't take my baby, please!*"

The caseworker let out a long sigh, tapping her finger against her phone. "You have to understand, Sally, I've seen too many cases like yours..."

Sally shut out the rest of Jordan Edelsmith's delivery, rushed into the kitchen and grabbed her cell phone from the counter.

"...so it's actually against my better judgement," Jordan continued,

Sally closed her eyes and forced herself to calm down while she pressed in the number.

"...but maybe, just *maybe* if you can convince me by starting with a *meaningful* apology...wait, who do you think you're calling?" Ms. Edelsmith stomped into the kitchen after Sally.

"Maria? It's Sally Miller, please, Maria, *please,* it's an emergency, is Mr. Tilley there? Oh, thank you, Maria, *thank you!*"

"You better hang up that phone," barked Ms. Edelsmith, "you're in big trouble, you know!"

As soon as she heard Charleston's voice Sally began crying again. "Mr. Tilley," she sobbed, "the caseworker, she says I'm in trouble, she's writing me up for child abuse, she's going to, to..." Sally could barely get the words out, "take Joshua away!"

"What?" Charleston sounded dumbfounded. "*What* caseworker?"

"Who came to inspect my home, you know, for David, she says they're going to come today and take Joshua away! Mr. Tilley, *please* help me!"

"Mrs. Miller, I'm confused. Why would the caseworker tell you such a thing?"

"She says my condo's too small, my kitchen's too small, I only have two bedrooms and, and one bathroom."

"Wait, you're telling me she's accusing you of child abuse...because your *house* is too small?"

"She says I'm an unfit parent, she thinks I bring men into the house and mistreat my son...Mr. Tilley, I love my son above all, I would never do anything like that, *never!*"

"I believe you, Mrs. Miller. Who is the caseworker?"

"Jordan Edelsmith."

"Is she still at your house?"

"Yes, she's right here."

"May I speak to her, please?"

"Here." Sally proffered the phone to Jordan, who stood with her arms tightly crossed, biting her lip.

"Who is that?" she asked.

"My lawyer," Sally sniffed.

"Your *lawyer?*"

"Charleston Tilley. He wants to talk to you."

Jordan Edelsmith hesitated and then took the phone and cleared her throat. "This is Jordan Edelsmith."

"This is Charleston Tilley, Mrs. Miller's attorney. Ms. Edelsmith, may I ask what's going on over there? Have you been authorized by the Department of Human Services to tell Mrs. Miller that her child is being taken from her?"

The color drained from the caseworker's' face. "Oh, heh, heh, no, no, just a misunderstanding. On Mrs. Miller's part."

"I see. So you didn't tell Mrs. Miller she was an unfit parent? Or that her son was going to be taken from her?"

"Oh, heh, heh, I just meant that, you know, I was telling her that she has to be careful if she has a baby in the house because, you know, I've, uh, heh, heh, just seen all kinds of, you know"

"So," Charleston cut her off, "there's no problem? With the home inspection?"

"Oh, heh, heh, no, no. She passed my inspection. I was just going to tell her."

"All right, then. Do you have the necessary paperwork on hand, Ms. Edelsmith?"

"Oh, yes, it's right here, heh, heh, ready to sign."

"I'll advise Mrs. Miller to sign it, then."

"Yes. I think that would be a good idea," Jordan Edelsmith chirped, sounding as pleased as if she'd come up with the idea herself.

"Thank you, Ms. Edelsmith. May I speak to Mrs. Miller again?"

"Certainly."

Jordan Edelsmith's smile turned to the sourest of expressions as she handed the phone back to Sally. Sally, meanwhile, stood in wonder at this woman's transformation from club-wielding Genghis Khan to tail-wagging Lhasa Apso.

"Mr. Tilley? Is everything going to be all right?"

"I believe so. Ms. Edelsmith is going to sign off on the inspection. You'll need to sign, too, and make sure that she gives you your copies."

Sally let out a sob of relief. "Oh, Mr. Tilley, thank you so much. My heart is still pounding!"

"You're all right, Mrs. Miller. It's a good thing you called me. If you have any more problems you'll call me back."

"Yes, thank you, thank you."

"In fact, give me a call after Ms. Edelsmith leaves, we'll go over the paper work, make sure everything is as it should be."

"Yes, I will." Sally wiped away tears of gratitude. "Thanks again, Mr. Tilley."

"You're quite welcome, Mrs. Miller."

After Sally hung up Ms. Edelsmith shoved the paperwork at Sally. "Here," she huffed. "You didn't need to go crying to your lawyer!"

Eat shit, bitch, Sally mentally responded as she signed the papers then handed them back to the caseworker. She waited in silence while Jordan Edelsmith arranged her papers then shut her briefcase one last time. She paused on her way out the door and gave Sally a poisonous look. "I don't even know why you need another baby."

Sally waited to answer until she heard Jordan Edelsmith's high heels clacking down her stairway. Then she stood with her back leaning against the door and said, softly, "Because, you fucking little upper-middle-class suburbia prep-school snot sucker, *I do!*"

Chapter Thirty-Seven

"It's twelve-fifteen and if I don't have a Reuben and fries from C and M's like right now I'm gonna end up smoking a cigarette!"

Sally chuckled without glancing up from her computer screen. "Go for it, Girl."

"For what? The Reuben or the cigarette?

Sally looked up at from her screen at Joanne. "*Not* the cigarette!"

"What are you eating?"

"Oh, I brought some" Sally reached under her desk into her purse and pulled out a zip-lock baggie, "cheese and crackers."

"*O-kay!* Did you bring some wine, too?" Joanne reached for the baggie and examined the contents. "Um, saltines and Velveeta in a baggie does not qualify to be called cheese and crackers." She plopped down the bag down on Sally's desk. "How much more data needs to be schtupped on that one?"

Sally typed a few more keys then hit "Enter." "There. Done."

"Come with me to C and M's for lunch. Unless you're seriously jonesing for Velveeta and saltines. And if you hit the lotto this morning then you're paying, otherwise my treat."

***

"So," Joanne asked as they settled into a booth at the crowded delicatessen with their sandwiches, "how's your messy life?"

Sally sighed. "Fine, I guess. Until I start thinking."

"Don't think, then. Just do."

"You sound like my mom again."

"Well, your mom and I do basically roll the same way, believe it or not."

Sally chuckled. "I'd say not. But I *am* taking her advice and just doing what needs to be done."

"Good. That's the best medicine. You're still going to foster your little Nicaraguan, right? You didn't flunk the home inspection or anything?"

Sally pressed her fingertips against her eyelids and shook her head. "Oh, my God, Joanne, I almost did!"

"What? How'd you almost do that?"

"I don't know, I…Ms. Edelsmith."

"Ms. *Whodlsmith?*"

"Ms. Edelsmith. The caseworker. She just kept saying things like my condo is too small and I bring men into the house and I abuse Josh."

"Wait, you're kidding me, right?"

Sally shook her head. "Then the worst thing, she said she was going to have me declared an unfit parent and have Human Services come and take Josh away." Sally began tearing up at the memory. "It was a nightmare."

"Well, what a motherless little *twat!* She was messing with you, right?"

"Well, yes, but I didn't know it at the time. I panicked and called Charleston on the spot."

"Good for you! Did he kick that caseworker's hiney for you?"

"He didn't even *have* to. The *second* Ms. Big-Shot-Just-Graduated-From-College realized I had my lawyer on the phone…"

Joanne burst out laughing. "I bet she about shit herself!"

"She about *did*," Sally laughed. "But here's the thing. I couldn't believe how quickly she turned from a fire-breathing dragon into a, I don't know, slobbering…*rabbit*. She just did a complete 360."

"Huh. I guess that's what a lawyer can do for poor slobs like us, right?"

"I guess," Sally replied thoughtfully.

They ate in silence for a moment then Sally said, "I'm going back to school."

Joanne stopped in mid-chew and stared at Sally in bug-eyed disbelief. "Uh, no, Hon, what you're…"

"Geez, Joanne," Sally laughed, "finish chewing first, you're gonna choke!"

Joanne finished chewing and swallowed. "I *said*, what you're *going* to do is take in another kid. And figure out how to make *that* work. "

"But you're the one who told me I needed go back to school and finish my degree. So I could get ahead and make more money in my job. Remember?"

"Yes I did say that, back when your life was only half as all-over-the-place as it is now. Hon, you have got the most impracticable sense of *timing.*"

When Sally didn't answer Joanne continued. "Okay, why would you even *consider* going back to school *now?*"

Sally shrugged. "I need to."

"I'm not arguing with that, all I'm saying is…Aw, screw it. Okay, fine. So you're going back to school. You've thought out a time line?"

"Not yet. But I guess if I start applying right now…"

"In your buckets of spare time"

"Maybe I could start next fall."

"Geez," Joanne sighed. "Okay, maybe I can give you some help. Once again I find myself yanked onto team Sally!"

Sally reached across the table and grabbed Joanne's hand. "Oh, thank you Joanne, thank you!"

"Don't thank me. Thank Ponti for being too cheap to send me to a shrink to get my head examined. What, you're crying again? I swear, girl, the rate you spill 'em you're gonna run out of tears."

"I'm sorry, Joanne, it's just that you've been"

"Oh, please," Joanne cut her off. "Look, I kicked my own four kids' butts through college, I guess I can kick yours through, too."

Sally laughed and wiped her eyes. "Be my guest."

"Okay, but you do know that I can't make any work-related exceptions for you, right? No missing days or any of that bullshit. I mean, I can't cover for you."

"Joanne, I would never ask. I'm thrilled you haven't fired me so far."

"Well, a good worker is a good worker. And I know you never expect any special consideration. Which is why I give it to you. I don't mind investing when I know my investment is going to pay off. Stop crying. Okay, listen. Money shouldn't be a problem. Money you can get easily enough. As long as you don't mind being up to your ear holes in debt until the day you die."

"Whatever."

"You've got to get into an adult education program."

"Like at Temple?"

"Exactly like at Temple. You know Mrs. McWilliams? Peg McWilliams from church?"

"My mom knows her. And I went to Little Flower with Megan McWilliams."

"Were you friends?"

"Facebook friends. For a while."

"That's good enough. Anyway, little Megan managed to scoop up a PhD and just got hired as assistant director of Temple's Continuing Ed department. I was going to point you in her direction back when I first suggested you finish your degree. Before you blew me off."

"Sorry. I was in kind of a bad place at the time."

"You're in a great place now?"

"Yeah. Right."

"Anyway, I'll talk to Peg McWilliams, she and I are on the Charitable Works committee together, I'll get her to tell Megan about you, and we'll all sit on Megan to help you get into Temple. Sound like a plan?"

"Like a great plan."

"Okay, now we've got the 'why', 'when' and 'how' figured out. That just leaves the 'what'. So what is it you're willing to sell you soul to the student loan empire for so that you can be a zombie slave and forego sleep for about the next six years?"

"Make that the next twelve years."

"What? Good lord, Child, what in the hell do you want to be? A doctor?"

Sally looked Joanne squarely in the eye. "A lawyer."

Chapter Thirty-Eight

"It's like I told you, there's no Band-Aid fix for this. We replace the pipe or we don't." Silvio listened patiently to the same protestations and pleas he always heard from the owners and managers of these old rental units with plumbing that had worn out long ago. "Yeah, I'm sure that's what it is, I'm right here in the apartment, we just ran a camera down the line, I see it all the time…You gotta understand, Bob, the pipe connected to the toilet is over seventy-five years old. It's corroded. The paper gets flushed and on its way to the sewer it's getting caught on the rust and metal splinters lining the inside of the pipe." Silvio waited again while the manager aired another round of skepticism. "Believe me, that's what it is. So now you got two options. Replace the pipe or tell the tenants not to flush any paper down the toilet. Or else let them keep flushing the paper and you can keep calling me every three weeks to clean out the pipe but that's gonna cost you, too." Silvio let the apartment manager complain, he knew there was no use cutting to the chase before he'd let them try out every argument they could think of against getting the work done. In the end they'd either get it done or they wouldn't. "Well, no, the owner isn't gonna like it, who would? But she wants her building up to code with working toilets she's gonna have to get it done, you know what I'm saying?" Next would come the question. "A building like this one? I'll have to take one more look, but I'd say fifteen thousand, to be on the safe side. Maybe a little less, but you want to be safe, say fifteen thousand…No, the owner's not gonna like it, but *you're* the manager, *you* have to deal with the tenants, *you* have to deal with the city, I mean that's what she pays you for, right?…Right, well, the owner wants to call me, sure, I'll talk to her, but I'll tell her the same thing I'm telling you…No, she can't call my Uncle Bud…yeah, I know she trusts Bud but Bud's getting ready to go on a cruise and he doesn't want to hear about how your boss doesn't want to deal with me…Look, you tell her she can go with me or she can call Kensington Gas And Sewer and they'll do the job for twenty-five thousand, whatever she wants…Yeah…No problem."

Silvio slipped his phone into his pocket as Ascensiòn wheeled the reel of fiberglass cable attached to the camera head from the bathroom into the living room of the old apartment. A young Hispanic woman followed behind him.

"We got us a big job here?" Ascensiòn asked.

"Eh, I don't know. Look, my Spanish isn't good enough, would you tell this lady her family's gonna have to not flush any paper down the commode for now?"

"Sure," Ascensiòn replied, "no problem."

The woman listened while Ascensiòn explained and then she nodded and shrugged indifferently.

Ascensiòn turned back to Silvio. "No problem for them. They're from Honduras."

"What do you mean?"

"Nobody flushes paper down the toilet anywhere in Central America."

"No?"

"Not even in the rich people's houses. Not even in the hotels."

"No?"

"Pipes down there, they block up like that." Ascensiòn snapped his finger.

"Huh."

They loaded the equipment into Silvio's van then Silvio climbed into the driver's side, Ascensiòn into the passenger's seat. They drove in silence for a few moments then Ascensiòn said, "Everything okay, Boss?

"Okay with me. You and Lupe all set to go?"

"One more week. How you gonna translate for your Spanish customers when I'm not here?"

"You'll be back. You could be back in six months."

"Maybe. Maybe more. How you gonna translate until I get back? Why you don't come over anymore to learn Spanish?"

"Too busy these days."

"That's what Sally said."

Silvio glanced at Ascensiòn. "What did Sally say?"

"That you don't come over anymore because you too busy. Too bad. Sally is getting better than you now." Ascensiòn chuckled, "Sally getting so good in Spanish, you will have to hire *her* to translate for you."

Silvio's fist tightened ever so slightly around the steering wheel. "That's not gonna happen."

"No," Ascensiòn sighed. "Me and Lupe, we think you and Sally..." Ascensiòn held his palms together then quickly pulled them apart.

"Happens, right?" Silvio swallowed against the tightening in his throat.

"Aw, man, what happens? You and Sally?"

"You tell me, I don't know. I just don't know. I don't understand. Women?...I just don't..." Silvio shook his head.

"No time for that, Maje, you have no time. Listen," Ascensiòn leaned closer to Silvio. He opened his hand out flat and pointed to the center of his palm. "You have a piece of gold in your hand, what do you do?" He closed his fist in a quick move, "You hold onto it tight! You don't, then it's gonna fall," he opened his palm again and turned it over, "right on the ground. Somebody else come and grab it," Ascensiòn snapped his fingers, "like that! You understand me, Maje?"

"Yeah, but"

"You got no time for bullshit, you know, Boss? Lupe and me, no time for bullshit now. We leaving our son. Maybe we don't come back."

"Aw, come on Ascensiòn, of course you're gonna"

"Maybe we don't right?"

Silvio sighed. "Right."

"I think Sally is a good person. We think she will be a good mother for David. What do you think, Silvio?"

"Aw, yeah, Sally, she'll be a good mother to David, you don't have to worry about that. Whatever else she is, she is a good mother. Real good mother. And Josh, he's a good boy."

"Yes, we think Josh will be a good brother to David. So we are happy to go back to…" Ascensiòn's voice cracked, "Leòn." He turned away from Silvio and stared out the window. He sniffed then ran his sleeve across his eyes.

Silvio kept his eyes on the road. "Yeah, you don't have to worry about a thing while you're" He grabbed his ringing cellphone. "Yeah?...What?...Geez. Right now?...Bustleton Avenue, you say? Aw, Ida, I can't, I've gotta go pick up my kids. What about Kevin, he's on call this weekend, right? Right, his kid's playoff's tonight. Great, well, let me think…"

"Hey, Boss, give me the job, I can take it."

"Wait a minute, Ida." Silvio turned to Ascensiòn. "Look, Ascensiòn, today was gonna be your last job with me. I mean, every time I pay you I'm risking both our necks, you know that, right?"

"No, no, you don't have to pay me anymore. I work for free this time. You need me I work for free tomorrow and Sunday, too, all weekend."

Silvio sighed. "Somebody threw a whole box of instant potatoes down a garbage disposal. And they got a dinner party tonight."

Ascensiòn laughed. "What? A whole box?"

"Yeah. You name it, right? Then they tried to flush it out by running water down the disposal. The thing's probably turned to concrete by now. You'll have to snake the drain. It's a row house at Bustleton and Levick."

"Yeah, I know Bustleton and Levick. You drop me off at the shop, I'll load the snake into my truck, I can be there, maybe an hour, hour and a half."

Silvio sighed again then turned back to his phone. "Okay, tell them somebody'll be there in the next hour or two. We'll be back at the shop in about twenty minutes, you can give Ascensiòn the address. Yeah thanks, Ida. 'Bye." He turned to Ascensiòn. "Your last job, okay?"

"Sure, Boss!"

Silvio helped Ascensiòn load the motorized snake auger into his truck then he reached for his wallet and pulled out three twenties which he proffered to Ascensiòn. "Here. Clearing out that drain'll probably take you an hour or so. Maybe two, who knows? It takes more than two you let me know. The rest is to cover the weekend rate."

"No way, you don't pay me for this. This I do for free."

"You're not doing this for free."

Ascensiòn grasped Silvio by the arm and pushed away the money. "You pay me, but not with this. You pay me by watching out for my son. You keep an eye on Sally, make sure everything is good with her so she takes care of David."

Silvio shook his head. "No, I don't …look, it's like I told you. Sally's a good mother. You don't have to worry. Sally doesn't need me watching out for her. She doesn't need me at all."

Ascensiòn's grasp on Silvio's arm tightened. "Please. You watch out for my boy, *please*." A tear rolled from the corner of his eye and Silvio couldn't stand it.

"Yeah, of course I'll watch out for your little boy. Of course I will. And here," he pushed the three twenties into Ascensiòn's hand, "for the job."

"No, no, I don't take any money."

"Yes you do. You work for me, I pay you. Period. Here."

Ascensiòn took the cash. "Thanks, Silvio. You're a good man. And Sally, she's a good woman. I'm sorry it don't work for you."

"Yeah," Silvio sighed, and he thought, *I just don't understand…*

Chapter Thirty-Nine

Trysta paced the bedroom floor, breathless from sobbing, the tears rolling down her cheeks. Darren paced alongside her, his voice pleading.

"Trysta, Baby, you've *got* to *stop!* All this crying, it isn't good for the baby!

Trysta stopped short and turned to Darren so that her face almost touched his.

"Do you even *care*? You, who won't even rescue his *own son* from that...*horrible monster!* She turned away from him and continued pacing. He continued pacing after her.

"Aw, Baby, you've seriously got to *calm down!*"

"Oh!" Trysta bounced down hard on the bed.

Darren cringed. "Oh, geeze, don't *do* that! You're gonna bounce something loose!"

She sat with her head in her hands, blonde hair streaming down over her arms and shoulders. "I can't believe you're talking to me like that," she whimpered.

"Talking to you like what?"

"Always taking *her* side!"

"I'm not taking"

"What goes on when you're over there?"

"*What?*"

"With you and Sally. What goes on?"

"Goes on? *Nothing* goes on, *Jesus!*"

"Then why won't you"

"I came to a decision is all."

Trysta looked imploringly into his eyes. "We came to a decision together. You and I."

"Oh, yeah, when we came to that decision your tongue was halfway down my *throat!*

Trysta grabbed her stomach and began moaning.

Darren hurried to Trysta and knelt before her, his hands caressing her arms. "Aw, Trysta, geez, Baby, what is it, what's...." He stopped short. Suddenly he had a stomach-churning sense of *déjà-vu*. Followed by a sense of *pas-encore-vu*. This wasn't life. This was some kind of merry-go-round existence that always came back, always *would* come back, as long as they lived, to him and Trysta in this bedroom, arguing, crying, joylessly copulating. He had to get off. Somehow. He stood up and backed away from her.

"*Oooh,*" Trysta moaned, doubling over, "*help* me!"

Darren ignored her moans. "See, I'm thinking a little more clearly at the moment..."

"*Oooh...*"

"...and I'm not suing Sally for custody. Not ever."

Trysta shot up straight and let out with a howl.

"Oh for God's sake, Trysta, what's with these pains?"

"Nothing," she sniveled, rubbing her hands across her eyes. "I'm all right."

"You're okay?"

"Yes I am. I just don't know what's the matter with *you!*"

"*Me?* Nothing's the matter with me!"

"Well then, when you say you're gonna do something you're supposed to *do* it!"

"Look I *told* you, I"

"You *know* I'm not one to think about myself! I'm only thinking about *Josh!* You *know* I am!"

"Trysta, it's like I told you, Josh needs his mother and I'm not gonna"

"*I'd* be a good mother! I'd be a *better* mother!"

"I'm not *saying* you're not a"

Darren was cut off by the slamming of the bedroom door. "Now what the...?" He opened the door to see Zach walking down the hallway.

"Hey, what was that, huh?" he called after the boy, but Zach continued down the hall then down the steps. He turned back to

Trysta. "What kind of behavior was that, huh?"

"Oh, now, Darren, you left the door open and you were being so loud they could hear you downstairs. That's what happens."

"You're talking about taking on another kid? You've got three of your own who need mothering!"

"What are you saying to me, Darren?"

"What I'm *saying*, is that you gotta get a handle on the kids you've *got* or they're gonna be completely out of control!"

Trysta sprang up from the bed up and stood close to Darren's face. "My children are *not* out of control! I have them *perfectly* under control! *I have everything perfectly under control!*"

The doorbell rang like a final note of punctuation on Trysta's pronouncement.

"Aw, now who's that?" Darren groaned.

Trysta gasped. "Silvio! Oh my God! What time is it?"

"Great. Silvio. Just what I need. You better go down there and handle him."

"Darren, come down with me! Otherwise he'll be just *horrible!*"

Darren put up his palms in a defensive gesture. "Oh no. Oh, no, I am *not* going to get into another"

"*Please,* Darren," she cut him off, grasping his wrists, *"please!"*

Trysta and Darren plunged into one quick final round of pleading and arguing into which Trysta injected a half-hearted attempt at seduction, while downstairs Zach opened the door to his father.

"Hi, Dad," the boy said sullenly. "You want to come in?"

"No," Silvio replied, "but I been waiting out there for fifteen minutes. I finally rang the bell. Where's your mother?"

"She's upstairs fighting with Darren."

"What? *Fighting?*" Silvio stepped through the door into the hallway.

Trina and Sam came bouncing out from the living room and jumped into Silvio's arms.

"Hey, how are my girls?" He laughed, giving each a quick kiss before setting them down again.

"Zach, what do you mean, fighting?"

"They always do that," Sam chirped. "Then they kiss and hug!"

Trina and Sam danced around, hugging each other and making

kissing noises.

"Would you quit being stupid?" said Zach, giving them a light shove.

"All right, that's enough rough stuff," said Silvio, putting an arm around Zach's shoulder.

Trysta appeared at the top of the steps, talking as she descended.

"Silvio, I don't expect you to show up early like this. It only causes problems with the children."

"I'm on time." He turned to Sam and Trina, who now stood watching their parents expectantly. "You girls need to get your things."

Trina and Sam began speaking at the same time.

"Mommy, we're not packed! We got a sleepover at Morgan's!"

"We got a sleepover at Morgan's! We're not packed!"

Silvio sighed. "Go get 'em packed, Trysta."

"Fine!" Trysta huffed. "Come, girls."

The two girls followed their mother as she swept back up the stairs. Sam looked back over her shoulder and said haughtily, "And *don't* leave, Daddy!"

Silvio chuckled then turned back to his son. "You all ready?"

Zach lifted the backpack leaning against the wall next to the front door. "I thought you weren't gonna come," he said.

"Not gonna come? No way! I told you, I was waiting out in my truck for you guys."

Zach stood looking at the floor.

"I gotta talk to you a minute," said Silvio, but his son didn't move. Silvio took his son gently by the arm. "Hey! Zach! Look at me now, I need to talk to you!"

Zach sniffed and rubbed a sleeve across his eyes then he looked up at his father.

"Okay, so how you been?" Silvio asked.

Zach shrugged then answered, "I'm okay."

"It's supposed to be sunny tomorrow, you bring your basketball, okay?"

"Okay."

They stood in silence for a moment then Silvio asked, "Your mom take you to see Dr. Cavanni?"

Zach shook his head.

Silvio blew out a sigh of exasperation. "Yeah, well, that's not so good."

"Darren did."

"Darren did? What? Took you to see Doctor Cavanni?"

"Yeah, I was supposed to go, but mom said I didn't need to go and then Darren said I did need to go and then they had a big fight like they always do and then Darren took me and the girls, too."

"What, he took the girls to see Dr. Cavanni, too?"

"No, he took the girls so mom could stay home and rest. He took them to the mall to buy a Barbie for their dumb friend's birthday party. Then he came back and got me from Dr. Cavanni's and he took us out to eat. Trina and Sam acted stupid, like always."

"Wow." Silvio was dumbfounded. "So Zach, are you telling me...I mean, does Darren do that kind of thing for you very often? I mean, do things for you, take you places, and all?"

"Yeah, he takes us to school when we miss the bus, makes us stop fighting when mom tells him to, stuff like that. He's always saying he doesn't have time because he's got too much work to do, but then he does it anyway."

Silvio could barely wrap his head around what his son had just communicated to him. Darren as home-wrecker, life-wrecker, some rich selfish big-shot creep who just reached out and grabbed whatever he wanted, yes, that Silvio understood all too well. But Darren as someone who actually cared about his children? Was that possible?

"Well, okay, that's all right of," Silvio could barely spit out the name, "*Darren* to do those things for you and your sisters."

"Yeah, I guess."

"Yeah. That's really all right of him."

"Darren's all right, I guess. Dad, do you like mom?"

"Your mom?" Silvio hesitated. "Sure, sure. I like her fine."

"But aren't you really, really mad at her?"

Again Silvio hesitated then sighed, "Yeah, Zach, I guess I am. Or I was. I'm starting to get over it." To himself he added, *Or I was starting to get over it.*

"Sometimes I feel really, really mad at Mom."

"Hey, it's only natural, you understand? To be mad at people when they...you know, hurt you."

"Dad, when somebody hurts you do you stay mad forever?"

Silvio shrugged. "I guess you could. But...I don't know, maybe that's not such a good idea, huh?"

"Dr. Cavanni says you gotta let people love you even when you're mad at them."

"Oh yeah?"

"She says being mad at people you love makes you feel lonely."

"That's for sure."

"She says you don't always understand why people do what they do. She says you gotta forgive people. I try, Dad, but it's hard."

"I know. I know. But I guess we gotta keep trying, huh?"

"I guess."

"Hey..." Silvio put his arm around his son. Zach wrapped his arms around his father and buried his head in his chest. Silvio held his son close and stroked his head and then he said, "Yo, don't forget your basketball, right?"

"Yeah, okay." Zach gave his father one more hard hug before letting go and then he bounced up the stairs. "I'll be right back," he called over his shoulder.

"I'm right here," Silvio called back, his heart feeling a surge of free-floating gratitude, though he could already hear from upstairs Trysta and the girls bickering and then talking all at once as they came down the stairs carrying backpacks and sleeping bags:

"But Mommy, this is me and Morgan's sleepover, and Sam is gonna bother us, I am *not* gonna use her dumb Barbies, I have my own Barbies..."

"Morgan is *my* friend, she invited *me* first and she said we could play Barbies, and Trina is gonna use *my* Barbies, she *always* wants to use my Barbies..."

"You girls stop this bickering over Barbies, you share your Barbies and you better not bicker over Barbies at the sleep over, or there'll be no ice cream, I'll call Morgan's mother and..."

"HEY!" Silvio shouted when they reached the bottom of the stairs. The girls and their mother immediately fell silent. Trysta shot him a cold look.

"That's better," Silvio said.

"Here," Trysta said, shoving the girls' pillows and sleeping bags at him.

Silvio took them from Trysta, trying to avoid her eyes, turning to his daughters.

"Okay, kiss your mom good-bye."

The girls hugged and kissed their mother and said their good-byes, and as Zach came down the stairs with his basketball Silvio called, "Zach, you, too. Kiss your mom good-bye."

Zach approached his mother, allowed her to kiss him on the cheek and then pulled back.

"Good-bye, Sweetheart," she said, ruffling his hair.

"Okay let's go." Silvio opened the front door and held it open for his children. "Everybody wait out in the van. I gotta have a word with your mother, I'll just be a minute." As they walked towards his van Silvio called out the door after them, "And no fighting, okay? Zach, you make sure there's no fighting, right?"

"All right," Zach called back. Silvio watched as he turned to his sisters and said, "Dad says no fighting, okay?"

"Okay," the girls chirped.

Silvio stepped back into the hallway and turned to Trysta.

"You want to talk to me, Silvio?" she asked coolly.

"Just for a minute."

Trysta stood with her arms crossed. "I don't think I want to talk to *you*! You said such *awful* things to me last time!" There was a slight lilt of seduction in her voice.

"I'm sorry about last time. I was, you know, upset."

"Huh," Trysta turned and walked away from him. He followed her into the living room and set the sleeping bags and pillows on the carpet.

"Trysta, I said I was sorry. I meant it. I'm sorry. Can we talk?"

She spoke with her back to him. "Why don't you go talk to Sally Miller?"

"Sally Miller? What do I want to talk to her for?"

"Well, you two *are* dating." She turned to face him. "*Aren't* you?"

"*Dating?*" Silvio laughed. "That time you saw me over there? I was fixing her furnace."

"Her *furnace?*"

"She called the company for a plumber. But her furnace needed fixing, too, and you know I sometimes do heating and electrical on the side." Silvio told himself he wasn't lying. Everything he said was true.

"But...you were drinking a *beer!* I *saw* you!"

Silvio shrugged. "She offered me one." This was true, too.

"Oh, come on, Silvio, I *know* you've been seeing Sally! Josh says you come over to their house!"

"Oh, that? Yeah, turned out her next-door neighbors wanted to learn English – the guy's a plumber, too – and while I was there the guy stopped over and asked Sally if they could start a language exchange."

"A *language* exchange?"

"Yeah. You know, we teach them English, they teach us Spanish."

"*Us?*"

"Yeah. I was there, I thought it was a good idea, I asked if I could be in on it. You know, to learn Spanish. I figured it'd be good for my business, with all the Spanish customers I got these days. So that's why I was going over to Sally's house. Or sometimes the Spanish people's house."

"To learn Spanish?"

"Yeah. To learn Spanish." Incomplete information, but still true.

"So you're *not* dating Sally Miller?"

Silvio hesitated and then said, "Nope." It was true.

Trysta brightened and her face lit up with a smile. "Gosh, Silvio," she giggled, "I should have *known* you wouldn't date someone like her! Trysta moved closer to Silvio and curled a lock of her hair around her finger. "You always had *much* better taste in women."

"I guess I have the same taste as Darren." He couldn't help looking at her, her body, her hair, those eyes. He unconsciously moved a step closer to her.

Trysta laughed seductively. "Now, what do you mean by that, Silvio. Do I look bad?" She took a small step closer to him.

Silvio blushed. "No, no, you look good."

"I do?"

"Sure, I mean...you always did look good when you were expecting. All glowing and...filled out."

Trysta frowned. *"Filled out?"*

"I mean the right way. A real...good-looking way."

Trysta giggled. She was so close now he could smell her hair. Like fresh flowers.

Silvio felt confused, tongue-tied, mesmerized by her beauty, the scent of her that used to drive him crazy. A flood of old feeling washed over him. "So, uh...how's everything? With you and Darren?"

"Fine," she giggled. She now stood so close that her stomach pressed against him. How many times had she pressed against him like that, captivating his body with hers, captivating his soul with her eyes? Suddenly he was on fire, consumed with the old desire.

"You happy, and all?" His voice was barely above a whisper.

"Uh-huh," she whispered back, her lips brushing his ear.

In a quick move Silvio wrapped his arms around her and kissed her passionately, hungrily. She fell into his embrace as naturally as if they'd never been apart, and pressed her breasts, her whole body, against him, allowing him to envelope her in his strong arms.

"Oh *Silvio*," she whispered breathlessly, *"devour* me!"

Silvio pulled away suddenly but she pulled him back. "Oh, Silvio, I forgot how good you feel!"

"Oh geez, Trysta, I, I'm sorry, I don't know what"

"It's all right." She pressed her finger tips against his lips. "Just 'cause we're divorced doesn't mean we can't be friends." Again they found each other's lips and fell into another passionate embrace.

"Trysta," he said softly, his hand stroking her hair, "Oh, Trysta..."

"Oh, Silvio," she responded breathlessly.

Silvio pulled suddenly away from her. "Trysta, I..."

"What Silvio?" she cooed, placing his hands back on her hips.

"I'm suing you for custody of the kids."

Trysta looked at him blankly. "What?"

"I need them. And they need me."

"What?" She giggled nervously. "Oh, that's just ridiculous!" She giggled again. "You can't sue me for custody!"

"You don't think so?"

"Wha...? Huh...?" Suddenly aware that his hands were still on her hips, she smacked his arms away. "I'm their *mother!*"

"I'm their father. This is the twenty-first century. I want custody of my kids."

"Well, you can't *have* custody! *I've* got custody! What would you do with them anyway in that dumpy little house"

"...that they used to live in?" he finished for her. "That they used to live in just fine before you left me and took them away?'

Trysta crossed her arms across her stomach and pouted. "Let's not get into that," she said fretfully. "It's all *settled*."

"No, it's not."

"*Yes...it...oh...oh!*" Trysta grabbed her stomach and groaned.

"I've already talked to my lawyer."

"*Ohhh...ohhh...*" she moaned.

"I don't want it to get ugly, for the kids' sake."

"*Ahhh...ahhh...*" she doubled over.

"But I'll fight you if I have to. Now, I want you to know that I'll be generous with visitation, real generous. You can see the kids as much as you want, and I mean that."

"*Silvio,*" she whimpered, "*Silvio...oh...help me...*"

Silvio continued ignoring her pleas. "Otherwise my mom will watch them while I'm at work. Mom'll be good for them."

Trysta bolted upright. "Your *mother?*" Taking over *my* children? I don't *think* so! Your mother never even *liked* me!"

"Well, let's not get into that. It's all settled."

Trysta stamped her foot. "*No...it's...not!*" She was breathing heavily. Then the anger in her eyes suddenly softened. He voice turned beseeching. "Oh, Silvio, Silvio...*why* are you doing this?" She moved close to him again. She rubbed her hands back and forth around his waist. Her voice was sweet now, seductive. "Why? Huh?" She turned her face up to his, she closed her eyes, ready to be kissed again.

"Because..." Silvio swallowed hard. He put his hands on hers and moved close, as if to kiss her. He paused a moment then removed her hands from his waist and stepped back from her. "Our kids are a mess. They're gonna grow up to be a pack of wild dogs if they don't get some guidance."

"But *I* give them guidance!"

"They need discipline."

"*I* give them discipline!" Her voice was desperate, pleading, "I'm their *mother!*"

"Like I said, I already talked to my lawyer, so..."

"NO! NO!" She screamed and pumped her fists like a child throwing a tantrum. "MY CHILDREN ARE *MINE!* YOU CAN'T HAVE THEM! YOU'RE NOTHING BUT A PLUMBER! GET OUT OF MY HOUSE! GO AWAY!"

Darren came running down the stairs. As soon as Trysta caught sight of him she resumed moaning and holding her stomach. Darren rushed to his wife.

"Trysta! Baby, what's going..." He turned to Silvio. "Hey, what'd you do to her? What'd you say to her?" He turned back to Trysta. "What'd he say to you?" Then back to Silvio. "What'd you say to her?"

"You ask her," Silvio snapped. He turned and pulled open the front door.

"He...he..." Trysta gasped.

Darren grabbed Silvio's arm but Silvio immediately smacked Darren's hand away and stepped up close to him, looming several inches over him. "*What?*" Silvio snarled.

Darren looked up into the stone-hostile expression in the eyes of this much bigger, much stronger man. He cleared his throat then turned back to his wife while Silvio turned and left.

"Oh, Darren, he, he..."

"What? What'd he do to you, Baby?"

"He...he...wants custody of the children! Darren, he wants to take the children away!"

"What? He does?"

Trysta stumbled into the living room then collapsed onto the couch while Darren ran out the front door and caught Silvio as he was climbing into his van.

"Silvio," he said breathlessly.

Silvio turned to Darren then climbed down from his van and slammed the door shut. "Look," he said, "I got my kids here."

"I know, I know, but, could we..." he motioned for Silvio to step away from the van.

Silvio stood with his arms crossed. "Okay, what?"

"You...you really want custody of those kids?"

"Yeah," Silvio said coldly.

"Like...you wanna take them away from here? To live with you?"

"Yeah."

"All three of 'em?"

"Yeah."

"Oh." Darren paused a moment then continued. "Well, of course, you *are* their father."

"Yeah," Silvio answered, warming up a few degrees.

"And Trysta...well, I mean, she's a good mother, a terrific mother, but, uh, you know, her condition, and all..."

Silvio was catching on. "And her pains, and all..."

"Yeah, that, too..."

"You're saying she needs a break?" Silvio uncrossed his arms.

"Yeah, sure," said Darren, "some help with the kids."

"So she can get more rest."

"Right, she's gotta get a lot of rest."

"Only..." Silvio stepped closer to Darren, "maybe she needs someone to convince her, huh?"

"Oh, well, of course, I'll have to convince her..."

"...that this'll be the best thing for the kids. And her."

"Oh, sure, the kids have to come first." Darren paused and then his voice took on a pleading edge. "Silvio...can we keep the lawyer fees...uh, I mean, the lawyers out of this as much as possible?"

"Hey, *I'm* gonna do whatever I have to. And I don't care about the cost. I might lose, but I'm sure gonna"

"Oh, *no*," Darren cut him off, "you *can't* lose! I mean, you've *gotta* have your kids, such ...wonderful... *terrific* kids! You gotta have 'em!" Darren took a step closer to Silvio, his hands folded in supplication. "*Please* take your wonderful kids!"

"Will you help me get them?" Silvio grasped Darren's arms. "Will you use your influence on Trysta?"

"Oh, God, yes," Darren cried, "every inch I can muster!"

Equal and Opposite Reactions

The two men fell into a spontaneous hug, quickly separated and then sparred for half a moment in a friendly, manly way before Darren headed back to the house and Silvio towards his truck. After a few steps Darren turned back to Silvio.

"Hey, Silvio," he called, walking back.

Silvio turned towards Darren. "Yeah?"

"Look, what you saw...you know, that last time at Sally's...me and Sally...it just...sort of happened. It was nothing. Really. Nothing."

"Yeah," Silvio replied. "I know."

Chapter Forty

It was Friday evening, the air had turned seasonably chilly and crisp, and the low-hanging clouds teased a suggestion of an early snow. It was the kind of Friday night that called for a warm cozy fire, a cup of hot chocolate, and a good movie or book to get lost in while wrapped in a comfy fleece throw. But Sally didn't have a fireplace or any hot chocolate in the house or even a good book, and she felt too restless to do anything but aimlessly pace the living room floor. It was Joshua who sat wrapped up in his blanket on the sofa, transfixed by the movie he was watching, "Finding Nemo," the tale of a little fish who'd been separated from his father. Josh seemed to want to watch this feel-good little cartoon fantasy all the time these days, though Sally could barely stand to look at it anymore. She finally picked up a magazine from the end table next to the sofa and flipped through a few pages and then she sat down on the sofa next to Josh and continued scanning the pages for something of interest, anything to take her mind off her mind. Josh cuddled up close to his mother and squeezed his eyes shut.

"Hey, what's this?" Sally chuckled. "You checking out the backs of your eyelids?"

"I was just making a wish."

"Oh, yeah? Well, make one for me, too."

"Mommy, are you sad?"

"Sad? How could I be sad when I'm with my best guy?"

"Isn't Silvio gonna come back?"

Sally paused a moment. "No, Babe, I don't think he is."

"I knew he wasn't gonna."

"Aw, Baby..." Sally held her son a little closer and kissed his forehead, willing herself not to tear up.

"Will Daddy still bring Zach over to play someday?"

"We'll try to make that happen. If we can."

Josh turned his attention back to the travails of Nemo for a while and then he said, "Mommy, why does everybody always have to leave?"

"Oh, Baby, everybody won't always leave, I promise you!" Her voice was breaking with emotion, but she continued, "And when you grow up, *you* be a person who doesn't leave, okay?"

"I'll never leave you, Mom." Joshua hugged his mother hard and again squeezed his eyes shut.

"Another wish huh? Well, go ahead, they're free." Sally held her son close, closed her eyes to the room around her and lost herself in a wish of her own.

"Mommy!" Josh was shaking her shoulder. "Mommy, wake up!"

"Huh?"

"It's the doorbell!"

"Oh." Sally went to the door, Josh following close behind, and then she hesitated, trying to fathom who could be at her door on a Friday night. The doorbell rang again. She was glad she'd gotten into the habit of locking her door ever since...well, ever since. "I don't know if I should open it," she said, more to herself than to Josh. "I mean, we're not expecting anyone..."

"It sounds like they're walking away, Mom."

"...unless maybe it's Lupe or Ascensiòn, huh? Lupe?" She called through the door, "Ascensiòn?"

There was the sound of footsteps returning and then from the other side they heard, "It's Silvio."

"Silvio, yay!" cried Josh.

Sally yanked open the door and stared, wide-eyed, into Silvio's face.

"Mom," cried Josh, "It's Zach! It's my stepbrother!"

"Oh," replied Sally, still too dumbstruck with surprise to take in the boy holding a basketball who was standing at Silvio's side.

"Hey, Zach, this is my mom. You can call her Sally."

"Hi," said Zach.

"Oh, uh, hi, Zach." Sally hesitated a moment then said, "Hi, Silvio."

"Hi, Sally."

Silvio and Sally looked at each other uncomfortably.

"Mom! Can Zach come in?"

"Oh, uh, sorry...sure, you wanna come in?"

Silvio and Zach stepped into the living room and Sally led them to the sofa while she and Josh doubled up on the only other chair in the room. "So, Zach, nice to meet you," she said with a smile. "I've heard about what a great guy you are."

Zach squirmed in his seat but smiled shyly.

"But don't you have a couple of sisters, too?"

"Yeah, they're at a sleepover." Zach tossed his ball from hand to hand.

"Yay!" Joshua piped up, "No girls!"

Silvio and Sally smiled and then Zach said to Josh, "You wanna shoot some baskets while my dad messes around with your mom's furnace?"

Sally looked inquiringly at Silvio, but Josh jumped off her lap. "Mom, can I shoot some baskets with Zach? *Please?*"

"Oh, well, I don't...I mean, it's already kind of dark out there."

"There's a light, Mommy, remember? Right by the hoop!"

"Aw, Sally, I'm sorry," said Silvio, "It's just I know how much these guys like to shoot baskets so I had Zach bring his ball. But, look, if you don't want"

"Please, Mommy, please!"

"Well...I guess it's okay."

"Yay! Yay!" cried Joshua.

"But you stay right out back by the hoop."

" And then we can come in and play video games! Mom! I need my coat!"

"Let me get it," said Sally, her heart swelling with gladness at the sight of her happy little boy.

"Get the one Zach gave me!"

"Okay, okay," Sally chuckled.

Joshua hurried after his mother to the closet and in his haste to get his coat on he kept missing an arm hole. "Wait a sec, Honey," Sally said, and while she was helping him configure his coat she turned to Silvio and said, "Mess around with my *furnace?*"

"Okay, Mom, that's good. Come on, Zach!" The two boys hurried out the door, Sally calling after them to remember to stay right out back, nowhere else. Then she and Silvio were left alone to share the silence.

"So, okay, my furnace is still in the kitchen, same as before."

Silvio walked back to the kitchen, opened the door to the alcove, glanced at the furnace and then shut it again. "Looks fine. Been working okay for you?"

"Working great. Warm as...Mexico. And I want to pay you for that part you put in."

"No, no, I don't want you to. Just so long as it's working okay, and all."

"Yeah, fine."

"Okay, well, uh...I just wanted to make sure everything was okay. With you, I mean."

Sally shrugged. "Why wouldn't it be?"

"Maybe I better go check on the boys."

"I'll go."

"They're probably okay out there, huh?"

"Sure, they're..." the words caught in Sally's throat, "right out back."

"Right. Well, if you're sure everything's all right. With you, I mean."

"With *me?*"

"Your furnace. Your commode. And all."

"Sure," Sally sniffled. "Fine."

Sally turned away from Silvio and crossed her arms, looking towards the ceiling and blinking back the tears. Silvio headed towards the door. "Okay, well, I guess I'll go get Zach, then." He stopped with his hand on the knob and turned back to Sally. "You have any trouble you'll call me, right?"

"Sure. Thanks." Then she whirled around, tears streaming down her face. "*Jesus*, Silvio, what the hell are you *talking* about? Of *course* I'm not going to call you! How could I ever call you again? About *anything?* Why are you *here?*"

Silvio rushed to her and took her into his arms, holding her close while she sobbed like a child.

"I'm sorry," He cooed, stroking her hair, "I'm so sorry. Take me back, Sally, please, let me back in. Give me back the key...to...to your heart."

Sally felt as though she'd collapse if he hadn't been holding her up in his strong arms.

"I want to talk about...you know...what happened."

"Silvio, please."

"Look, Sally, I gotta tell you"

"Silvio, I don't...I can't..."

"No, please, Sally, please, I didn't get it before. But I get it now. You don't really love Darren anymore."

Sally pulled in a deep breath. "No. I don't."

"You fell into the trap, is all."

"Yeah. I did. And for what it's worth, I'm sorry, okay? I'm sorry I hurt you, sorry I hurt myself...sorry one meaningless moment could bring everything we had crashing down. I'm sorry for being too damn dumb to realize that what we had was that fragile. I'm..." She broke down, sobbing too hard to continue.

"Sally," he cut her off, gently touching her arm, "stop. You've spent enough time being sorry."

"Sure. Tell it to my heart." She tried to pull away but he still held her close.

"Aw, come on, please. Look...it's my turn now. To be sorry."

She looked up into his eyes. "What do you mean?"

"I mean, I'm sorry. Sorry for making you suffer so long. And for not understanding what was going on that day with Darren and you...that it was just one meaningless moment, like you said. Sally, look, if anything I'm was being too damn dumb. But I'm not anymore."

Sally felt light, fluttery wings of hope beating in tandem with her heart. "Does that mean you want to...to forgive me?"

"No. It means I hope you'll want to forgive me. I'm sorry, Sally. See...I fell into the trap, too."

"You...?"

"Yesterday. With Trysta. While I was picking up the kids."

"What?" Sally pulled away and this time Silvio let her go.

"Yeah. You know, we were talking, and then she was being so

friendly, and she looked so, so..."

"I know..."

"And she was moving closer and closer, and then the next thing you know..." Silvio's face was a study in shame and sorrow. His eyes filled with tears.

"Silvio...how far did you go? With Trysta?"

Silvio wiped his sleeve across his eyes. "Well, about as far as you and Darren."

"Huh. Not very far, then."

"No, no, not at all."

"But maybe you could have, right?"

"I don't know. I swear, I don't even know how it happened at all!"

"I know. I mean, *I know* you don't know!""

"It's not like I was planning it, or anything."

"I know."

"And I swear, Sally, I don't love her! I don't feel a thing for her. I mean, not a thing that means anything."

"I know, I know."

"But I'm *glad* it happened with me and Trysta! I'm thanking *God* it happened. Because it made me realize that when you've been married to person for that long, something like that *can* just, just *happen*."

"Yeah, it can."

"But it doesn't mean..."

"Oh, God, no, it doesn't mean..."

"Doesn't mean you don't..."

Silvio sunk to his knees and buried his head in Sally's waist, sobbing. "I thought you didn't love me anymore!"

Sally knelt and took Silvio into her arms. "Silvio, I do. I really do love you. I want you. I need you. Oh God, when I thought I'd lost you..." Sally broke down into sobs and they sat on the floor for a few moments, holding each other, tears of sadness turning to tears of joy that what was lost was once again found.

They lay down on the carpet and held each other until a warm calmness settled over them. Then Sally rolled onto her back on the floor while Silvio rolled onto his side facing Sally, propped on his elbow and resting his head in his hand. Sally sighed. "You know this isn't going to be easy. We're each of us still so twisted around our feelings. Our hurts."

"I know," Silvio sighed.

It's just weird, though."

"What is?"

"How I spent all those days, all those nights, crying over Darren. He treated me like dirt under his feet and instead of kicking him out of my heart all I could do was want him back."

"You couldn't help it. You spend years loving a person, it gets to be a habit, you know? You're hooked, even after they stop loving you.

"Yeah, I know, but that's what's so weird now. All that…yearning and burning…all that…stupid, hopeless *longing*…love, whatever…it's gone now. Took off somewhere. Maybe it just flew back to wherever it came from in the first place."

Silvio laughed humorlessly. "Or maybe it was all wiped out by that kiss."

"Oh hell, it wasn't even a real kiss!"

"I know, I know. Aw geez, I know! Only…well, at the time it looked real to me."

"Believe me, it wasn't."

"I know."

Sally sat up on the floor and wrapped her arms around her knees. "It was just another empty, stupid-assed game we had to play one more time, and me the sucker like always. But that was the last time."

"Sally, it's okay. Let it go. What happened with you and Darren, what happened with me and Trysta. We both gotta let all that go."

"Can we, Silvio? I mean, are you sure? Because this is Sally you're talking to. I'm not Trysta, you know? Trysta you would've forgiven anything. Kissing another man…sleeping with another man…leaving you for another man, breaking your heart into a million pieces, and you'd of still taken her back in a heartbeat. You know you would've."

"Yeah. I would've. Once upon a time. But now, Sally, it's"

"Wait, Silvio." She put a hand on his arm. "What I mean is, you wouldn't have left Trysta because she's not the type you'd leave. She's your classic damsel in distress. The type who can always find a man to take care of her. Knows how to play the deck for all it's worth. Me, I can't even hold onto the damn cards."

Silvio rose to his knees.

"Sally…"

Sally wiped her eyes with the back of her hand. "So I guess what I'm saying is, before we give this another shot, make sure it's me you want."

"Sally…When a person is all, like you said, twisted around inside it's hard to know what he wants. And when a guy isn't thinking clear he isn't seeing so clear either, you know? But I'm seeing clear now. And I don't want Trysta. I know who she is and I know who you are, and I know who I am, too, and I'm not such a perfect guy myself. But I swear to God I don't want Trysta. Not anymore." His voice was breaking with emotion. He bent over her and caressed her face with his hands. "Sally…I want *you*."

He leaned close to her and kissed her face hungrily then stood and gently raised her to her feet.

They were still standing wrapped in each other's arms when Josh came bounding through the door holding the basketball. Zach followed behind him. They stopped short at the sight of Sally and Silvio, who quickly let go of each other.

"Hey, guys," Silvio chuckled nervously.

"You done playing?" Sally asked, running a hand through her hair.

"I *knew* they were gonna do that," said Josh with mock exasperation. "C'mon, Zach, let's go to my room and play videos!"

But Zach stood frozen, a deer-caught-in-the-headlights expression on his face, until Josh yanked him on the sleeve.

"Come *on*, Zach," Josh cried, pulling Zach by the sleeve towards his room. Zach followed robotically, allowing himself to be pulled along by Josh while he stared back over his shoulder at his father.

"Oh, boy," Silvio sighed. "This isn't gonna be easy."

"Hasn't been easy and it's not gonna *be* easy." Sally wrapped her arms around Silvio's waist and grinned. "Just a helluva lot more fun."

Silvio looked into her eyes and smiled. He pulled her close and held her there, next to his heart.

Chapter Forty-One

Darren lay on his side in bed, wide awake in spite of the athletic sex he'd just had with Trysta. He knew he hadn't been performing well lately with his wife, but tonight had been good, almost as good as at the beginning.

He was feeling good. God, better than he'd felt in, well, who knew how long? But not only good. Energized. Motivated. Hopeful. And who'd believe that he had that schmoe Silvio to thank!

He rolled over onto his back and stared at the ceiling. Ah, old Silvio wasn't so bad once you got to know him. But good, bad, or indifferent, Silvio was going to be his salvation. His ticket to liberation. Liberation from Trysta's out-of-control kids. And, dared he think it? From Trysta. Darren glanced over at his sleeping oblivious wife, her mountainous belly slowly rising and falling with each breath.

My God, was he really thinking of leaving her? Now that she was, what, eight months pregnant? No, of course he wouldn't do that. He'd wait at least until the baby was born. In fact, He'd wait until Silvio got custody of the kids.

He felt a sudden chill. What if Silvio didn't get custody?

But of course he would! For one thing, the son-of-a-bitch had the money, right? And, of course, though Darren had promised to help Silvio get his kids back, really, what was there for him to do? All he really needed to do was sit back and do nothing. Let Silvio duke it out and pay the lawyers. Wouldn't cost Darren a penny!

At least not until after his divorce. Then there'd be the child support – of course, Trysta would want custody of the baby and he wouldn't deny her that…in truth, he didn't want to drag the thing out in court, he couldn't afford it, especially right now when he was just barely getting on his feet financially.

But unless he could get Trysta to play ball in a really spectacular way – and not a snowball's chance in a South Jersey summer that she would – he was going to end up having to hire an attorney. He'd get the guy he used with Sally, that guy was pretty good, got the whole deal squared away and over with pretty quick. But then, of course, all it took to get Sally on board was offering her custody of Josh. Darren glanced again at his wife. He wasn't so sure with Trysta.

Well, hell, any way they cut it he was going to end up saddled with two child support payments before this thing was over. Just no getting around it. He swore he'd never again have sex without a condom. Or a vasectomy would be better. He'd definitely look into a vasectomy. Once all this bullshit was over.

But if he could unload this big fucking monster of a house, he'd have half the battle won. And then…hell, maybe he'd just grab one of the Manayunk units for himself, work out a deal with whoever he ended up selling the building to. Yeah, that would actually work. The Manayunk location would be a whole lot better. Definitely a whole lot better for getting over to the Northeast to pick up Josh for visitations. He'd be able to just shoot up the Roosevelt Boulevard. No more trying to negotiate that fucking Schuylkill Expressway during rush hour.

Unless, of course Trysta opted to stay out in the West suburbs with the baby. Then, of course, he'd have no choice, with the visitation. But housing was so expensive out in the West Philadelphia suburbs, he bet Trysta would move back to Cornwells Heights to be closer to her family and her kids once Silvio got custody of them. That really would be best. For all of them.

He wondered how visitation with a newborn would work, if Trysta was going to be nursing, and all. Maybe they'd just have to put off the visitations 'til the baby was a little older. But he definitely wanted to be in this child's life, just like he was in Josh's life, and he'd be just as good a father to this child. And even to Trysta's kids, whenever he saw them. He liked them well enough. They were just a handful. Too much.

But they'd all work it out, Darren would cooperate, any way Trysta wanted it, he'd go along. He was feeling magnanimous.

And then he'd be a whole lot closer to where he needed to be for work, closer to Highland and Erskerberg, closer to the Drexel property, closer to South Philly and Angelo Barbieri's interests.

Angelo Barbieri. The worm in the rose. Or more like the spider spinning the web. A golden web, but a web all the same. And he, Darren, the fly. Not that he was the only one stuck and squirming on Barbieri's web. The shock of finding out about Jeremy Andrews still hadn't worn off…Jesus, the head of Global Acquisitions! What could Barbieri possibly have on him? Well, hell, any number of things, actually. And upset as he'd been at learning that it was because of Barbieri and not his own worth that he'd gotten his job back, if Barbieri was in fact pulling strings all the way up to Jeremy Andrews then what difference did anyone's worth make, except their worth to Barbieri?

But wait…could it be possible that Highland and Erskerberg with all its clout and prestige in the real estate world was in truth just a pawn company for Angelo Barbieri? Who knew how many strings Angelo Barbieri was actually pulling? Darren chuckled ruefully. At least he was in good company.

But he'd get out, he swore to God he'd get out of Barbieri's maw somehow, someday. But that was a problem for another day. Today he needed to work out a more pressing escape plan. His escape from his wife and her children. Darren rolled back onto his side and drifted off to sleep.

***

Trysta woke up suddenly. She was too hot. Or maybe just too uncomfortable. She got up to use the bathroom then when she returned to bed she turned this way and that but couldn't fall back to sleep.

Darren was sound asleep, snoring softly. Trysta bounced the bed a little but he wouldn't wake up.

"Darren!" she whispered loudly, shaking his arm.

"Wha….?" He muttered.

"Wake up!" She shook his arm again.

Darren popped up. "What?" he asked in a sleep-fogged voice, "Is it time?"

"*No*, it's not time!" Trysta answered petulantly, "I can't sleep!"

"Go back to sleep," he muttered and then lay back down and turned back onto his side.

"But I *can't* sleep!"

"*Jesus*," he grumbled and then a moment later he was softly snoring again.

"Huh!" Trysta threw off the covers and hauled herself out of bed. She put on her bathrobe and slippers and went downstairs to the living room where she plopped down onto her plush, fairly expensive living room sofa.

She felt like crying, but suffering the frustration of the consummate actress who needs her audience to bring her emotions to life, found herself at this moment unable to dredge up any tears. Still, Trysta knew that if there was anybody who deserved sympathetic tears it was herself. But who was ever around to feel sorry for her *except* herself? And when did she ever have time to think of herself, with a house, husband, three children of her own plus her husband's child and one on the way to take care of? When, in fact, in her whole life, or at least in her life since high school, had she *ever* put herself first? She was always doing, doing, doing for others. Trysta reached for a throw-pillow and began absently playing with the fringes. Doing for men. Doing what men wanted her to do, being what they wanted her to be. Always looking good for them, always putting on a happy face for them no matter how she felt inside, always keeping them happy with what they loved most, that is, sex, sex, and more sex. Sex even when she didn't particularly feel like it, which was most of the time, even when she was nine months pregnant, back, legs, shoulders, everything aching, thoroughly uncomfortable and dead exhausted and sex was the last chore in the world she felt like doing, still she always had to dig in and go to work, let them paw her and man-handle her and slobber, drool, and ooze all over her while she pretended to melt like warm milk chocolate all over them. God, she worked hard. And then sometimes for nothing. Her thoughts wandered back to high school where the sex had all started. Of course, she wasn't counting all the little "boyfriends" she'd had along the way, the cute, harmless kindergarten kisses through middle-school spin-the-bottle, you-show-me-yours-I'll-show-you-mine stuff.

No, it was high school where the boys turned into men. She remembered Jeremy DeCiccio, her first real love. Maybe her only real love. What man had she loved as much as she'd loved Jeremy? Hadn't she done everything he'd wanted her to do, given him everything? What more could she have done to show her love for him? And yet when she told him her period was late how fast he'd dropped her! Shattered her heart to pieces, told her to get an abortion and didn't even offer to pay for it. So where was she supposed to get the money for an abortion? Her parents? Her father would have killed her. All the gallons of tears and bushels of sweet talk she'd had to pump out during her adolescence just to keep her father's ex-marine temper at bay wouldn't have been enough to keep her from getting kicked out of the house this time. No, she'd had to fend for herself, to which end she'd had no choice but to stake out Silvio Jablonski. Trysta smiled at the memory of seducing Silvio back when he was a cute, clueless football player who'd been following her around since freshman year like a big, waggy-tailed puppy dog. In fact snagging Silvio had been almost effortless. And how surprised had she been, absolutely shocked, when, upon telling Silvio that she was pregnant he not only would hear no talk of getting rid of the baby, but wanted to marry her and raise their child together, no questions asked! So marriage to Silvio had seemed like salvation at the time, he had a job and could provide her with a home and a life and, most importantly, a child born comfortably within the safety-zone of wedlock. But then before she knew it she was chasing after three children, who were, of course, the most important thing in her life even if they wore her out and drove her crazy. And of course there were times she wished she could get away from them. But she loved her children as much as a mother could, which is why she would never give Silvio custody, not even more visitation, not a minute more, let him beg and plead and spend a ton of money trying to make her. Let him just suffer, mean as he was to her these days. What right did Silvio have to be so mean, anyway? Hadn't she been a good wife? A wonderful wife, really. She'd given him three beautiful children, kept a nice home for him, worked full time, and kept him more than happy in bed. And when had she ever complained about anything? Silvio had had it good with her and he knew it. And what's more, she'd been faithful. Even with men at the office constantly pursuing her, fat old married slobs, most of them. But who would have blamed her if she'd have given in to one of these men, one of the powerful, important, wealthy ones? No, she'd been one-hundred-percent faithful. Until Jeremy Andrews. The second Jeremy of her life, whom she'd found as irresistible as the first. Handsome in the way that a middle-aged man could be, charming, well-dressed – and *single* – he came in as new chief of Global Acquisitions with a powerful business-world pedigree and a whopping big salary. And a seductively burning desire for Trysta from day one. But once he'd quenched his desire this Jeremy turned out to be as cruelly false-hearted as her first Jeremy. Except that this Jeremy gallantly offered to pay for an abortion if the baby Trysta was carrying was in fact his. It probably was Jeremy's. That had been her plan when she'd gone off her birth control: to have Jeremy's heir as the living line that would reel him in once she'd snagged his high and mighty heart. Except that it turned out that she hadn't snagged his high and mighty heart. Only his high and mighty penis. And even that only temporarily. Of course, the baby could possibly be Silvio's, too. It wasn't Darren's, that was for sure. But Darren would never figure it out. Men like Darren and Silvio – unlike men like Jeremy Andrews – were so dumb about those things. Darren would just assume, as Silvio had before, that the baby was a little early. In truth she was about to deliver any day now, overdue, even. She probably should have gotten the abortion...Oh, God, no, what was she thinking? She didn't mean that, she'd never, ever, kill her child! Trysta rubbed her hand protectively over her belly. Well, what was so wrong with wanting a better life for herself and her children? She wasn't eighteen anymore, people move on, and she'd moved on to a new level personally, far above the working-class existence she'd grown up in then re-planted herself back into with Silvio. And how lucky had it seemed when Darren came along and kissed away the tears she couldn't stop crying over Jeremy...Darren, who, after his promotion to Global Acquisitions, was making a salary that, while below Jeremy's, soared above Silvio's. And then one thing very quickly led to another. She'd had to make things move quickly with Darren: when she sprung it on him that she was pregnant with his child she knew she was already a good three months along with somebody else's. (And it was only a little white lie: Darren *was* sleeping with Trysta, so if she hadn't already *been* pregnant he certainly could have *made* her pregnant, so he was just as responsible as anyone). But conquering Darren had required only slightly more effort than conquering Silvio had, and Trysta could still recall the heady, happy, victorious feeling of conquest followed by the love that welled up in her heart when Darren chose her to be his wife. His new wife. His true soul mate, the woman who had rescued him from the loveless hell of a marriage he'd been trapped in with Sally the Shrew. Yes, she had rescued Darren as much as he had rescued her. Theirs would be a marriage made in heaven, living the good life together, the life Trysta was meant to live, with a man who adored her. And now here she was, all the pieces in place, except…what was wrong with the picture? What was wrong, of course, was that by some kink in the natural order her ex and Darren's had discovered each other and were now dedicated to destroying Darren and Trysta's dream life, dragging Darren and Trysta down to the level of their own miserable existence. Trysta threw the pillow down. Who was she kidding? The real problem with her life with Darren was that they were broke. The real problem was that no sooner had Darren won her heart than he lost his job. And by that time her pregnancy was an undeniable, unendable, visible-to-the world reality, and she'd already broken it off with Silvio. They all pretended that Darren quit his job to "strike out on his own." But Trysta, though she'd been only a receptionist, knew how to untangle the office grapevine well enough to know that Darren had in fact been fired. And she'd have to be an idiot not to have figured that Jeremy Andrews was behind it and she was at the meaty heart of the matter. Trysta smiled wryly over the power of her presence to steer men's actions. Still, Darren should have been sharp enough to know how to hold on to his job, for goodness sake. Trysta heaved a great sigh. What was *really* wrong, most painfully ironically wrong, was that now, *now*, Silvio's Uncle Bud finally decides to turn the plumbing business over to Silvio. Not a year ago, when Trysta could still have benefited, but *now*. All the heartbreak, all the problems, this huge life change she'd undergone, she was sure all would have been avoided if only Silvio had taken over the business a year ago. As owner of the company Silvio could expand the business as he'd always dreamed of doing and would soon be making three times as much as he'd made as an employee. And he'd do well. He'd succeed. And she could have shared in his success, and probably would have ended up with a big new house every bit as nice as this one, vacations to places even better than excruciatingly hot, filthy Puerto Vallarta, over which Trysta would much have preferred to honeymoon in breezy Cape May, New Jersey, or the Poconos, but Darren just *had* to have his honeymoon in Mexico. Trysta shook her head. *Darren.* Oh, she still loved him, of course, but...well, she had to be honest, the thrill was gone. And the baby was here. She was stuck. Once again, stuck by a baby.

Unless...what if the baby turned out to be Silvio's? Surely Silvio would want his child...and if Trysta made herself available to him once again, free and clear of Darren, surely he'd want her back, too...after all, the only reason Silvio was so bitter was because she'd left him for Darren...but if she left Darren and returned to Silvio with their child, Silvio would take her back in a second, she was sure of it. And wait, Trysta wouldn't even have to prove the baby was Silvio's, all she'd have to do was prove it wasn't Darren's, which it wasn't, and since nobody knew about Jeremy...as far as anyone would know it could *only* be Silvio's!

Trysta maneuvered onto her back on the couch and shifted the mental wheels into high gear. Now how would she go about getting all this testing done? Darn, she'd probably need Darren's co-operation... she could tell him...she could tell him...what could she tell him? Oh, she could tell him that, well, she thought they should have proof to show that this child was beyond doubt Darren's...because...because...because *why?* Oh, because with Silvio acting so crazy these days, wanting to take her children away from her, he just might get the crazy notion that *their* baby was his, and try to take it away, too, and if they had the positive proof of a paternity test that Darren was the father...only, of course, the test would prove the opposite, which would open a big can of worms and get the ball rolling in Trysta's direction. Then one day, a few months from now when she was back in shape, she'd arrive at Silvio's door surrounded by their children, their baby in her arms, she'd beg his forgiveness, tears of sorrow and love rolling down her cheeks and Silvio would hesitate only a moment before rushing to take her into his arms, tears of forgiveness rolling down his cheeks as they vowed to rebuild their life together. Actually, the whole thing seemed like an awful plan and an exhausting one, but it was the best Trysta could think of. She'd have to somehow make it work. But for now she'd bide her time, relax, have the baby – what else *could* she do? – and see how things continued to play out. Maybe she wouldn't have to do anything after all. Maybe Darren's real-estate schemes would quickly start making some serious money and then maybe things would get better between her and Darren, they'd have enough money to be able to stand up to Silvio together, and everything would work out in her favor. She'd be busy with the baby for a few months, she'd need to get back into shape herself and then she could work it all out. But she felt tired now. Trysta returned to her bedroom and climbed into bed and her eyes were drifting closed when it hit her. Oh God, was that a pain? A *real* pain?

Chapter Forty-Two

Sally, Silvio, Sally's mother, Joanne and Maria sat or stood around Sally's dinette table nursing mugs of coffee while Charleston stood looking out Sally's front window at the light snow blowing through the air.

Joshua, who'd insisted the night before that he wanted to be woken up on this Saturday morning to say good-bye to Lupe and Ascensiòn, lay on the couch where he'd fallen back asleep with his blanket, a stuffed toy dinosaur held against his chest.

Charleston checked his watch and turned to Sally.

"It's seven-o-five. Do they know we need to be on our way no later than seven-ten? Between this weather and the traffic..."

"I told Ascensiòn. He said they'd be here by six forty-five, but..." Sally shrugged.

"Yeah, well, they don't get over here they're gonna miss their plane," said Silvio.

"Maybe I should go knock on their door?" Maria offered.

"I'll go with you," said Charleston.

"How about I come, too," said Joanne.

"Me, too," said Silvio.

"Mom, will you stay with Josh?" said Sally.

"Of course, Dear. That's what I'm here for."

"But I want to go, too," Josh said groggily.

"You stay here with Gram," said Sally's mother, "you can watch a little TV while I fix you some French toast."

"Yay," said Josh, hopping off the couch and bouncing towards the stack of DVD's on the stand next to the television.

Sally shot her mother a look of dismay. "TV? Really, Mom? It's seven a.m."

"We'll watch something educational."

"Grammy," Josh cried, holding up a video game case, "can I play Super Mario?"

"Yes, you can, Sweetheart."

"Mom..."

Joanne put a hand on Sally's shoulder and whispered in her ear, "Let it go, Sweetheart. Go put on your coat."

The little group then walked across the way to Lupe and Ascensión's apartment. They stood outside the door, hesitant, each wondering which of them was going to ring the doorbell.

Finally Sally pressed her thumb against the bell and called through the door, "Lupe? Ascensión?"

"Guys," called Silvio, "gotta go!"

They heard a loud sob and a moment later Ascensión opened the door. His face was tear-stained and looked ravaged by grief.

"She can't do it," he said softly, tilting his head back towards his wife, who sat in the only chair left in the living room in her coat and hat, holding David close and rocking him while the tears streamed down her face.

Charleston stepped into the apartment and the others crowded in behind him. They stood with Ascensión and watched Lupe in anxious silence, unsure of what to do, each of them looking to Charleston for guidance. But he stood in silence, too, offering no cue regarding what to do next.

"Well, shit," Sally mumbled under her breath. She went to Lupe and knelt next to her chair. "Hey, Girl," she said softly, rubbing Lupe's arm, "It's time."

"No," Lupe sobbed, "no puedo. No puedo dejar a mi bebé."

"Yes you can, you *have* to give him to me, you *have* to, come on, you're about to miss your"

"Sally," Charleston cut in, "she does not have to do this. It's got to be her choice." He looked at his watch. "Maria, would you let Lupe know this, and that we'll leave in two minutes?"

"No tienes que hacer esto si no quieres, puedes quedar aqui," Maria translated, "pero vamos a salir en dos minutos."

"Por favor, Mi Amor," Ascensión begged softly, "for our son."

Lupe shook her head. "No puedo, no puedo." She repeated it over and over, like a dirge.

"Then we have to go now," said Charleston as he walked to the door with Maria following behind him. "Good bye, Ascensiòn, Lupe. Good luck to you both."

"No!" cried Ascensiòn, "Wait!" He knelt before his wife next to Sally. "Lupe, por el amor de dios, esto es una locura! It's *crazy!*"

"Sally, Silvio, Joanne, you should come too," said Charleston curtly.

Sally slowly stood up and walked away from Lupe, Ascensiòn and David. She wiped her eyes wither sleeve.

"Adios," she said softly and then followed Charleston, Maria, Joanne and Silvio out the door.

"No!" Lupe sprang suddenly from her chair and hurried out to Sally just before she closed the door. Ascensiòn grabbed the suitcases and hurried after her.

Standing in the breezeway outside the apartment Lupe wrapped David's blanket close around him, carefully covering his head and shoulders against the snow which was beginning to fall more steadily. Then she handed him to Sally. "Aqui," she said, "take my baby, take him."

Sally took David and held him close. Silvio put an arm around Sally's shoulder.

"Now is time for his bottle," said Lupe.

"I'll fix him one right now. Lupe, I promise to love him. And I promise that Josh will love him. Better than anything in the world." The tears were streaming down her cheeks.

"And I'll be there," added Silvio. "We all will, right?"

"We will," said Charleston and Joanne while Maria nodded.

Sally leaned close to Lupe and kissed her cheek. "Go ahead, Hon. It'll be all right."

"Yes." Lupe brushed David's cheek and smiled weakly then took her suitcase from Ascensiòn and followed Charleston and Maria down the stairs to the parking lot.

Ascensiòn kissed his son then Sally. "Our angel." He hugged Joanne and kissed her on the cheek. "Thank you, good friend. You watch my son, too?"

"You know I will," said Joanne, rubbing at her eye.

"Thank you, again, Silvio. We come back. You hold on to Sally. Never let her go again."

"I never will." Silvio rubbed his hand gently along Sally's arm.

"He ever does I'll kick his hiney," said Joanne. "I'll kick both their hineys."

"She will," chuckled Sally.

"I will," said Joanne.

Ascensiòn stood in the doorway and looked back into his old apartment one more time. "I like this place," he said and then shut the door and followed after the others.

With David wrapped in her arms Sally stood with Silvio and Joanne on the landing and watched Lupe and Ascensiòn load their meager belongings into the trunk of Charleston's car. Lupe and Ascensiòn both gazed up one more time at their son with a look of heart-breaking longing then climbed into the back seat. A moment later they were gone.

Sally sobbed while Silvio pulled a handkerchief from his jeans and wiped his eyes. "Here," he said, wiping Sally's eyes for her with the dry end of his handkerchief then offering it to Joanne.

"Uh, no thanks," said Joanne, "I don't like sharing the goods. I got my own snot rag." She pulled a Kleenex from her coat pocket with a flourish then wiped her eyes and blew her nose loudly as Sally and Silvio laughed through their tears.

Bouncing David in her arms, Sally asked, "do you think they'll be back?"

Silvio hesitated a moment then he said, "Yeah. I think they will."

"Yeah, they will," said Joanne, wiping her eyes again.

"I think they will, too," said Sally.

They stood looking out at the snow now falling steadily onto the parking lot until they heard Sally's front door open. They all turned to see Joshua standing in the doorway with Sally's mother standing behind him.

"Sally?" her mother called softly, "are they…?"

"They're gone, Mom," Sally replied.

"Are you…?"

"We're okay."

"Speak for yourself, Hon," said Joanne, "my tushie's about to freeze."

"Did Lupe and Ascensiòn go back to Nicaragua now?" called Josh.

"Yes, Babe, they're gone."

"Is Baby David my brother now?"

"Yes, he is."

"Well, bring him into the house so we can start being together!"

Joanne motioned to Sally and Silvio. "You heard what the man said. Come on, kids."

Sally and Silvio smiled at each other then followed Joanne back into the warmth of Sally's apartment, closing the door tightly against the cold outside air.

View other Black Rose Writing titles at www.blackrosewriting.com/books and use promo code **PRINT** to receive a **20% discount** when purchasing.

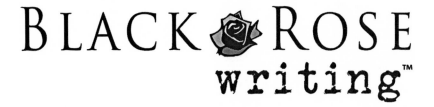

CPSIA information can be obtained
at www.ICGtesting.com
Printed in the USA
FFOW03n0524120617
36572FF